DND# 6
The Worth of Souls In Jesus' Name

McCartney Green

ISBN- 9798351706191

Copyright©2022 McCartney Green

Originally published as:
Expendable Book 6 of The Dandelions Series
Copyright© 2010 McCartney Green/Dandelions Publishing

All rights reserved. Except for use in any review, the reproduction or utilization of this work in whole or in part in any form by any electronic, mechanical or other means now known or hereafter invented, or in any information storage or retrieval system is forbidden without the written permission of McCartney Green.

This is a work of fiction. Names, characters, places and incidents are either the product of the author's imagination or are used fictitiously, and any resemblance to actual persons living or dead, business establishments, events or locales is entirely coincidental.

"Do not repay anyone evil for evil. Be careful to do what is right in the eyes of everyone. If it is possible, as far as it depends on you, live at peace with everyone. Do not take revenge, my dear friends, but leave room for God's wrath, for it is written: "It is mine to avenge; I will repay," says the Lord."   Romans 12:17-19

Everyone who does evil hates the light, and will not come into the light for fear that their deeds will be exposed.   John 3:20

Note to Reader:

Come, let us talk of what you are about to read. Firstly, the title. In this book the main character, the heroine, has come to learn that she is expendable, worth almost nothing, but God feels differently about that, for we are His children and to Him we are worth a great deal.

"Are not two sparrows sold for a penny? Yet not one of them will fall to the ground outside your Father's care. And even the very hairs of your head are all numbered. So don't be afraid; you are worth more than many sparrows."
Matthew 10:29-31

Next- the villain in this book is one of the most evil I've ever written. Once I wrote him, I had to go back and soften it, but I left it somewhat edgy for a reason. You see, I've met real evil. His name was Ted Bundy. But God had other plans for me. (Praise God, thank you, Jesus.) There is so much evil and darkness in this world. It is everywhere. It permeates everything. It is why and how we are heading into the tribulation. But why write about it?

    The answer to that is in a page from my life. There was a time that I had turned my back on God, but He didn't turn His back on me. He, being God, knew exactly how to bring me back to Him. He gave me the ability to see past the veil into the darkness, to see that the dark evil forces are real. They are there, constantly badgering and beating, waiting with their jaws open wide. They are looking for the cracks in our armor, or for us to fall, off the sidewalk, or off the curb, or off the high wall. And this evil is beyond anything you can imagine. The horrific perversions of Satan carried out by fallen man.

    Once God allowed me to literally see it AND see its carnage, I had to admit it exists. And if the dark side exists, then logically my brain and my hard heart had to admit that the light also exists. The moment I allowed that tiny thought into my brain, (the faith of a mustard seed,) amazing things began to happen. Actually, amazing things *continued* to happen, I just began realizing them— acknowledging them. And funny thing, the more we acknowledge God's hand in our lives, the more He will bless us with interaction with Him.

    So, in my books I'm showing a little of this evil to wake some people up. But don't be afraid and don't be discouraged. Because Jesus IS coming back, sooner than some of you may realize, and he's not a little baby anymore. Until then, God has placed His warriors here on Earth to help and defend and protect the innocent. These warriors are mere humans. They are fallible. Yet, they do the best they can, and will continue to do so until the Divine intervention. These warriors come in all shapes and sizes, male and female, (yes, only those two,) and they wield a vast array of weaponry; hands, swords, guns, knives, brains, speech, pens, talents.... a vast array.

    You may be one of those warriors. I pray you will seek God's will for your life. I pray for your complete healing if evil has touched your life in any way. I pray you to be filled with love and the absolute joy that comes from connection to God. In Jesus mighty and powerful name, Amen.

Keeping Tabs

At the beginning of *The Worth of Souls* it is the end of May and ...

Eric Kino is 56

Shelley Adams Kino is 51

Ricky Kino is 38

Breanna Adams Kino is 34

Eric Kino III is 6

Taylor Kino is 3

Mark Adams is 25

Little Joseph (JoJo) Adams is 6

Joey Adams is 23

June Flower Kino is 15

Jason Lee is 44

Angel Lee is 42

Kimberly Lee is 13

Justin Lee is 53

Lori Lee is 39

Toby (Smith) Nash is 41

Caroline Jones Smith is 39

Grace Smith is 11

Brody Smith is 7

Lisa Lewis Stewart is 33

Chaz Stewart is 36

Melaynah Stewart is 6

John Appel is 37

Jodi Appel is 35

Jacob Appel is 7

Maddie Lewis is in her 70's and still going strong!

Keegan Tanner is 36

Lizzy Anderson Tanner is 29

Heather Anderson is 10

Rose Anderson is 9

Violet Anderson is 9

Daisy Anderson is 8

Lily Anderson is 8

Gabriel Tanner is almost 4

"It is difficult to know at what moment love begins; it is less difficult to know that it has begun."

~ Henry Wadsworth Longfellow ~

The Worth of Souls-In Jesus' Name

Prologue

Seattle, Washington

Mickey sniffed hard, then used the back of her hand to wipe up any residue. She drew in a couple of sharp breaths, choked and sputtered, and then the tears started anew.

"Young lady you stop that mewling. You have absolutely nothing to be crying about. You know sometimes Daddy has to punish you so he can teach you."

Mickey's fierce eyes darted to her mother's. "He's *not* my daddy."

Wringing her hands, Marion Benson knelt down in front of her daughter, her expression softening. "Well, of course he's not your real daddy, sweetheart," she cajoled. "But Talmond and I are getting married today and you really need to try to accept that. Can't you just try?"

"I hate him."

Her mother's eyes hardened. "Well– I love him, and that's all that matters now, isn't it?" She took Mickey by the shoulders and gave her a shake. "I swear sometimes you are such a selfish little brat. Don't you care about anyone but yourself? What about me, Mackenzie? Don't I deserve some happiness in this life?"

Mickey didn't know how to answer. Of course she wanted her mom to be happy, but did it have to be this way? Was getting married to a horrible man the only way her mom could be happy? She remembered seeing her mom cry back when her daddy first went away and she felt really bad about that. Well, maybe she *is* just a terrible kid, maybe she *is* selfish, but there is just no way she can be happy about her mom getting married to such an awful old man. He is mean and ugly and bossy and . . . why oh why did my daddy have to go away?

Her mother gave up waiting for an answer, gave her a final shake, stood, glanced at herself in the dresser mirror and brushed some hair off her forehead. "Besides you don't see your real father hanging around here, do you? No. You know why? Because he doesn't give two figs about you,

Mackenzie. He didn't call on your seventh birthday and I guarantee he's not gonna call when you turn eight. He doesn't care about you so I don't know why you're so loyal to him."

Mickey closed her eyes. She hated when her mother talked about her daddy in a bad way. He was the one person in her life she'd ever loved. And her father loved her. He did. Mickey refused to listen when her mother spoke about him like this, which was most of the time. Glaring at her mother, she put her hands over her ears. Mickey wouldn't tell her mother she was wrong because then she would only say more bad things about her father. No, Mickey wouldn't argue about her father.

Marion pulled Mickey's hands down from her head. "Why are you so stubborn, huh?" She grabbed Mickey's face, squeezing her cheeks together. "You'd better start listening to me, you understand? Why can't you just see that I know what's best for you? Now that we're marrying Talmond you won't have to go to that crummy school anymore and you'll have lots of nice clothes to wear."

"I don't care. I like my school– and I hate him," she sobbed. Accusingly, Mickey glared at her mother. "You l-let him h-hit me."

"Oh, stop it. He didn't hit you. He spanked you and you darn well deserved it. You're just gonna have to accept that Talmond is your new father and what he says goes."

Mickey wiped more tears from her face. "I didn't do anything wrong."

"He told you to make your bed, clean your room and get your bath, didn't he?"

When Mickey didn't answer her mother went on. "And he comes up here and catches you lying there on the bed reading a book. You blatantly disobeyed him, knowing this is our wedding day and we have a million things to do. Knowing that in doing so you would make me unhappy."

Mickey shook her head. "I didn't mean to make you unhappy. I found the book when I was making the bed. I just opened it for a second."

"Mickey, just stop. No more excuses."

"Is there another problem?"

Mickey turned fearful eyes toward the dark figure standing in the threshold.

"No of course not, dear," Marion said quickly. She offered a weak smile.

Talmond Daley walked slowly into the room, put his arms around his bride and kissed her thoroughly. "Sweetheart, why don't you go take care of what you need to do and Mackenzie and I will have a little talk."

Marion frowned. "But—"

"Now don't you go worrying your pretty little head. It's always hard on kids when their parents remarry. I'll talk to her and she and I will get along just fine. You'll see. Now run along. I know you have all those little female rituals to attend to. I'll join you in a few minutes."

Marion smiled. "Okay, but you two play nice."

"Absolutely," Talmond said softly.

He waited for her to leave before he turned to Mickey. He had to admit she was a beautiful child. Thick brown hair and large brown eyes. An adorable little heart-shaped face with a turned up nose and an alluring pouty mouth which at the moment was drawn up tight. The child stood defiantly before him, her hands clenched into fists, her chin lifted. However, her stance didn't fool him. There was fear in her eyes. Shifting his gaze, he took in the hand-painted floral design on the fine French provincial furnishings, the expensive designer bedding, the Persian rug, the custom drapes. He made his way to an antique chair he was sure was unappreciated and sat down.

"Mackenzie, come here," he ordered.

When she didn't move he crooked a finger at her. "Now."

Swallowing, Mickey moved slowly toward the man her mother would marry. When she got close she expected him to grab her, shake her, hit her again, but he did none of those things.

His knees spread open and he pointed to the floor between his legs. "Right here, Mackenzie."

Taking another step she moved between his legs, her heart pounding.

He rubbed the back of his hand over her upper arm. "There now, that wasn't so hard, was it?"

Warily, without taking her eyes from him, she shook her head.

"You and me are gonna have to come to some sort of an agreement," he began. "I don't want us to spend the next eleven years fighting, and you don't either, do you?"

Mickey shook her head. "No."

"The fact of the matter is, I'm going to marry your mother, and you and your mother are gonna be living here in my home. And in *my* home, Mackenzie, what I say goes. Now, you're gonna have to accept that. Do as I say and we'll get along just fine. Cross me, and it will be a lot worse than what you experienced earlier today."

She bit her lip and scrunched her eyes as she tried to figure out how far she'd get if she ran away. Of course, she knew that wouldn't really help her. She knew they would eventually find her, bring her back. Thoughts of what would happen then, made her shudder.

She startled as his fingers closed around each of her arms.

"I'm a fair man, Mackenzie. All you have to do is obey me. Do what is expected. When you don't, it makes your mother unhappy and I won't have your mother walking around like a zombie simply because you couldn't behave." He lifted her chin so she had to look him in the eye. "So, do we have an understanding?"

His eyes bore into hers. Inside her head and her heart Mickey felt like screaming. Outside though, she merely nodded her head. "Yes sir."

"There. Now that's been taken care of we can get on with our day. Give your new daddy a big hug," he said, bending forward slightly.

Swallowing back the tears that threatened anew, she reached up and lightly put her arms around his neck while he wrapped his strong arms around her waist and pulled her snug against him. Mickey knew true gratitude when he finally released her and set her back from him.

He stood. "Now, I want you to make your bed and get your bath, and remember, no more problems with you, young lady. The next time it will be with a belt and on your bare bottom."

Her eyes blinked as she envisioned what he promised.

"Am I understood?"

Her jaw clenched. "Yes sir."

Chapter One

Los Angeles, California

Jeff yawned. Laura's attempts at getting his attention were working. He'd had a tough day and hadn't gotten home until almost eight. He'd been tired and not in the mood for much of anything, but she'd ordered pizza and bought wine and finally he'd begun to loosen up.

The movie they'd watched had been boring and it had been all he could do to stay awake. It seems though, she knew just how to get to him. Yes, his energy was definitely surging. He rose slightly off the couch, just enough to push Laura down onto the cushions.

"Finally, I have your attention," she cooed.

Her statement made him think. She often complained about him not giving her his full attention. She had a point, he had to admit. They'd been a couple for several months now. She'd even moved in with him, yet they were not getting closer. If anything he was drifting farther away. However, it was the times like right now, when she was able to pull him from his shell that kept him in the relationship. Besides, it was too much trouble to find someone new. But really, what was the purpose of that kind of relationship?

He lowered himself to kiss her when his cell phone went off.

"Oh, no," Laura said, a warning tone in her voice. "Absolutely no," she ordered.

"Honey, you know I have to answer."

"No, you don't. It's just that you care more about everyone else than you do about me."

"Not true," he argued. Shaking his head, he moved toward the dining room table where he'd tossed his wallet, keys and phone when he'd come in a scant four hours earlier. Laura grabbed his arm as he passed.

"I'm serious, Jeff. Let it ring. Come back here and finish. Whoever it is can wait."

"Laura, let go. I'm on call. I have to answer. Besides, it's almost midnight, it must be important." He twisted his arm away from her grasp and rushed to the phone but it stopped ringing by the time he scooped it up. Peering down at the number, his brow furrowed. "It's Jeffy."

"Who's Jeffy?"

"Eric and Shelley's teenage daughter." When she appeared to not recognize the name he shook his head at her. "Laura, we've been together over six months. How can you not know who I'm talking about? Eric and Shelley Kino, you know Ricky Kino's father and Breanna Adams mother? He didn't wait for her reply as he hit the call back button. Jeffy answered quickly.

"Jeff?" she cried into the phone.

"Yes, Jeffy, what's wrong, sweetie?" he asked, trying to keep the worry out of his voice. He could hear her sobbing, sniffling, trying to get her breath. "Jeffy, answer me. What's happened?"

"Jeff, c-can, you come get me?"

"Where are you?"

"I'm at the *Best Western* on West Coast Highway near Newport Beach."

"What are you doing there?" he barked.

Another loud sniffle. "Don't yell at me."

"Okay, okay. Just calm down," he said, not sure if he was speaking to her or to himself. "I'm not yelling at you, sweetie. I'm just worried about you. I mean, you're fifteen-years-old and you're out at a motel at midnight. Where's your father?"

"No!" she cried. "You can't tell my father. You can't tell anyone in my family. That's why I called *you*."

Jeff ran a hand through his thick blond hair, a sick feeling settling in his gut. Jeffy's father was the legendary martial arts master, Eric Kino. Her brother, the famous martial arts movie star, Ricky Kino, and her sister was another movie legend, Breanna Adams. Her mother was a martial arts champion. Jeffy had two more brothers, Mark and Joey, also both champions, and all were friends of his.

He knew them because he worked as an agent for Ameritech Security, a company run by Jason Lee who was a long time friend and student of Eric Kino.

He'd first met them eight years ago when Jeff was a twenty-two-year-old newbie agent. He'd been asked to help bodyguard the Kino family. An agent had been assigned to each family member because some sicko had threatened to kill them. Jeff had drawn Breanna, the movie star, which had almost been his demise. She'd drugged him, left him unconscious on the beach and taken off. She'd almost lost her life that day. And he'd almost lost his job, probably would have if she hadn't intervened with Jason.

Jeffy, who's real name is June Flower, had only been seven back then and had been very attached to him because, as she put it, he was cute and had the same name as her. Now, she is a teenager. She is also a genius. A child prodigy. At fifteen, she is halfway through her college stint and will be a doctor by the time she's twenty. Add in the fact that she's psychic, has visions, is a 4th degree black belt in more than one discipline, plays concert piano and is startlingly beautiful one could say, oh yes, Jeffy is special. And now she's calling him at midnight and asking him to keep it a secret from her extremely lethal family. Geez.

"Jeff, will you come and get me or not?" she cried.

"Of course I will. I'm on my way," he said, blocking out Laura's loudly indrawn breath. "What room are you in?" She gave him the information. "Jeffy, listen. I'll be there in about thirty minutes. Is there a peep hole in the door?"

She sniffed. "Yes."

"Okay. Do not open the door to anyone but me. You got it?"

"Yes. Hurry, Jeff."

"I'm on my way, and when I get there, you and I are gonna have a long talk."

"Okay," she said petulantly.

Pocketing the phone, he sat on the couch and began putting on his socks and shoes.

"I can't believe you're leaving me to go see that spoiled brat."

Sighing, Jeff shook his head. "She's not spoiled. She's actually a good kid."

"Oh, yeah, great kid, out at midnight and asking you to come rescue her. Let me tell you something about that kid. She has her sights on you."

"Don't be ridiculous. Jeffy is only fifteen. I'm twice her age." He finished tying his shoes and turned toward her. "You're acting as if you're jealous." He stood, went back to the dining area, grabbed his wallet and stuffed it in his pocket.

"I'm not jealous of that little kid, Jeff, but I am of your job. You're always on call."

"That's an exaggeration. I'm not always on call. Still, I will admit, Laura, my job is important to me. It's all I've ever wanted to do, and being on call is part of the job."

"It's ridiculous."

"Ridiculous? Would you act like this if I were a doctor being called away to cure a patient?" He didn't wait for a response. He turned away and she followed him into the bedroom, watched as he strapped on his shoulder holster and gun.

"At least if you were a doctor I'd have a good excuse for being alone all the time. My friends would at least understand that, but not this stupid rent-a-cop thing you've got going."

He froze, his jaw clenched. Great. He'd had no idea that's how she thought of him. The truth comes out. "Do you know that Ameritech is a highly respected security consulting firm that handles extremely important accounts worldwide? Did you know we've been asked to work with the FBI many times and that we've been held up as an example for law enforcement agencies across the country, that the owner of the company trains the people who train the Navy SEALs? I've worked my way up to be one of Jason's top agents. Do you understand what that means?"

When she didn't answer he turned away. "No, Laura, I'm not a doctor. I am what I am. I'm sorry if that disappoints you."

She shrugged. "All it means to me is you're never here."

His eyes focused on the far wall. "Look, I have to go. We can talk about this when I get home."

"And when will that be, Jeff?"

He only shook his head at her, started toward the front door.

"If you leave tonight I won't be here when you get back."

Jeff stopped. "I have to leave. If you can't handle that, I'm sorry." He opened the door and left the apartment, forcing his mind to focus on the situation at hand. Jeffy.

~~~

"Jeffy, open the door, it's—"

The door swung open and Jeffy threw herself against Jeff. He wrapped his arms around her. "There now, you're okay. Everything's okay." Gripping her arms he pulled her away long enough to satisfy himself that what he'd just said was true. She appeared to be fine.

"What happened, Jeffy? Why are you here?"

"Oh, Jeff, it was so terrible. I'm so stupid."

"Now, I'm sure that's not the case. Come on, step inside and we'll talk a minute."

He backed her into the room, making sure the door closed solidly. Jeffy slumped down on the bed. Jeff pulled a chair out from the small table by the window, turned it backward and sat down across from her. "What happened?"

She shook her head, gathered her long, curly, dark tresses in one hand and flipped them back over her shoulder. "It's so hard, you know, being so young and being in college. I just wanted to know."

"You wanted to know what?"

"What it was like, you know– sex."

Jeff swallowed. "Sweet Jesus, Jeffy. What did you do?"

"Oh, don't start getting all crazy on me. I didn't think you would judge me."

"Judge you? No, Jeffy, I'm not judging you. I'm worried about you. And I'm worried about what your parents are gonna say."

"Well, you don't have to worry about me. It didn't happen."

He blew out a breath, raised his eyes heavenward. "Thank you," he whispered.

Tears welled up in her eyes, spilled over onto her beautiful cheek.

"Oh, come on now, Jeffy, why are you so sad?"

"Try to understand, Jeff. It's like having a grown up brain inside a child's body," she said softly. "College kids, they talk about sex all the time. How great it is, how they crave it, how good it feels, how it makes you want to scream."

Jeff did his best to keep a straight face.

"I understand the physiology of it, and of course I've seen movies and read books, but I've never experienced it for myself. I just wanted to know what all the fuss was about. I wanted to know how it felt to turn yourself over to another person and allow them to give you mindless pleasure in such an intimate way, you know?"

Jeff swallowed. "Uh, yes, I understand where you're coming from."

Jeffy sighed heavily. "So, I talked Blake into bringing me here."

"Blake, huh? *You* talked *him* into it?"

"Well, it didn't take much talking."

"I'm sure. What's his last name?"

"Why?"

"Because I'm gonna kick his butt and then have him arrested."

"You can't do that, Jeff. It wouldn't be right. He didn't know I'm only fifteen. How could he? He's a senior and I'm in his biology class. No one at school knows my age. Besides, I told him I was eighteen."

Jeff sighed, shaking his head. "So, he brought you here?"

"Yes. I sort of, you know, came on to him, suggested the motel. After that everything happened so fast."

"I bet."

"Once we got here, I sort of, well, lost my courage. Something didn't seem right. He started taking my clothes off me, and, I guess I felt ashamed when he looked at me. So, I stopped him. He wasn't very happy about that."

Jeff sat up straighter. "Did he hurt you?"

"No. I wouldn't let that happen."

Jeff realized it was a silly question. This girl was the daughter of Grandmaster Kino. She could probably kill with a touch like Uma Thurman in *Kill Bill*. Still, all males have a huge physical advantage over females, even highly trained females. "Jeffy, if he did things you didn't want him to, you can tell me."

"It wasn't like that. I don't know why I acted the way I did. It's supposed to be fun, right? Fun and exciting and pleasurable, right?"

He blew out a breath. Jeff suddenly felt way out of his league. "Maybe, you should talk to your mom about this. Or Bree."

She shrugged. "Just tell me, Jeff, what was I suppose to feel? He kissed me, and it was just cold and slimy. He took my clothes off and saw me in my underwear and I was really embarrassed. And he tried to do stuff, you know, like touch me intimately, and I had to stop him because it just felt too weird. Was that bad? Should I have let him do it and just get it over with?"

Jeff ran a hand through his hair. "No, sweetie, you did the right thing. Your first time should be special. And when it's right, you'll know. You won't feel weird or embarrassed." He pressed his lips together firmly. "So, what did this guy, Blake, do when you made him stop?" Jeff asked, even though he felt sure he already knew the answer.

"He got real mad. He called me a tease. Yelled at me about him having to buy dinner and pay for this motel room. I told him I would pay, but he was so mad and he cursed at me so much it finally made me cry. Then I tried to explain to him why I did what I did. When I told him I was only fifteen he just totally freaked. He grabbed his keys and took off."

"Oh, hon," Jeff said, shaking his head. He moved to the bed and put his arms around her. Jeffy crawled up in his lap like she used to when she was little and let him hold her. "I'm sorry you had to go through all that. Guys can be real jerks."

She shook her head. "It was all my fault. I don't know what I was thinking."

He stroked her hair as he held her. "You were thinking it's time you grew up and learned all about life. I understand that."

She looked up. "You do?"

"Of course I do."

She sighed heavily and sat quietly for a few moments. Finally, she looked back up at him. "Jeff?"

"Yes?"

"*You* could teach me."

"Hm? Teach you what?"

"You could teach me. About life. About sex."

"Oooh, no." He stood up so fast he practically dropped her on the floor. Tossing her back onto the bed, he went to stand by the door, instinctively intending to put as much space as possible between them. "Jeffy, uh, Jeffy, that's very sweet. Really it is, but, hon, you're only fifteen. I'm thirty."

"So? Back in the fifteen hundreds that would make us both adults."

"We don't live in the fifteen hundreds and in our time that makes you a child and me a criminal."

When she looked as if she might cry again, he moved forward and knelt down in front of her. "Jeffy, you flatter me, sweetie. I'm not kidding, or making light of anything, but that's not gonna happen so just wipe those thoughts out of your brain. Now, we need to get you home and I guess I need to speak with your father."

"No!"

Another deep sigh from Jeff. "Sweetie, you need to talk to your parents. You need to let them know how you're feeling about things. They'll help you work through this. You have to know that."

"But you don't understand."

"Maybe not, but I know your mom and dad and brothers and sister love you very much."

"I know they do. It's just that, well, I can't tell them what I've done. They'll be so disappointed."

"I think you're wrong there, Jeffy."

"They're all so perfect, you know?"

Jeff nodded. There was no arguing there.

"And I don't want them to know what an idiot I am. Besides, one of my brothers would probably try to murder Blake. Please, Jeff. Please promise me you won't tell them."

"Jeffy, you're putting me in a very bad position."

"Please, Jeff. Don't tell them."

"Your mom would be devastated if she knew her own daughter didn't feel like she could come to her."

Sighing, Jeffy nodded. "You're right, and I never want to hurt my mom." Tears welled in her eyes. "Ugh! This growing up thing is so hard." She wiped the tears from her eyes. "Okay Jeff, I promise, I'll tell mom."

Jeff smiled. "Good, Jeffy. I feel so much better. Don't you?"

"Just not right away. I need time to think about things first."

Jeff blew out a breath.

"You promise you won't say anything to my parents until I have a chance to do it."

"Okay, I promise," he said with a sigh.

She smiled at him.

He rolled his eyes. "So, let's get you home. I can get you past the security gate, but sneaking in is all up to you. How in the world did you get out of the house in the first place?"

"I'm supposed to be spending the night with a friend."

"You outright lied to your parents?"

She hung her head. "Yes. It's the first time, I swear. And it feels terrible."

"Good. It should. Come on. Get all your stuff and get in the car."

He opened the door and stood there waiting on her. When she approached she smiled, stood on her toes, leaned close and kissed his cheek. "Thanks, Jeff."

"I must have a death wish," he muttered.

~~~

Consciousness came back to Mackenzie slowly, easing in as a soft gray around the fringes of her mind. She knew she was still in the van, the big black one that had pulled up in front of her as she'd jogged down the street in her own safe neighborhood. She knew because she could feel the motion of the road beneath her back and could smell gas and exhaust. Not yet daring to open her eyes and interact with her captors, she tried to calm her racing heart.

Her head pounded. Tears burned her eyes and she ordered herself to get control. She wasn't a little girl anymore. She was a full grown woman with a master's in English, working on her second novel. She remembered she'd been ecstatic to get published. She grasped onto that happy time in her life to block out what was presently taking place, but she couldn't hold onto it. Suddenly none of that seemed very important.

Someone's shoe tapped her leg.

"She alive?" a man's deep voice asked.

"For now," another answered.

"Good, 'cause I need her alive for what I have in mind."

Oh Lord, help me.

"This isn't like that, man. We don't touch her. Our orders are to hold her secure until we get the word to off her."

"Yeah, well, what the boss man don't know won't hurt him, right? I mean, she's dead anyway. We may as well have our fun."

"I said, you don't touch her. Sex leaves evidence."

"Butch, you're such a pussy. Maybe it's you I should s–"

She heard an indrawn breath, a scuffle, grunting and the sound of flesh hitting flesh. Someone tripped over her legs. The van swerved.

"Hey, you two idiots, give it a rest before I shoot both of ya."

The voice had come from farther away and Mickey assumed it was the driver. It sounded familiar, but she couldn't place it.

"Let go," she heard the one with the deep voice say.

"Better watch what you say," the one called Butch warned. "Next time you open your mouth like that, you're the one who's gonna be screwed."

There was a grunt as Mickey supposed the Butch guy was letting go of the other one. The excitement over, Mickey forced herself to think. Who was this 'boss man'? And why would anyone have her kidnapped? Of course, her family had plenty of money, at least, her stepfather did. He was in the middle of a campaign for his second term as Senator of the great state of Washington. After that, President, he kept saying. Yeah, right. Mackenzie had no idea how much he was worth, but she assumed he was rolling in it from the lifestyle he'd provided for her, her mother and her little sister, Marissa.

Marissa. The thought of her sweet little sister had her grimacing. She supposed if someone had to be ransomed for her stepfather's money, she was glad it was her and not little Marissa who'd been born when Mackenzie had been thirteen. Sweet Marissa. Everyone loved Marissa. She was everything Mackenzie was not. Quiet, calm, obedient, content, kind and nonjudgmental. As far as Mackenzie was concerned, Marissa was the only good thing that had come from her mother's horrible decision to marry Talmond Daley, the bane of Mackenzie's existence.

Just the thought of Marissa having to go through this ordeal made Mackenzie so sick, her stomach heaved. Lord, she hoped she didn't throw up, because now that she was more awake, she realized she was gagged. She'd drown in her own vomit. Trying to move her arms to remove the gag made her realize her arms and legs were also bound.

The predicament she found herself in seemed so very surreal. This kind of stuff didn't happen, did it? Not in real life. Yet it *was* happening. She'd been going for her morning run, a van had pulled up in front of her and stopped. Two men had jumped out and grabbed her. She'd been inside the van in about two seconds. She'd fought, but one of them hit her in the jaw and that's the last thing she remembered. Until now. And now it was all she could do to stay calm and think, yet all she could think about was she didn't want to die and what she wanted probably wasn't gonna make a bit of difference. Someone kicked her leg again.

"You're awake, aren't you?"

It was the one called Butch. When she didn't answer, he kicked her again. She opened her eyes.

~~~

They'd been driving for over twelve hours. The only reason she knew that was because it'd been around six in the morning when they'd taken her and it was dark now. Twelve hours meant they could be as far as two or three states away by now, supposing they'd driven east or south. Surely there was no way they could've headed north and crossed over into Canada. Not with a hostage lying in the back of their vehicle.

The ride was excruciating. Her head felt as if it may explode and she feared she soon would lose control over her bladder. When she heard the crunching of gravel under the tires she hoped that meant they had arrived at their destination, but it turned out to be at least another thirty minutes before they rolled to a stop.

She'd been so uncomfortable she almost cried with relief, except that arriving at their destination also meant she was one step closer to her death. The side door opened and the men stepped out. Mickey gratefully breathed in the fresh air. It was Butch who turned, lifted her and carried her toward a small cabin that appeared to be in the middle of the woods. He carried her through the main living area into another small room and tossed her none too gently onto a single old-fashioned bed with a metal headboard. Then, he turned and closed the door.

Her body trembling, she watched him as he approached. He looked her over. Terror overtook her and she found herself struggling to breathe. He came forward, placed a knee on the bed and bent over her.

"I'm gonna take the gag off. I want you to be very still. If you scream, the only one who will hear you is Richard, and believe me, you don't want him to come in here. Do you understand?"

She nodded her head.

Leaning over her, he released the gag and pulled it away. She drew a large breath.

"Thank you," she whispered.

His hand gripped her cheeks. "Don't thank me. Later, you'll wish you hadn't."

"I– I need to use the bathroom."

He nodded his head, drew a knife and cut through the duct tape that bound her, then pulled her into a sitting position. "Can you stand?"

"I think so."

He took her wrist in a steely grip and pulled her up. She swayed and he put a hand out to steady her. "Come with me."

Butch led her out of the room and pushed her toward a door on the left. She glanced around, trying to take in as much detail as possible. As far as she could tell, the cabin had three rooms, a main living area, a bedroom and a bathroom. The living area held a sofa and a chair, facing a fireplace. There was a small niche in the left corner of the room that was a tiny kitchen with a table and two chairs. The man Mickey supposed was Richard was sorting through boxes of supplies. She heard the van drive away.

Butch opened the bathroom door and shoved her through. Mickey looked around the small room. There was no window, which she figured was why Butch had let her in here without being watched. As she quickly used the facilities, she took note of the rest of the room. There was a standup shower and a tiny sink with a used cake of soap lying on the edge. No real towels, however, a small aluminum bucket sat under the sink, holding a roll of paper towels. Rising, she glanced in the mirror that hung over the sink. There was a bruise on the side of her face and her eyes appeared to be those of a stranger.

She knew if she didn't come out of the bathroom soon, Butch would come in after her, but, dear Lord, she didn't want to go back out there with those men. They were her killers, waiting for an order to off her from some person playing God. No, she sure didn't want to leave this room. She felt like giving in to her grief, sinking down onto the floor and having a good cry, but that wouldn't help anything.

Slowly, she turned the knob and opened the door a crack. Butch was talking to Richard, his back to her. Eyeing the front door to the cabin, she wondered if she could make it outside. No way for her to sneak. She'd have to just make a dash. She had to try, didn't she? And she had to act quickly before Butch turned back toward her. Heart pounding, she counted to three and took off.

Mickey flew from the bathroom, crossed the main room in two steps, grabbed the door and jerked it open. Jumping off the porch she was in the woods in mere seconds. It was pitch black and she ran blindly. Either instinct or too many movies had her running a zig-zag pattern. It felt so good to run, to be free, could it be this easy?

Maybe it was because of the rushing sound of her heart in her ears that she didn't hear Butch behind her. The next thing she knew she was tackled from behind. She hit the forest floor, the air leaving her lungs in a giant whoosh. Butch wrestled her around to her back and straddled her. Mickey flung her fists out at him, swinging wildly at his face.

"Stop it," he barked.

Like she would listen. She kneed him in the back and kept right on swinging. He tried to gather her hands together but her movements were too frenzied.

"I said stop," he yelled just before he slapped her.

Mickey winced at the sting, yet she couldn't let a little pain deter her from her goal. She bucked, trying to dislodge him from her stomach. Unfortunately, he finally got control of her hands and pinned them beside her head. He leaned close to her, placing his mouth right beside her ear.

"Listen to me. You can make your last days on earth torture, or you can pass them in relative peace. The boss man hears I can't control you, Richard gets a shot, and all he wants to do is drill your fine self. You got me?"

"Please let me go. Please. I can tell you don't want to hurt me.

Please."

"You can't tell squat."

"But what if my stepfather pays the ransom? You keep acting as if he won't pay. What if he does? Then you'll let me go?"

"Either way, you're dead."

"Why? Can't you let me go once the ransom is paid? Please, I don't want to die," she pleaded, her eyes boring into his.

"Don't give me that scared little girl look. Bad things happen. That's life."

He jerked her to her feet and drug her back to the cabin. This time when they got to the room he slammed her on the bed, pulled out a set of handcuffs and cuffed both her hands over her head to the antique metal headboard.

"Will you tell me why, or at least who?" Mickey sobbed. "Who is this man who wants me dead? Who is he?"

He stared at her in silence, his jaw tense. "You're better off not knowing." He turned away, then turned back. "I'll be back with something to eat later." He left the room.

～～～

Jeff hurried to the door, wondering who would be pounding on it this early in the morning. Normally, he'd be worried that whoever it was would wake Laura, but she'd been true to her word. She'd been gone by the time he'd returned the night he went to rescue Jeffy Kino.

She'd come back the next day all haughty, along with some guy she worked with, to retrieve the rest of her belongings. She'd brought her co-worker along as if she'd had something to fear from Jeff and that really got to him. Jeff had wanted to shoot the guy right between the eyes. That would've gotten rid of the self-righteous look on his yuppy face. Oh, yeah, Jeff thought as he imagined that look of surprise when the bullet first struck. He'd entertained himself with the thought many times over the past two days. If this was Laura again, he was gonna give her a piece of his mind.

He snatched the door open. "What do you—" He stopped cold because Ricky Kino stood at his front door, his arms folded over his chest.

"Ricky!"

Rick nodded. "Jeff."

Jeff sighed, waved him in, turned from the door and headed toward the kitchen. Ricky stepped in, closed the door behind him and followed Jeff.

"Uh, to what do I owe this honor?" Jeff asked as he spooned coffee into the coffee maker Laura had purchased for the apartment.

Ricky took a seat at the bar that separated the kitchen from the tiny dining room and tossed a scandal mag on the counter. "I thought you might want to explain this."

Jeff poured in the water, hit the button and sauntered over to the counter, focusing in on the paper in front of him. On the front page was a slightly out of focus picture of Jeffy and him, standing in the doorway of a *Best Western* motel room. The headline read: *Kino's kid sister rendezvous with lover.*

Jeff's face paled as he took a step back. "I swear, Rick, it's not what it seems."

"Let's talk about what it seems, Jeff," Ricky said calmly.

Jeff eyed him suspiciously. He knew the calm voice could be deceptive.

Ricky went on. "It seems to be the middle of the night. It seems you and my little sister are at a motel. There are more pictures on the inside of the paper that make it seem like the two of you are quite cozy. One where you're all wrapped around her and one where she's kissing you."

Jeff swallowed hard. "Rick, I'm no rocket scientist, but I'm also not stupid. I swear to you, I would never mess around with Ricky Kino's baby sister or Master Kino's under-aged daughter."

Ricky grinned. "Hell, Jeff, I know that. I just wanted to watch you squirm for a minute."

Jeff heaved a sigh. "Great. Well, so glad I could offer you some entertainment." Shaking his head, he gestured at the magazine. "When did that come out?"

"Yesterday. I've already tracked down the shooter. It was the hotel clerk. Apparently Jeffy and some guy checked in near the end of his shift and he recognized Jeffy. Thinking to have the scoop of the day on a celebrity's little sister, he waited until the end of his shift, drove his car around to have a clear shot of the room and waited. Then you showed up. He says you were there about fifteen minutes, and then you and Jeffy left together. He has no idea what happened to the other guy."

"I do. He freaked and ran when Jeffy finally told him she was only fifteen."

Ricky drew a deep breath. "So, what's the rest of the story?"

"She hasn't told you?"

"No. And I'd like to find out before Dad and Shelley see this thing."

Jeff shook his head. "I can't tell you."

"Excuse me?"

"I promised her I wouldn't tell her parents. I have to keep my word. I'm sure you understand that since you're all about honor."

"I think you have me mixed up with my father."

"Bull. Play it off if you want. I have eyes in my head. Ricky Kino is honor personified. Anyway, she promised me she would speak to her parents. She said, she needed to wait, to think about things, but she would tell them– or, her mom, anyway."

"Well, I'm not them, savvy?"

Turning his back, Jeff poured himself a large mug of coffee and faced Ricky, leaning back against the kitchen counter, one ankle crossed over the other. He didn't bother offering some to his guest. He knew Ricky never touched the stuff. "I'd offer you some tea or some other weird crap like that but I don't have any."

"I'm good, and you're stalling."

"I'm trying to decide if I'm breaking my word by talking to you."

"Jeff, do I need to find this guy, have him arrested, kick his butt?"

Jeff shook his head. "Not his fault. Poor guy had no idea Jeffy was as young as she is."

"Are you kidding me? She looks like a baby?"

"Are *you* kidding me? She has breasts and curves and a tight body, not to mention that long, curly mass of dark hair and those huge brown eyes. She's like a young Shelley but with your coloring. She's a knockout."

"Okay, I'm not comfortable with this conversation."

Jeff laughed. "She's growing up, Rick. Admit it."

"Geez, time is flying by."

"Yeah, way back when I first met you eight years ago you weren't even married. Now, you're what—?"

"Thirty-eight, married, with two kids. It doesn't seem like it though. I feel like I'm still twenty."

"Guess it's all that clean living."

"Whatever. Back to the story, Jeff, and bottom line– is my sister still a virgin?"

"When I delivered her back to her home she was. What she's done since then I can't say."

Ricky's brow furrowed as his mind went to work. "So, it was her idea to go to the motel. She's trying to lose her virginity?"

"Something like that."

"And the guy somehow found out how old she is and took off and she called you for a ride home because she didn't want any of us to know what she'd done."

"Pretty close. Only, it was Jeffy who decided she couldn't go through with it and the guy got pretty mad."

Ricky's scowled. "Did he hurt her?"

Jeff chuckled. "You and I think more alike than you know. No, he didn't hurt her, but he did upset her enough to tell him the truth about her age and when she did, he took off. She called me and asked me to come and get her."

Ricky nodded his head. "Hey, thanks for being there for my sister."

"No problem."

"So, Jeffy wants to know about sex."

"Yeah. She even asked me to teach her."

Ricky looked up quickly. "Really? That's interesting." He began to chuckle. "Put you in a predicament, didn't she?"

"To say the least."

"Guess it runs in the family."

"What do you mean?"

"When Bree was eighteen, she practically begged me to relieve her of her virginity."

Grinning, Jeff shook his head, thinking about the beautiful movie star. "Wow, every man's dream. And so I'm guessing you were the one who did the deed?"

"No, I wasn't. I don't do casual sex. So, I turned her down. It was a heck of a hard thing to do."

"You're a better man than me."

Ricky laughed.

"No, really, I'm sure turning down the finest piece in America was difficult."

"Hey, watch how you talk about my wife."

Jeff shrugged. "There are worse things to be labeled."

Rick sighed. Thinking about his first time with the woman who was now his wife, made him want to head home. He cleared his head. "Shelley needs to know about Jeffy's newest obsession. She's gonna be upset that her own daughter didn't feel she could come to her about it. Guess I'd better have a word with Dad, put the burden on him."

"Great idea. When all else fails, turn it over to someone else."

"He's the only one that can handle Shelley."

"Handle Shelley, hmm? Do you think she knows that's how you feel?"

"No, and I'd appreciate those words staying between you and me." Ricky looked around. "So where's Laura?"

"She left me," Jeff said, shrugging it off. "She was mad when I had to leave the other night to rescue Jeffy. When I got back, she was gone."

"Oh, man, Jeff. Sorry about that."

"For the best. I don't think there was any love lost. We were used to each other and it was easier to stay together than go looking. However, the other night she let me know my career was an embarrassment to her."

"Ouch. You're a top agent. Pretty respectable in my book."

"Yeah, well, thanks. You wanna be my new girlfriend?"

Ricky grinned. "Sorry, I'm taken. So, you got anybody else in mind? I'm sure Bree can fix you up on a blind date or two."

"Oh, yeah, that's just what I want to do. Let me give you an emphatic, hell no."

Shrugging, Ricky raised his eyebrows. "Bree knows some real lookers. I understand you're not interested right now, but who knows, down the road on a lonely night—" He let the implied sentence go.

"Yeah, I'll keep that in mind. When I'm ready should I look that up under 'Bree's call girl services'?"

"Funny. So what now?"

"I've got a couple weeks of vacation coming. I'm gonna drive up to the lake home I bought last year, do some work on it, get in some shooting."

"Going alone?"

"Guess I am now."

"That place is pretty isolated. Leave an itinerary and check in."

"Will do, mommy."

Chapter Two

They'd come south, Mickey thought. It had to be south. The sun was just coming up and it was already warm. Even in June, mornings in the state of Washington are cool. She tugged on the cuffs just to make sure they hadn't miraculously come undone during the night.

Peering down toward the foot of the bed, she looked to see if Butch was still there and was relieved to find she was alone. He'd surprised her last night by staying in the room with her. Arriving with a peanut butter and jelly sandwich and a bottle of water, he'd un-cuffed her, allowed her to sit up, and then cuffed just one hand to the bed so she could feed herself. When she'd finished, he'd told her to lie back down. She'd begged him to leave the cuffs off. Patiently, as if she were a child, he'd gently pushed her down and cuffed both her hands to the bed again. He then turned off the overhead light, sat down in the chair at the foot of the bed, propped his feet up, turned on a flashlight and opened a book. A few hours later it woke her when he'd switched off the light.

She hadn't expected him to stay and she wondered if he was actually guarding her, or possibly protecting her from Richard. After all, it wasn't like she could go anywhere with her hands cuffed to the bed. So, she reasoned, Butch must be protecting her, and that meant he just might have a heart or a conscience and she might be able to appeal to him, wear him down and talk him into letting her go. The idea bolstered her mood.

She definitely needed something to bolster her mood. She'd never thought about how vulnerable someone is when they are bound in some fashion. The feeling of being absolutely and completely dependent on whoever is supposed to be seeing to her needs, she found terrifying. From the smallest thing like being unable to scratch her nose, to the biggest thing like not being able to defend herself against an attacker. She was helpless. Not only that, but claustrophobia was becoming a problem. Just lying here thinking about it right now, knowing she is not free to run, was making her want to scream.

Her heart began to beat faster, beads of perspiration popped out all over her body, tears welled in her eyes. She tugged on the cuffs, lightly at first, then harder. Choking on a sob, and panicked, she twisted her body until her arms crossed and she was on her stomach. Then she rose up onto her knees. The panic began to subside. She sniffed, leaned forward to wipe her eyes on her wrist.

The door opened and Butch stepped in. He carried a cereal breakfast bar and a bottle of water. Setting them down on the table beside the bed, he leaned over her.

"What are you trying to pull?"

"Nothing," she said softly. "I, uh, I was afraid you weren't coming back and I panicked."

His lips pressed tightly together as if he didn't believe her.

"Really, I'm just glad to see you."

He frowned. "You won't say that in a few days." He leaned over and unlocked the cuffs.

Keeping in mind her plan to convince him to let her live, she offered a timid smile. "That feels better. Thank you."

He rolled his eyes at her, pocketed the cuffs, grabbed her by the wrist and pulled her out the door. She stumbled against his back when he stopped abruptly to open the bathroom door. Glancing around quickly she found Richard sitting on the sofa scarfing up doughnuts. He looked up at her, his eyes sweeping over her body before he turned back to watch the small, older television.

Butch shoved her into the bathroom. "Don't bother to try running this time. I'll be right here next to the door."

"I won't," she assured him meekly.

When she emerged from the bathroom a few minutes later he grabbed her wrist. He'd started to push her back into the bedroom when she looked up at the television and gasped.

Glancing over, he saw Mickey's family being interviewed on TV.

"Can I see? Please?"

He didn't let her move any closer, still, he allowed her to stay there beside the bedroom door while she watched the eight o'clock news. Her mother spoke into the camera, asking the kidnappers to please not hurt her daughter. Marion's hand rested on Marissa's shoulder. The camera zoomed in to show the tears coursing down the young girl's cheeks. "Oh, Rissa," Mickey said softly, her throat clogging with emotion.

The camera pulled back and focused in on her stepfather who was now speaking. "We'll do anything you want," he said. "Just bring her back."

Mickey's brow furrowed. He sounded emotional, like he was just sick over her. She knew that wasn't true. He'd hated her as long as he'd known her. And she hated him. Still, they'd lived somewhat civilly together for eleven years, mostly ignoring each other. Except for the times she'd angered him. As was her habit, she forced those memories away.

He's a good actor, she thought as she watched him. She'd realized that over the years. Of course he couldn't let the world know theirs was not the perfect family. The world believed he'd fallen in love with a poor, single mother whose husband had deserted her and her child. The mighty Talmond Daley had stepped in and rescued them, and in his most charitable of hearts, he'd adopted the child as his own, changing her name from Mackenzie Leigh Benson to Mackenzie Leigh Daley.

Pushing the ugly thoughts from her mind, she listened as the press was allowed to ask questions of the local chief of police even though Mickey was sure the case was being handled by the FBI.

"Sir," one reporter asked, "have you received a ransom note yet? Can you tell us how much the kidnappers are demanding?"

"We've not received a ransom note yet," the chief answered.

Mickey looked quickly back up at Butch. "Why not? Who's supposed to send the ransom note? How long are they gonna wait?"

"That's enough," Butch snapped. Grabbing her wrist he jerked her into the bedroom and cuffed one hand to the bed. Shoving the breakfast bar at her, he turned and left the room.

She felt sick, yet she knew she needed to keep up her strength if she was gonna somehow escape. She had to believe she could. She had to act as if that time is coming. And so, she forced herself to unwrap the breakfast bar and eat every single crumb and drink every drop of water.

As she ate, her mind raced back to the fact that no ransom note had been sent thus far. That didn't mean one wouldn't be sent. Surely someone would ask for a ransom. Yet, what if they didn't? And then she remembered that it didn't really matter one way or the other because Butch already said she was dead either way. Well, if no one intended to bargain for her life, then she would bargain for it herself. She was bound and determined to soften Butch up enough to make him want to save her life.

She didn't see him again until lunchtime. He brought her more water and another peanut butter sandwich.

"Thank you," she said sweetly.

"Stop saying that," he ordered as he took a seat in his chair.

He watched her as she ate. She looked up and smiled at him. "Can I ask you a question?'

"What?" he grumbled impatiently.

"Have you killed anybody before me?"

At first she thought he wouldn't answer, then he gruffly said, "Yes."

"Any women?"

"No, but don't get your hopes up. I'll do what I'm ordered to do."

"And whoever's in charge is going to order you to kill me eventually, right?"

"Yes."

"Whether the ransom is paid or not."

He remained silent.

"Butch? Is that right? I'm dead either way?"

"Yes."

"Then, why wait?"

"What?"

"Why wait for the order? If I'm dead either way, why not just get it over with? You wouldn't have to babysit me or feed me or worry that I'll escape."

"I was told to take you and hold you until the order to kill comes down. That's what I'm gonna do."

"Maybe there's a chance this guy will change his mind. Maybe, since he wants to wait, maybe it's because he thinks there may possibly be a change of plans."

Butch looked into her eyes for several seconds as he considered the idea. His eyes hardened. "And maybe it's because he needs to prove you're still alive in order to get the money," Butch returned. "Listen, kid, don't get your hopes up." He picked up his book and opened it.

"Well he certainly won't get any money if he doesn't send a

ransom note, right?"

Butch didn't answer.

So maybe there will be a ransom note, she surmised, and maybe there will be a bargain for her life. And maybe the ransom will be paid and maybe they will work it where the kidnappers get caught and she gets rescued and maybe her stepfather really is upset about the whole thing and maybe somewhere deep down inside he actually cares enough for her that he will pay the ransom . . . yeah, and maybe the moon is really made of bleu cheese. He didn't care, she wasn't worth a wooden nickel to him.

She was quiet for awhile. Pushing herself up against the metal headboard, she stretched her legs out in front of her and looked Butch over. He had short dark hair and light eyes. Gray maybe. His nose was large and crooked like it'd been broken a few times. A scar ran across the top of his forehead as if someone had tried to scalp him. His mouth was a firm, straight line. He was a large man, with large hands. Suddenly, she could see those hands closing around her throat. Swallowing, she looked away. It'd grown quite warm and sweat trickled down her forehead and between her breasts. After an hour or so of silence and heat, Butch put his book down, rose and went to open the window.

"Thank you," she said as he sat back down.

He only rolled his eyes at her.

"Butch?"

He blew out an angry breath. "What?"

"Do you have a family?"

He didn't answer.

"I mean, everyone has a family. Mother, father, brother, sister, aunt, uncle, cousin. Everyone has somebody. You were born so you had to have a mother."

"If I did I don't remember her."

"Anyone else?"

"Nope."

"Who raised you?"

"Some crack head lady who used me to help her get her fix for the day."

"What happened to her?"

"Some guy cut her heart out."

Mickey had to regroup after that answer. Still, she felt she was making progress. He was at least talking to her. She had to keep going. "Is there no one you ever cared about? Like maybe a girlfriend?"

He kept his eyes focused on the pages of the book while he spoke.

"Had one once. Met her when I worked for a landscaping company. The daughter of some rich guy."

"What happened to her?"

"Her father found out I was banging his daughter and had me arrested."

"How old was she?"

"She was seventeen and knew plenty well what was what. I wasn't her first."

"How old were you?"

"Eighteen."

"So, really it wasn't like her father tried to make it out to be. You were both really just kids."

"Go figure," Butch said sarcastically.

"That sucks," Mickey continued commiserating. "It's not like you were taking advantage of a young innocent or anything. You were barely older than her."

Butch looked up, his eyes boring deep into Mickey's. "Crap like that happens every single day. Innocent people get messed up. That's life, princess. Accept it. I did."

"Did you ever see her again?"

"Nope. I went to prison over that. She actually wrote me for a while. Then the letters just stopped."

"So you hate her now?"

"Naw. She told her father the truth. He chose not to believe her. Guess it disturbed his sensibilities that his little girl could fall for a commoner. He made sure the commoner would never get close to her again." He shrugged. "No, I don't hate her. Can't blame her for having a life. Hope she's happy. Really."

"So you're not such a hardened bitter guy after all, are you?"

He stood. "I'm also not stupid. Sorry, little girl. You're going down. Accept it. All the talk in the world is not gonna make me change my mind. I follow the orders."

~~~

Mickey's days in captivity had become a blur of monotony. Butch came in the room with a breakfast bar and water, took her to the bathroom, cuffed one hand to the bed for the day and sat with her while she tried to talk to him. Peanut butter sandwich for lunch, and a can of beanie-weenie for dinner rounded out her menu. Another trip to the bathroom, then she was forced to lie down and both hands cuffed for the night.

He stayed with her for the most part, reading his book or sometimes just staring out the window. Mickey wondered why he stayed. Maybe he thought it was the least he could do, keep her company until the time came. She wondered if at the end he would give her a nice meal, like they give death row inmates. Maybe he stayed because he thought he needed to keep an eye on her. Maybe he preferred her company over Richard's whom she'd barely laid eyes on since they'd arrived at the cabin. Not that she was complaining. She'd heard them arguing with each other several times, but she couldn't quite make out what they were arguing about.

How much time did she have left? Would her stepfather even pay the ransom? He wouldn't want to, but he would do it to appear saintly in the public's eyes. It was these things Mickey pondered early one morning when everything drastically changed.

She looked up when the door opened, expecting to see Butch, but her heart filled with dread when Richard appeared in the doorway, his slick smile in place.

"Hey gorgeous," he said with a grin.

"Where's Butch?" Mickey asked shortly, trying not to let him know how much he scared her.

"He's taking a walk before breakfast. Said you were driving him crazy. And I was out there thinking, you know like, while the cats away this mouse is gonna play."

"You're not supposed to touch me. If you do, Butch will hurt you."

"I ain't scared of him. You and me, we're about to be great friends."

Mickey's breath hitched in her chest. Richard moved close to the bed, placed his hand on her knee. She jerked her leg, trying to knock his hand away, but he just laughed.

"It's okay if you fight me. I like it when they fight."

Tears welled in her eyes and she cursed herself for being a big baby.

"You wearing those tight little running shorts and that short little shirt that shows your bellybutton, you know it tempts us guys. You do it on purpose. You ain't got no one to blame but yourself. I bet you ain't even got any underwear on under that."

She didn't dare answer, because he was right. Her running shorts were made to wear alone. He grabbed her, she tried to use her leg to kick him away from her. He only laughed. She tried again and ended up clotting him in the head.

Furious, he was on her in seconds, straddling her waist. He reared back and punched her in the mouth. Mickey saw stars. Her eyes started to close, but she forced them back open. He tried to kiss her but she bit him. Cursing, he punched her again.

This time she realized she was losing consciousness. On the fringes of her awareness she knew he was trying to remove her clothing. It didn't really seem to matter as she felt herself slipping away. She tried to cry out. To scream. She wasn't sure if she accomplished it. She heard a crash. Then suddenly, he was off her.

Mickey struggled to raise her head to see what had happened to Richard. Butch had him up against the wall and was bashing him with his fists. Lord, he was gonna kill him. Richard's face was covered with blood. Butch had his hands around Richard's throat, just like she'd imagined them around hers. Then suddenly he let him go and Richard slid to the floor. Butch bent over, hauled the prone man over his shoulder and left the room.

When Butch returned, he came straight to the side of the bed and peered down into her face. Blinking up at him, she couldn't think of anything to say, and it was a good thing because she probably couldn't speak anyway. She looked into his eyes and—wait; did she see a shred of compassion?

Only then, his eyes left hers and traveled the length of her body. He didn't say anything, yet his breathing became heavier. Mickey suddenly realized he was considering finishing what Richard had started.

Mickey didn't speak. Somehow she realized he waged an internal battle and she was afraid if she spoke, he would lose that battle. And then, suddenly, he reached up and unlocked her cuffs. "Fix yourself," he said gruffly.

Mickey immediately straightened her clothing. She started to cry tears of gratitude. "Thank you," she sniffed.

He stilled, looking straight ahead. "I told you not to say that."

Wisely, she stayed quiet while he took her through the morning routine. When he led her to the bathroom, she glanced around quickly, looking for Richard, but she didn't see him. Once she'd eaten her breakfast bar she curled back up on the bed, hugging her knees with her free arm.

Butch sat in his chair but remained silent. Mickey's mind strayed over Richard's visit. Shuddering at the thought of his hands on her, she wondered where he was now. Glancing at the large man in the chair, her eyes welled with tears. It was weird that she could feel grateful to a man who intended to leave her for dead very soon. Lord, but she didn't want to die. Grown woman or not, she was terrified. Wiping at her tears, she cleared her throat. "Butch?"

"Yes?" he said softly.

His answer took her aback. Usually he answered in a gruff monotone 'what.' When her eyes looked up at him he was looking right at her instead of past her, but she wasn't gonna fool herself anymore. She felt drained, defeated. She had no more energy to put toward thoughts of escape. Blowing out a breath, she realized that somewhere along the line she'd accepted that it may happen, that she is going to die. What did it matter. She was obviously expendable. She cleared her throat again. "When it's time, I want you to be the one to do it." she said quietly.

His gaze remained calm as he looked into her eyes. Slowly, he nodded his head.

~~~

Jeff Davis pulled his truck up to the large ranch style house he'd bought a year earlier. Since that time he'd been up to work on it only twice. No problem because he wasn't in any hurry. The house was a dingy, pale yellow with white trim. No front porch to speak of, instead a few concrete steps led up to the door.

Inside was a great room, a large open kitchen, three bedrooms and two baths and that was all, but he'd gotten a great deal. Included in that deal was the large lakefront that met his property in the back. Both times he'd been up to work on the house, it was actually the back deck and dock that had occupied all his time. And it would again, for the next two weeks.

Smiling, he jumped from the cab of his truck, grabbed his bags and headed inside. He'd unhitch the trailer and unload the building materials after lunch. It'd been a long, tedious drive. Shoving the front door open, he dropped his bags and began opening windows to air out the stale smell. Flicking a switch, he was happy to see the power company had already turned on the power. Jeff turned his phone to some tunes, hooked it up to the mini speakers and cranked it up, then went to put away the kitchen supplies. He used his handy dandy

Clorox wipes to clean the counter, then peeked cautiously into the fridge since he couldn't remember if he cleaned it out before he left the last time he was here. Whew, coast clear.

It took him only thirty minutes to get unpacked and make some good old bologna and cheese sandwiches, with sour cream and onion chips on the side. He rummaged through the cooler, bypassing the beer for now, and grabbed a soft drink. Popping the top on a Coke, he slid open the glass door that led out back to the deck he'd rebuilt on his last visit. He eased down onto the only piece of furniture, a wooden Adirondack chair. Sighing with pleasure, he took a few swigs of his Coke, sat it on the wide arm of the chair and bit into his sandwich.

There was a breeze blowing in off the lake. It ruffled his hair, cooled his body and eased his mind. This was the life. Sunshine, fresh air, lake, fishing, building something with his own two hands. Once he finished building his dock he intended to purchase a gorgeous Proline fishing boat he had his eye on. He breathed deeply as he imagined pulling that boat up to his newly built dock. Birds sang overhead as if they too imagined how nice it will be. He smiled. It was quiet here, at least on this part of the lake.

He'd brought Laura up here with him on his last visit around Christmas. He remembered she'd talked incessantly about the fancy subdivision on the other side of the lake. The one with the three-story dwellings, the elaborate docks and 2.3 luxury speed boats per home. He'd described to her his plans for his little home on the lake. She had been duly impressed because at the time theirs had been a new relationship. He realized now she'd merely been being polite. Apparently, the simple life was not for her. Money and prestige were more her game. More reasons why ending the relationship had been for the best.

After lunch, he decided, he'd unload the trailer, then take a swim, then scout out a good place to set up his shooting range. He glanced out to the left of his property. About a hundred yards of open field blended into the far tree line. He could still see the old wood plank he'd nailed to one of those trees last time he was here. He'd wanted to show off for Laura. Again, she'd been duly impressed. He shook his head at the thought.

He'd come better prepared this time. Brought targets and guns and his favorite rifle. Shooting was his thing. He hadn't been in the military, but when he'd done sniper school with Ameritech, he'd graduated at the top of his class. He could hit any target, moving or not. He chalked it up to the video games he'd played as a kid. It just came easy to him. He'd won a dozen or so awards in state and national competitions. Stuffing the last crust of bread in his mouth, he stood. Enough dreaming. For now, there was work to do.

~~~

The day was a scorcher and Mickey thought she'd melt before the sun started on its downward trek. Eyeing Butch, she wondered if he would allow her a shower. Man oh man, it would feel so good. Why wouldn't he, she reasoned? It couldn't hurt to ask. He obviously liked to be clean. Each morning she could tell he'd showered and shaved. Contrary to how one would picture a criminal, he always dressed nicely, usually in black slacks and a white shirt.

"Butch?"

His eyes drifted from the window to her. "Yes?"

There was that answer again. His attitude toward her had definitely changed. "I was wondering, it's so hot and I've been stuck on this bed for days now. Do you think I could take a shower? I promise not to try to run. It would feel so good, to get clean. One last physical pleasure." She'd added that last part as a guilt trip. It must've worked.

He rose, came to her, unlocked the cuffs and pulled her up. She swayed briefly, dizzy since Richard had knocked her in the face. Breathing deeply, she cleared her head and nodded. He led her out of the room and toward the sofa where a towel lay over the back. Richard was there on the sofa. He glanced up at them briefly, then turned away. Mickey was surprised at the extent of his injuries. His face was one massive bruise.

Butch grabbed the towel and handed it to her. "It's been used, but it's the only one I have. And I don't have any girly shampoo, but you can use what's in there."

"Thank you," she said, smiling. "I'm gonna wash out my clothes so don't come barging in if you think I'm taking too long."

He nodded, pushed her into the bathroom and closed the door.

Mickey wasted no time. She kicked off her running shoes and socks. In just a few seconds she was in the shower, the warm water running over her face and hair. It felt just as good as she'd imagined. Grabbing up the cheap shampoo that sat on the floor of the tiny shower, she lathered up her long, brown tresses. The shampoo smelled so good and she groaned with pleasure as she leaned her head back, closed her eyes and rinsed her hair. Next, she scrubbed her body with good old Dial soap. It smelled heavenly. When she finished with that, she did it again. "Lather, rinse, repeat," she chuckled softly.

When the water started to turn cold, she quickly used the shampoo to wash out her shorts, sports bra and shirt. She didn't wash her socks because she didn't want to put them back on wet and going barefoot was not an option. Not when she wanted to be ready to run. The water was freezing now, so she stepped out, dried her body and wrapped the towel around her head. She wrung out her wet clothes the best she could and pulled them back on then sat on the floor and put on her socks and shoes. Finally, she stood, moved to the sink and gazed in the mirror.

Her lip was swollen from being punched. It was the eyes that caught her attention, like the last time she'd gazed in the mirror. She didn't recognize herself. Everything had changed. Who was this person staring back at her with the haunted eyes? She continued to stare at the mirror, unable to look away. She felt as if she was supposed to be getting something. Grasping some enlightenment. Maybe it was the writer in her trying to be philosophical. It was as if someone was trying to tell her something.

Reaching out her hand, she placed it on the mirror, blocking out everything but her eyes. She leaned closer, looking deep into her own eyes. "You're gonna die soon," she whispered. It was so unfair, she thought. Yet was it? Butch told her to get over it. It happens all the time in life. And she was certainly no more special than anyone else. But darn, she wanted to live. Her hand balled into a fist and softly punched the reflection of her face– and then it hit her.

She could break the mirror! If she could break it and take a shard of the glass, she'd have a weapon. She'd have to work quickly. The second Butch heard the glass break, he'd come barging in. It was worth a try wasn't it? She didn't want to go down thinking she could've done more to try to save her own life. She scanned the room. What could she use to break the glass?

Eyeing the aluminum bucket sitting under the sink, she picked it up and tested it's weight. It just might work. It was light, but if she swung with all her strength, she might be able to break the glass. She removed the paper towels and held the bucket up, made a couple test swings, like a golfer getting ready to make the million dollar putt. You can do this, she told herself. This could mean life or death. Don't think about it too much. Just do it. With that in mind, she reared back and swung. The glass shattered. Mickey dropped the bucket and grabbed at the glass, snatching the first shard she could as Butch came charging in.

"What the hell?" he barked.

She stood still, her hand beside her, inching the piece of glass up under the stretchy material of the leg of her shorts. "I'm sorry," she said, as pitifully as she could. "I guess I just lost it. I was staring at my face, wondering how my life had come to this and I guess I had a little temper tantrum. I'm sorry, Butch. I'll clean it up."

Sighing, he shook his head. "No. You won't."

He jerked her arm, drug her back into the bedroom, cuffed her, then turned and left the room. Mickey quickly used her free hand to retrieve the precious shard of glass out from the leg of her shorts and push it between the mattress and box springs. Drawing a deep breath, she tried to calm her racing heart. She'd done it! She'd succeeded in procuring a weapon. Now she just had to find the right time and the courage to use it.

She could hear Butch in the bathroom, tossing pieces of glass into the metal bucket. Her mind shifted to a time in the near future when she'd have to use her weapon on him and felt guilty about having to hurt him. Then she shook her head. He's been calmly talking about killing me, she thought. The only difference is at least I have a conscience about it. She wrinkled her nose. Then again, I won't feel a thing about hurting Richard.

The moment Butch came back into the room Mickey apologized again for the little mishap.

Calmer now, Butch shrugged his huge shoulders. "I can't blame you for feeling like breaking something. You've been through a lot this past week. You're holding up pretty well. Better than some I've seen."

Her eyes met his, realizing he was speaking of other's he'd killed. She felt sick. Butch sat and looked out the window.

"Have they sent the ransom note yet?"

Butch continued staring out the window.

"How much did your boss ask for?"

He turned back to her, abruptly stood, moved the chair close to the head of the bed and sat back down. Mickey swallowed hard, thinking she'd angered him by asking the questions. Still, she wouldn't cower. She raised her brows and looked him in the eye. "Well?"

"There isn't gonna be a ransom note, little girl."

Moisture immediately gathered in her eyes but she blinked several times, forcing back the tears. "What do you mean? Why not?"

"Look, I think you should know the truth before you die. It's a hard truth. I don't know why, but I feel like I gotta be straight with you."

"I know why. It's because killing people is not really you, Butch. I told you, I think there's something good inside you."

"Stop it," he barked. "Just keep your mouth shut and I'll answer your questions." He stopped, drew a deep breath. "There isn't gonna be a ransom note to get money from your stepfather because the man who kidnapped you, the man who's paying me to off you, *is* your stepfather."

Mickey felt all the blood rush out of her face. Felt her heart thudding in her chest. Her mouth fell open, but she couldn't speak. Thoughts raced through her mind. Glancing up at Butch she could see that he spoke the truth. She shook her head at him, as if in denial.

He nodded at her. "Yes, it's true. He wants you dead."

"But why? I mean, I know we never liked each other very much, but I didn't know he hated me so much that he would pay someone to kill me. What did I do to make him hate me so much?" Her voice sounded pitiful, even to herself. She was on the verge of a breakdown. A big one. She knew he was a hateful, dominating, horrible, even sicko man, but she never thought he would stoop to murder.

"There's several reasons why, little girl. From the way he talks, it started when you snooped in his office a few weeks ago and found information on the arms deal he made with the Saudis. It was then he decided to figure out a way to get rid of you."

"What are you talking about? I have no idea what you're talking about," she cried.

"Look, he don't talk that much to me. I only know what I've gathered from other conversations. All I know is, he came home one day and you were in his office going through his files."

"I've never– wait. A few months ago. I was looking for a copy of my birth certificate. I'd used my last copy for some classes I enrolled in and misplaced it. I thought to grab one from his office. He always kept several copies. He came in while I was there and asked me what I was doing. He was so huffy about it I told him to kiss my butt."

"He says you were snooping. Says he couldn't take any more chances with you. You had to go. And he says what better time than an election year. He got excited as he realized he'd have all the free publicity he could handle and the sympathy vote along with it."

"My stepfather is having me offed to get votes? This is crazy."

"It's real."

Panic set in as she realized this ordeal won't be over until she's dead. Somewhere deep inside she'd actually thought there was a chance that once the ransom was paid the police would close in and she'd be rescued. But dear Jesus, she *was* gonna die. Heart pounding, she eyed the large man. He was her only way out. "You don't want to do it. I can tell. You don't want to kill me."

He frowned. "I'll do what I have to do."

"Why, Butch? Why do you have to do it? For the money? How much did they pay you?"

When he remained silent she jingled her arm against the metal headboard to get his attention. "I have the right to know, don't you think?" she said, almost yelling now. "That's what you said when you decided to tell me all this. You said I should know. How much, Butch?"

"Two hundred."

"Two hundred? What? Two-hundred thousand? That's it? That's all I'm worth? Wow, Butch, how could you? Huh? I don't understand," she cried. "It doesn't make any sense. This isn't you. I know deep inside you're a good person. You're not a killer."

He stood abruptly. "You don't know what I am. I've killed before, and I will again. You're not gonna be able to reach inside me like I'm some Darth Vader person who still has some good in him. You have no idea who you're dealing with and we'll just leave it at that." He drew a deep breath. "Look, little girl, you're upset. You're angry. And you should be. Someone you trusted, someone who's supposed to like, taking care of you, decided you're expendable. He sees you as a necessary loss for his greater good. That's upsetting. So you go ahead and vent all you want, but it won't change anything."

Wiping tears from her cheeks, she blubbered at him. "I don't want to die, Butch. Please, let me go. Please. I won't turn you in."

"Stop it."

"Butch, you speak as if you have an education. You don't sound like some guy off the streets."

"What does that have to do with anything? So I read a lot. So what?"

"Most educated people understand the value of a human life."

"I said to stop begging."

"Why? Because I'm getting to you? Is my begging for my life making you uncomfortable? Then let me go. You can let me go. Or– or—" Her eyes lit up as an idea struck her. "We could stage my death. Oh, Butch, we could stage the whole thing! And I won't resume my old life. I'll go off and be someone else. That could work. Don't you see? It really could work. Please, just let me go. We'll stage the whole thing and that'll get you off the hook."

"I said stop it."

"Why, Butch? It could work."

He shook his head. "He'll want to see a body. He'll want to ID you."

"Butch," she pleaded now, her voice low. "I don't care what you say, you have goodness in you. And you're intelligent. Just think about it. Please. Just give it some thought."

He shook his head. "There's nothing to—"

"No! Don't say it. There are things to think about. Don't say 'no' yet. Please. Please, Butch. Just say you'll think about it. Go over all the options. Just try to see if there is another way out. Please."

He stood. Closed his eyes. Shook his head.

"Bu—"

"Okay," he interrupted. "I'll think about it."

"Oh thank—"

"Don't get your hopes up." Turning his back he moved toward the door. "I'll be back later with your food," he said without turning around.

Mickey immediately did what Butch had told her not to do– got her hopes up. She dared to hope that Butch might actually switch sides. That she might actually live. That one day she might even write the entire episode into one of her books. Then her mind went back to what she'd just learned. Her stepfather actually hated her enough to have her killed. How could she instill that kind of hate in a person?

No, she refused to believe it was her. It was him. He was evil personified and always had been as far as she was concerned. He believes he will profit from her death. Well she intended to fight to the bitter end.

While Butch was gone, Mickey used the time to practice pulling her weapon from underneath the mattress. If she were to take out both men, she would have to strike at a time when Butch unlocked the cuffs and both hands were free, like when she used the restroom or when he unlocks her at night to get her situated on the bed before he locks up both hands.

She tried to make her mind think of a plan, like who she should try to kill first. That one was easy. Richard. Once he was down, maybe Butch would be more willing to listen to her ideas, but how could she get to Richard when Butch had him terrified to come near her? Mostly, how would she be able to use this small, jagged piece of glass to get herself out of this predicament?

All afternoon she went over every possible scenario in her mind. Unfortunately, she was no closer to figuring a way out than she was earlier. Butch came back into the room as the sun set. For dinner he gave her a can of ravioli. As she gulped it down, she realized she was starved. Never would she have dreamed a can of ravioli could taste so good.

Butch was back to being silent, but his eyes never left her as he watched her eat.

When she finished she looked up at him. "Thank you," she murmured.

He only sighed.

They sat in silence. She knew he would take her to the bathroom soon and lock her down for the night. Had he considered her idea? Him being so quiet made her think he'd already vetoed it. She'd been here over a week. There probably wasn't much time left.

"It'll be soon, won't it?" she asked, knowing he would tell her the truth.

"Yes."

"Once you, I mean, once I'm, I'm gone, what will you do with my body?"

"Dump it." He shook his head. "I mean, we'll take you somewhere so someone will find you. Then Daley will identify you, the world will mourn your loss and you'll have a funeral fit for a queen."

"And you'll be two-hundred thousand dollars richer," she said bitterly.

"It isn't for the money," he said softly.

Her head sprang up, her body alert. "Then what's it for?"

He stood, unlocked her cuffs. "It's for my brother."

"What? What about your brother? You said you didn't have any family."

"I lied," he said as he grabbed her wrist and led her to the bathroom.

Mickey hadn't been able to get Butch to say any more. He'd let her get freshened up, locked both hands over her head and told her to sleep. Then he'd taken his place in the chair, propped his feet on the end of the bed, flicked on his flashlight and opened his book.

Hours past in silence other than the low murmur of the television in the other room. Mickey lay in the semi-dark, listening to Butch's breathing and the occasional page turning. Finally, she had to ask one more question.

"Butch?"

"Yes?"

"Will it hurt?"

He didn't answer right away. He clicked off the light and sat in the dark for several minutes. "It'll hurt for just a second. One bullet, in the head. It'll be over quick. I won't let you know when it's coming. You'll never know what hit you."

She sniffed. "Thank you."

He cursed softly.

~~~

The air was warm and dry, making Jeff smile. Targets set with nothing but miles of woods behind them, rifles and handguns primed and loaded Jeff took a deep cleansing breath. He started with his Glock, squeezing off the first shots easily. He loved the way the sound echoed around his head. He loved the smell. He loved the kickback. It was gonna be a good day.

After target practice, he'd clean his firearms, eat some breakfast, and work on the large dock that was his ongoing project. Eventually he'd have to get some buddies up to help with the bigger projects, but for now it was nothing he couldn't handle. Thanks to Ameritech's regimen, he was solid muscle, so lugging around some timber and bags of concrete was nothing. Switching the gun to his left hand, he emptied it at the next target and then smiled. Oh, yeah, a great day.

~~~

Mickey opened her eyes as Butch set a breakfast bar and a bottle of water on the table beside the bed. Beginning the day as usual with a trip to the bathroom, he unlocked the cuffs and stood back to give her room to rise, watching her as she rubbed the feeling back into her arms and hands.

"Ready?" he asked.

She nodded. "Did you think about what I said?"

"I said I would, didn't I?"

"Yes. Have you made a decision?"

He helped her up. "We might be able to figure something out."

There was a sharp intake of breath as Mickey threw her arms around his neck. "Oh, thank you, Butch. Thank you. Thank you so much." The tears spilled over.

He pulled her away. "Don't thank me yet. I don't know if it will work. We'll take the day to plan. We'll have to work fast. The order could come down anytime."

"It'll work," Mickey said, a huge smile on her face. "I just know it will."

Taking hold of her left wrist he pulled her to the door, opened it and stopped. That was unusual, Mickey thought. Why are we stopping? She tried to peer past Butch, but he seemed to be purposely blocking her with his body.

"You're making a mistake," she heard Butch say, his voice fierce.

"No I'm not. You made the mistake. We got the order. It's time."

Mickey gasped. Jerked on her wrist, but Butch had her held fast.

"Back up," Butch ordered.

"I'm not going anywhere," Richard drawled.

Mickey screamed as two loud blasts filled the air. Butch jerked, let go of her wrist and fell backward. Mickey stood face to face with the man who would take great pleasure in killing her. He grinned at her.

"I guess that takes care of that problem," he sneered.

Mickey turned and dashed back toward the bed with Richard right behind her. She shoved her hand between the mattresses, felt the glass slice through her palm. Grimacing through the pain she grasped the crude weapon tightly in her fist.

Richard grabbed her, turned her around and pressed her back onto the mattress. Grabbing her hair with his hand he held her still while he covered her mouth with his. Her stomach lurching, she pretended she wanted him, reciprocating the kiss. She could tell he was startled at first, then he relaxed.

As a sob rose in her chest, Mickey raised her weapon and sliced it deeply across his neck, aiming the best she could for his jugular.

He gasped and tried to pull away, but she wrapped her other arm around the back of his neck to hold him in place and sliced again and again, terrified that what she was doing wouldn't be enough to stop him. Time seemed to slow. She could feel Richard's warm blood spray over her face. She could feel his legs kick. Then she realized a gurgling sound was coming from his throat. Her strength leaving her, she loosened her hold on him and he slid off her and rolled onto the floor, holding his neck.

Richard stared up at her with furious eyes. Blood seeped out from under his hand. Mickey couldn't move, couldn't take her eyes off him. His mouth was moving yet no sound was coming out. Finally, her flight instinct kicked in. She inched away from him. He reached out toward her. Shrieking, she darted toward the bedroom door and landed flat on her face as she tripped over Butch's legs.

Sobbing now, she scrambled to her feet. Her eyes took in the prone man, who would've been her savior, his sightless eyes staring blankly. Blindly she ran to the front door, threw it open and scampered down the porch steps. At first she started to run down the road then remembered her plan. If she ever got free she couldn't let her stepfather know. She couldn't let anyone know until she could figure out what to do. Turning, she darted into the woods. It was the same woods she'd run into the first day here when Butch had caught her. Butch. Butch was dead. She cried for him as she ran.

After several minutes, she stopped, trying to get her bearings. She noted the early morning sun on her left and figured she was headed south. She was pretty sure she was in California, though where in California she had no idea. She ran everyday in her old life which seemed very distant now. The most she'd ever run was a ten mile mini marathon. As her mind started functioning again she realized she didn't bring any water. Hopefully it wouldn't be a problem finding some. She may be in the wilderness for quite some time. Drawing a breath, she took off.

As her body slipped into a running rhythm, her mind went back over the last half hour. She'd probably killed a man. If not, she'd hurt him bad enough to keep him from running after her. But Butch, poor Butch, was dead for sure. He'd wanted to help her. Maybe he'd wanted to change his whole life around. So much was lost, but she couldn't think of that now.

She was alive. Throwing her head back she started to laugh. She was alive! She laughed hysterically, as she ran without seeing. That proved to be her undoing. When her foot came down in a hole, the pain in her ankle sobered her immediately. She tumbled onto the soft forest floor, lay flat on her back, panting.

The blue sky and sunshine shimmering through the trees

somehow seemed to be the most beautiful thing she'd ever seen in her life. She'd seen it before, but never had she felt so much a part of the earth, so much a part of the essence of life.

Her ankle throbbed and sweat poured from her body as she lay there catching her breath. Common sense told her she had to keep going. Groaning, she rolled over, pushed herself up and moved onward in a half trotting- half limping broken gate. As she ran, however, she thought she heard gunshots. Oh no, he was following her. Heart racing she picked up her pace.

Chapter Three

Jeff's eye squinted as he peered through the sight of his *Browning BLR takedown*. A gift from his boss, the rifle was a prized possession. At the flash of brown and gray, he lowered the rifle and looked off past the target he'd been aiming at. He thought he'd seen a small deer or dog, or something. A human?

Stuffing his Glock inside the front waistband of his jeans, he carried his rifle loosely by his side and stealthily made his way past his targets and into the woods. He stopped just past the last target and stood very still, listening. The sound he heard was human, someone trying to catch their breath.

Jeff placed his rifle against a tree, pulled his gun and moved forward. Ten feet. Twenty feet. Swinging his gun around quickly, he cornered his prey. He had his gun trained on a woman who cowered behind a tree, her face, hands and clothes covered in blood.

She looked up at him through dazed eyes. He shoved his gun away into his waistband and knelt by her side. She tried inching away.

"Whoa, now, it's okay. I'm not gonna hurt you. I promise. I'm gonna help you."

She shook her head. "Are you, are you—? Who—" Turning on her hands and knees she tried to crawl away.

"Hold on there, I swear I'm not gonna hurt you." He grabbed her by the waist and pulled her back to sit. It appeared she was about to scream and he let go, throwing his hands in the air. "See? I'm not gonna hurt you. Shh, now, calm down. You're hurt. Please, let me help you. Can you tell me what happened? Why are you hiding behind this tree?"

"You, you were shooting at me."

"Oh, no, hon, not at you. I was shooting at targets. See?" He pointed out a nearby target nailed to a tree.

Big, brown eyes blinked up at him, a story so tragic in their depths that it took his breath away. "Oh Lord, I know who you are." She shifted her gaze to the ground but he took her hand, forcing her to look at him. "You're Mackenzie Daley aren't you?"

She began to cry then shook her head furiously.

His brow furrowed. "You're not?"

When she didn't answer he touched her face gently. "Okay, now. You're safe now. Shh, you're safe. I won't hurt you." His eyes scanned the woods behind her. This was MacKenzie Daley, and if she's hiding out here in the woods there might be someone chasing her.

She calmed a bit and he took a moment to look her face over carefully. "Mackenzie, I've seen your face enough over the past week to know it's you."

She shook her head.

"Your face has been plastered all over the news. You got away from your kidnappers? They were holding you somewhere near here?"

He looked around, trying to figure out from which direction she'd come. He reached into his pocket for his cell phone. "I have to call this in."

"No!" she finally said. "No, you can't. Please, don't! Wait!"

The panic in her voice startled him. He raised his eyes, quickly doing a search of the surrounding forest. Realizing there was more here than meets the eye, he put the phone away. "Okay. I'm not calling, see?" he said in a gentle tone, holding his hands out for her to see. "I'm gonna need for you to calm down so you can talk to me. Tell me why you don't want me to call and let them know you're alive."

"You have to believe what I'm about to tell you," she whispered.

He nodded his head. "I have a feeling I will."

She drew a deep breath, nodded her head. "Yes, I am Mackenzie Daley."

He nodded. "So far so good."

"My stepfather," she began, but stopped as the tears came again.

"Talmond Daley. Yes," Jeff urged.

"It was him."

"What was him?"

"He was the one who ordered those men to take me."

Kneeling silently beside her, Jeff blew out a breath as his trained mind took in the full meaning of what she was telling him. He repeated the words back to her to make sure he had it right. "Your stepfather, Senator Daley, ordered men to kidnap you and hold you hostage?"

She nodded. "Not just hold me hostage. They had orders to kill me."

"How do you know this? Did they tell you?"

"Yes. Well, one of them did. They've been waiting on the orders to kill me. It was supposed to be today, but I, I–" She stopped, moaned as the vision of what had occurred ran through her brain.

"You got away?"

She nodded. "Yes, and, so, he can't know—"

He cut her off. "I understand. He can't know you've escaped. He can't know you're alive or he'll come after you. He can't know you're alive until the authorities are able to put a case together against him."

She nodded again, looking up into his face, her brow furrowed. "You believe me?"

He nodded. "Yes, I believe you."

"Just like that?"

He smiled. "Someone in your condition usually doesn't think up elaborate lies to tell."

Relieved, she drew a deep breath and offered a small smile. "I thought my biggest problem would be to get someone to believe me. Who are you? Are you a cop?"

"No, much better. My name is Jeff Davis. I'm a security agent for Ameritech Security." His eyes scanned the forest again. "Do you think someone followed you?"

Her eyes opened wide. "No! Did you hear someone?" She started to scramble away again.

Laying a hand on her shoulder, he stopped her. "No, I'm just trying to ascertain the situation. You're safe with me, I promise. Mackenzie, where were they holding you and do they know you've escaped?"

Raising a trembling, bloody hand, she pointed north. "There's a cabin, that way. I'm not sure how far I've run."

"The only place I know of in that direction is an old hunter's cabin about three miles."

"I think that's it."

"How many men and are they armed?"

Her eyes filled. "There were two. R-Richard, he sh-shot Butch." Her body began to shake, her teeth to chatter. "And, then, and then I–

I, he– he tried to– I think I killed him."

Jeff took her face in his hands, tilted it up toward him. "You're doing real good, Mackenzie. Real good. How did you kill him, sweetie? Did you shoot him?"

She shook her head. Slowly, her eyes turned to look down at her right hand. She held her fist out to him.

"Oh, boy," Jeff uttered softly. He gripped her tightly around the wrist. "I want you to open your fist, okay? Go slow. Open, that's it." He examined the long, sharp shard of glass, its base deeply embedded in her palm. Her body began shaking violently. Quickly, before she had time to resist, he removed the glass from her hand. He took off his t-shirt and used it to wrap the wound tightly. "Mackenzie, you're going into shock. We need to get you inside."

Her teeth chattering, she nodded.

"Are you hurt anywhere else?"

She shook her head, and then changed direction. "I think I s-sprained my a-ankle."

"Okay, we can deal with that." He rose, then reached down for her. "Hold on around my neck," he instructed.

She did as he said, flinching slightly as he lifted her from the ground as if she weighed nothing. How lucky, she thought, that she'd run into this knight in shining armor. How unlikely. She stiffened. It *was* unlikely. What if he also worked for her father? What if he was taking her to him right now? She panicked, suddenly, tried to push away from him.

He stopped, looked behind him, and then down at her. "What's wrong? Did you see something?"

She looked deep into his eyes. "You, what are you doing out here?"

He understood, set her down, took his wallet out of his pocket, showed her his security I.D. "I don't know what else to do to convince you that I'm one of the good guys, except, if I worked for your father, I'd go ahead and kill you right now, wouldn't I?"

She blinked up at him, tears welling in her eyes and running over her cheeks. "I guess so. I don't know."

"Mackenzie, look at me, trust me. I'm gonna help you. I own this property. I bought it a few years ago and I come up here to relax and shoot."

Her entire body trembled. "I don't know what to do." She gave a soft moan before she collapsed.

He caught her, lifted her back into his arms and walked toward the house. "I swear to you, you are safe with me," he said as he walked.

Something in his voice, the conviction maybe, it got to her. "I'm sorry for doubting you," she whispered. "I think I do trust you."

Everything seemed blurry, foggy, and as he carried her, the temptation to rest her head was too great and she laid it on his shoulder. Safe. She was safe! She nestled her face into the crook of his neck, listening to his breath as he walked and it seemed to give her amazing comfort. He smelled so good. Clean. Pressing her nose against his skin, she breathed deeply.

"I'm very lucky," she mumbled against his neck.

"Why's that?" he asked.

"The first person I come across after I get away is someone who can actually help me. Not a frantic housewife, or some backwoods hunter or a by-the-book sheriff, or anyone else. I find you. I mean, the company you work for, I've heard of Ameritech. You guys are kind of like the FBI, right?"

"Close enough," he said. Only we're a private company. He stopped by the tree to grab up his rifle.

She gasped when he bent over, her hands reaching out in startled reflex.

"It's okay," he murmured. "I've got you."

Her eyes filled again, at the sound of his masculine voice, this time in gratitude that she was in the arms of one so capable.

Jeff, breathing hard by the time he got to the back deck, entered the house and took her immediately to the bedroom. Setting her down gently on the bed, he spoke quietly. "Mackenzie, I have a lot I have to do. We can't stay here. I have to get stuff in the truck, make some arrangements. I'm gonna have to leave you here for a little while. You rest while I get everything done, and then we'll leave, okay?"

She swallowed hard, looking down at her bloody clothing. "Can I use your shower?"

"Umm, are you sure you're up to it?"

She nodded. "I feel better already. And I've stopped shaking."

"Okay, hold on."

He pulled his phone from his pocket and snapped off several shots of her, then placed the phone on the dresser, opened a drawer and pulled out a t-shirt and a pair of his boxers and placed them on the dresser. "After your shower you can put these on. We'll get you some clothes later today."

She nodded.

Next, he pulled out a dark brown t-shirt and pulled it over his own head. "Do you know how to fire a gun?"

She shook her head.

"It's easy really." He pulled the Glock from his waistband, gave her a quick lesson. "I'm gonna leave this with you, just in case. Anyone but me comes through this door, you fire. Got it?"

Eyes wide, she nodded her head.

Eyeing her hand wrapped in his t-shirt, he frowned. "Are you gonna be able to get undressed and shower with your hand the way it is?"

She nodded again. He doubted it. It was gonna hurt like heck, but it's not like she was gonna let him undress her and wash her. Silently reprimanding himself for even thinking that, he shook his head to clear it of the images. The poor kid had been through hell. In his own defense, he could blame his male reaction to her on the way she'd snuggled her face up against his throat as he'd carried her. Her breath on his skin, her lips moving against him as she spoke, the intimacy of it, he admitted, it got to him. He blew out a breath.

"Don't leave this room until I get back."

She nodded again, looking around the room as if seeing it for the first time.

He touched her shoulder, made her look at him. "Listen to me, Mackenzie. I may be gone a while, so don't get worried."

She nodded. "I understand," she said softly.

He started to leave.

"Jeff?"

He stopped, turned, brow raised in question.

"Thank you."

He nodded, smiled. "I'm just glad I was here."

He picked up his phone and left the room, then knocked on the door. "Mackenzie, lock the door," he called. He stood there until he heard the click. Then he took off.

He would have to deal only in cash, so he would need money, and he would need an untraceable car. All of that would be no problem as soon as he called his boss, Jason Lee. In order to do that, he needed to get a disposable phone. Talmond Daley being a Senator means he is a powerful man. Once Daley knows Mackenzie survived her ordeal and is gone, he'll have a manhunt out and they'll make their way to

Jeff's house pretty fast. They'll find out he owns the place and trace him to Ameritech. Jason will deny knowing where he is, but Daley is powerful enough to get Jason's phone records which he would do, looking for a call from Jeff. There won't be one.

Hopefully it will be several hours before Daley sends someone to the cabin to find out why his thugs haven't checked in with him. Why did he want his own daughter dead? Though, she's not his flesh-and-blood daughter, is she? She's his adopted child. His stepchild. Jeff blew out a pensive breath. He would have plenty of time to talk to the girl later. Right now he had to get going.

It was over an hour later when he knocked on the bedroom door. When she didn't answer, he called out to her. A few seconds later she opened the door, the gun in her hand. Removing it from her quickly, he placed it on the dresser.

He looked her over. She was pale but clean. Her straight, brown tresses were almost dry. She was a looker. The bruise on her cheek didn't take away from her beauty, nor did his black, Jack Daniels t-shirt which was long enough to completely cover the boxers she wore. She had on some Nike shoes that were spattered with blood, but no socks.

"You okay?" he asked.

"I think so," she answered.

He gathered her discarded clothing. "Come into the kitchen."

Following him obediently, she glanced around the sparse home. Not much to it. There was a chair by the sink in the kitchen and he motioned her into it. Her eyes rose to his in question.

"We're not gonna be able to get you to a doctor any time soon so I'm gonna have to disinfect that cut on your hand and bandage it up the best I can."

He took her hand, held it over the sink as he examined it. "Man, that is deep," he muttered. He looked up at her. "This is gonna hurt, and I'm sorry about that."

"It's okay," she murmured.

She grimaced as he washed the cut under warm water. Next, he poured vodka over her hand, gripping her wrist tighter when she instinctively tried to pull it back. He watched her face as she scrunched it up and started blowing out big puffs of air.

She winced, moaned a little and then went silent.

"The worst part is over."

"No it isn't. It's still burning."

He smiled. "It'll ease up some soon," he said as he leaned close and placed a row of butterfly bandages along her palm. Next he wrapped her hand with gauze, then taped it securely. "We'll look at it again later to make sure it doesn't get infected."

"You sure come prepared," Mickey said, motioning to all the first aid supplies.

He shrugged. "Yeah, I'm a regular boy scout, huh? Okay, we have to get going," he said as he gathered up the supplies including the vodka into a plastic grocery bag. He took another grocery bag and placed her bloody clothing in it and tied it securely. "Come back to the bedroom again for just a second."

Mickey followed him back, still slightly limping, and sat on the bed while he threw everything into a duffel bag including more guns and the bag of medical supplies. Finally he picked up the gun he'd loaned her, checked it over and placed it in the front pocket of the duffel. She noticed he had another one in a holster strapped to his chest. Next he grabbed the two pillows from the bed and held them out to her. "You hold these."

Silently, she wrapped her arms around the offered pillows and hugged them to her body.

Jeff pulled the comforter and top sheet from the bed, threw them over his shoulder and nodded at her. "Let's go," he said. Wrapping his hand around her arm to allow her to take some weight off her ankle, he ushered her out of the room.

Opening the passenger side door, Jeff threw the duffel and bedclothes he carried into the back seat of the brand new F-150 and then took the pillows from Mackenzie and stuffed them over the console between the two front seats to make it more like one long seat, easier for her to lie down to rest. "Be right back," he said as he ran back inside to do a sweep of the house and back deck area. He didn't have time to put his tools away, and sighing, he ran back to the truck.

Within seconds they were speeding down the gravel road. Jeff glanced over at the quiet girl who was obviously still dazed from all that had happened. He'd been to the cabin, taken pictures. The man she'd killed had a huge jagged hole ripped in his neck. His blood was everywhere. It was apparent he'd been on top of her when she cut him since there was an outline in blood of her upper body on the sheet. The thought of what she'd been through made him wish the guy wasn't dead just so he could have the pleasure of killing him. Instead, she'd been the one to kill him and that was gonna be a hard thing for her to deal with. Really hard.

Mackenzie looked over at him, gave a tentative smile.

"You okay?" he asked.

Nodding her head, she bit her lower lip. "This gravel road seems so long. Last time I was on it, I couldn't see it. I was on the floor of the van. We'd already driven for so long and the whole time they had me tied up and gagged. I thought my bladder was gonna burst. When we hit the gravel road I remember thinking that we were finally at our destination and any minute now they would let me use the bathroom, but it was a lot longer before we finally stopped."

"Yeah, it's actually ten miles. I'm sorry you were so mistreated. So, tell me, about the van, do you remember what it looked like?"

"Big and black. With a side door that opened wide. No windows in the back."

"Do you know what they did with it?"

Brow furrowed she looked at him. "They?"

"The guys at the cabin. What did they do with the van? It wasn't there."

"You went to the cabin?" she asked, her voice shrill, her chin trembling.

"I had to see what was there before anyone tampered with the evidence."

"Was, Richard– was he—"

"Dead? Yes."

She swallowed hard, placed her hands down on the seat beside her as if to hold herself in her seat.

Jeff reached over and placed his hand on top of hers. "You did what you had to do, Mackenzie. What you did, it saved your life and that's a very good thing."

She turned her hand over and squeezed his hard. "Thank you.

"Mackenzie where—"

"Mickey."

"'Scuse me?"

"My name, people, my friends, they usually call me Mickey."

"Okay then, Mickey it is." He paused for only a second. "So, Mickey do you know what happened to the van?"

"There was another man driving. He dropped us off and left. I never saw him, but I heard his voice and it sounded familiar. I couldn't place it though."

"If he dropped you off and left, that means this guy could be hanging out close enough to get here in a hurry if he needed to."

As if saying the words made it happen they saw the dust and heard the gravel crunching of an approaching vehicle.

Mickey watched as Jeff quickly unbuckled the shoulder holster he wore and pulled it off, placing it in the floorboard. He drew the gun and placed it between his knees.

"Lie down," Jeff ordered. She was moving too slow for him so he grabbed her head and shoved it down on the pillows he'd placed over the console.

"Oh no, oh no, oh no," she uttered, her voice tight with fear.

Softly, he placed his hand on her head. "Shh, now, you're safe with me. And lookee there, it's a black van."

"No, oh no," she squealed. Her hand grabbed his thigh, her nails dug in.

He patted her head. "Stay very quiet." Jeff slowed the truck.

"What are you doing?" Mickey shrieked obviously panicked.

"I'm gonna talk to him."

"No! Oh God, please no!" Her hand gripped his leg in stark terror.

"Shhh, Mickey, you're safe. Just stay down."

Jeff hit the button and his window automatically lowered. He waved his hand out the window.

The van slowed beside him. "Hey, buddy," Jeff said, his voice slow and friendly.

The man in the van only rolled his eyes.

"You lookin' for a dog?"

"No, I'm not looking for a dog," the man grumbled.

"Shame, cuz I found one. She looks like she's part Golden Retriever. Gorgeous breed. I got her tied up back at the house. Figured the owner will come lookin' for her sooner or later. It'd be a shame to let a dog that pretty go missin', ya know what I mean? I don't think she's a purebred, got a little something else in her. I dunno, if our dog went missin' my kid would have a fit. I'm sure I wouldn't see a moment's peace until I got that dog back home where it belongs. I've driven all around this darn lake askin' folks if they're missing their dog, but —"

"I haven't lost a damn dog."

Jeff pretended the gruffness went right over his head. "Okay, well, here, let me see if I can find something to write with, yeah here we go." He scribbled down a phone number. "If you don't mind, if you come across someone who's missing their dog, just give me a call."

The man jerked the paper out of Jeff's hand and took off.

"Have a nice day," Jeff mumbled sarcastically. He watched the van leave, got the tag number. The driver appeared to be alone, he thought. He could take him easy enough. Rolling his window up, he gunned the engine, jerked the steering wheel and whipped a u-turn.

Mickey's head popped up. "What– what are you doing?"she shrieked.

"I'm going after him."

"No! Please, no," she cried.

"It's okay. He's alone. I can take him right now."

"Oh no, please don't do this. Please!" The terror took over. Throwing herself against the passenger door, she jerked the handle. The door flew open and she prepared to jump.

"Dammit," Jeff cursed as he slammed on the brakes. Reaching across the seat he grabbed her and pulled her back toward him.

She fought him, arms flailing, fists flying. Holding her firm, he pushed her head against his chest and held her fast with the other arm. "Okay, I won't go after him. Shh, it's okay, you're safe. I won't go after him. Mickey, stop fighting. We won't go after him. I promise. We'll leave, okay? We'll take off right now."

It took a minute before his words got through to her brain and she stopped fighting and began to calm. She was crying hysterically but she didn't care. She felt no shame and she didn't even try to stop. Wiggling her head closer into the crook of his neck, she breathed deep. There was something about the smell of him, the strength of him that had a tranquilizing effect on her. Her heartbeat slowed. The tears eased.

His hands cupped her face and pulled her away from his chest so he could look at her.

"Better?"

Sniffing, she nodded. "Please, don't go after him," she whimpered.

"Okay, I won't. Listen to me. We're gonna leave, right now. Put your seatbelt on and promise me you won't try to jump out of the truck again."

She sat back in her seat, pulled the strap across her and clicked it in place, drew a deep breath. "I promise, as long as you go in the right direction," she said in a tiny voice.

Jeff made another u-turn and headed out.

The gravel road finally ended and they headed north. He needed to get to a town where he could buy a prepaid phone. His mind went over everything he had to do. Her soft voice broke into his thoughts.

"Where are we?"

"We're near Honey Lake."

"Where's that?"

"Wow, I'm sorry, Mickey. You have no idea where you are, do you? You're in California. We're headed to a town called Susanville. There's a Walmart there. I need to get some things for you and a phone for me. Then we're headed to Red Bluff which is about two hours more. There's literally hundreds of motels there and we'll find an obscure place to hold up until I hear from my boss."

"Your boss?"

"Jason Lee. He's the head of Ameritech Security. He'll be able to help you."

"But how do you know he won't tell anyone I'm alive?"

"He won't. Trust me. What he *will* do is launch a covert investigation on Daley. He'll expose him. And then, you'll be safe. I have faith in Jason."

Her pensive expressions told him she wasn't as sure as he was. She said nothing more, only turned her head and stared straight ahead. Jeff's eyes kept wondering over to her, catching glimpses of sleek legs, a turned up nose, a flawless complexion and a sweet mouth. Her hair and eyes were almost the same color, a rich, shiny brown. He found himself wanting to touch that hair and look into those eyes.

Shaking his head, he forced his mind back to business. He thought of the cabin and what the van driver would be looking at in a few minutes. It was a hideous scene. Blood everywhere. Bloody footprints leading out of the only entrance and into the woods straight toward his house. It wouldn't take them long to figure out she'd come to his house and that he'd left in a hurry. A few phone calls later they'd know who she was with and they'd try to find them. He was gonna make sure that didn't happen.

As they approached Susanville, Jeff realized it would be very easy for someone to recognize Mackenzie Daley who hadn't spoken since they'd hit the highway.

Jeff cleared his throat and she immediately looked over at him.

"Do you think you can reach in the back there and grab that Dodger's cap in that black bag?"

Without speaking, she did as asked then handed it to him.

He shook his head. "It's for you. I need you to put all your hair up inside the hat. We don't want anyone to recognize you. And here–" He leaned over and pulled a pair of sunglasses out of the glove compartment. "Put these on."

She arranged the hat then put on the glasses. "How do I look?" she asked, falling into a playful act, which gave a brief glimpse of her personality when she's not under duress.

Jeff smiled. "It'll have to do, for now."

A few minutes later he pulled into the Walmart parking lot and took a parking space near the back of one of the middle rows. Turning to Mickey, he realized she was about to panic again. He took her hands.

"I'm not gonna be very long at all. You do not get out of the truck."

She nodded, her eyes wide.

He brushed his hand over her cheek, a worried frown on his face. "You look like you're about to pass out."

"I'm okay," she said, offering a tiny smile.

He didn't buy it though because her chest heaved with each breath she took. "Try to stay calm, slow your breathing."

"What if he comes back this way, looking for you?"

"The guy in the van? We could've turned three different ways off that road. He'll assume we headed south, toward L.A. He certainly won't think that we decided to go on a shopping trip to Wallyworld. Look, Macken– Mickey, I'll just be a minute. I promise. Stay down and take this." He reached in the bag and pulled out the same gun he'd given her earlier. "You remember how to use it?"

She nodded. "I think so."

He showed her again.

Mickey took a huge breath. "Okay. Just go, but, please– hurry back."

He touched her face. "I'll hurry."

She watched him jog the length of the parking lot and disappear inside. Setting the gun down on the seat next to her, she tried to get her racing heart to slow down. Why she was being such a wimp she didn't know. She admitted she was terrified. Maybe even more now that she was free then before. The thought of them recapturing her, ugh, her stomach turned over.

It seemed Jeff had been gone forever when she saw the van. Sucking in a horrified breath, she threw herself down into the floorboard of the truck, grabbed the gun and began to whimper. "Oh, no, no, no," she cried. "I knew this was gonna happen. Oh, please Jeff, where are you?"

Then she discovered a new problem. From her perspective down in the floorboard of Jeff's truck, she realized she couldn't see what was happening. Was the van still coming toward her? Rising slowly, she peeked up over the dash ever so slightly. Oh, no, he must've seen Jeff's truck because he was headed straight for her! Ducking back down, she heard the sound of the van's engine as it approached and knew it had pulled into the space just opposite, nose to nose. Closing her eyes, she wondered if she should shoot first or wait for him to try to grab her. Or, maybe he wouldn't grab her. Maybe he would simply point a gun through the window and kill her right now and get it over with so there would be no more mistakes.

Her heart pounded. There was a rushing sound in her ears as she waited for him to appear, her eyes shifting from the driver's side window to the passenger side window, expecting him at any second. She couldn't stand it. She couldn't stand hiding there like a sitting duck. She couldn't stand being trapped, pinned down like she had been all week, like she had been just a few short hours ago this very day. She had to do something, only, what? Run. She had to run. She needed to get out of the car and run.

Keeping her head low, she eased her body from the floorboard and onto the seat, moved to the driver's side door, unlocked it, counted to three, threw the door open and ran toward the store as fast as she could go.

Jeff saw her when she jumped out of the truck, but she obviously didn't see him since she was running toward the store as fast as her bad ankle would allow. He stepped in front of her and scooped her up. She screamed.

"It's me," he said, quickly. "It's me, honey. Shhh, now, I'm back."

Her arms were around his neck, squeezing until he could barely get his breath. Her legs wrapped around his waist. He held her tight. To onlookers it would probably look like she'd been so happy to see him she'd run into his arms. To him she was more like a terrified puppy clinging to its owner.

"He's here, we have to go," she sobbed.

"Who's here?"

"The van. He pulled in right in front of us. Please, Jeff we have to run."

Jeff's eyes took in the truck and the van parked in front. He sighed. "Listen to me, Mickey. The van parked in front of the truck is dark blue with white accents down the side. And it's a woman with a kid. See? She's putting her kid in a stroller right next to the van."

Without letting go of her, he turned around so she could see what he saw. "Okay?" he asked.

"I thought— I mean, I could've sworn—"

She never finished. She only laid her head on his shoulder and began to cry. He held her tight as he walked to the truck. Her entire body trembled and he realized she was still in shock. He had to get her calm. Clumsily opening the passenger side door he sat her down on the seat and tossed his bags with the purchases he'd made over onto his seat.

Pulling the comforter from the back, he wrapped it around her shoulders, then rubbed her back briskly. She looked up at him, tears making tracks down her cheeks. He used his thumbs to wipe at them. "Doing better?" he asked.

"I must be losing my mind," she whispered.

"No, you're having a normal reaction to what's happened to you."

He reached into the backseat and pulled the bottle of Vodka out of the medical bag. "I want you to take two good belts, okay?" he said, holding the bottle up to her lips.

She took a gulp and made a face. "Yuk, that stuff tastes horrible by itself," she said, scrunching up her face.

Jeff smiled at her. "Are you kidding me? This is the good stuff. One more time," he urged.

She obeyed and handed him the bottle. He put the "good stuff" away, reached down into the floorboard in front of her feet and retrieved his gun, had her swing her feet inside the truck and securely closed her door.

Mickey kept her eyes on him as he rounded the truck and opened his door. He pulled a packaged cell phone from one of the bags then tossed the rest of the bags into the back. Pulling a knife he quickly opened the package, activated the phone, got in the truck and started down the road.

Jeff punched in the number, hit send.

"Yes?"

"Jason, it's Jeff. We have a situation. Get to a clean phone and call me." He hung up, looked over at her.

Mickey listened as he spoke, amazed at the difference in his voice between the times he'd spoken to her so kindly and the all-business in his tone now. His words were short and to the point.

"How long do you think it will take for him to call you back?" she asked.

"A minute or two." He looked her over. "Hungry?"

She shook her head.

"Well, if you get hungry, I bought some junk food. It's in one of those bags in the back. We need to stay on the road until we get to Red Bluff."

"Thanks, but I don't think I could eat."

He patted the pillows beside him. "Then lie down and sleep. It will help the time to go by faster."

"I don't think I can sleep either."

"Okay, you don't have to sleep, but it might be a good idea for you to lie down anyway."

Unbuckling her belt, she complied, snuggling down into the pillows, her eyes immediately drifted shut.

They snapped back open the next second when Jeff's phone went off. Rolling onto her back, she watched him from where she lay. He had a strong jaw, at least he did from this angle. He was movie star handsome, in a rugged sort of way, she thought. A cross maybe between Brad Pitt and GI Joe. His blond hair was streaked with sunlight, like he spent a lot of time on the beach, although, his eyelashes, which were very long, were black in color. His eyes were hard to tell from this angle, possibly hazel. She stopped her inspection when she heard him say her name into the phone and remembered she wanted to hear this conversation.

"No, I'm not kidding, she's lying on the seat of my truck as we speak . . . I don't have the whole story yet, I had to move quickly and she's been too shocky to talk, but we can debrief her tonight when we stop . . . nutshell, she believes it was her stepfather who had her kidnapped . . . yeah, that's pretty easy to see the benefits for him in that area . . . he held her in a cabin near my lake property, she got away, I found her in the woods near my house. She was pretty shaken up. She had to kill one guy to get away, the scene was pretty bad . . . yeah, I got pics . . . I stopped the driver of the van involved in the snatch. I couldn't take him because Mackenzie freaked out on me . . . tag number is KLM 9935 . . . I thought you'd say Red Bluff. I'm already headed there . . . yes, car, money . . . we'll need a wig, clothes for her, I need more ammo just in case. ..Got it . . . I intend to take very good care of her. One more thing, put a trace on your private line. I gave the driver of the van your number to call in case he came across someone who lost a dog. He'll put two and two together eventually and realize the guy he spoke to is the one who has Mackenzie and that I gave him my number because I want to deal... Yep... Later."

He pushed a button, glanced down at her. "I feel much better now that we have that out of the way."

"He's gonna help?"

He smiled. "There was never any question of that. A case like this, I'm sure he's in the zone. Ameritech is like renting your own FBI slash CIA. Jason used to consult for the FBI and also for the military. He knows what's up. He implemented a lot of the military special ops training. He decided to open his own company instead of being caught up in government red tape. He uses the newest, hottest, technology, he trains his agents thoroughly. He's very much into righting wrongs. An equalizer, so to speak."

"An equalizer. That's exactly what I need." She looked up at him from where she lay on the car seat. "And you're an agent?"

"Yes."

"So, what were you doing up at the Lake?"

"Taking a vacation."

She frowned. "I'm sorry."

He smiled. "For what? For ruining my vacation? I think taking care of you is a little more important."

Smiling, her eyes drifted shut again. "Thank you."

She'd said she couldn't sleep, but he knew if she just let her body relax for a second she'd be gone. The after effect of an extreme adrenaline rush is complete exhaustion. Looking down at her as she floated off to sleep, his heart stuttered. Man, she was lovely. She lay on her back, her chest rising and falling with each breath. He let his hand reach down and touch her face. She sighed and turned onto her side, causing his hand to slide down her back. He kept it there while he drove.

Thinking of the actions Jason would be taking gave him a little satisfaction. Talmond Daley, the SOB, would kill his own family, his wife's flesh and blood while he is revered as a United States Senator. Jeff hoped he would get a shot at the guy.

He'd driven an hour when she stirred, rose up and laid her head on his thigh instead of on the pillows beside his leg. He swallowed hard. He'd had the A/C cranked up pretty good, yet suddenly there were beads of perspiration popping out on his forehead. Gripping the steering wheel with both hands, he tried not to think about it, and then she stretched and tried to burrow her hand up underneath him. He grabbed it quickly, placed it on his knee and covered it with his hand to hold it there.

Chapter Four

"Mom?" Marissa said softly as she entered the den.

Marion Daley looked up at her youngest daughter. She'd been sitting in the designer chair Talmond had presented her with on their second wedding anniversary. He'd always provided the best for them and Marion had always believed marrying him had been the best thing for her and her little girl. Yet sitting here in the chair, her feet tucked up under her, she'd been reconsidering.

One time, when Mackenzie had been nine, Marion remembered, and all curled up in this very chair, she'd been working on a homework assignment, making a diagram of the human body, when she'd been called into dinner. Being obedient for once, she'd quickly stood, placed the papers and markers on the seat and joined her mother and stepfather for the evening meal. When they'd re-entered the room after dinner, Talmond found the marker Mackenzie had been using had rolled off the stack of papers. Apparently, she hadn't bothered to cap the red marker and it had bled into the upholstery.

He'd calmly called her to him, pointed to the chair. Her daughter's mouth had dropped open. Marion had watched him take her hand and lead her upstairs. Marion hadn't intervened. Mickey needed to learn responsibility. She'd turned and glanced at her mom as he'd taken her from the room. Marion could still see her face now, clear as day. There had been fear in her eyes, but something more. An accusation of betrayal.

Now that her daughter was missing, all those little things kept surfacing, one after another, a constant montage of memories that made up her daughter's life. Sitting here, Marion realized most of them were bad memories whenever Talmond had been involved. Had she betrayed her eldest daughter? Had she traded her daughter's happiness for a comfortable life? Marion had a right to some happiness too, didn't she? She was so confused.

Her husband and that FBI agent, Special Agent Dodge, who was handling the case, didn't know she'd overheard them speaking last night in his study. She wasn't allowed in the room. No one was allowed in there unless he'd invited them and the only one Marion had ever known him to invite, was her youngest daughter Marissa. Last night though, Marion had stood just outside the door in the hallway. Talmond had demanded to know why there hadn't been a ransom note. He'd asked the agent to explain to him what the kidnappers could be thinking. The answer is what had sent Marion into a tailspin.

Agent Dodge had said it was possible the kidnappers had no idea who they took. That it may have been a quick snatch for no other reason than to do her harm or sex trafficking. Then her husband had asked what Mackenzie's chances are of survival. He'd asked the agent to just tell him what he thought, no padding the truth. The agent had said, realistically, it'd been over a week since the abduction and no ransom note, no contact, more than likely, she's already dead.

She'd heard no response from Talmond. If he'd made one, her head was too full of sounds and images to hear it. Up until that moment, she'd truly believed they would get Mackenzie back. The truth was a bitter pill. Her first born child was probably dead, probably raped and tortured and killed by some mad man who could care less that she was smart and beautiful and loving and brilliant.

"Mom!"

Marion shook her head. "Oh, I'm sorry, Marissa. Did you say something?"

"Mom, you're scaring me. Are you okay?"

Marion sighed, shaking her head. "I was just thinking about Mickey."

"That's why I came in here, Mom, to ask if you've heard anything. Has there been a ransom note, a phone call, anything?"

"Honey, don't you worry your pretty little head," Marion answered lightly.

"Are you kidding me?" Marissa shrieked. "Don't worry my pretty head? Good grief, Mom, we're talking about my sister. Do you understand what that means?"

"Honey, I know the two of you were close but—"

"Were? You're talking about her as if she's not coming back."

Marion stared off toward the window. "There's a possibility that, oh dear, how do I say this. There's a chance she could be—"

"Don't say it! Don't you dare say it. Mickey is not dead. She's not. She's coming home. I can't lose her mom. I can't lose her, I just— " She stopped abruptly, holding her hand against her mouth as tears welled up and spilled over.

Marion rose, went to her, hugged her close. "Oh, my dear little baby girl, I understand. I miss her too."

Marissa pulled away. "I'm not a baby. I'm fifteen. And I very much doubt you understand."

"Sweetheart, how can you say that?"

Marissa took in her mother's pale face, thinner now than just a week ago, and felt ashamed. "I'm sorry Mom. I'm just upset. Just please, Mom, please don't talk about Mickey as if she's not coming back. She has to. Don't you see? I love her more than anyone in the world." Turning, she fled upstairs.

~~~

In the study, Talmond Daley sat quietly, waiting for his phone to vibrate. Any minute now he expected a call from Kurt Wells. Kurt had been Talmond's man almost since the beginning and was as dependable as the sunrise. Of course, there was a reason for that. Daley had given the order to put Mackenzie down this morning. Richard was to take out Butch first thing. He would then walk Mackenzie out to the grave he'd dug in the woods and fill it with her dead body. Then Kurt would arrive in the van to make sure Richard would rest in peace in the second grave he'd unknowingly dug for himself, thinking it was for Butch.

Now, it seems things were not going as they should. Richard had not checked in at the appointed time. Over an hour had passed before he'd called Kurt and sent him in. Now two more hours had passed as he anxiously awaited news. Honestly, he couldn't wait to be able to celebrate the death of that little brat. She'd given him trouble for over twenty years. Defying him, taunting him, and when she got older she'd teased him with her woman's body. His only regret was that he hadn't had the chance to take care of that little piece.

When her book had been picked up by a publisher she'd flaunted it. When it made it to the New York Times best-sellers list, she'd been downright cocky. Well, she's not cocky anymore, he thought smugly. He really should thank her, for all the free publicity and the giant sympathy vote he's gonna get for all this. Poor Talmond Daley, his beautiful daughter, whom he loved so much he'd adopted her, treated her like she was his own, and now she's gone. He chuckled, then snatched up his phone as it made a buzzing sound against the expensive wood of his desk.

"Yes," Talmond said brusquely into the phone.

"Sir, we have a problem," Kurt answered.

"What kind of a problem?"

"Butch is dead. Richard is dead. Mickey is nowhere to be found."

Talmond could feel the blood drain from his face. His heart began to race, his head to pound. "That can't be. How did she manage to get away? How did she kill two grown men? He let out a string of curses. What took you so long to call back?"

"I've been searching the woods and surrounding areas. There was blood leading off south. I figured it was her."

"And?"

"There's a house a few miles south. There's a bunch of lumber and other building supplies out back along with some tools. I think whoever was there left in a hurry because the tools are scattered all over the place. No one's home, but I believe this is where she went."

"What makes you think that?"

"There's blood on the door jamb just outside the back sliding glass door."

"Have you been inside?"

"Not yet."

"Well, what are you waiting for?"

Kurt sighed. "I'm going now. Hold on."

Talmond waited while Kurt broke into the house.

"It almost looks like no one lives here. There's a bed and dresser in one bedroom, other than a table, there's no other furniture. Still, someone has been here recently. The bathroom is wet."

Talmond blew out a breath, closed his eyes as he thought. "So you think she made it to that house. Some guy was working there, he saw who she was and took her to safety? Only, we would've heard something by now. It should be all over the news that the Senator's daughter has been found alive. Maybe the guy has his own plans for little Mackenzie."

"Or maybe she knows the truth and told him not to tell anyone," Kurt said. "Maybe that's why we haven't heard anything."

"Find out who that house belongs to. Whoever was there may be the owner or may be just a hired contractor. I want to know who was there."

Mickey woke when the car slowed and pulled into a parking lot. Yawning, she turned onto her back, realizing her head rested on Jeff's thigh.

"Oh, gosh, I'm sorry," she mumbled as she rose to a sitting position.

"No problem," Jeff said softly. "Feel any better?"

"Actually, I have a headache, but I always do when I drink. Maybe I took more than a few shots. I drank straight out of the bottle. It's hard to tell how much I had."

Smiling, he nodded at her. "Maybe. I'll ask inside for some aspirin or something."

His words made her realize they were parked outside the front office of a motel. "Are we in Red Bluff?"

"We are. Look, this isn't like a real high class place, but in order to keep a low profile—"

"It's okay," she said quickly, cutting him off.

"You stay in the truck. I don't want the clerk getting a look at you."

Nodding, she bit her lower lip.

Jeff realized her reluctance. "You'll be able to see me through the glass the entire time. We'll lock you in."

He left her. What is the problem, she wondered? Why is she suddenly so afraid of being left alone? She knew she was acting crazy, but she couldn't seem to control the panic that overtook her every time Jeff said he'd be right back. She watched him talk to the clerk, sign some paper, pull out his wallet, pay in cash, pick up a key from the counter and turn toward the door. The relief was instant. She sighed. She was losing her mind.

They swung around to the back side of the motel. Instead of parking just outside their assigned room, Jeff parked several doors down. Quickly, he ushered her down the walk and inside the room. He tossed the few things he carried onto one of the beds. Looking around he sighed. "Accommodations aren't great, but they'll do," he said.

"It's way better than where I spent the past week," she answered.

"Gotcha," he said with a nod. "I'm just gonna get the rest of the stuff from the truck." He left quickly, not giving her any time to fret.

When he returned a few minutes later she was in the bathroom. He placed his bag near the head of the bed closest to the door, then went about unloading the rest of the shopping bags. He looked up when she emerged from the bathroom. Immediately concerned he rose, went to her. It was obvious she'd been crying.

"You okay?" he asked, reaching out to touch her arm.

"I think so. I don't know what's happening to me. I looked into the mirror and the tears just started coming."

"Mickey, it's gonna be hard for awhile, you know, with all the memories, but it *will* pass."

Her eyes blinked up at him, as if in slow motion. She smiled. "I believe you."

"Good. Come sit a minute, I have some things for you."

She sat on the edge of the bed Jeff had designated as hers.

"This one is for you," he said, handing her a phone. "In case we get separated for any reason, it has two numbers already programmed in it. The first one is me. The second one is my boss, Jason Lee."

She nodded blankly.

"Mickey, I need you to understand that you can't call anyone else. Not a friend, not your mother. Do you have a boyfriend?"

"Not really."

"Good," he said, realizing he truly meant that. "You can't call anyone. This is only for an emergency. Got it?"

"Yes."

"Okay, good." He reached for another bag and began to empty it. "I bought some things for you for now. I was almost out of cash and in a hurry, so I was only able to get a few essentials. Once the money gets here, we'll get you some more things. For now, I grabbed a couple of shirts and shorts, a package of socks, a toothbrush and a hairbrush."

He handed her the things. She looked down at them then back up at him. "Thank you," she said softly.

"I, uh, didn't know what size, so I guessed. How did I do?"

As if in a daze she examined the articles. "I think these will fit," she said absently.

"Mickey?"

Her eyes met his.

"I know you've been through a lot today. I know you're hurting. I want you to know that you're safe now and that everything's gonna work out."

She nodded. "I believe you. Really I do. I'm not sure what I'm feeling. I feel weird, like everything is happening in slow motion in a movie."

Reaching out, he took her hand. "I know just what you're talking about. Part of that is because you're in shock. The other part is because your mind doesn't want to accept everything."

"How do you know all that?" she asked, her head bent, as if examining his hand.

"I just know." He squeezed her hand. "Mickey," he hesitated, knelt down in front of her so he could make eye contact but she averted her eyes immediately. "Honey, did they rape you?"

Her eyes darted back to his. "No."

"You can trust me."

"I think I know that. I don't know why, but I do trust you. Really though, they didn't. Richard, he tried, but Butch pulled him off me and beat him up pretty bad. You went to the cabin," she said, biting her lip. "Richard, he's the one I—" Shaking her head, she grabbed her stomach as if she would be sick.

"He's the one you killed. Mickey, it was you or him. You know you did the right thing?"

Nodding, she breathed deeply. "I know, but I don't think I'll ever forget the feel of slicing through his neck and—" She put both her hands to the sides of her head. "Oh, my God," she wailed.

He reached out and pulled her to him, held her close until she calmed again. "Listen to me now, Mickey. It's a hard thing, sweetie, but we need to give Jason as much information as possible, so I'm gonna need you to tell me everything that happened from the moment you stepped out of your house that morning to when I found you behind that tree. Do you think you can do that?"

Sighing, she nodded her head.

"Okay. First things first. You like pizza?"

"Huh?"

"Pizza. I'm starved. And I don't want to leave you to go get anything else and I don't want you out in public, so the easiest is either pizza or Chinese. And I'm leaning toward pizza."

"I like pizza."

Moving toward the phone on the small table between the two beds, he looked over his shoulder. "Loaded?"

She gave a slight smile. "Of course."

He grinned at her. "My kinda girl."

Mickey waited patiently while he made the call. When he replaced the receiver he held his finger up. "One more minute."

She nodded and he headed to the bathroom.

When he emerged he motioned toward the tiny table in front of the window. "Let's sit over there."

She followed him and took a seat. Jeff pulled out his new phone. "We're gonna kill two birds with one stone and let Jason listen in so I won't have to go over everything with him later. Besides, he may have some questions to ask you. Is that gonna bother you?"

She shrugged. "I guess not."

Jeff punched in the numbers. "Ready for a debriefing?" Jeff asked.

Mickey assumed the answer was yes, since Jeff placed the phone on the table and nodded at her. "You're on speaker," he said. "What time did you leave your house?"

"It was just before six," she began.

Jeff watched her face as she spoke. She told of her initial terror, of Butch and Richard fighting in the van, of the routine they'd fallen into at the cabin and Richard's botched attempt at rape. Jason asked questions in his quiet, unassuming voice, one, Jeff knew, was a facade. Jason was one of the deadliest men in the country. Mickey answered his questions, her voice shaking at times.

She told how Butch had become her protector and how she'd asked him to be the one to take her life when the time came. The irony didn't escape any of them. Jason asked for detailed descriptions of the men, which she gave. It was when she told of Butch's decision to fill her in on her stepfather's culpability that Jason asked the most questions.

"Tell me about you and your stepfather's relationship," Jason asked.

She gave a heavy sigh. "I hated him. And obviously he hated me. I just never thought he'd actually want me dead."

"Of course you didn't," Jason said kindly. "Tell me, Mickey, why did you hate him so much?"

"When I was young, he beat me constantly. He called it necessary discipline. My mother called it spankings, but it was much worse than that. He hit me hard and often. So hard sometimes, I truly couldn't sit down for the pain." She gave a short bitter laugh. "You hear that, don't you? You hear parents say, 'do what I say or you won't be able to sit down for a week.' It doesn't sound so bad when you hear it. Most people don't even think about it. But it *is* bad."

"Why did he hit you? What did you do that was so bad in his eyes?"

She shrugged nonchalantly. "Spilled my milk, tore my dress, made a mess, didn't move fast enough, broke a glass, got a bad grade, late coming home. You name it, he'd take me upstairs to my room, lay me on my bed and whale away."

Jeff muttered a curse as he stood and began to pace the room.

"Ms. Daley, I know this is hard on you," Jason continued, "but I'm asking because I need all the dirt I can get to bring him down. You understand?"

"I understand," she said.

"When did the beatings stop?"

"Stop?"

"What I mean is, as you got older, as you turned into a young lady, did he switch his mode of punishment? Did he turn to restrictions, or no allowance?"

"Oh sure, those things got added in."

"Yet he continued to hit you also?"

"Yes."

"Mackenzie, did he ever touch you inappropriately?"

"You mean sexually?"

"Yes."

"Not really. I mean, I know he wanted to, but somehow he kept himself from giving into the temptation."

"How do you know he wanted to?"

"When I was about fifteen, I was wearing a little blue jean skirt. I'd come home from a party and I was a few minutes late. When he got me upstairs and laid me down on the bed, he pushed my skirt up. I just laid there silently waiting for the impact, but it didn't happen. I could hear him breathing hard and then I realized, he was turned on. He just stood there like that for what seemed an eternity. I remember thinking, if he tried anything I was gonna bite and kick and scream and go straight to the police."

Jeff circled around behind her, placed his hands comfortingly on her shoulders. "And did he try?"

She shook her head. "No. Finally, he snapped out of it and just whaled away. I remember screaming into the pillow because it was the worst ever. I never wore anything but pants after that, but he never stopped hitting me until I finally left home."

"And when was that?"

"The day I turned eighteen."

"And so, there's no love lost between the two of you," Jason said.

"Does he think that you would go to the media and sabotage his political career?"

"I'm not sure what he thinks. It'd actually never occurred to me. I was busy living my own life. Writing books, enjoying a life out from under his thumb."

"Can you think of anything else? Anything that seemed odd to you?"

"There is one more thing Butch told me that didn't make any sense. He said my stepfather was sure I knew about the arms deal."

Jeff and Jason both came to attention. "And do you?"

She shook her head. "I have no idea what he's talking about and I told Butch that. He said something about me being in his study and my stepfather knows I know." She shook her head. "It doesn't make any sense. I think he's paranoid. I've only been in his study once or twice in my entire life. No one is allowed in there."

"Then how were you in there?"

"I went in one day a few months ago. He wasn't home and I was in a hurry. I needed an extra copy of my birth certificate and I didn't want to go wait in line at the vital statistics building and I didn't want to wait two weeks to send away for it so I went through the file cabinet looking for our family documents."

"And you didn't see anything suspicious?"

"No– but really, I wasn't being very observant. I only had eyes for what I was looking for and I didn't even find that."

"I need to get into that study," Jeff said.

"No. I want you to stay with Ms. Daley until I get her to a safe house," Jason stated firmly.

Jeff nodded. "Of course."

"Mackenzie, you did a good job," Jason said once they'd sewn up all the loose ends. "You're a trooper. Now the question is, do you want to go all the way with this or do you just want it all to be over?"

"I'm not sure what you means."

"We can go straight to the press right now. You can tell your story, it'll ruin him politically, but there's no guarantee he'll do any jail time with no witnesses to corroborate your story. He'll claim it was a vindictive act on your part. Revenge for a strict upbringing or something to that end. The up side of going that direction is once you're in the public eye, you're safe. They wouldn't try to touch you after that. The alternative is you stay hidden while we try to build a case against him for both the kidnapping charges and this arms deal.

The down side is they're gonna hunt for you to try and finish the job they started.

"Just from the fact you haven't already gone to the media they should be able to deduce that you know your stepfather was behind the whole thing. They're gonna want to silence you."

Mickey leaned forward, rubbing her thighs with her hands as she thought over her options. "I think you're wrong about something," she finally said.

Jeff came around, sat in front of her. "Go on."

"If I go public now, I still won't be safe. He'll be furious that I finally won. He'll be in ruins. I wouldn't put it past him to try to off me anyway, you know, make it look like an accident. I still won't be safe."

"You know him better than us," Jason agreed. "Are you saying you want us to take this all the way?"

"Yes. I do."

"Have you thought about your mother and sister?"

"My sister will be better off without him in her life even though he dotes on her. My mother will have to learn to get along. I have no idea how she'll react or cope, but I can't concern myself with that. You know, just once I wish she'd stepped in to defend me. Just once."

"Okay, that's it," Jason said.

Jeff picked up the phone, took it off speaker, finished up the conversation. Just as he hung up someone knocked at the door.

Mickey jerked upright, gasping in fear. Standing, she stumbled back away from the door.

"Probably just the pizza," Jeff said quickly. Drawing his gun from his holster, he moved toward the door, peered out. Quickly replacing his gun, he opened the door. "Ah, just the man I wanted to see." He pulled a couple of bills from his wallet, shoved them in the waiting hand, took the box and the two liter Coke and closed the door.

Mickey retrieved two plastic cups from the dressing area. They sat down and dug in.

"I didn't think I'd be this hungry, but man, it smells so good," Mickey said, lifting a slice from the box and sinking her teeth into it.

Jeff watched, fascinated. Her lips were shiny from the greasy toppings and a tiny dot of sauce stayed just above her upper lip. Then her tongue darted out to lick it away.

"Mmm, heavenly," she moaned.

Jeff filled both cups with Coke and drank his down immediately.

He too was starved and yet suddenly, he'd much rather be doing other things. Forcing himself away from his thoughts, he grabbed the biggest slice and stuffed two thirds of it in his mouth.

Finishing off his first slice quickly, he grabbed another piece. "So," he said, his mouth full, "tell me about your sister."

Mickey took a swallow of her soda, licked her fingers and nodded. "Her name's Marissa. She's fifteen. She's beautiful and smart and the only good thing that came from that marriage."

Jeff had to shake his head to snap himself out of the trance her sucking on her fingers had put him into. He commanded himself to focus. "And Daley, he didn't abuse her too?"

She shook her head. "If he had, I would've intervened, but he totally seemed to love Marissa. Everyone does. She's a great kid. Sharp, funny, gentle, you know? Like the personification of Snow White or something."

"So, if you would've intervened for her, why didn't you intervene for yourself?"

She looked down for a moment, feeling embarrassed. She certainly had nothing left to hide from this man. Finally, she shrugged. "I'm not sure why. Telling someone my stepfather spanked me, it just seemed so pathetic. Besides, there were veiled threats that he would hurt my mother, or make her suffer somehow if I were to cause trouble. It was pure manipulation on his part, I realize that now. Look, I don't sit around crying about my step-daddy being mean to me. I'm grown and I've been out of his reach for ten years now. I don't let him affect my life. Well, at least, that's what I thought."

"You're a strong woman, Mickey, in more ways than one. What you've been through in your life and what you've been through this past week, and you fought long and hard and you survived. Do you realize how amazing that is?"

She merely shrugged, not sure what to say.

"Think of it this way. You were taken hostage by three men. Two of them are dead and you escaped. I'd say a guy better think twice before he messes with you. See what I mean? I'm proud to know you."

She gave a soft smile. "Thanks. Really. Those are very kind words. I'm just grateful it was you there at that house. I don't know what would've happened had it been someone else. You acted so quickly. You got me away from there. You've taken care of me as if I were your own sister or something."

He grimaced, shook his head. "No, not like a sister." He watched her face as she grasped his meaning. Her cheeks turned pink and he again reprimanded himself. He pointed at the box. "You want that last piece?"

She laughed, obviously grateful for the tension breaker. "No, you go ahead."

"Thanks," he grinned as he scarfed it up.

Mickey stood and began clearing up the table. Jeff's eyes followed her every move. Her hands still shook ever-so-slightly. Her brow was furrowed as if she were concentrating very hard on the small chore. He'd almost told her he'd do it, but realized she needed to do something. Anything. When she finished she glanced around the room, nervously twisting her hands together. Finally her eyes met his.

He smiled, trying to put her at ease. "Do you want to try to rest?"

"I slept almost the whole way here. What time is it? I've lost track."

"It's almost four in the afternoon."

"Oh." She moved toward the window as if she were about to look out.

"Don't do that."

She stopped. "What?"

"Don't go near the window. Please."

Nodding, she drew a ragged breath, glanced around the room.

Realizing her dilemma, Jeff patted the bed. "Mickey, come sit down."

She obeyed immediately. He wondered if she'd always been so obedient during her life or if she was still in hostage mode."

"Tell me how you're feeling," he ordered.

She swallowed hard. "Uh, I feel, I don't know, maybe a little trapped. I feel like I can't breathe. I need to go outside."

That was out of the question. "Do you know how to play spades?"

"Huh?"

"Spades. Or Rummy or Hearts or poker, or hell, Go Fish, anything?"

She gave a small smile which was one of the most beautiful things he'd ever seen.

"Yes, I know them all."

"Good. Let me get my cards." He moved quickly while he had her attention, trying not to give her anytime to think– or remember. Fishing the deck out of his bag he came back to the bed, instructed her to sit with her back against the headboard, and sat facing her, his legs crossed in front of him.

"I'll deal," he said.

"What are we playing?"

"Spades."

"Okay. Don't you want to take off your shoes?"

"Not now." He didn't tell her it was because he liked to be ready to move fast.

They played several games of Spades until he could tell her attention was waning. He changed it to Rummy, and then to War, and finally to a game called Spit, which was a game of speed. When she lost several times in a row he coached her a bit. "Focus, concentrate. I want you to beat me."

"Why?"

"Just trust me. Now try, Mickey. Show me how smart you are. I'm told you're a brilliant writer. I don't believe it. How could you be with a mind that moves so slow? Show me."

Her eyes narrowed. "Fine."

They played again. She did better but still lost to him. The next time it was close. The third time, she won. She threw her arms up in victory. Yelled "woo hoo," nodded her thanks to the invisible crowd.

Jeff grinned. "Good job."

She laughed and then frowned. "Did you let me win?"

Jeff blinked. "No, of course not."

"You did! You let me win," she said indignantly. "How could you?"

"I swear I didn't. You beat me fair and square."

She rose up on her knees. "Liar. You are lying to me."

He chuckled, shook his head in denial.

She raised her left fist to punch him in the shoulder.

He raised his brow, pointed at her. "I wouldn't do that if I were you."

"Or what?" she questioned. "I doubt there is anything you could do to me that hasn't already been done."

Jeff seriously doubted that.

She swung. His hand snapped out and caught her wrist. She tried to pull free, but he held it firmly. She swung her injured hand at him. He caught it easily. She pulled and then pushed trying to free herself. Jeff fell over backwards, still holding onto her wrists. He grinned up at her as she knelt over him.

"Let me go," she commanded, her brow raised in mock threat, her eyes twinkling.

Jeff nodded, chuckled. "If you promise not to hit me."

She tried briefly to free her hands again, tugged hard, but his grip was like steel. "Let me go," she said again, this time her eyes fierce with anger.

Jeff watched her face as he realized what was happening.

Her face crumpled. "Let me go," she said again as she collapsed onto him, sobbing.

He let go immediately, wrapped his arms around her, held her tight against his chest. "There now, sweetie. It's okay. You go ahead and cry." He turned to his side, making her slide off of him and onto the bed, but he kept his arms around her and kept her pressed against his body. He ran his hands over her back and shoulders which heaved with anguish. She cried her heart out for at least fifteen minutes. When she began to quiet she moved her head, angling her face up toward his neck, burrowing in like some kitten looking for warmth. He smiled when she pressed her nose and mouth against his skin and he felt her breathe in deeply.

Several minutes later, he'd thought she'd fallen asleep when she spoke.

"I'm sorry."

He pulled away so he could see her face. "There's nothing to be sorry about."

"Yes there is. I'm sorry for falling apart on you."

He smiled. "Let's see, you're upset because you were forcefully taken off the street by thugs who were hired by your own father to kill you. You were tied down to a bed and terrorized for a week. You were forced to kill someone to keep him from raping and killing you. I'd say you're entitled to a few minutes of falling apart." He smiled down at her, tenderly stroked her cheek with the back of his knuckles.

She sniffed. "Maybe if it were only a few minutes, but this isn't the first time I've fallen apart today."

"And it won't be the last."

He cupped her face, his eyes searching hers. She blinked up at him in complete trust and it moved him. She licked her lips and his eyes traveled there, lingering. He was so close to her he could feel her moving softly against his chest as she breathed. He wanted her. He admitted it. God forgive him, but he wanted this woman. He leaned forward, his lips hovering over hers. She looked into his eyes and he knew she was as caught up in the need as him. She would allow a kiss, she was practically offering herself. She was so trusting, so vulnerable. Vulnerable. Darn it. Swallowing hard, he leaned even closer, tilted her face down, and kissed her forehead gently before he moved away.

She watched him as he stood, went to the window, used a finger to make a tiny opening in the curtains and peer out. Her eyes couldn't help but follow the line of his broad shoulders to his slim waist, to his muscular backside and thighs to the way his feet were placed shoulder width apart as if he were always in the ready. His thick, dark blond hair glinted in the little bit of sunlight that flickered across his face as he stood at the window. He wouldn't let her by the window, but he stood there bravely, her shield.

How lucky was she that she'd come across him, that he'd been on vacation, that he'd been at his house, even that he'd been alone? Lucky. Right. Yet, she was, wasn't she? Because somehow she'd survived against great odds and she was alive, eating pizza, playing cards. Would her luck hold? She still wasn't out of the woods, but with Agent Jeff Davis on her side she somehow felt everything really is gonna be okay, just like he keeps saying.

Jeff turned away from the window, glanced at her, ran a hand through his hair, looked toward the door. They'd spent a couple of hours playing cards. They had the rest of the night to go before they would be on the move. Nothing to do but keep her talking which at least was something he seemed to enjoy doing. He sat in a chair by the small table near the window. "So, tell me about your books."

~~~

"Do you mind if I turn on the television, maybe watch the news?" she asked. "It's almost eleven."

Jeff grimaced. He'd done his best to distract her. They'd talked for hours. He now knew all about the book she'd published and the one she was working on. She now knew about his family, his work and even Laura, his most recent botched relationship. They'd talked politics and discussed movies and music. They'd played more card games. He'd even done his "magic" tricks for her.

She'd complained that she was stiff and sore from all she'd been through and he'd thought about offering to give her a massage, but decided he couldn't chance it. His attraction to her was too strong and too out of place. He frowned now, at her question. "Jason will have told the Feds about the cabin and it will be all over the news. You think you can handle it?"

She nodded. "I need to know what's going on."

Rising, he walked around to the table in between the two beds, grabbed the remote and flicked on the television while Mickey sat nervously on the end of a bed, her hands gripped tightly together in her lap. It didn't take him long to find the news. And it didn't take long to find the news about her since it was the top story that was already underway.

Reporters stood on the gravel road down from the cabin where she'd been held. "A gruesome scene found here today. We're told a brutal double homicide, took place in the cabin just down the road here. FBI officials speculate Mackenzie Daley had been held here. How the two men died is still under investigation. The question remains, where is Mackenzie Daley? Talmond Daley states that he and the family still hold out hope that she is alive. Back to you, Helen."

"Yeah, right," Mickey murmured. She stood, walked toward the dressing area on the far wall then turned abruptly and walked toward the door, coming to a stop just in front of it. Leaning her forehead against the surface she banged it softly. When she turned, Jeff was there.

The look on her face when she peered up at him tore him apart. "Okay, hon," he said softly.

This time she leaned her head against his chest. His arms came around her, squeezing her tight against him.

"It hurts so bad, Jeff," she said, her mouth moving against his sternum. "But I don't know why I hurt or even what hurts. I just feel so bad. I mean, I know it's over. I know I'm safe now. I'm dealing with the fact it was my stepfather who tried to have me killed. That part doesn't even really surprise me. So why do I feel so much pain in my heart? I should be happy. I'm safe, safe here with you, yet instead it feels as if the world has come to an end." Her arms crept slowly around his waist and pulled him harder against her.

Jeff stroked her back then moved his hands up to her shoulders to massage the tension away. When she gripped him suddenly and desperately and pushed her face up toward his neck he cupped the back of her head, murmuring soft words of comfort against her ear. "Oh, sweetie, it's gonna fade, I promise. This pain won't last forever. Your body is reacting to a severe physical and emotional trauma. It's gonna hurt, but Mickey, I'm here, and I won't let anything else happen to you."

She drew a deep breath and gazed up at him. He moved away

slightly so he could look into her eyes. She glanced at his mouth, licked her lips. He wanted to taste her more than anything he'd ever wanted, but knew he couldn't do it. Wrong time. Absolutely wrong time. Notwithstanding, there would be another time. He would make sure of it.

Touching her cheek, he smiled. "You're tired. You need to rest. In the morning things will seem better."

They both jumped when someone knocked on the door.

Chapter Five

Marissa came flying into the den. "Dad," she cried. "Why didn't you tell me? I told you I want to know everything that's going on. Why didn't you tell me?"

Talmond Daley politely excused himself from the group of people he'd been meeting with. His publicist and campaign manager nodded politely. The FBI agents stepped back to observe. Marion remained seated in her special chair as she had been for hours.

"Marissa, honey," Talmond said, putting his arm around his daughter. "I didn't want to upset you."

"Upset me? I've been more than upset already. Don't you know that I'd want to know that Mick might be alive? I just heard a report on the news. Do you think she got away? Do you think she's alive?"

"Sweetheart, it's hard to say. I don't want you to get your hopes up."

Impatient with the way her father always tried to placate her, she pulled away and approached the agents. "What do you think? Did she get away? I've got to know. Please, tell me."

Agent Dodge smiled kindly. "It's possible. Dogs have tracked her from the cabin where she'd been held through the woods to a home a few miles south. We'll have more information very soon. We're tracking down the owner of the house now."

"She's alive," Marissa said defiantly. "I know she is." She turned toward her father. "She's alive so stop telling me not to get my hopes up." She spun on her heel and left the room.

Talmond joined the group again, apologizing for the interruption.

"It's no problem," Agent Dodge answered. "She's upset. That's understandable. After all, they are sisters," the agent said pointedly. "Everyone who loves Mackenzie is upset."

Talmond's eyes narrowed in anger. What was he trying to imply? He wasn't sure he liked the attitude of this guy. Maybe a call to his superior officer would bring him down a peg or two. Looking around he smiled congenially at the group. "Of course. I've been trying to shield her from the whole ugly affair. I suppose at her age, she'd only see that as me trying to keep things from her." He sighed dramatically. "I've already raised one teenager, you'd think I'd know better by now." He shook his head sadly for affect, then looked up. "Back to what I was saying. I want to be kept informed of every move the bureau makes. Whatever information you uncover about the owner of the house, I want to know it. Our daughter means everything to us, so I'm sure you can understa—"

A cell phone went off. Agent Dodge placed it up to his ear. "Dodge," he said gruffly.

Agent Dodge's eyes made brief contact with his partner as he backed away from the group. He placed his hand over the phone as he nodded at Daley. "Uh, personal call. I'd better take it in the other room. Excuse me."

Talmond shook his head as the agent left the room. "We're in the middle of trying to find my daughter and he's getting personal calls. Such incompetence shouldn't be tolerated."

"I'm sure he won't be but a minute," Agent Stevens put in.

Looking for a place to have a private conversation, Agent Dodge slipped into the large kitchen, however, it was occupied by the housekeeper who was arranging small cups of coffee on a silver tray. She looked up at him, startled by his presence.

"May I help you, sir?" she asked politely.

"I'm sorry to bother you. I just wanted to step out for some fresh air," he said, nodding toward the kitchen door. He opened the back door and stepped out onto a gorgeously landscaped veranda complete with a pond and fountain. It was early evening and getting dark, but the place had lighting around the whole set up so he was able to see his way. He walked around the back side of the fountain out into the grass, making sure he was alone.

"Okay, sir, I'm clear. Fill me in."

The agent was silent as he listened to his superior, offering occasional yes sirs and curses. "What you're telling me," he finally said, "fits exactly with what I'm seeing. "The old man says all the right things, but he's cold and hard as a slab of concrete. It doesn't surprise me a bit he planned the whole thing, and yet, I doubt you're gonna find a connection between the dead men and the Senator. He's too smart for that. Pull his phone records, pull his bank records see what we can find."

He listened again for some time before he spoke. "It's a stretch to think he planned her kidnapping and death for publicity alone, don't you think? . . .Well, if he wanted her dead for whatever reason he's gonna be anxious to find her and finish the job. We can feed him some info and see how he responds, hopefully we can give him enough rope to hang himself. . . .Yes sir, will do." Ending the call, he slipped the phone into his jacket pocket and made his way back inside.

He didn't see the young girl curled up in the elaborate tree house just above his head. Marissa wiped the tears from her face, while the gist of what she'd just heard swirled around in her mind. It sounded as if the agent was saying something that just couldn't be true. Her father was a hard man, she knew that. And he'd been particularly hard on Mick, which had always bothered her, yet she'd never thought he could actually be involved in her sister's disappearance.

Her mind worked hard, trying to find another explanation for what she'd overheard. He wouldn't really hurt Mick, would he? And then she remembered, he had hurt her. There had been an incident, just before her sister had left home. Marissa had been five or six and she'd run into Mickey's room to tell her all about her being student of the month at school. When Marissa had burst through the door she'd found her father standing in the middle of Mickey's room, his hair all messed up, breathing hard, the breast pocket on his suit coat torn and hanging down and he was in the process of taking off his belt.

Then she'd heard a sound from the corner of the room and shifted her gaze. Mick stood in the corner, also breathing hard, blood trickling from her nose.

"Marissa, go on now. I'll be out in a minute," he'd said to her, his voice the same calm, stern voice she'd always known.

"What's happening?" she'd asked stupidly as if she didn't know. Yet, she *had* known.

Her sister had spoken then. Marissa now remembered clearly, how her voice shook. It made Marissa want to burst out crying now, ten years later.

"Baby girl," Mickey had said. "Do me a favor sweetie, and run ask Ms. Dora to get us a little picnic together. I thought you might like to have dinner with me in the park tonight."

Marissa had looked to her father, who'd nodded. She'd then

slowly backed out of the room and closed the door. She'd gotten all the way to the stair landing when she'd heard the loud "swack" and then a little whimpering sound. Until this minute, she'd blocked all of that out of her mind. Suddenly she realized her father loved *her*, but he'd never had feelings for Mick. Now it sounded as if he'd planned Mick's kidnapping, and if he did, then is her sister dead, or had she actually escaped somehow? And if she was still alive, what would happen to her? And more importantly, what could Marissa do to help her sister? She needed more information.

~~~

Jeff's arm snaked around Mickey instinctively, pulling her away from the door while he looked through the peek hole. Sighing in relief, he unlocked the door.

Mickey stood back as Jeff admitted a huge man into the room. He had to be six foot eight, Mickey thought, with a Hulk Hogan physique. He had long, scraggly black hair, a beard and mustache, two earrings in one ear and a gold tooth. He wore jeans and a sleeveless shirt and big, clunky boots. He smiled broadly at her, showing off dimples and the twinkle in his eyes.

Locking the door behind the man, Jeff held out his hand. "Good to see ya, man," Jeff said.

"The heck with that," the man said. He dropped a large canvas bag on the floor, and crushed Jeff to him in a giant bear hug.

Jeff grunted then chuckled as the man let him go. "Mickey, this is Jack, he's a good friend and an agent at Ameritech."

"Hi," Mickey said brightly, offering her hand which Jack took and gently pressed between his two large paws.

"Hello, beautiful," Jack said, his eyes filled with concern. "You doin' okay?"

She smiled warmly at him. "I'm okay, thanks to Jeff. I don't know what would've happened if not for him."

"Right time right place, is how I see it," Jack answered. "And he *was* there, and you *are* safe, so no reason to wonder what would've happened."

Jeff laughed at the puzzled look on Mickey's face. "Jack's just a big ol' teddy bear. At Ameritech keeping everyone positive and focused on good things is one of Jason's priorities. Jason is a very strong Christian, a very positive guy, and also incorporates Zendo Ryu into everything."

"Zendo Ryu?"

"The complete school of thought. It's Grandmaster Kino's art. Jason believes it can be applied to everything."

"So, Jason not only incorporates the normal skills and training, like martial arts, marksmanship, criminology, but also high science, the newest technologies and anything spiritual," Jack added.

"Yeah, but Jack here is much better at positive thinking than I am."

"Jeff's major talent is in marksmanship. He's what they call a 'crack shot,' or an "expert sharpshooter," or like I like to say, a hot shot."

"Whatever," Jeff said with a grin.

"Jack's mind is uncanny. He has what I call amazing luck and he says it's all from the uncluttered way he thinks."

"It's not luck. I'm just truly blessed. God is good. Give it a try, Mackenzie. You won't regret it." He grabbed the canvas bag from the floor and tossed it onto Jeff's bed. "Okay, let's see what Santa brought for you."

Mickey watched as Jack began pulling items out of the bag and handing them to Jeff for inspection. Two lethal looking guns, ammo, a leather shaving kit filled with money– lots of money. Cell phones, some computer chip looking things, a small microphone type thing and finally a styrofoam dummy head sporting a long, curly blond wig, covered in plastic. This last item he handed to Mickey.

Eyebrows raised, she took the offered item, looking it over with obvious distaste.

"It's safer to change your appearance. It's either the wig or change your actual hair and I didn't think you'd want to do that," Jeff said.

"I guess not," she said quietly. She set the dummy carefully on the counter in the little dressing area, removed the plastic and fluffed the hair out while Jack and Jeff spoke quietly.

Turning, Mickey watched them talk. They exchanged keys. Next Jeff plugged one of the chips into his phone, copied the pictures he'd taken, then handed the chip back to Jack. "Pics of Mackenzie and the scene at the cabin," he said.

Jack nodded.

Mickey's mind flashed to what pictures were on that chip. Pictures of her all bloody when Jeff first found her, pictures of the cabin, of Butch and– and Richard lying there with a gash in his throat.

Even though she knew the two men were in the same room with her, it seemed as if they were very far away. Their voices sounded as if they were coming to her from deep inside a tunnel. She was tired, she realized. So very tired and suddenly all she wanted to do was lie down and sleep. Her head began to spin and she reached out to steady herself against the wall. Her eyes closed while she tried to get her bearing. It dawned on her briefly that she was passing out.

She felt strong arms wrap around her and then her feet were no longer on the floor. Drawing a deep breath, she knew it was Jeff holding her. It was the same smell from early that morning when he'd carried her into the house. She wanted to bury her nose against his skin and stay there forever.

When her eyes fluttered open, she realized they were all alone and Jeff was sitting beside her on the bed, pulling the covers up over her shoulders. "What happened?" she asked.

"I think the day has just caught up to you. Sleep now."

"You won't leave?"

"I promise, I'll be right here."

Mickey's eyes drifted shut.

~~~

Either it was still dark outside or the insulated curtains over the single window did a heck of a good job. Mickey stretched her arms over her head and realized immediately they were secured there. Gasping in panic, she tugged on the restraints and felt the cold metal, heard the jangle of the cuffs against the headboard. Terror had her heart pounding, had her throat clogged, had her eyes tearing. Lifting her head, she searched for her protector but he wasn't anywhere to be seen. "No," she cried. "No, this can't be."

Then the door to the bathroom opened, letting light into the room. Mickey watched in horror as Richard stepped up to the bed, his stare filled with accusations and hatred. Her eyes went to his hand which he had clamped to the side of his neck, blood oozing out from under it. His knees hit the end of the bed then eased up onto it. Mickey tried to scream, but the sound froze in her throat. Eyes wide in horror, she watched as he crawled his way up toward her. His blood dropped in spatters on the spread, then on her chest as he loomed over her. Richard pulled his hand away from his throat revealing a gaping, black hole. Mickey screamed.

Jeff sprang from his bed and flew to Mickey's side, grabbed her and pulled her into his lap. Her arms swung at his face, her feet kicked at him. She fought hard, but he was able to wrap his arms around her and press her head against his mouth so he could talk into her ear.

"I've got you Mickey. Come on, now. Wake up. It's me, it's Jeff, shh, now, wake up honey."

Her motions slowed, then her body stiffened and she opened her eyes.

She still gasped for air even though she'd stopped fighting him. "Jeff?"

"Yes, Mickey, it's me. You had a nightmare. It's okay, you're safe. I've got you."

"He was here."

Jeff held her tight, rocked her back and forth. "Who was here?"

"Richard. He was here and he was angry for what I did to him. He was on top of me."

"It was a dream."

"I'm losing my mind," she whimpered.

"No, you're having a normal reaction to a horrible experience."

He held her silently until he could feel her body start to relax and her respiration slow.

She sniffed loudly. "This is ridiculous. I am not a sniveling, sissy type of girl. I swear I'm not. What's happening to me?"

"Your actions are normal, sweetie. Believe me, I know." He leaned over and scooted her off his lap and back onto the bed, then stood and fetched her a glass of water. "Here, drink this."

Taking the plastic cup, she sipped some water, then looked up with a half smile. "Why do people always do that?"

"Do what?"

"When someone's upset, people are always offering them a glass of water."

He smiled. "There's actually something behind that. Doing something relatively normal and mundane helps to bring you back to a functioning level. In this case, your body remembers drinking water thousands of times and it helps to align your emotions. You do feel better don't you?"

Sniffing, she nodded her head. "I think so."

Leaning over, he pulled the covers back up over her. "You need to rest."

When he started to pull away, she grabbed his hand. "Wait, Jeff, please. I don't want to be alone. Will you stay with me? What I mean is, will you hold me? God, I know it sounds so wimpy, but I can't seem to help it."

Jeff swallowed hard, ran a hand over his bare chest, tugged on the shorts he wore. "Uh, of course I will." Sighing, he sat down on the side of her bed. "Scoot over," he commanded.

Mickey moved and Jeff eased in beside her, mentally telling all his body parts to behave.

"Face the wall," Jeff said. She turned over and he scooted up behind her and wrapped his arms around her.

Mickey wriggled back against him trying to get comfortable. When she finally settled, Jeff spoke into her ear. "How's that? Any better?"

"Much. I think I can actually sleep now."

That makes one of us, Jeff thought. He lay very still, listening to her breathe, wondering what his problem is that he can't keep his mind on business. He was holding a kidnap victim who'd been through amazing atrocities over the past week, who needed comfort and warmth from another living being, and he couldn't stop thinking about what it would be like to kiss her. He lay spooning with her and it was taking every ounce of will to keep his mind on her well-being.

"Jeff?" Mickey asked softly.

"Hmm?"

"Do you think I'm silly or a crybaby?"

"No, of course not. Believe me, I understand your need for closeness.

"So you don't think I'm losing my mind?"

"Not at all. Some traumas take time to overcome."

"You've faced a trauma, haven't you?"

He drew a long, slow breath. "What makes you think that?"

"You keep telling me I'm acting normal. You keep telling me you understand what I'm going through. It just makes sense. Have you been through some sort of trauma?"

"Yes," he said quietly.

"That's why you understand."

"Yes."

"Does it hurt to talk about it?"

"Not anymore."

She turned around to face him. "Will you tell me?"

He peered into her eyes, which were black, glossy pools in the darkness of the room. "I don't think you want to hear about it."

"But I do. I really do. I want you to share it with me. Actually, I *need* you to share it with me."

Sighing, he nodded his head. "I guess I get that." He did get it.

The next day after he'd been kidnapped and tortured, his best friend had held him in almost this same position and confided that he'd been through the same thing. It helped tremendously. Jeff touched his forehead to hers, then brushed his hand over her face. "I was also a hostage once. Several years ago. By Muslim terrorists."

"In Afghanistan?"

"No. I was never in the Middle East. They were Muslim terrorists, but they were right here on American soil. Well, actually, they were on a ship, harbored in Savannah, Georgia. I was only held for one very long night, but it was the worst night of my life."

"What happened to you?"

"I was careless and let someone sneak up behind me. We'd been searching for some kids, babies actually, who'd been kidnapped and were scheduled to be taken by ship to be raised by an ISIS satellite group. We'd just found them in an old warehouse and I was so focused on the elation of finding the kids I never heard the guy come up behind me. He knocked me out."

"Oh my God, I remember something about this. This happened about four years ago?"

"Closer to five. You remember it?"

"I remember about the babies, and two agents who were missing."

"I was MIA. The other agent wasn't really missing. He just hadn't reported in because he was busy trying to rescue me. He was the one who found me. Keegan Tanner. One of my closest friends."

"Keegan Tanner, I remember him. Oh, you're Jefferson Davis!"

"You remember my name?"

"That name kinda sticks in your mind."

He groaned softly. "My mom, she's a southerner, born and bred. Named me after the general."

Mickey giggled. "Cute."

"Whatever. I can't believe you remember my name."

"I remember because I was writing at the time and thought both names would make interesting names for characters." She took a moment to snuggle in closer. "So, I didn't mean to interrupt the story. Tell me what happened. Please. You said they knocked you out."

"Yeah, they hit me in the head with something. I'm not sure how long I was out, except that it was long enough for them to take me from the warehouse to the ship. When I woke up, I was lying on the floor in what looked like an old laundry room. I was very disoriented and it took me some time to realize I was on the ship."

"Were you free to move around the room?"

"No. My hands and feet were bound and they'd taken my clothes."

"Oh." She shivered as she imagined his situation.

"Are you sure you want to hear this?"

"I'm sure. Were you alone?"

"Not for long. I'd only been awake a few minutes when the misery began. These two guys lifted me up and hung me on some sort of hook, like a meat hook or something. And this other dude, he started asking me questions."

"Like what?"

"My name, who I worked for. They thought I was CIA and they wanted to know who I was with. I kept telling them I wasn't CIA, but they didn't believe me. I didn't want to tell them anything else because I wasn't sure what happened to Keegan and I didn't want to give him up in case he was sneaking around trying to find me– which was exactly what he was doing. I'm not sure that they actually needed the information they were asking about. I think they were simply enjoying causing me pain. Anyway, I wasn't giving them the answers they wanted so they weren't real happy with me." Jeff drew a deep breath before he continued.

Mickey remained silent, realizing he was gathering the courage to speak about it.

Jeff cleared his throat. "They used a car battery and jumper cables." He shuddered. "I'd never felt so much pain in my life. Not before, and not since. They shocked me until I fell unconscious and then took me down and immersed me in a tub of ice water. The cold revived me and then they started over. I lost track of time. I was so out of it I forgot who I was and couldn't have told them anything anyway. I didn't want to die, yet at the same time I wished for death, hoping it would bring relief. The torture, it seemed to go on and on, hours and hours without a break. That's how it seemed. I really don't know how long it was between sessions. I do remember the exact moment when I accepted I was gonna die. And then the moment I did, Keegan showed up and got me outta there."

"Oh, Jeff," Mickey uttered softly, her voice hitching on a sob.

"I don't remember much about anything else until I woke up on the bank of the Savannah River. All I really remember about that is I was so freakin' cold. Keegan was in bad shape too. He'd been shot sometime during our escape, but he put his arms around me trying to give me his warmth and then— then I just lost it. I broke down, so don't you be embarrassed when you cry or have a nightmare, because believe me, I cried. And it took me months of therapy before I could talk about it without getting pretty damn upset."

"Jeff," Mickey said, bringing her hands up to cup his face. "What you went through, I'm so sorry you had to suffer like that. I hurt so much for you, it makes me want to kiss all the pain away. Can I do that? Will you let me?"

With a curse, he grabbed her hands, pulled them away from his face and pushed her over onto her back until he was practically on top of her. "Will I let you kiss me out of sympathy or pity?" he asked incredulously, his tone biting. "No. Don't do me any favors."

"But—"

"Oh, don't get me wrong. I want you to kiss me, and I sure as heck want to kiss you, and I've pretty much given into the fact that that *is* going to happen. Just not now and certainly not out of pity. When I kiss you it's not gonna have anything to do with sympathy and a lot to do with how a man wants a woman."

"I'm sorry, I didn't mean, well, I, I'm just sorry."

He sighed heavily. "Look, I know you didn't mean to insult me. You were just being sweet and compassionate and I appreciate that because that's the type of person you seem to be, but believe me when I say, I'm okay now. I understand what you went through, Mickey, and I'm here for you, to protect you, to listen to you, to help you in any way I can. For now though, I want you to sleep. I want to get on the road early."

He looked down at her, her chest heaving, her mouth slightly open, her eyes blinking up at him and the words, 'just give into it,' kept shouting in his brain. Just bend down two inches and kiss her. He'd just decided that would be his course of action when she spoke.

"Okay, I'll sleep. Do you mind getting off of me?"

His eyes closed briefly while he got himself under control. "Sorry," he murmured, quickly moving to the side.

Mickey turned away and scooted her bottom back up against him. Jeff's arms tightened around her and they lay silently. Only Jeff's entire body was thrumming with need. Closing his eyes, he willed himself to relax, not an easy thing to do when a woman as beautiful as Mackenzie Daley had her backside pressed against him. If he'd let her kiss him as she'd asked, he'd probably be doing things right now he couldn't take back. It took some time to unwind but he finally relaxed. Just when he began to drift off, Mickey's soft voice intruded once more.

"Jeff?"

"Yeah?"

"I know what you mean when you said you accepted you were gonna die. All week long I cried and fretted because I didn't want to die. Then near the end, I accepted it."

He squeezed her tighter. "When you get to that point, it changes you. I understand that."

She lay silently for a moment, then spoke softly. "Thank God for Keegan Tanner."

"I do. Every day."

"I guess I owe him my life too. I mean, if he hadn't saved you, then you wouldn't have been there to save me."

"Then thank God double for Keegan Tanner," Jeff agreed. "Except I didn't save you. You saved yourself. You're an amazing woman, Mackenzie." He placed a chaste kiss on the crown of her head. "Now, sleep."

~~~

Jeff's eyes blinked open. A glance over his shoulder at the window told him it was morning as he could see a tiny outline of light around the room darkening drapes.

Mickey had turned during the night and now had her body curled up close to him, her face pressed against his neck. Her breath tickled against the hollow of his throat. He tried to slowly pull away but she moaned and nestled closer, rubbing her nose against him as if she were a kitten.

The room A/C was functioning well enough, yet he began to feel his temperature soar. Giving into temptation for just a second he ran his free hand lightly over her shoulder, down her side and pulled her in close.

Dear Lord, please help me to be what I'm supposed to be. How he wanted to touch her. He wanted to watch her come awake, to see her eyes open as he touched her. He sighed. He also wanted more than just a quick tumble and there was definitely no time this morning. Taking a deep breath, he pushed away from her, swung his legs over the side of the bed and headed for the bathroom.

As he emerged Mickey yawned, stretched and opened her eyes.

"Good morning," he said.

She smiled sweetly. "Hi."

"We need to get on the road." Realizing his words sounded brusque probably due to his pent up emotions, he added a smile to the mix. "Would you like to shower first?"

Rising, she nodded. "That would be great. Thanks."

He watched her pad around in the boxers and t-shirt he'd given her yesterday, gathering some of the new clothes he'd purchased and other supplies and slip into the bathroom. While she bathed and he tried to keep his imagination from running amuck, he re-packed and organized their bags, making mental notes of supplies they needed. Realizing her bandaged hand would need to be redone, he set out the medical supplies.

He looked up as she emerged. She'd chosen the khaki colored shorts and the yellow tank top and she looked sweet and fresh and clean and totally hot and man oh man what was his problem? Motioning for her to sit at the table, he quickly applied clean dry bandages.

"It looks good. I don't think there'll be any infection."

She grinned. "How could there be after wasting your expensive Grey Goose on it yesterday?"

He smiled. "All for a good cause. How's the ankle?"

"It's sore, but already feels a lot better."

"We can wrap it if you'd like."

"I think I'll be okay."

"Let me know if it starts hurting. I'll be just a minute." Grabbing some clothes, he entered the bathroom and came out ten minutes later, showered, shaved and dressed. He stopped short at the sight of Mackenzie sitting on the bed in her blond wig. Apparently it didn't matter what shade her hair was, she was amazingly beautiful. He frowned though as he realized she was acting strange. Mickey sat on the edge of the bed, stunned into complete stillness. Her mouth hung open, her eyes blinking at the TV.

"What?" he asked, turning to gaze at the screen.

A picture of him stared back, the one from his latest driver's license. He caught the words, "wanted for questioning in the disappearance of Mackenzie Daley." Next came a description of his truck, which thankfully was no problem, since Jack had brought him a clean car the previous night. The odd thing was instead of asking citizens to contact the police or FBI they were directing them to some 1-800 phone number.

He mumbled a curse. Grabbing one of the bags, he swept

everything he hadn't already packed into it. "We gotta move fast, Mickey. No telling who here at the motel office remembers me from yesterday. Make sure you have your phone," he barked. "Here, take this bag. Leave the room key on the dresser."

Mickey reached out to take the offered bag and searched the room for anything they'd missed, while Jeff donned shoes and socks, strapped on a holster and gun and shoved two phones in his pocket. He threw the two other bags over one shoulder, grabbed the new car keys and peered out through the peek hole. "You ready?" he asked.

Eyes wide, Mickey nodded.

"Okay, let's go."

Jeff threw the door open and started down the walk with Mickey following just behind.

Five rooms down, Jeff slowed.

"Oh no, the truck is gone," Mickey cried.

"Jack took it. We're here," he said unlocking the driver side door of a silver Camry. He hit the button and her door unlocked as he tossed his bags into the back seat. Twenty seconds later they were pulling onto the main drag.

"How did they find out I'm with you?" she asked.

"They traced you to my house. It's not hard to find out the owner of a home. I knew they would find out who you were with. What I can't believe is that they've plastered my face all over the news as if I have something to do with your abduction."

Jeff drove the speed limit as he pulled out a cell phone and pushed a button.

"Did you see the news?" Jeff asked Jason the moment he picked up.

"I didn't, however, I've been informed. I just got off the phone with the bureau. It's not them and it's not the police. I believe it's gotta be Daley taking matters into his own hands. That's why the 800 phone number. All he needs is for some concerned citizen to spot you and call in and he'll be able to zero in on you pretty quickly."

"Fortunately, they gave a description of the truck. At least we're one step ahead of him."

"For now. Listen, forget heading east to the safe house. I want Mackenzie Daley near me."

"You want us in a Los Angeles safe house?"

"No. I'm putting her in with Eric."

"With Grandmaster Kino?"

"They would never think to look for her there. Besides, the Kino's house is a fortress. No one comes in and no one goes out."

"Huh, no one except Jeffy," Jeff said.

"Yeah, I heard about that little excursion of hers. She's now Kimmie's hero."

Jeff thought about Jason's thirteen-year-old daughter. Jason being Korean and his wife, Angel, a gorgeous blonde bombshell, Kimmie was destined to be the total looker she was. She was thirteen going on twenty-one and Jason definitely had his hands full with that one.

"Kimmie could do worse. So, I'm headed south on I-5?"

"No, I don't want you two on the road. I'm deploying a chopper. Take Hwy 99 south to the medical center in Chico."

Jeff listened as Jason explained his plan of action. His eyes darted to Mickey, knowing she would have a hard time with it, but it couldn't be helped and he needed to get the job done and over with ASAP.

"A little over an hour," Jeff said. "I'll be there."

"Take care of our girl. She's the star witness."

"I got that. Later." He glanced at the star witness as he tossed the phone onto the console. "Ever been in a helicopter?"

"No. Why?"

"Because Jason's decided it's not safe for you on the road. He's sent a chopper to pick you up."

"Oh, well, this should be fun, huh?"

"Sure. No problem at all."

~~~

The moment Jason hung up from speaking with Jeff, his private cell buzzed. Noting the unknown caller, he pushed the button, held the phone up to his ear. "Yeah."

"You the guy who found my dog?" a voice asked.

"Yeah, that's me," Jason answered, using the slight drawl Jeff spoke with so they would think they were speaking to Jeff.

"I want her back."

"Where are you? Still up at the lake?"

"Of course I'm not still at the lake. I'll give you the address, but no cops. You got that?"

"Cops are the farthest thing from my mind. Hold on, let me get something to write with." Jason punched a special little button on his phone, waited a few seconds before he spoke again. "Okay, go ahead."

The man rattled off some address in Reno, Nevada.

"Reno? I was halfway to L.A.," Jason complained. He wasn't of course. He was in L.A., en route to his office, but he wanted to buy Jeff some time.

"I suggest you turn around if you want this meeting to happen. Oh, and Agent Davis," the man added, "bring the dog with you."

"I'm afraid that won't be possible, but we'll talk. I got something you want and you got something I want." He disconnected.

Jason hit another button and peered at the read out, giving him the coordinates of the incoming call. He then pushed a button on his dashboard. "Call Mina."

His secretary answered on the first ring. "Yes sir."

"Mina, get me the address of these coordinates." He read them off to her. "I'll be at the office in fifteen minutes. Just give it to me when I get there."

"Yes sir."

"Thanks, Mina. And good morning."

"Good morning to you too, sir."

~~~

Kurt Wells hung up the phone, and then immediately called Talmond Daley who picked up on the first ring.

"Yes," Daley said.

"I spoke with him. I can't believe he actually gave me his own freakin' number. He's on his way to our little meeting."

"He gave you the number because he knew who she was and he thinks he can profit."

"Guy has balls of steel."

Talmond remained silent while he thought over the direction things had taken. "Even though he's on suspension, he's still a security agent for that Ameritech group. He has an inflated ego. Make sure you deflate that ego a bit. He'll be expecting a confrontation."

"And he's getting one. I got four ready to help me take him."

"Make sure they don't kill him, I need him to give up where he's stashed Mackenzie."

"They have their orders and I'm here to make sure they follow them. I've sent Angelo and Yin to Los Angeles to get some information out of this Ameritech place."

"Don't underestimate them. They've got a big reputation," Daley warned.

"They're a rent-a-cop security agency."

"You mess up, I don't rescue you. I don't even know you."

"I won't mess up." Kurt ended the call.

The moment Daley hung up, the house phone rang.

"Daley," he said sternly after reading the caller ID.

"Agent Dodge here, Senator."

"What can I do for you?"

"Sir, I'm gonna have to ask you to not take matters into your own hands. You plastering this Jeff Davis' face all over the media doesn't help."

"It doesn't help, huh? The FBI has been sitting around with their thumbs up their butts. At least putting it out there might get something going."

"It will also warn Davis and send him into hiding," Agent Dodge responded, acting as if catching Jeff Davis was his primary goal, when instead he was keeping Daley pacified while they procure the evidence against him.

"Yes, well, we'll just have to see which one happens, won't we?" Daley disconnected.

~~~

Thirty-five minutes later Jeff pulled inside a fifteen foot high chain link fence across from a hospital. A small building stood near the entrance, but Jeff didn't stop there. He drove to the far side of a large empty field with a big white circle painted in the middle.

"Chopper's not here yet," Jeff said.

He put the car in park, but left it running for the sake of air conditioning. Pushing his seat back to give himself more room he turned to his passenger. "Sorry, we had to skip breakfast. I'll make sure you get something to eat soon."

"It's okay. I'm not too hungry."

Jeff nodded, his eyes sweeping over her. It was time. He leaned toward her, cupped her face in his left hand. "Remember last night when I told you me kissing you is gonna happen?"

"Yes," she whispered, her eyes blinking up at him.

"Well, I hadn't planned on it being this soon, but it seems it can't be helped. If you don't want this, you need to tell me now."

Mickey swallowed hard, looking over Jeff's gorgeous face, her eyes flickering down at his athletic body, his broad chest, his muscular thighs, his flat stomach. She'd known him only twenty-four hours and maybe it was because she'd been through a traumatic event and he was her knight in shining armor, but she had to admit, she wanted him. She wanted his kiss, yes, but she wanted much more than that. The chemistry between the two of them was palpable. She linked her gaze with his and gave an almost imperceptible nod.

That's all he needed. His hand moved around to the back of her neck and pulled her toward him, his thumb caressing her jaw. Leaning closer, his mouth touched hers gently. She was warm, and soft and oh so sweet and he sincerely hoped the chopper was running late. Increasing the pressure on the back of her neck, he deepened the kiss.

His heart sped up, his respiration doubled. Her hands reached out toward him, grabbed his t-shirt and held it tightly in her fists. He felt her body melt toward him. She gave a soft moan which only encouraged him. She tasted so sweet. He hadn't thought it would be possible, but his need for her increased, doubled, tripled.

Pulling away, he shook his head at her. "Mickey, you are amazing. I don't want to stop."

She grabbed him by the shoulders and pulled him forward. "Then don't. Don't stop."

Complying, he kissed her again quickly. The heat rose immediately. She moaned again. Mickey's head fell back, and she arched, encouraging him onward.

"I should stop," he mumbled. She whimpered.

He kissed her a long time, listening to the soft sounds she made in the back of her throat. "I want you, Mickey," he muttered when he lifted his mouth from hers. "I know I shouldn't. I know you're vulnerable right now, but heaven forgive me, I want you more than I've ever wanted anything in my life."

"I don't feel vulnerable right now," she whispered. "I feel powerful. I want you too, Jeff. I need you. I need you so much." The ever-present tears welled and spilled over onto her cheeks.

"Don't cry, Mick." He leaned closer, kissed her deeply.

"I'm not crying. It's just that I need you so much. I need that closeness, that, that–"

"The intimacy?"

"Yes, the intimacy. I need to feel it. I can't seem to get close enough."

He completely understood the need to reach out, to be close to another person after having been through a traumatic, life and death situation.

She, leaned in, nuzzled against his neck. Her eyes lifted to find him smiling at her.

"What?" she asked, smiling back.

"You are so very beautiful." He cupped her face and kissed her slowly and deeply. "Sweet Mickey," he sighed when he ended the kiss. "You are amazing."

She sat up straighter. "Make love to me."

He shook his head. "I want to, but this not the right time. I know it feels like we've known each other a long time, but it's only been one day. Trust me, it wouldn't be a good thing. It could ruin whatever the dear Lord has planned for us."

"You think God has plans for us?"

"It seems pretty evident to me."

"Please," she said, reaching out, placing her palm on his chest.

Softly grunting, Jeff pressed her hand harder against him before he removed it from his body. "Soon, sweetheart, but not now. We have company."

Brow furrowed, Mickey rose up to see Jeff's truck parked a little ways away and the chopper appear overhead.

She gasped. "How– how long has—?"

"He just got here."

Jack got out of Jeff's truck. "Is Jack coming on the helicopter too?" she asked.

"Yes." He opened his car door and sighed heavily. This was about to get ugly. "Let's go."

Mickey got out of the car while Jeff rearranged things in the three bags in the back seat, taking things out of one bag and placing them in another. Mickey watched as the chopper landed and Jack tossed his bag into it and climbed in. Jeff finally pulled out only one bag, took Mickey's hand and guided her toward the chopper.

He tossed the one bag up next to Jack's then turned and took Mickey's face in his hands and kissed her soundly. When he pulled away her look of confusion gave way to understanding and a few seconds later to panic.

"No!" she cried. She reached out, grabbed onto his shirt. "Don't leave me. Please, Jeff."

"I can't come with you right now. I have to take care of business."

"What business? What are you gonna do? You can't go anywhere, your face is all over the media. Someone will see you and report you."

When he didn't answer, she became frantic. "That's what you want, isn't it? You intend to use yourself as bait." Tears spilled over onto her cheeks. "Please, don't do this, Jeff. What if something happens to you?"

"That's a chance I have to take. I'm an agent, baby. You know that. I have to catch these guys who would see you dead. And I intend to bring Talmond Daley to his knees for what he did to you."

"I don't care what he did, Jeff, don't send me away."

"Mickey, listen, I know you've become attached to me. It's a completely natural reaction. But—"

"Please, Jeff, please come with me or let me stay with you."

"Mickey, do you trust me?"

She shook her head.

"You don't?"

"I do," she said softly, her eyes cast downward in defeat. She raised her head quickly. "But you're the only one I trust."

"The people where you're going, they're like family to me and they'll take good care of you. You say you trust me, so I want you to prove that by going with Jack. He'll escort you. I swear Mickey, I wouldn't send you anywhere I thought was unsafe."

She shook her head.

He tilted her head up to get her to look into his eyes. "Yes, Mickey, and I promise to come back to you soon. I promise."

She capitulated by leaning her forehead against his chest. He held her for a few moments. "I have to go now," he said softly.

She looked up. "Earlier, you said you hadn't planned on kissing me this soon. The reason you did was because you were telling me goodbye?"

"Yes, sweetheart. I didn't want to leave you without having kissed you just once."

"You're about to do something dangerous, aren't you?" she asked, the panic rising in her heart.

He gave a slight shrug. "It's what I do. I'm an Ameritech agent, my job is dangerous."

She stifled the tears that threatened again. "Are you afraid?"

"It's a good fear. One the keeps me alive. But, I'm pretty good at what I do, so, fear is not really a part of it. I have to go, Mickey. So, yes, I am kissing you goodbye, but just for a little while. I promise. I'll be back." He took her in his arms and kissed her again then quickly lifted her up into the chopper. He leaned in, nodded at Jack. "Take care of her."

Jack nodded. "You know I will."

Chapter Six

Jeff stood and watched as the chopper rose into the air, then pulled his phone from his pocket as it vibrated. "Davis."

"Jeff, someone is looking for their lost dog."

"Cool. Now I don't have to drive around trying to get someone to spot me."

Jason read off an address. "It's in Reno. I bought us some time by telling them you were halfway to Los Angeles. You're about three and a half to four hours away."

Jeff grabbed his bags from the Camry and tossed them into the truck. "I'm on my way." He started the truck and pulled away. "So how do you want me to play this?"

"They won't want you dead. Not right away anyway. They'll want you to tell them where you're hiding Mackenzie."

"Right. So do you want me to take them, or do you want me to let them take me and see what I can milk out of them?"

"I'm not sure how rough they feel like playing."

"I can play rough."

When Jason didn't answer immediately, Jeff cursed. "That was a long time ago. I'm over it. When are you gonna get over it?"

"Just want you to understand what you could be in for."

"I understand full well."

"I have your backup on their way. Rendezvous with him before you go in. You have a feed?"

"Yeah, I got one."

"Okay, then. So, we let them take you. The back story goes like this; you've crossed over to the dark side due to your need for money, lots of money– for a gambling debt. You were out at the lake house on unpaid leave while I was thinking about giving you a second chance. I can't have my agents dealing in anything shady."

"Got it."

"Jeff. Be careful and check in."

"Okay, mommy," Jeff chuckled as he pushed the end call button.

~~~

Mickey eased down onto the foot of the bed and took in her surroundings. Much to her surprise, the friends Jeff sent her to were Eric and Shelley Kino, the famous martial artists who also were the parents of Ricky Kino and Breanna Adams the even more famous movie stars. They lived in a beautiful home on a giant oceanfront estate near Crystal Cove south of Los Angeles. Mickey was not a stranger to wealth, but she had to admit, the place was breathtakingly beautiful.

She'd been given "the blue room" because it was next door to the Kino's bedroom and they wanted her in close proximity. The blue room was actually many shades of blue. The walls were painted in varying giant sized horizontal stripes of different shades of blue which accented the white crown molding The luxurious bedding was white satin trimmed in blue, giving Mickey the illusion of sitting on a cloud, which was probably the intent of the designer.

The headboard was white leather, and a soft taupe and navy blue rug broke up the monotony of the brilliant hardwood floors. A gorgeous seascape hung on the wall opposite the bed and Mickey felt as if she could get lost in it. Or more accurately, she felt just plain lost.

Shelley Kino had greeted her warmly, fed her and escorted her to the room. Then the kind woman had gathered toiletries and a thick terry robe and clothing and brought them to her. Mickey hadn't meant to break down and cry at the kind gesture, but she had, just like she'd been doing often over the past two days with Jeff. When Mrs. Kino had tried to comfort her, Mickey had withdrawn completely. Mickey was sure she'd insulted Mrs. Kino, or Shelley, as the woman kept insisting she call her, even though she said she understood.

Once Shelley left, Mickey had jumped into the shower and scrubbed and cried and scrubbed and cried some more. Finally, she stepped out of the shower, pulled on the robe, combed her hair and found her way out to the bedroom. Now she couldn't find the energy to do anything but sit.

She missed Jeff, wondered what he was doing, wondered if he was in danger and worried that he wouldn't make it back to her. She knew her attachment to him was just a little crazy. She knew she was off balance, all the out of character crying jags being a giant telltale sign, but it was like, well, like she didn't care how crazy it seemed. Jeff was the only one who really understood what she'd been through. She wanted him to hold her, to talk to her, to tell her everything was gonna be okay, because when he said it, she believed it.

Her eyes on the picture of the sea in front of her, she stretched out on the bed and went over and over in her mind the kiss they'd shared that morning. She replayed not only his kiss, but his touch, his soft words spoken in his deep voice. She wanted him so badly it hurt. She longed for his arms to be around her. She needed him. This need will drive her insane, she realized as she laid there. Doing her best to push him out of her mind, she closed her eyes.

The next thing she knew Shelley Kino was asking her to move up on the bed. Mickey complied in her half awake, half asleep state. Shelley pulled the covers up over her, tucked them under her chin. Then Mickey felt a soft hand on her cheek and heard softly whispered words.

"Father, thank you for this sweet girl and please heal her heart. In Jesus' name, amen. Sleep now, sweet child. Everything is gonna be alright. You're safe here with us. We promise we won't let anything happen to you."

Mickey sighed, snuggled down into the pillows and slept.

~~~

"Yes, in answer to your question, I went against the wishes of the FBI. I didn't see any reason to keep things hidden. I believe in being honest and open in all my dealings. I put that Jeff Davis's picture on the news because he either knows what happened to my daughter or he has her himself. I want her back and if I made some bureaucrats at the FBI angry, then so be it."

Agent Dodge tried very hard not to roll his eyes as he watched Talmond Daley conduct the press conference. His eyes met his partner's who only shook his head.

"We understand this is the same Jeff Davis who helped to save all those kids five years ago. Were you aware of that?"

"I've become aware of that, however, I can't let the fact that he was once a hero cover up what he's become. I don't care who he is. I want my daughter back. Surely you can understand that."

"Senator, do you think not being able to get out and campaign has hurt your chances of re-election?" a reporter from the Seattle Times asked.

"No, I don't think that at all. I think the good people of Washington understand what our family is going through and would expect nothing more than I be here with my family until all this ugliness is behind us."

"Senator, some people have suggested that you and Mackenzie were not on the best of terms," a female reporter remarked, her mic bearing the Fox news insignia.

Talmond frowned at the woman. "Those people would be mistaken. Our family is extremely close. Mackenzie came home frequently to spend time with us. That hardly sounds like a child who's not on good terms with her family. You have only to ask my wife or my younger daughter, Marissa, and they will confirm the closeness of our family unit. I will not give credit to those who seek to give Mackenzie a bad name. Next question?"

Marissa stood nearby watching her father answer questions while her mother stood smiling beside him. The perfect family? Hardly. Yet she'd always been taught that. And she'd believed it. She'd wanted to believe it. She'd been happy in her little golden shell. Now she realized her mother was a ghost, barely aware of what went on around her. Probably on antidepressants. And her father was a monster. The question still remained, is Mick still alive? He certainly acts as if she is. He acts as if he's desperate to find her. And if he is, then as Agent Dodge said, it's because he wants to silence her.

Glancing over at the two FBI agents she realized they weren't buying her father's act any more than she was. She wondered if they would take her into their confidence, if they would let her know what was really going on. She decided she would try to find a moment alone with them.

~~~

Jeff met with his backup, attached his mic feed, a tiny dot secured under the ribbing of his t-shirt. He checked his guns, stuck one in its holster and one under the seat in his truck along with his phone, wallet and knife.

Agent Nate Hawk spoke into his mic. "Test. You getting this?"

Jeff nodded.

"Jason wants me to let you know the perp who'd called to set up the meeting did so from the given address and not from a remote location."

Again, Jeff nodded. That told him, even though he was knowingly walking into a trap, the building wouldn't be set to blow.

Nate took Jeff by the shoulders. "The location being so remote, I'll have to stay a few minutes away to remain unseen. I won't have eyes on you."

"I'll be okay. They want Mickey more than they want to kill me."

Nate nodded, placed his hand over his heart.

Jeff smiled at the gesture from the Native American and jumped in his truck. "See ya on the flip side, pony boy."

Fifteen minutes later he arrived at his destination. The place was on the west side of Reno, out in the middle of nowhere. Jeff pulled into a gravel parking lot outside of what appeared to have once been a plant nursery and garden center. Now it was a large deserted building. He pulled up next to a Ford Explorer, pocketed his keys and stepped down out of his vehicle.

First things first, he mumbled to himself. He leaned into the truck, grabbed his knife from under the seat and quickly sliced through all four tires on the Explorer.

He replaced the knife and turned toward the building. The trick, he thought as he moved toward the glass door entrance, is to be bad enough to make them think they had him, and good enough to not let them accidentally kill him in the process. "I'm headed in," he mumbled to Nate.

Gun in hand, Jeff eased through the glass doors, entering nothing but a small empty room. He made his way to the open doorway that led to the larger portion of the building. Gun first, he edged his way inside, trying not to glance at the man flattened against the wall to his left. It seemed to take the man forever before he finally made his move. He stepped up toward Jeff and held his gun to Jeff's head.

"Hold it right there."

Jeff stopped. Three other men approached. One grabbed the gun from his hand while another twisted his arm behind him and shoved him against the wall, holding him there with a forearm to the back of Jeff's neck.

The third man ran his hands over Jeff, removing his keys. "That's it," the man said as he straightened.

"That's it? I figured you'd be loaded down with weapons."

Jeff shrugged. "Not for small time crooks like you."

He received a quick kidney punch for the remark. Jeff grunted, but before he could retaliate, his arms were grabbed by two of the men and they began to drag him toward the far side of the room.

"You guys are awfully sensitive," Jeff quipped.

"You think you're smart, don't you?" the one who'd hit him said. "Though it looks like you're not too smart since we got the upper hand so quickly. Now, shut your mouth until we tell you to speak." The man hauled off and kicked Jeff in the back of the thigh.

That was it. He might let them take him, but first he was gonna teach this guy a little lesson. In a split second he twisted his arms from the grasp of the two men who held him, grabbed the bully, rammed his knee into the guy's nose, spun and kicked to his head and sent him down unconscious.

Two guns pointed at Jeff's head and he threw his arms up. "Okay, okay. I'm good."

"Bring him here, you idiots," Kurt's voice sounded from across the room.

They pulled Jeff forward. His eyes met the man who'd been driving the black van on the lake road. The man approached Jeff, brows raised. "I'm not gonna fool around here, Davis. You know what I want. Where is she?"

Jeff tilted his head. "If you're speaking about Mackenzie Daley, she's alive and she's somewhere no one will ever find her."

Kurt drove his fist into Jeff's stomach. Jeff doubled over, but stood back up, his chin held at a defiant angle.

"Did you turn her over to authorities?"

"Are you kidding me? She's my meal ticket."

"She's not anything for you except your death. Where is she?"

"Unless you work out a deal with me, you'll never know."

This time the punch was to the face. Blood spurted from Jeff's lip. He licked at it then spat the blood at Kurt's feet which earned him several more punches followed by a kick to the groin. Jeff crumpled. They lifted him back to his feet. Jeff's purpose here was to get information, so he allowed the rough treatment. However, he was definitely looking forward to the time when this guy would get his comeuppance and he sincerely hoped it would be him giving it to him.

Kurt motioned toward a support beam. "Tie him up over there." Memories of another time washed over him and Jeff's stomach turned for just a second before he got himself under control.

Once he was tied securely to the post, the questioning began again.

"If you don't turn her over to us, you will die."

Jeff laughed bitterly. "I'm gonna die anyway, man. She's my only ticket out of the mess I'm in."

"What mess is that, Davis?"

"I, uh, I got myself into some trouble at the casino. They're gonna kill me if I don't pay them."

"You expect me to believe that? You're supposed to be some hero agent for some fancy company."

Jeff nodded. "I was. You're right I was, 'was' being the operative word."

"So what happened?"

Jeff shrugged. "I guess with all the fame and stuff, I sort of went overboard. Let it go to my head. I got in deep. The first time, my boss, he helped me out, but this time he says I'm on my own. I was up at my lake house because I was given an unpaid suspension. I swear. Call Ameritech. They won't have anything good to say about me."

"So what do you think holding the girl is gonna do for you?"

"First, when I saw her, I thought, I'll rescue her and that would get me back in good with the boss man, you know? But then I realized that still wouldn't get me out of trouble. Then she started spilling her guts about not letting her father know she was alive because he was the one who wanted her dead and I knew, she was worth a lot of money. She was like an angel sent to help me, ya know?"

"And so you think you can extort money from us for her? You're gonna ransom her to the original kidnappers?"

Jeff smiled. "When you put it that way, it sounds kind of silly, doesn't it? However, it's more like– I want in."

"In? Maybe you don't understand. We're not getting money for the girl."

"Oh, I understand plenty. She told me about the arms deal. Keeping her quiet about that would be the most important thing, don't ya think? And all I ask is for a small percentage. Let's say ten percent."

"Ten percent? You're outta your mind. You think Daley is gonna pay you eight million dollars?"

Eighty million, Jeff thought. Geez. Jeff shrugged in answer to the question. "There is no deal if the girl talks, so I think eight million is worth it."

Kurt moved up close to Jeff, put a gun to his forehead. "I could just blow you away right now."

"Yeah, you could, however, if anything happens to me, five packages get mailed. Video of Mackenzie telling all about what she knows will go to the FBI, CIA, Department of Defense, CNN and

FOX."

Kurt eased the gun away from Jeff's head. "You got this all planned out, don't you?"

"I think I do."

"How do we know she's even still alive?"

"She is. I've got her stashed with a friend. If I don't come back, she goes public. As long as I'm alive, she remains hidden and silent and you guys have nothing to worry about. When I get my money, I deliver her to you."

"I want proof she's alive."

"I'll send video to your cell phone by this time tomorrow. By the way, I'm gonna need my money by next Friday or I'm dead."

"Then I guess you're dead, Davis. This deal isn't going down for three more weeks."

That worked easy enough, Jeff thought. "Well, then tell Daley I'm gonna need an advance in order to keep Mackenzie quiet. Tell him I'm gonna need three hundred thousand by next Friday."

"You got balls, Davis."

"Yeah, what's left of them. Where is the big deal gonna take place?"

"I wouldn't tell you even if I knew."

"Come on, you're the good Senator's right hand man. Don't tell me you don't know all the details."

Kurt shrugged. "I don't give a damn if you believe me. No one knows except Talmond himself. He's got all the documents, all the details and I've never seen them."

"When you know, I want to know."

"What makes you think I would tell you?"

"Because I hold all the cards."

"You know all you're gonna know. You keep the little brat quiet, you'll get your freaking money. I want that video."

"And I want the money, so rest assured, you'll get the video."

Kurt stood staring at the man. "What if we decide to take our chances on finding Mackenzie and just kill you now?"

Jeff smiled. "Why don't you ask Talmond what he wants you to do?"

Kurt frowned in frustration. They'd been working this arms deal for almost a year. It was finally coming to fruition and they couldn't afford to let it get messed up by some spoiled brat little girl and a crooked security agent. "Daley is gonna ask how we know you really have her."

"Tell him to wait for the video. Or, you can tell him how much I enjoyed his daughter, especially the sweet mole on the side of her left breast. If he knows her as well as she says he does, he'll know I'm telling the truth."

"He's never had her that way and if she's telling you that, she's lying."

"He's never had her, however, he's wanted her. He's spied on her enough to know that what I'm saying is true."

Kurt had no response to that.

"Oh, and one more thing, I'll know if anyone follows me. You do, and the deals off."

"You don't want this deal to be off, Davis. Not if you want to stay alive."

"You're right, I don't. So don't follow me and we'll all be happy in just a few weeks. Tell Daley he got lucky."

"How's that?"

"You're boys at the cabin messed up majorly. If I hadn't been there to take up where they left off, Daley would be in federal lockup right now."

Kurt rammed his fist into Jeff's gut. Jeff grunted with the pain.

"What was that for?"

Kurt smiled. "Just because I don't like you." He nodded at his men. "Cut him loose."

"Can I have my weapon back?"

"No, I think I'll be holding onto it." He tossed Jeff his keys.

Jeff made his way out of the building, quickly started the truck and peeled away.

~~~

"Yes," Jason said as he depressed the button on his desk phone.

"Mr. Lee, two men tried to enter the building carrying weapons. They've been disarmed, but they're demanding to see someone about information concerning Agent Davis."

Jason smiled. These guys are idiots. "Send them up."

"Sir?"

"Send them up, Gail. Have Agent Sykes escort them."

"Yes sir."

Jason grinned. He carefully tidied up his desk, removed the picture of his wife and daughter and placed it on a bookshelf to keep it safe, then checked to make sure the camera was operational. Mina buzzed him a minute later.

"Send them in," he answered her.

His door opened and Agent Sykes led two men into the inner sanctuary of Jason's office. One of the men was Chinese. The other maybe Latino, Jason surmised. Sykes closed the door and stood against it, his arms folded across his chest.

Jason smiled at him. "You can wait outside."

"Sir?" Agent Sykes questioned, clearly concerned for his boss.

Jason nodded. "It's okay."

The agent left as instructed and the two men's demeanor changed immediately from submissive to challenging.

"Have a seat," Jason ordered as he came around the front of his desk and leaned on the edge.

The men sat.

"My name is Jason Lee. And you are?" He waited.

The Chinese spoke first. "Yin Chu."

"Mateo Martin," the older man said.

Jason purposely didn't offer his hand, but simply nodded. "Now, I understand you want information about one of my agents."

"Jeff Davis."

"I see." Jason turned his back, moved to the window. "Why do you want to know about Agent Davis?" he asked, without turning around.

"He's suspected in the kidnapping of Talmond Daley's daughter."

"Yes, I saw that on the news." He turned slowly to face the men. "So you're with the FBI?"

"No, we work for Senator Daley."

"I see. So you're here with no authority."

The men sputtered on about Daley being a Senator while Jason smiled at them.

"I assure you, working for an elected official gives you no authority here."

"Then you're covering for this guy who could be a felon?"

Jason laughed. "Jeff is stupid, but he's not a criminal."

"Do you know where he is?"

"No. I've put him on unpaid leave for reasons that don't concern you. I gather from the news report this morning that he went to his lake house to work some things out."

"Yes," Yin Chu said. "And while he was there, he became involved with the abduction of Mackenzie Daley."

"I doubt that seriously."

"Maybe you don't understand the seriousness of the situation," Martin said, a warning tone in his voice. "Daley wants his daughter back. He'll leave no stone unturned and– no one unpunished. Perhaps you'd better think about cooperating."

Jason moved forward to lean on the front of his desk once more. "Are you threatening me?"

"Take it any way you want."

"I don't know where Jeff is and if I did I wouldn't tell it to a couple of Daley's flunkies."

The two men rose.

Jason eyed their stances calmly. "You two are making a big mistake."

"We think maybe it's you making the mistake."

Jason had to keep himself from grinning. He decided he would get them a little riled. "What?" Jason prodded. "You think you can rough me up, force me to talk? How do you think you can do that? You," he pointed at Martin, "are a make believe MS-13 wannabe and you," he said gesturing at Yin, "the Koreans have always outclassed you. You are nothing but a filthy, dirty, Chinaman." Of course Jason had no problem with the Chinese people, still, he knew mentioning the man's ancestry would stir him easily.

The man rattled off a string of threats in Chinese, demeaning Jason's Korean ancestry.

Jason surprised him by answering him also in Chinese. Apparently, being told off in his own native language was more than the guy could take. He sprang at Jason, who merely blocked the punch Yin threw and grabbed him by his Adam's apple.

"I can kill you in one motion," Jason said softly. "And I want to. So be very careful and very still."

"Maybe you'd better let him go," Martin threatened as he wiggled his arm and a switchblade fell from his sleeve into his palm.

Jason straightened. "Maybe I should." In a split second he'd let go, clipped his hand over Yin's throat and stepped over him as he fell to the floor choking.

Martin smiled, eyes gleaming. Two seconds later he lay disarmed and unconscious at the foot of the book shelf. The picture of Jason's wife and daughter wobbled precariously for a moment and then fell, glass shattering as it landed on Angelo's head. Agent Sykes came bursting through the door.

Jason looked up. "Call our friends at the bureau and tell them we have two to take into custody."

"Yes sir."

"And then we need to have a little talk about places to hide weapons."

Sykes swallowed. "Yes sir."

Jason lifted the broken picture frame. "Well, darn," he sighed.

~~~

Mickey turned at the knock on the door. She'd been staring out at the ocean all day. She'd been so disappointed when she woke this morning and realized Jeff hadn't come back yet. Of course, he hadn't actually given her a time frame, still, she hadn't thought it would be more than a few hours. It'd now been well over twenty-four.

Shelley had come first thing in the morning, asked her to breakfast. Mickey had politely refused. Then the sweet lady had tried again in the afternoon, asked Mickey to do some online shopping with her for some clothes, but Mickey told her she just felt too tired and wanted to sleep. Shelley asked Mickey for her sizes and left her to rest. Mickey supposed it was time to pull herself out of the funk she was in. She couldn't hide in the blue room forever. "Come in," she called softly.

What appeared to be the fantasy version of a Hawaiian princess walked through the door. She was a little over five feet, with a slim, well-muscled, bronze colored body, and long, black hair that fell to her waist in large, voluptuous curls. She wore a tiny pink and white floral bikini with a matching sarong style skirt that rode very low on her hips.

The girl smiled sweetly, showing beautiful white teeth. Her entire face lit up, and her brown eyes showed such warmth and compassion it belied the girl's age. Mickey knew that this was Jeffy, June Flower Kino. Shelley had spoken of her several times.

"Hi," Jeffy said. "I was on my way up to change for dinner and Mom asked me to tell you dinner will be ready in about thirty minutes."

"Thanks," Mickey replied.

"Oh, and by the way, I'm Jeffy, well, I mean I'm June Flower, but most everyone calls me Jeffy." The girl smiled brightly at her. "Do you feel like talking?" Jeffy asked.

She was mesmerizing and Mickey felt drawn to her. Mickey shrugged, smiled back at her. "Sure."

Jeffy came in and sat on the edge of the bed. Mickey took a chair and waited for her to speak.

"I, um, just wanted to say that I'm sorry for everything that's happened to you."

Mickey's eyes moistened immediately but she blinked several times to make it stop. "You know everything?"

"Yes. Uncle Jason told Mom and Dad and they believe there should never be any breakdown in communication, so everyone in our family knows. Joey knew anyway because he's been working with Ameritech for a few years now."

"Joey? I thought he was the little boy."

"That's little Joey. He's my nephew, my brother Mark's little boy. I meant my brother Joey. He's twenty-three."

"Oh."

Jeffy smiled. "Our family is a little confusing."

"Maybe a little."

"Would you like me to tell you about them?"

Mickey smiled. "That would be great. Maybe it will keep my mind off my troubles."

"Okay. Well, there's my mom."

"She's very kind. I really like her."

"Yeah. She's like that. Everyone feels the same way. She met my dad when he trained her for the MART, which is a big martial arts tournament."

"I've heard of the MART. I've watched it a few times."

"Cool. She already had Bree and Mark and Joey when she met my dad. My dad had Ricky. Ricky's mom died of cancer. Then my dad and mom got together and had me. And Mark's girlfriend had a baby but she died of brain cancer and that's why we have little Joey. And Bree and Ricky finally admitted they were in love with each other and they got married and they have two kids now."

"Wow, and Bree is Breanna Adams the famous movie star and Ricky is Ricky Kino, also the famous movie star?"

"Yeah, though to me they're just my brother and sister."

"Gotcha. My little sister would go crazy to be able to meet them."

"How old is your sister?"

"She's your age actually."

"Really?"

"Yes," Mickey said softly. "I miss her so much. She must be devastated by all this."

Jeffy frowned. "Because she thinks you're dead?"

"Yes. We were very close. I can't imagine what she must be going through."

"I wish there was a way we could get a message to her," Jeffy said.

"I know, but Jeff says no contact. It will destroy everything he's working on to catch my stepfather."

Jeffy shook her head. "Bree and I, we're really close too. If I thought she was dead or hurt, I don't know what I would do. Ricky was kidnapped once a long time ago. Waiting to hear if he was dead or alive was one of the worst nightmares our family has ever been through. Of course, I have to say that I knew he was alive."

"You did?"

Jeffy nodded her head. "I can— feel things. I— know things."

"You mean like you're psychic?"

"Yeah, like that, only, I'm not in control of it. I never know when it will kick in."

"Have you always been like that? I mean, how old were you when you realized you 'knew' things?"

Jeffy shrugged. "Mom and Dad say it's been like that since I could barely talk. Like, they said I went crazy one night as we drove home saying, 'bunny, bunny,' and they kept saying they didn't see a bunny, but when we pulled into our drive there was this huge rabbit sitting on the driveway just past the gate. I mean, that's no big deal, but like, I knew Ricky was alive. I could feel him."

"I remember when that happened. When they found him he was pretty messed up."

"Severe contusions and lacerations of the face, fracture of the second, third, and fourth proximal phalanx, numerous knife wounds, first and second degree burns and severe testicular trauma, fortunately not ruptured."

Mickey's mouth dropped open.

"Uh, sorry. I'm studying to be a doctor."

"Oh, that's right. Jack told me you're like a genius and you're already in college."

"Yeah, right now I'm at the Keck School of Medicine at USC."

"You don't sound so excited. What is it? Would you rather be at Harvard?"

Jeffy smiled. "No. First I'm too young to be away from my family and second, I know Harvard is where everyone thinks the best and brightest go– but our family is pretty big on not being swayed by the conventional."

"What do you mean?"

"It's kinda like the Hummer."

"You mean the car?" Mickey asked, her expression puzzled.

"Yeah. I mean, everyone says they're the thing to have. The most luxurious, the best made, the most expensive. Before the gas crunch they were the totally cool thing to have. Why? Because someone, somewhere with a little bit of pull said they were and the sheep of the world followed suit. Everyone trying to keep up with everyone else. So silly. I mean, really look at the Hummer. Yes, they have luxury, as do a guzillion other vehicles, but really look at them. Big, ugly boxes taken from the design of military ATV's. I just bet some dudes sat around one Saturday afternoon and decided to do a test. They decided to design the ugliest car they could come up with, tell the public it's the best, the most expensive, and sit around and laugh while all the people clamber over each other to own one."

Jeffy shook her head in disgust, then looked up at Mickey. "Oh! Oh, I'm sorry. Sometimes I get a little long-winded. It's been a problem for me most of my life. I didn't mean to get carried away."

Mickey laughed. "No problem, Jeffy. This has been an extremely enlightening conversation."

"You're not put off?"

"Not at all."

"Good." Jeffy blew out a breath. "Anyway, about school, it's okay I guess. I do love learning. Sometimes, the teachers can't teach me fast enough and it makes me crazy, so I read quite a bit. My problem though, is the social thing. I'm having a difficult time. Well, what I mean is, sometimes I just wish I was a normal girl in a normal school getting ready to have my first date or go to prom, you know what I mean?"

Mickey smiled. "I think I do."

"Mom and Dad, they encourage me to make friends with kids my own age, and I try, I really do, but they talk about stuff that's so, well, so stupid that I can't relate. So the other kids think I'm a snob and I just bury my nose in a book and try not to think about it."

"Oh, Jeffy," Mickey said moving closer and taking her hand. "You're in a difficult spot, bless your heart. You have the mind and knowledge of an adult stuffed inside the body of a teenager."

Jeffy's eyes welled with tears. "You understand. No one outside my family has ever understood. Not really."

"I do understand. Maybe it's because I'm a writer and I immediately think of what someone would be thinking or feeling. You're in a grown up world and you not only haven't been able to experience the things a kid gets to experience, you also haven't experienced the things an adult experiences."

Jeffy nodded. "Like sex."

"Sex?"

"Yes. No one wants to talk about it with me. I mean Mom and Dad, they're pretty open about things and they understand my need to learn and they try to help me to understand things, but you see, I'm reading and learning about the workings of the human body and I've never even experienced an orgasm. How stupid is that?"

Mickey swallowed, not quite sure what would be the right thing to say.

Jeffy grinned. "I snuck out of the house a few weeks ago intending to remedy the virgin thing, however, things went a little astray. If it hadn't been for Jeff being so kind and gentle the whole episode could've been a lot worse."

"Jeff? Jeff Davis?"

"Uh huh. Isn't he just the cutest guy in the world?"

"He's good looking enough," Mickey said stiffly. She was afraid to ask but she had to know. "What exactly did he do?"

"He rescued me of course."

Jeffy went on to tell the whole story and Mickey found herself greatly relieved. When Jeffy finished telling about the pictures in the scandal magazine and Ricky confronting Jeff they had a good laugh. So why did Mickey suddenly feel like crying. She didn't want to have one of her stupid crying spells right here in front of Jeffy, but the tears started and she couldn't hold them back.

"Oh, Mickey, I'm sorry. I didn't mean to make you cry. You've been through so much and here I am talking about my stupid problems. Please don't cry."

Mickey swiped her eyes with her fingers. "It's not you," she said as she sniffed and smiled through her tears. "I don't know. I just keep getting these crying jags. Jeff says it's normal. I really miss him, and I miss my little sister too. You're so much like her. If only I could tell her I'm okay."

Jeffy stood and put her arms around her. "We'll think of something, don't you worry. Everything is gonna work out, I just know, and Jeff is coming soon."

"You've heard from him?"

Jeffy shrugged. "No, I just know it. You need to talk to my dad, Mickey. He's a psychologist and he helps people work through trauma."

Mickey sniffed. "I thought your dad was a martial arts instructor."

Jeffy laughed. "He's not just an instructor. He's a grandmaster. He's the best. He owns schools in every state and he teaches big important people, who train the military special ops people, and he's also a psychologist. He became one so he could help his students to become one with themselves. He's very kind, and people love to talk to him. You'll see what I mean when you meet him."

Jeffy bent to give Mickey one more hug. "I gotta go get dressed, but I have to say, I just love you already."

Mickey laughed.

The door opened and Shelley Kino stepped into the room. "Everything okay in here?" she asked.

"Oh, hi Mom," Jeffy said brightly. "Sure, Mickey and I were just getting to know each other."

"I didn't mean to barge in, but I knocked and you didn't answer and you know how I worry."

"Yes, I know. Is Bree here yet?"

"They just got here and dinner's ready. Why don't you hurry and dress and Mickey and I will be right there."

"Okay. See ya Mickey," Jeffy said. "Thanks for letting me talk your ear off."

Mickey grinned at her. "No problem."

Shelley sat down next to the beautiful girl whom she thought could be compared to her own daughter, Bree, known as one of Hollywood's most beautiful actresses. Shelley took Mickey's hand. "Jeffy has a tendency to talk a lot. I hope she didn't upset you."

"No, not at all. She took my mind off things for a while. She's sweet. I really like her."

Shelley reached up and smoothed some hair away from Mickey's face. It was a tender, motherly gesture which, darn it, brought more tears to Mickey's eyes.

Shelley stood, retrieved a tissue and held it out to her.

"Thank you," Mickey said, dabbing at her eyes.

"Your heart is tender now," Shelley said. "You cry all you want. It's good for you. You've not only been hurt physically, but you've been betrayed by people close to you. That hurts more than the physical. I'm here for you to talk to if you want. I want to hear all about everything that happened to you, but I'll wait for you to tell me in your own good time. Just know that I understand. And let me encourage you, if you don't want to talk to me, you need to talk to my husband. I promise, if you do, you'll feel better."

"You have a kind heart," Mickey said, smiling at the pretty woman. She knew Shelley Kino was in her late forties but she looked to be no older than thirty-five. She wore no makeup, though really, she didn't need any. She had gorgeous brown eyes with incredible gold colored lashes. Her hair was dark blonde or light brown with golden streaks through it. It was long and thick judging from the width of the single braid she wore. She had on blue jean shorts and a sleeveless shirt which showed off amazing biceps, and killer legs. Her smile was kind, her eyes wise and a little sad.

Shelley smiled. "You have a kind heart too. Takes one to know one. Now, you may not believe me, but sometimes it helps to do normal things like coming downstairs and eating dinner."

She smiled. "Jeff told me that same thing the other day."

"Jeff was right." Shelley eyed the young woman. "He's a good guy, isn't he?"

Mickey sighed before she spoke which told Shelley what she wanted to know.

"I've never met anyone like him," Mickey said. "He's so kind and tough and strong and fearless and intelligent. You don't meet many men with all that going on."

"No, you certainly don't." She smiled kindly. "Tell ya what, come downstairs with me and we'll all tell you funny stories about Jeff. It'll make you feel a lot better."

Mickey stood. "I think I'd like that."

They went downstairs together and Mickey was suddenly surrounded by a wild, loud mass of some of the most attractive people she'd ever seen.

The Breanna Adams came forward without speaking a word and hugged her tight. "Welcome to our home," she said softly. "Everything's gonna be okay."

She pulled away and Mickey smiled at her. "Thank you."

Ricky Kino approached, a look of compassion on his gorgeously handsome face. He took both her hands in his. "Hi, Mickey. We rhyme!"

Mickey giggled while everyone else groaned.

"No, really, we're glad you're here. Thank goodness Jeff was at his lake house."

"Amen," someone in the background said.

Ricky looked her over. "And I'm gonna guess that Jeff is just as thankful."

Mickey blushed and Ricky smiled knowingly.

"These little munchkins are Eric and Taylor," Ricky said, introducing his children.

Mickey smiled down at two of the most beautiful children she'd ever seen. They were like exotic fairies from a storybook. Both had thick, dark brown hair, with a slight wave to it. The girl's hair was very long. They each had beautiful golden skin and large eyes. The boy had dark, brown eyes like his father. The little girl's eyes were almost gray. She was mesmerizing. Truly, they nearly took her breath away. "Hello," she said.

Little Eric smiled kindly, a complete twin to the look that'd been on his father's face a moment ago. He held out his small hand in a very grown up gesture. "Hi. I saw you on TV. I'm glad you got away."

"Me too," she said. "How old are you, Eric?"

"Six. I'm in the first grade."

"That's wonderful."

"I'm three," a tiny voice said sternly.

"Well, then," Mickey laughed. "I thought you were much older than three. I thought maybe you were, umm, about a hundred."

The little girl giggled, a sound like tiny bells tinkling.

"You're funny," Taylor said. "Like my daddy."

Mickey smiled up at Ricky who was looking down at his little girl with so much tenderness Mickey's heart lurched.

"Hi, I'm Mark."

Mickey looked up at the owner of the deep voice. He was taller than all the rest by a few inches. She remembered he was Shelley's oldest son from a previous marriage. He had light brown hair and big brown eyes like his mother. He was big and athletically built and had his hand resting on the top of a little boy's head.

"And this is little Joey."

Obviously the family taught the children impeccable manners because the child offered his hand with a giant smile.

"Hi! I'm six too, but I'm older than Eric, but that's okay because he's my best friend. He's also my cousin, but we don't care, we're still best friends."

"How lucky for both of you," Mickey offered.

"Joey couldn't be here," Shelley added. "He's still at the office with Jason. Come on everyone, let's sit down."

Jeffy came running in and they circled around the large table. Mickey looked around at all the happy, smiling faces and people who were obviously at ease with each other and compared it to the horrible family dinners she'd had to endure as a child. She was beginning to realize she'd missed so much. Which meant Marissa was missing out too.

They were all seated by the time the man Mickey presumed to be Grandmaster Kino walked into the room. He went straight to his wife, stood behind her chair and placed his hands on her arms.

"So sorry, I'm late," he explained. "I had Jason on the phone and wanted to get some details on a few things."

Mickey watched as he leaned down and kissed his wife. Not a quick nip of the lips but a slow, sweet kiss. When he pulled away there was promise in his eyes.

"I would say the old 'get a room' thing," Ricky said, "but they'd probably do it."

Bree smiled. "They're in love," she explained to Mickey.

"So are we," Ricky said. "And there are plenty of rooms upstairs."

"You guys stop," Jeffy complained. "You're gonna make Mickey think we're weirdos."

"I think it's great," Mickey said dreamily. "You know, to be so in love."

Eric came around the table to Mickey's side and offered his hand. "Mickey, I'm Eric."

Mickey gazed up into a noble face. He smiled the kindest smile she'd ever seen and he took her hand in his. She felt warmth and love immediately flow into her body and felt the now familiar sting of tears. "We'll talk later," he assured her. "Please, feel welcome in our home."

"I do, thank you."

"I promised her," Shelley began, "that we would tell her all the funny stories about Jeff we could think of."

"That'll take all night," Ricky laughed.

"Let me tell you about the time I drugged him," Bree said.

As she spoke Jeffy smiled up at Mickey. Mickey smiled back.

Ricky winked at her. Bree chatted on. Mark added color to the story. Shelley smiled at her husband who smiled back at his wife with complete devotion on his face. Mickey sighed. Maybe everything really was gonna be okay just like everyone kept saying.

Chapter Seven

At least she didn't scream this time. She did wake up panicked and sweating and shaking with thoughts of seeking out Shelley. Two things stopped her, a dark, unfamiliar house and the fear of disturbing the lovebirds. She'd thought for just a moment she'd heard voices or maybe a door shutting, but she knew she was safe. She'd been assured by Master Kino that the house was not penetrable.

She thought of the long talk she'd had with Eric Kino in his study earlier that evening. She was welcomed into his study, unlike her stepfather who never allowed her in his domain, not even once during her life. Eric spoke with her as if what she had to say was utterly important to him. He nodded and made comments as she told the story of her abduction, letting her know he completely understood what she'd been through, understood her fears and her coming to terms with her own mortality.

He'd asked her about her relationship with her stepfather, about her mother, about her sister. He'd understood her feelings of betrayal by both her mother and her biological father who'd never come back for her. He'd commended her on her writing career, on her strength, on her calm thinking under pressure when she'd been in captivity. He had a presence about him, a powerful presence. He was a wonderful man and Mickey understood completely why his family was so full of love and kindness and respect for each other.

Rising, she made her way into the bathroom, splashed water on her face, glancing down at the cut on her hand. It was healing well, thanks to Jeff. She sighed. Where is he, she wondered. Is he safe? Would the Kinos keep her informed? Drying her hands and face, she wandered out onto the balcony.

The warm ocean breeze blew her hair back from her face, calming her as she walked to the edge and leaned over the railing. The ocean was powerful and beautiful and she would normally be captivated by the moonlight on the water, but all she could think about was Jeff. So strong. So kind.

The way he took control of the situation when he found her in the woods, the way he lifted her and carried her to safety, she couldn't get him out of her head. Her heart skipped a beat as she thought of how he'd kissed her in the car. She missed him. How could she be so needy?

~~~

He slipped into her room. The bed was empty and he knew a moment of irrational fear, but he turned his head toward the open balcony door and she was there, standing in a sheer pink gown, leaning over the railing in the moonlight. He marveled at her beauty. Moving quietly he went to the door and stepped out onto the balcony.

"Hello, Mickey," he said softly.

Gasping, she whirled, her hands flying to her face in startled surprise. "Jeff?"

He smiled.

"Jeff," she cried running at him.

He caught her, scooped her up. She wrapped her legs around his waist as he crushed her to him and fiercely kissed her mouth. When he finally pulled back she hugged him to her, burying her face against his neck.

"I can't believe you're here," she cried.

"Why not? I told you I'd come back to you."

"I thought it would be days or even weeks before I saw you again. And now you're here. You're really here." She pulled back to look at him and took his face in her hands. Her brow furrowed. "Jeff, what happened to your face?"

"Had a little confrontation with the boys. I'm okay."

"What boys?"

"The ones you don't want to hear about."

"The guy driving the van?"

"Him and a few others." He set her on her feet. "But we're not gonna talk about that right now."

"Why not?"

"Because I've been having a hard time trying to put you out of my mind while I work. Now I'm here, with you in my arms, and I don't want to talk about the bad guys."

She smiled up at him. "Oh, I'm sorry I've been distracting you," she lied. Of course the news didn't bother her a bit because she was having a hard time herself, keeping her thoughts from him.

He pulled her close. "Mickey—" He stopped, sighing deeply.

"What?" she asked. "What's wrong?"

He shook his head. "It's just that, I want to make love to you, Mick. I can't get you out of my head. I know I shouldn't do it and still, you are all I can think about."

She kissed his cheek. "Then just do it, Jeff. I want you."

"I know you do, and I want you, but you're not yourself."

"But—"

"You've told me so yourself. You said you don't usually cry at the drop of a hat. You don't usually cling to anyone. You were quite self-sufficient before you were abducted. You didn't need anyone. You've said all those things. So, knowing that you've been traumatized, that you're vulnerable, I should just walk away. I should leave your room right now."

"But—"

"But I can't seem to make myself do it. I'm drawn to you. I'm a weak man, Mickey."

She smiled. "Oh, thank goodness."

He scooped her up, carried her inside to the bed and stretched out next to her.

"Jeff, I missed you so much. While you were gone I felt so empty."

"I missed you too, Mick," he murmured as he nibbled at her lips. "All I could think about was getting back to you, spending time with you, sleep with you wrapped in my arms knowing you're safe and protected."

Mickey moaned as he kissed her deeply.

Jeff understood her moan. The taste of her, the feel of her, was like salve to a wound. He felt ultra-sensitized to every nuance of her, the scent of her hair, the pulse beating at her throat, her soft sighs. There was so much pleasure, just in her kiss alone.

"I can't stop kissing you," he murmured.

"Then don't," she whispered. She sighed in contentment as he continued. Each kiss soothed a place in her soul. Each kiss subdued the want, the deep pulsing need she had to be close to him, to feel his masculine power and trust that power to take complete control of her. She was lost in his kisses, lost and found.

"Mick, you are beautiful."

He rose and toed off his shoes. Moved closer to her and dropped his forehead to hers. "Sweet Mickey, it feels so good to be with you like this. It feels so right. Nothing should feel this good. Nothing has ever felt this right in my life." Jeff lifted his head, kissed her long and slow and moved to her side.

Mickey curled up close, pressing her face against his throat, breathing him in. He wrapped his arms securely around her and they lay silently for some time. It was Mickey who finally spoke.

"I know there are a lot of things wrong in my life right now, Jeff, but somehow, with you by my side, I can't seem to feel anything except euphoric."

Jeff chuckled. "I'll take that as a compliment."

Mickey giggled.

Jeff rose slightly to look at her face. "That was beautiful."

"What?"

"That sound. I think it was you, laughing."

"I think it was. Imagine that. There were times over this past week I thought I'd never laugh again. And here I am feeling almost happy, feeling pleasure, feeling alive. Lord, it's like I'm falling in love with you." She gasped at her own words, placed her hand over her mouth. "Oh, Jeff, I, uh, I didn't mean that. Please, don't pay any attention to me. It's just part of the trauma thing you were telling me about. Some sort of transference of something or another. I'm sorry. Please don't let my inane rattling push you away. It's just that—"

He placed his hand over her mouth. "Shh, baby. I'm not going anywhere. It's okay. It's okay if you didn't mean those words and it's okay if you did mean them. The crazy thing is, I'm feeling the same way. Maybe it is just the trauma thing for both of us, or maybe it's the real thing, or whatever. Let's just be honest with how we're feeling. We'll take it slow, we won't rush just in case this is, what'd you call it? Transference of something?" He gave a small laugh. "Until we figure it out, let's just be happy with what we have, and I'm telling you right now, I love being with you and I miss you when you're not around."

"Me too, Jeff."

~~~

Mickey woke, stretched her pleasantly fatigued muscles. Smiling, her mind quickly did a rewind of the night's events. Jeff beside her, holding her, soothing her. His kisses were delicious to say the least.

She turned her head to watch him sleep, however, he wasn't there.

Sitting up quickly she peered around the room and breathed a sigh of relief when she spotted him on the balcony. It was only dawn and he couldn't have slept but a few hours all together so how could he be up so early? Wrapping the sheet around her she went outside to join him.

He turned as she neared him. The smile on his face melted her.

"Good morning," he said softly.

"Hi. What are you doing up?"

"Just use to getting up early I guess." He crooked a finger at her. "Come here."

She edge forward into his arms and raised her mouth for the kiss. He smiled down into her face. "Want to see something really cool?"

She smiled. "Sure."

He pulled her in front of him and pointed down just past the pool area to the first strip of white sand. Six amazing people moved in sync to the rhythm of the waves, ebbing and flowing. It was beautiful.

"They're doing that Tai Chi stuff, huh?" Mickey whispered.

"Tai Chi Chuan. Then after that they'll go into the lesson for the day. Tai Chi used to be an actual fighting style handed down from the Chen family in China but it evolved into like a form of gentle exercise. Grandmaster Kino uses it to warm up."

"Do you do all that stuff?"

"Sort of. I mean, my boss, Jason learned from Eric and Jason teaches his agents or teaches the teachers who teach his agents. We agents tend to center in a more lethal way. Don't get me wrong. These people," he said pointing at the family below, "are lethal, or, I guess I should say, can be lethal. I go against Grandmaster Kino, I'm dead. I just haven't developed all the other sides. You know all the being one with the universe and one with God stuff. I do work a little on that. Like I said, Jason follows Zendo Ryu and encourages his agents to become totally whole."

"Totally whole. I like the way that sounds." She turned to watch the family. They were now running through kicking drills. Mickey was completely astounded when Shelley went through a series of kicks against a kicking pad held by her son Mark while at the same time Jeffy did the same against a guy Mickey presumed to be Joey, the agent she hadn't met. Eric was on his knees before little six-year-old Joey, instructing and correcting.

"They are amazing," Mickey said softly.

Jeff nodded. "Yeah, they are."

Mickey glanced up at him. "You really like these people. You said they are like family to you."

"They are, but it's not like I'm special. I mean, they treat everyone like that, like family. I have great respect for them. All of them are at least like fourth, fifth, sixth degree black belts in more than one style of martial arts. Except for little Joey, but he'll catch up, I have no doubt. And you should see Ricky. He is the stuff. He's a seventh dan in Tae Kwon Do. I don't know what dan Eric is. He's a grandmaster and you have to be ninth dan to be a grandmaster but he may be higher. I'm not sure if it goes up from there. I think it does. And that's just Tae Kwon Do.

"They do Karate, Hapkido, Judo and Ninjutsu. They are deep into the Chinese Shaolin Kung Fu art, but there are no belts determining rank in that one."

"Then how do you know they are deep into it?" Mickey asked in jest.

Jeff smiled down at her. "They take trips, or sojourns they call it, to stay with and train with Shaolin monks. The Shaolin don't let just anyone into their midst, but they do the Kinos. Master Kino will tell you it has helped him greatly to achieve his "oneness" because that is a big part of the Shaolin teaching– body, mind and spirit are as one."

Jeff shrugged. "May seem boring to some, but it's all pretty interesting to me, since I've trained so much. It would be cool to progress so far." Suddenly thoughts of Laura's disdain for his career choice jumped into his brain and he hoped he wasn't boring Mickey, but the thoughts fled at her next statement.

"Maybe you could teach me some stuff. Maybe it would help me to feel a little bit empowered."

He smiled, his heart turning over with contentment. "That is a great idea, Mick. You know, that's why Shelley became a martial artist."

"What do you mean?"

"A long time ago, back when Mark and Joey were little, Shelley was raped. It sent her into a tailspin until she took it upon herself to take Tae Kwon Do. That's how she met Eric."

"How do you know all this?"

"I accompanied her and Bree when Shelley spoke at a women's conference several years ago. That woman has been through hell and back. A lot like you." He touched her cheek. "Anyway, at the time I was Bree's bodyguard."

"Oh, yes, I heard all about that," Mickey said, her face shining with amusement.

Jeff shook his head, rolled his eyes. "Of course you did. They take every opportunity to tell the story." He smiled, turned to Mickey, pulled her close. "Did the story help to cheer you up?"

"Immensely."

"Then it was worth it." He motioned over his shoulder to the family below. "They invited me to join them this morning, but I knew I'd be busy so I turned them down."

"Really? Busy doing what?" she asked, smiling provocatively.

He ran a finger across her collar bone, which was the only bit of skin that wasn't wrapped up in the sheet. "You know." Bending down he kissed her softly.

When he raised his head he frowned, which frightened Mickey. "What?" she asked.

"What, what?"

"You're frowning. What's wrong?"

Grimacing, he touched her nose. "I admit, it's something terrible. I want to go back to bed, hold you, kiss you, but I have several things I have to take care of today and Jason will be here soon for breakfast. I don't know if there's time. I need to shower and dress and write up a report before he gets here."

Mickey forced her calm, responsible side to emerge. "You go take care of business. I'll be okay."

~~~

He came out of the bathroom already dressed. She watched him tuck in his shirt, put on a tie, buckle his belt. "Where did you get the clothes?" she asked.

"I stopped by my apartment last night."

"Oh." She sighed. The only clothes she had were the shorts and shirts Jeff had purchased for her. Shelley had purchased some things online for her but they weren't supposed to arrive until sometime this afternoon. She really needed some underwear.

Jeff finished dressing, pulled a leather case from his bag and drew out a laptop computer which he set on the small desk in the corner of the room. Mickey watched him as he logged into a secure site. She realized she loved watching him. He was adept, it seemed, at everything he did. Again she thought of how lucky she was that he'd been at his vacation home.

He was dressed nicely this morning. Shirt and tie. She guessed that meant he was going to work. He'd said he had things to take care of today. What did that mean exactly? Frowning, she moved forward, placed her hands on his shoulders as he worked.

"Jeff?"

He smiled up at her, his brows raised. "Yes?"

"Are you," she took a deep breath. "Are you going away again?"

His lips pressed tightly together. "I'm not sure. It's up to Jason."

She stroked her hand over his face that had several cuts and bruises. "You never did tell me what happened to you."

Sighing, he held a finger up, hit a few more keys on the computer to save his work and then turned back to her, gesturing toward the bed. "Sit down."

She did as directed.

"I had a meeting with your stepfather's flunkies. The guy driving the van and four others."

Nausea overwhelmed her. She clutched at her stomach.

"Hey," he said softly. "It's okay. You're safe and I'm here and I'm fine. Everything went as planned. I got lots of important information at the cost of a few bruises."

"What did they say?" she asked, her voice quivering.

"There *is* an arms deal. An eighty million dollar arms deal. That's big stuff. More than likely the FBI or CIA are not gonna want to wait on this one. I'm guessing they're gonna raid the Senator's study and office, confiscate everything and find out all the details. Then they're gonna put him away for like, two hundred years."

"Really?"

"Well, I may be exaggerating a bit."

She leaned against him. "So, my sister and my mother will soon be on their own?"

"Will that be hard for them?"

"For my mom, yes. I guess I sort of feel sorry for her. For my sister? I don't know. She thinks Talmond is this wonderful father. I hate to burst her bubble."

"He's an evil man, Mick. Who's to say what he may do to her eventually if she were to get in his way."

"Of course you're right."

Moving forward, he placed his finger under her chin and tilted her face up. "It will all work out, Mick. Trust me. Now, how about letting me finish this report and then we'll go down to breakfast."

She smiled sweetly. "It'll cost you."

"How much?"

"What about when I'm free to be seen in public you take me out somewhere for dinner and a movie."

"Cheap date are ya?"

"Huh, we'll see about that."

~~~

"Please Agent Dodge. You have to tell me what's going on. I can help."

"Marissa, you're a very smart and mature little girl, but you are a little girl. There's no way I can involve you in our investigation. Now, if you want to help, the most you can do is tell me everything you know about your father. I understand you're the only one he'll let into his study."

She shrugged. "I don't know why. Maybe he trusts me."

"Have you seen anything in there you would consider suspicious?"

"No, but I wasn't looking for anything. I'll go back home and I'll go through everything in there, but please tell me what's happening. Is my sister alive?"

Agent Dodge stood, shaking his head. "I don't want you going through things in your father's study. I can't tell you anything at this stage of the game. You're a minor, I can't involve you. You seem like a good kid, Marissa, with a good head on your shoulders. I wish I could say something to help you but I can't right now. I can only tell you what you already know. We found a cabin in the woods near Honey Lake in California with two dead men. Evidence shows your sister had been there at some time and that she left through the woods headed south. She arrived at a vacant home owned by a Jefferson Davis. What happened to her after that, we're not sure." He blew out a breath. He hated lying to the kid, but no way could he blow the investigation by confiding in the young lady and then she accidentally slips up and tells her father what they know.

Marissa sat quietly. "Honey Lake?" she finally asked.

"Yes, why?"

"I thought I heard my father say something about Honey Lake a long time ago."

"How long?"

"Maybe last year some time."

"We can't find any link between the owner of that land and your father."

"If my father doesn't own it then who does?" Marissa asked.

"An older woman by the name of Ruth Carter. It was given to her upon the death of her grandfather, Seth Wickerman."

"There's something on the edge of my memory," Marissa said.

"Like what?"

"Something about that property. I have to think about it." She pulled out her cell phone, noted the time. Sighed. I have to go. If I don't show up for school they'll contact my father."

"Do you need a ride back to school?"

"No sir. I got a friend to bring me here. He's waiting for me. Listen Agent Dodge, there's something I need to say. My father was not very nice to Mickey. He hurt her. He beat her. Living with him was like torture for her. I pretended not to know, not to see. She didn't want me to see, but still, I let her down. Ask Ms. Dora. She can tell you. Anyway, please, if there's anything you can think of for me to do, you let me do it."

"We'll let you know, Marissa. Thanks for coming down." He watched her leave, looked over at his partner.

"Poor kid."

"It won't be much longer," Agent Stevens said. "I can't wait to get this guy."

~~~

Jeff and Mickey arrived downstairs at the same time Jason arrived at the front door, so Jeff let him in. Jeff quickly made the introduction and Jason took Mickey's hand in his.

"I know you've been through a lot. Things are gonna get better from here on out."

Mickey nodded. "Thank you for all you've done, Mr. Lee."

"Please, call me Jason." He held a newspaper up to Jeff. "Shall we get this video made? I have to go into the office to get it sent in so that it can't be traced."

"What video?"

"One that proves you're alive," Jeff said. "Your father's men think I'm working with them to keep you hostage until after the arms deal. They want proof I really do have you. Hope your acting skills are up to par."

Unable to find a blank wall, they went upstairs to hold a sheet up as a background. Jason made the video quickly, using the newspaper as proof of it being current. That little piece of business taken care of, they went back down to join the Kino family.

Breakfast was a free for all. Everyone cooking or fixing cereal or putting cream cheese on a bagel or chopping fruit or adding protein to the blender mix. Once everyone had their preference for their morning meal they sat around the large table and went over the day's plans. Mickey did her best to try to follow along.

Mark would drop Jeffy at school, she's working on a project that will take most of the day and then will be spending the night with a friend. Shelley would take little Joey with her on a shopping trip for some things for Mickey. Eric had several appointments. Joey was headed into Ameritech the same time as Jason. Jeff would stay here with Mickey until further notice. Mickey's happy sigh of relief was audible and caught everyone's attention. She blushed a bright red.

Jason told Eric what had transpired at Jeff's meeting the day before and assured him it would only be a few days to a week before the FBI made a move of some kind on the Senator.

Eric patted Jeff on the back and offered his compliments and congratulations. Jason then told about the two men who'd come to visit him. They'd been taken into custody and spilled their guts. Unfortunately they didn't know much. All documents on the arms deal were supposedly kept in Talmond Daley's study.

Jeffy stood and said she really needed to get going. She went around the table kissing everyone goodbye. When she got to Mickey, she hugged her close. "Don't you worry, I have a feeling something really good is gonna happen."

Mickey smiled and hugged her back. Jeffy turned to leave, then stopped, her eyes moving from person to person.

Eric frowned. "What is it, baby girl?"

Jeffy smiled, shrugged. "It's you all, my family. You're all so awesome, you know? Sometimes I just feel so grateful for you. I guess I just wanted you to know how much I love every single one of you."

"We love you too, sweetie," Mark said first.

They all joined in.

Mickey almost couldn't believe the scene as it unfolded. It was like something out of a sugary holiday movie. Were there really families like this? A group of people who live peacefully together with love and respect for each other? She snapped out of her reverie when Jeff reached under the table and squeezed Mickey's hand.

Jeffy left with Mark, breakfast ended and everyone helped clean up. There was a flurry of activity as each member of the family went about pursuing their schedules. While Mickey helped with the dishes, Jason pulled Jeff aside in a corner of the huge great room. He was frowning which put Jeff on alert.

"You and Ms. Daley have something going?"

"Something going?" Jeff asked nervously.

"You know exactly what I mean," Jason said.

Jeff looked down. "Uh, yes sir."

"What?"

"What?"

"Yes, what. What do you have going?"

Jeff blew out a long breath. "We're, well, we're not sure yet."

"You're sleeping with her?"

Jeff looked down. "Yes sir. I mean, I slept with her last night, but I didn't SLEEP with her."

Jason shook his head, drew a breath urging himself to be patient. "I guess I don't need to tell you she's in a vulnerable state and I'm not sure your decision in this is the best for her. You are supposed to be protecting her. Not seducing her."

Jeff swallowed hard. "It's not exactly like that."

"If you're trying to justify sleeping with her because it's something she wants then your reasoning is flawed. You rescued her. You're her hero, so to speak. She's gonna feel the need to cling to you and she may interpret that as a sexual attraction. After a trauma like she's been through she's not exactly thinking clearly."

"I understand that and we've considered all those things."

"Considered them and discarded them?"

"No sir, not discarded."

Jason's eyebrows rose.

"I'm just saying that I'm not trying to seduce her or take advantage of her for the sake of an easy lay and I'm a little surprised you would think that of me. It's not like that."

"Then how is it?"

Jeff sighed because he knew it would sound ridiculous. "I think– I'm in love with her."

"In love with her." Jason repeated. He shook his head and did his best not to roll his eyes.

"I know it sounds crazy, sir. It sounds crazy to me too. It feels crazy."

"Well, then, that should tell you something."

Jeff nodded. "I know." He blew out a breath, scrubbed his hands over his face. "It feels crazy but it also feels right. I mean, look, I've never felt this way before about a woman. I don't know what to think. The chemistry, it's strong, ya know? We both feel the same way but we have talked about the extenuating circumstances and that this may blow over once we get back to normal living."

"And you don't think that the right thing to do would be to wait until you and she *are* back to 'normal living'?"

Jeff nodded. "I *do* think that– in my head. Yet, the feelings in my heart, they were like, so strong."

Sighing Jason shook his head and then stood silently, peering into Jeff's eyes. Finally he nodded. "Look, you know I'm not one to invade your privacy except when what you do affects our company and its reputation. This matter of the heart, I have no choice but to trust you in this, but Jeff, be careful with her. She's a victim *and* she's a witness."

"Yes sir."

"And don't be insulted by this interview. I didn't really think you would take advantage of a vulnerable girl. As owner of this company though, there are certain things that have to be said, regardless of my personal feelings about an agent."

Jeff nodded. "I understand, sir."

Jason smiled. "And, by the way, one of the things that need to be said is, you did a great job assessing the situation and getting Mackenzie Daley safely out of there. You also did a great job yesterday getting information out of Daley's flunkies. Keep up the good work."

"Thank you, sir," Jeff said with a grin.

~~~

Talmond Daley's hand balled slowly into a fist. It did something to him to see her standing there alive and well when he'd so carefully planned her death. He couldn't tell where she was. A white sheet hung on a wall behind her. The floor she stood on was hardwood. She could be anywhere.

His eyes zeroed in on her face. She appeared a little banged up. He could see a few bruises. The hollow, haunted look in her eyes was pleasing. He could only hope that this Jeff Davis had some issues that he might take out on Mackenzie though he doubted it. All the guy was interested in was getting his hands on some money.

Her hand was wrapped in a bandage and he wondered how she injured it. He listened carefully as he heard Davis order her to hold the newspaper. She told him to hold it himself. The camera pointed at the floor for a few seconds, he heard a soft grunt, then heard him threaten her with more bodily harm and then it was back on Mackenzie, the paper in her hands. The camera zoomed in on the date and the headline.

"Looks legit," Kurt said, stating the obvious.

Talmond nodded in response.

"I hope he knows how to keep her under control until the deal goes down. She's a hellion."

Talmond looked up at his man. "He couldn't do any worse than the rest of you."

Kurt's lip curled in disdain for his boss. "I told you to let me off her in the beginning. I knew keeping her around would make trouble."

"I had to make sure the timing was right, you fool. Do me a favor and try not to think."

Kurt didn't say anything else, but he knew the real reason Daley waited so long to kill Mickey. In his own pathetic, distorted, deranged, sick way, he was in love with her.

~~~

Jeffy glanced at her cell phone, rolled her eyes. Kimmie Lee had been her friend for as long as she could remember. Jeffy had been two when Kimmie was born to Aunt Angel and Uncle Jason, neither one of them actually related to Jeffy except through extreme close friendship to her parents.

Jeffy thought Kimmie's mom, Angel, was one of the most beautiful women she'd ever known. She was a natural blonde, with a beautiful face and killer body. She was the head of a national women's group for empowerment and self-defense that was apparently inspired by Jeffy's own mother. Korean born Jason Lee was one of her father's best friends and was always saying he owed his success with Ameritech Security to her father. And so, Jeffy and Kimmie had practically grown up together as sisters.

Jeffy loved her as a sister, but Jeffy's mind had come between them many times when Jeffy would lose patience. Kimmie was no slouch. She was a straight 'A' student, high school freshman class president, captain of the debate team, ambassador for the *Stop the Bullying* children's organization and could sing like an angel, but sometimes she demanded entrance into Jeffy's strange half adult half teenage world when Jeffy didn't have the time or authority to allow her.

This was one of those times. Jeffy punched the button on her phone. "I can't talk right now, Kimmie."

"Why not? You're usually out of class by now."

"It's just not a good time."

"Jeffy, what are you up to?"

"What makes you think I'm up to anything?"

"I can tell. First, you always want to talk so you saying you can't talk sounds weird. Second, you were supposed to come by the house for lunch today."

Jeffy grimaced. "Oh, Kimmie, I'm sorry. I totally forgot."

"Yes, I can see that, which is what makes me know you're up to something. You never forget our weekly get-togethers. I may be younger than you, Jeffy, and not as brilliant as you, but I'm not a dolt either. Something's up and I want to know what. Besides, I just heard thunder and there's not a cloud in the sky here. Where are you?"

"Okay, okay, yes, something's up. I'm in Seattle."

"Seattle? What are you doing there?"

"I don't have time to tell you about it now."

"Do your mom and dad know where you are?"

"No."

"Jeffy—"

"Listen, Kimmie, I can 't talk right this minute. I'm in a cab and I need to pay attention to where I'm going."

"But—"

"I promise to call you a little later. Don't say anything to anyone, especially not your dad."

"I won't."

"Thanks, Kimmie. Talk to you soon." Jeffy pocketed her phone, drew a deep breath and watched as the cab cruised slowly through the pouring rain like a boat on a lake.

They drove down a street lined with beautiful trees. Jeffy sat up straighter when the cab slowed and pulled into a drive. It was a large mansion off a fairly busy street right in the center of Seattle. Luckily the gates were standing open and the cab just pulled right up. That would never happen at the Kino house. Jeffy paid the driver and got out of the cab, pulling her giant shoulder bag with her that had everything she would need for an overnight stay, money, ID's, change of clothing, toothbrush, hairbrush, and other toiletries. She stood tall and eyed the house, gathering her courage.

Drawing a deep breath, she dashed up to the door, trying to keep from getting too wet. She pushed the doorbell. Nervously she waited, pulling at her skirt, smoothing her hair that was gathered into a clip at the back of her neck. Her heart skipped a beat when the door knob started to turn, having no idea what she would find on the other side.

A pleasant looking woman who seemed to be of either Latino or Native American descent answered the door.

Jeffy smiled at her brightly.

"Yes, may I help you?" the woman asked.

"Hi, yes, I'm here to see Marissa," Jeffy answered.

The woman frowned. "Please step inside."

Jeffy walked in and stood in the foyer. It was very elegant, very posh, very formal.

"One moment please," the woman said.

Jeffy watched her walk up the stairs. While she was gone she peered around the foyer, gazing at pictures, peeking into a formal living room, pulling open a drawer in a secretary.

"What do you think you're doing?"

Jeffy turned suddenly at the stern male voice. She recognized Senator Daley from the research she'd done on the internet. She smiled sweetly at him. "Oh, hi! Uh, sorry, I've always been nosy. I'm just waiting for—"

She looked up as Marissa came running down the stairs. Jeffy charged at her.

"Oh, Marissa," Jeffy cried running to her and throwing her arms around her neck. "Girl, it is so good to see you!" She leaned close to her ear. "Play along."

"Hey– Chris, wow, where have you been? I haven't seen you since last, uh, what?"

"Last October remember? At that party?"

"Oh, that's right! Gosh, it's so good to see you. Come on upstairs and I'll catch you up on all the gossip." Marissa looked down at her father. "I'm sorry Dad, if we disturbed you. Did you need me for something?"

His gaze narrowed at the newcomer then moved back to his daughter. He sighed. "No, dear. You and Chris go do whatever it is little girls do."

"Dad, I'm not a little girl anymore."

"Yes, dear, if you say so." He turned and went inside a room, closing the door soundly behind him.

"Would you girls like a little something to eat?" the woman

who'd answered the door asked.

"Oh, yes, please," Jeffy said. "I'm starved. I haven't eaten all day."

"Ms. Dora, this is – Chris."

Jeffy held out her hand to the woman who smiled and took it.

"It's a pleasure to meet you, Chris. I'll be right up with some goodies."

"Thank you, Ms. Dora," Marissa said, then took Jeffy's arm and led her up the stairs.

Once they were safely ensconced in Marissa's room with the door closed soundly, Marissa folded her arms across her chest and stared at her unknown guest.

"Who are you?"

Jeffy smiled at her. "You did a great job covering. I was really nervous that you would give me up, but you didn't. Mickey said you were smart."

Marissa gasped. "You've seen Mickey?"

Jeffy placed a finger on her lips, took the girl's hand and sat her down. "Shh, not so loud. Yes, I've seen her. I had breakfast with her this morning."

Marissa eyes filled with tears.

"Listen, I'd rather not talk here in this house. Can you go out?"

"Do you have a car?"

Jeffy frowned, shaking her head. "No I'm only fifteen."

Marissa smiled excitedly. "I have a friend. I'll call him. He'll come pick us up."

"Sounds great."

"But can't you at least tell me something now?"

Jeffy grinned. "She's alive and well," she whispered.

Marissa reached out, embracing Jeffy. "Thank you. Oh, thank you."

Jeffy hugged her. "You're welcome. Now, let's get some food and get out of here."

~~~

While Shelley shopped and the rest of the family took care of their business, Jeff and Mickey romped on the beach. Mickey wore a borrowed suit from Shelley and Jeff wore his own shorts. He did however, borrow a surf board and showed off for the girl. She was highly impressed.

Jeff took her out and taught her some basics and they played in the surf until Mickey gave out from exhaustion. They came in and laid on the beach, soaking up the sun while they caught up on their missed sleep. When their energy returned they walked, holding hands, stopping to kiss every few minutes. They talked and talked. Jeff told her more about his family. She told him everything, from her father leaving her and her mom, to the dreadful wedding day, all the terrible beatings, the birth of her sister and their close relationship.

When she thought she was talking too much, she hesitated and then he prodded her on, sensing her need to tell someone the things she'd kept bottled up inside for so long. He reciprocated, telling her about what he considered to be his boring, non-eventful life, though it was a life filled with love and a life for which he was extremely grateful.

She teased him about Bree drugging him and he'd gone on to tell the rest of the story, walking her around the bend to the rocks where Bree had climbed and almost lost her life.

Jeff eased down inside one of the crevices and leaned back against a rock. He crooked a finger at Mickey. She came to him, sat on his lap facing him.

"Well this is nice and cozy, isn't it?" she said.

"The perfect hideout," Jeff agreed. "I bet lil' Joey and Eric will use these rocks one day as their fort to hide from girls or to be pirates. I wonder if Mark and Joey and Ricky ever did."

Mickey laughed. "I bet they did. It's a great place for kids."

"It's a great place even when you're all grown up," Jeff said.

Mickey sighed in contentment.

He smiled at the sound. "What's that sigh all about?"

"It's about everything. This time a week ago I was living in terror, cuffed to a bed, wondering which moment would be my last. Now I'm cuddled up on the beach, safe, secure and–, dare I say it– in love. And then to think of how we found each other, like it was fate or destiny. Everything is just so amazing. And my feelings for you– the feelings are just so strong, it's so hard to believe. I find myself wondering if it's even real. What if this isn't real?" she whispered. "What if I wake up tomorrow or next week and don't feel this way about you anymore."

He frowned, shrugged his shoulders. "Then, we'll go our separate ways, better people for having known each other."

"That's not what you were supposed to say," she whined. "You were supposed to say, that won't happen because—" She stopped realizing she almost made another blunder.

"That won't happen because I love you too and I'll never stop loving you no matter what?"

"Please don't make fun of me, Jeff."

"I wasn't making fun of you, sweetheart. I was saying what I really feel. Look, I don't know what to think. I've known you only a few days. I've never felt this way about anyone. It's not supposed to happen like this. So, I'm thinking, it's not real. It can't be. We're just feeling attached to each other because of the crazy situation, but then I look at you, I look into your big, brown eyes and I can't imagine being without you."

"That's how I feel too, Jeff. Intellectually, I know this is crazy, but in my heart, I don't want what we have to end. I'm in love with you, Jeff. It feels so good just to say the words. I love you. I love you, I—"

He brought her mouth to his, kissed her deeply. "And I love you, Mick. I don't understand how it can be. I don't even know you, yet I feel like I've known you forever. I love you and you're right it does feel good to say it. I love you, Mick."

She smiled. "Other than my sister you're the only one who's ever called me that."

"What? Mick?"

"Yes." She looked down. "I miss her. I can't imagine what she must be going through."

"She's probably saying the same thing about you."

Mickey smiled, ruffled his thick blond hair. "You're so very insightful."

He grinned. "How's this for insight." He kissed the top of her head. "It's been three days since I met you and I still love you," he assured her with a smile. "It hasn't gone away yet."

~~~

The two giggling girls squished themselves into the front seat of Cameron's shiny black Mustang. Knowing the ropes, he took off before Marissa's dad could stop them. Once they were on the street and a few blocks away, Jeffy looked over at the boy driving the car.

"Hi, I'm Jeffy, but you'll have to call me Chris."

Cameron glanced over at her, did a double take, then smiled at her. "Hi. You have two names and their both male names."

She smiled. "I guess it seems that way, but I assure you, I'm all female."

"Oh, I can see that," he said smoothly, causing Marissa to snort.

"I'm here under false pretenses," Jeffy explained. "Marissa's the one who came up with Chris. We told her dad my name is Chris. My real name is Jeffy Kino."

"Jeffy? Interesting," Cameron said. "Where to?"

"We have to talk. Go to the back of the football stadium," Marissa ordered. She turned to Jeffy. "No one will be there in the summer at this time of day. We go there to hang out sometimes."

He sped up now that he knew where to go, causing the girls to squeal in delight. It took only a few minutes to arrive at their destination, park and pile out of the car. The three strolled underneath the bleachers until they found a spot dry enough to sit.

"Okay, Jeffy, tell me," Marissa coaxed.

Jeffy glanced over at Cameron. "Are you sure he's okay?"

"Hey, don't talk about me like I can't hear you."

Jeffy laughed. "Sorry."

"He's like my best friend," Marissa said. "You can trust him."

"Okay. Well, like I said earlier, Mickey is alive and well. The guy who found her up at the lake is a good friend of our family. I guess you already know he's an agent with Ameritech."

"Yeah, but they made it sound like he was involved with her kidnapping."

"Yeah, but he wasn't. He's just acting like that to get more information from your dad. He rescued Mickey and brought her to our house to stay for now."

"Mick's at your house? Where's your house?"

"Just south of L.A."

"Good grief. How'd you get here?"

"I flew, then took a cab to your house."

"Do your parents know where you are?"

Jeffy grinned. "What do you think?"

"Oh– my– Gosh," Marissa exclaimed. "You are sooo cool!"

Jeffy shrugged. "I know what it's like to have someone you love missing and not know what happened to them. When my brother Ricky was kidnapped, I thought I would die."

"Your brother was kidnapped?" Cameron asked.

"Yes. He got—"

"Hold it. Ricky– Ricky Kino? You're freakin' kidding me? You're Ricky Kino's little sister?"

"Yeah."

"That means you're Breanna Adams sister too?" Marissa added.

"Yeah."

"Oh– my– Gosh!"

"Whatever. Back to the subject. No one is allowed to know where Mickey is but when I spoke with her yesterday, she was so worried about you, Marissa. She was crying and stuff and I just hate that, so I told her maybe I could figure something out. And I did. I decided to come and tell you myself. They might trace a phone call, or anything else, but no one would suspect some little kid. So here I am."

"But aren't your parents gonna be furious when they find you gone?"

"Yes, they are. I'm gonna call them in a little while and check in. They think I'm spending the night with a friend which is sort of the truth, so they won't expect me home until tomorrow."

"You are amazing," Cameron said reverently.

Jeffy smiled at the cute boy. "Thanks."

"But where are you gonna stay tonight?" Marissa asked. "My father won't let anyone spend the night."

Jeffy shrugged. "Hmm, well then, I guess I'll stay at a motel."

"Don't you have to be eighteen to get a room at a motel?"

"There are ways around that."

"Like what?"

She grinned as she rifled through the giant shoulder bag, finally pulling out her wallet. She thumbed through it, pulled out several cards, held them up one at a time. "This is my fake ID. This is a student ID at USC. This is my gym pass at USC." She opened up the side, pulled out several hundred dollars. "And this is for anyone who needs a little convincing."

Cameron chuckled. "You definitely came prepared."

Jeffy shrugged. "I've never done anything like this before and I wasn't sure what I would need. Money is always helpful. I admit, I thought I'd be able to stay the night with Marissa, like an old friend, but hey, we go with the flow. So, it's a motel. No problem."

"I'm sorry my dad is such a butt. I've never been able to have anyone spend the night. Though, I don't know about you all alone in a motel. I don't like this," Marissa said.

"I'll be okay. I can take care of myself."

"You do all the martial arts stuff too, don't ya?" Cameron asked.

"Yes."

"I think I'm in love."

Jeffy giggled.

"I don't want you to stay in a motel all by yourself," Marissa said again. "Cameron, you stay with her."

"What? I can't do that. She's like a girl and all. Besides, she won't want some guy in her room."

"You won't mind, will you Jeffy? It will make me feel so much better if Cameron stays with you. I'm already so nervous about Mickey. Don't make me have to worry about you too. Please."

Jeffy looked at Cameron, and then shrugged nonchalantly. "Sure. He can stay with me if that's his preference. I would appreciate the company, however, won't your parents want to know where you are?"

"My parents don't care where I am as long as I'm not bothering them."

Jeffy shook her head. "They don't know what they're missing."

Cameron's eyes met hers. She smiled brightly. "Okay, then, that's settled, you're staying with me. Now, listen, Marissa, I haven't told you everything."

Heads together, Jeffy filled them in, telling Marissa that her father hired men to kidnap Mickey, telling her about the arms deal and how she wishes she could get into Senator Daley's office and look around, hoping she could find something. Jeffy was pleased to hear that Marissa had figured out what a bad guy her father was because she didn't want to be the one to tell her. She couldn't imagine what it would be like to feel such animosity toward her own father.

They talked more about Jeffy's famous family, about life, about hopes and dreams. Jeffy felt right at home with the two of them. They weren't shallow or stupid like some kids she'd met. She realized she really liked them and when this was all over, she hoped to remain friends with them somehow. Of course, she hadn't told them about her IQ or about her actually studying at USC, and she had no intentions of doing so. For once, she wanted to just be normal. They thought her USC passes were fake, and that was okay with her.

As they chatted Jeffy couldn't help but steal glimpses of Cameron. He was very cute with his black hair and blue eyes and dimples. When he mentioned he played football in high school, she told him all about her brother Mark who Cameron had heard of because Mark had been a Heisman candidate.

They talked football for some time until Marissa got bored with it. As it got later in the day, Jeffy told them she had to call her mom and asked everyone to be very quiet.

"Hi, Mom," she said cheerfully when Shelley answered the phone.

"Hey sweetie. Are you having fun yet?"

"Not yet, things haven't quite begun yet."

"Well, you behave and no going out, after dark, okay?"

"Okay. I won't. Well, bye. Miss you."

"Miss and love you. Bye baby girl."

She hung up and smiled at her two new friends. "Well, I guess that takes care of that."

"You have balls of steel," Cameron said.

Jeffy laughed. "I've been told that before."

"Well, we need to get Marissa back to her house and you checked into a motel."

Marissa frowned. "I wish I didn't have to go."

"It's Friday night, can't you stay out?" Jeffy asked.

"Last Friday my father tried to get me to go out with some friends and get my mind off Mickey for a few hours but I refused. I can't all of a sudden change my attitude."

"You're right," Jeffy said. "Anyway, listen, it's okay. When this is all over we're gonna spend an untold amount of time together. I certainly don't intend to let our newfound friendship fall through the cracks."

Cameron frowned. "Are you sure you're only fifteen?"

Jeffy's face paled. "Yes, why?"

"You sure don't talk like a kid, ya know what I mean?"

"Oh, well, sorry about that. My dad is real big on speaking properly like an adult."

"Oh, no, it's okay. Just sometimes, you sound weird."

She laughed. "Ricky says I *am* weird."

They stood and started back. At the car Marissa hugged Jeffy fiercely. "Thank you so much for coming and letting me know about Mickey. I'll never forget what you've done."

"It's nothing, really."

They piled into the car and in fifteen minutes pulled up in front of the Daley mansion.

"Are you sure you're okay in there with that monster?" Jeffy asked.

Marissa smiled. "I'll be fine. I'm his flesh and blood. He wouldn't hurt me."

"Don't be so sure," Cameron warned.

"Noted," Marissa said as she closed the car door and leaned inside the window. "You take care of our new friend."

"With pleasure." Cameron said with a smile. He sped off.

"Where's your friend?" Talmond asked as Marissa came through the door.

"Cameron is taking her home," Marissa said, her heart in her throat.

"I don't know where you met her, but I don't think she's the kind of girl you should be associating with."

"Oh, Daddy, why not? I met her at school. She's very nice."

"She's low class."

"What makes you think that?"

"I can just tell. Besides I caught her going through the drawer in the secretary in the foyer."

"I'm sure she didn't mean anything by that. She's just, you know, open and curious."

"She's trouble and I don't want you seeing her again."

Anger flared in her heart. "Stop trying to control me. I can choose my own friends," she said shortly. She turned and ran up the steps to keep from having to say anything else.

Chapter Eight

"Hey," Marissa whispered into her cell phone. "What are you doing?"

"We're lying here in bed talking about you," Cameron said.

"What about me?"

"Well, remember how you said you hate breakfast because your father makes such a deal out of it and it's like this boring, hour long ordeal?"

"Yeah, so?"

"Well, Jeffy here has this idea that she can scout your dad's office while you guys are at breakfast."

"Oh– my– Gosh, you've got to be kidding me!"

"I'm not kidding," Jeffy said.

"Am I on speaker?"

"Yes, you're on speaker," Cameron mocked in a little girl voice.

Marissa giggled. "How would you get in, Jeffy?"

"Just leave a window or door unlocked for me somewhere. I mean, everyone, even Ms. Dora is gonna be in either the kitchen or dining room, right?"

"Well, yes."

"My flight doesn't leave until eleven. What time do you eat breakfast?"

"On Saturday it's nine o'clock on the dot and we must stay to have 'family time' until ten on the dot. Sometimes we just sit there and stare at each other. Well, except Dad, he gets to read the paper."

"He's a sick man, Marissa. I don't even know him and I hate him. I'm sorry. I know he's your dad and all, but geez, OCD aside, what a pervert."

"I think I used to love him," Marissa admitted. "He'd always been so good to me, but now that I know what he did to Mick, I realize what a monster he is. Now I can barely stand to be in the same room with him."

"I'm sorry, Marissa. I know this has to be hard on you."

"I'm okay. Especially now that I know Mick's okay too. I just can't wait for everything to be over."

"That's why I want to do this. If I can find something incriminating, it could actually be over as early as tomorrow."

"That would be so awesome."

"So, are you gonna do it?"

"Yes. I'll leave the library door open. There's a veranda off the left side of the house just outside the library. Come in there. When you come out of the library turn left. His office is two doors down."

"Okay. It's a date. Don't let me down."

"I won't. I hope you find something big."

"Me too."

"Well, I'd better hang up. You two don't do anything I wouldn't do."

"I don't know, Marissa. Jeffy here is definitely a hot babe."

Marissa laughed. "You two behave."

Cameron closed the phone. "She practically forces me to spend the night in a motel with a looker like you and I'm supposed to behave."

Jeffy grinned. "A looker, huh?"

"Yes. Don't you know that?"

"Most people just like me for my brains or for my brother and sister."

Cameron laughed. "Your brain is nice and all that, and it's cool you have a famous family, but, Jeffy, I swear you could drive a guy crazy."

Jeffy smiled. "Really? I think I like that."

He moved closer to her. "Do you now? What else do you like?"

She looked up at his face that was just inches from hers, but looked down again, shrugged.

"Hey, I was just like, flirting, you know. No big deal."

Jeffy smiled at him. "Yeah, I know. That's no problem. It was your question. 'What else do I like?' Well, the problem is, I don't know what I like. Can I ask you a personal question?"

Cameron scooted back to lean against the wooden headboard attached to the wall. "Okay, shoot."

Jeffy moved up to sit beside him, mostly so she wouldn't have to look right into his eyes. "Are you– a virgin?"

His mouth opened. "Wow, you get right to it, don't ya? Look, I didn't mean anything by what I said a second ago. Like I said, I was just flirting a little."

She looked over at him, gave a comforting smile. "Oh, sure, I get that. Still, I want to know, are you a virgin?"

When he didn't answer right away, she felt bad for asking. She looked down. "Sorry. You don't have to answer if you don't want to."

"No."

She blinked. "No? You've had sex?"

"Yes."

His eyes met hers and she couldn't look away. He was looking at her in a way that made her feel funny inside. Not a bad funny like Blake a few weeks ago, but funny in a pleasant way.

"How old are you?" Jeffy asked.

"Sixteen, almost seventeen actually. When did you turn fifteen?"

"Just a few months ago in March."

"Man, I'm almost two years older than you. Marissa will be sixteen in August. That makes you the baby of the three of us."

"Oh." She looked down.

Cameron took her hand. "I didn't mean to call you a baby. Not in a bad way. I sure don't see you as a baby. I think I see you as the coolest chick I've ever met."

Jeffy beamed. "Thanks."

"You're welcome. So tell me, do you have a boyfriend?"

"No, I sort of keep to myself at school. Do you have a girlfriend?"

"Nah. We broke up."

"What about Marissa? The two of you seem pretty close."

"We're just friends. We've known each other since first grade. We're like, there for each other whenever one of us is going through a hard time."

"That's awesome to have such a good friend."

"Yeah it is."

"So, can I ask you another personal question?"

"Sure."

"The first time you had sex, what was it like?"

Cameron swallowed hard. "Uh, it was, uh, it was really, like, great."

"Was she a virgin?"

"No."

"When you say, great, what do you mean?"

"Uh, darn Jeffy, I don't know."

"Please, Cameron, I want to know. I need to know." She leaned against him. "Please, just tell me a little more than 'it was great.'"

He sighed. "It was kind of like that first kiss, you know? That warm feeling in your stomach when you kiss for the first time and you feel like you don't ever want to stop. It was kind of like that only a hundred times stronger."

Jeffy's big brown eyes blinked up at him as she considered his description.

Cameron's brow furrowed. "You don't know. You've never been kissed, have you?"

She shook her head. "Well, not really. There was this one guy, but he was so rough and it didn't feel good, it was just cold, wet, and slimy. I hope it's not supposed to be like that."

Cameron laughed. "I don't think it is."

Jeffy's eyes opened wide with excitement. "Cameron, will you show me? I mean, will you show me what a kiss is supposed to be?"

"Jeffy, you hardly know me. I'm not sure if it would be right for me to kiss you yet."

"Well, logically speaking, we don't have a lot of time. I'm leaving tomorrow morning. This is one of those now or never kind of deals. Don't you want to show me?"

He drew a breath. "I'd be crazy to not want to kiss you. And I do want to, Jeffy. But—"

"Then don't over analyze it. Just do it."

He smiled. "You're doing that weird kind of talking again."

"Oh, uh, sorry. Habit." She smiled at him, while she went over in her mind the words she'd spoken and how she should've changed them so she wouldn't sound so weird. When she couldn't figure it out, her mind moved onto the problem at hand. "Are you gonna kiss me or not?"

"Yes. Okay. Don't rush me."

She smiled. "Okay. I'll just sit here and you let me know when you're ready."

"Fine." He sat silently for a few moments, and then turned slightly toward her. He used his left hand to position her head. He watched her eyes as he moved his mouth close to her. His heart pounded a mile a minute. Her eyes were wide and it made him chuckle a little, but when she frowned he corrected himself. Slowly, he touched his lips to hers, moved them gently over hers until finally her eyes drifted shut. He opened his mouth a tiny bit and she responded with the same motion.

When he pulled away, Jeffy stayed there, her eyes closed, her mouth slightly open.

"So, what do you think?" he asked.

She opened her eyes. "It was nice, but, I mean, not earth shattering like everyone says."

He smiled. "Well, I didn't want to freak you out."

She nodded. "Okay. I appreciate the sentiment. Still, I mean, can you try again? I mean like, it certainly wasn't like the way my father kisses my mother."

"You've seen your parents kiss?"

"They do it quite often. Ricky's always telling them to 'get a room.'"

Cameron laughed.

Jeffy put her hand on his face. "So, kiss me like my father kisses my mother. Show me what it's really like."

Cameron's stomach tightened and he was all too willing to continue the lesson this time. "Okay, but you have to follow my lead. Whatever I do, you do it too."

Jeffy nodded. "I understand that. It's an intimacy that shows you trust each other and want to be close to each other."

Cameron shook his head. "Whatever."

"Doing it again?"

"Yes."

"Sorry."

"'Sokay." He tilted her face up, lowered his mouth to hers. He kissed her as passionately as he knew how, and he knew she understood when she gave a soft moan in the back of her throat.

Though he was sure she was beginning to understand, he wasn't willing to end it just yet. He angled his head differently and deepened the kiss, thinking he was the luckiest guy in Seattle tonight. He kissed her so hard she began to slide down and suddenly she was on her back and he was half way on top of her. Not wanting to frighten her, he broke the kiss, but she grabbed him by the shoulders and pulled him back down.

This time he really kissed her, deeply and thoroughly. Her arms moved up to circle his neck and one of his hands moved down her arm accidentally touching the side of her breast. She gasped and sat up.

"I'm sorry," he said immediately. "I didn't mean to do that. Really. You're safe. I won't go any further."

"No, no, it's okay. I know I'm safe. I just wasn't ready for the feelings. I seem to be ultra-sensitive to touch right now. Wow. I mean, wow. I've never felt that way before, like, I don't know, like I wanted you to be closer to me. Like I never wanted you to stop kissing me. Wow."

"It was pretty good for me too," he said.

She smiled at him. "Did you want to keep going?"

"Um, only if you want to."

"I do," she said, closing her eyes and lifting her face for more kisses.

He went to town. Making out with a gorgeous, willing girl had been far from what he'd thought he'd be doing tonight, yet who was he to argue with fate. She slid down again, just like before, and he moved half way on top of her just like before and she locked her hands behind his neck just like before.

They only broke the kiss for short intervals to catch their breath. Jeffy decided kissing was awesome. She began to understand the intimacy of it. She paid attention to her body, to the way it responded to what Cameron was doing. When he moved, when he made a sound, each thing he did, her body responded. How very intriguing, she thought.

She thought about how he'd accidentally touched the side of her breast a little while ago and found herself wishing he'd do it again. As a matter of fact, she wondered why he didn't, and then she realized he was being honorable. She hadn't given him permission to do anything but kiss her. He was honorable! Her father would like that. Hmm, she'd better put her dad out of her mind for now. Anyway, she so wanted to know what it would feel like for Cameron to touch her, she'd just remedy the situation real fast. She broke the kiss. "Cam," she whispered.

"Hmm?"

"You can touch my breast again, I mean, if you'd like to. It's okay."

He merely stared at her.

"Cam?"

"Uh, yeah, I don't think that's a good idea."

Sighing, she accepted that. She just concentrated on kissing him back. They kissed for a long time. Finally Cam raised his head. "Do you like that?"

"Oh, yes," she purred at him. "Don't stop."

"Okay."

She didn't know how long they'd been at it. He kissed her and she was in heaven and couldn't stop moaning over the feelings. She thought maybe making the moaning sounds was encouraging him to keep at it, and so she let the sounds come.

Taking time to read her body though, she realized something was happening. She felt hot, and had a funny feeling in the pit of her stomach. She knew she was having the symptoms of a body's natural response to foreplay. Her body was readying for the act of sex!

Just the thought of the act, wow. She found herself imagining it. She was starting to understand. Suddenly, having sex was all she could think of. She wanted it. Craved it. Had to have it.

She broke the kiss and rose up. "Cameron, do you want to have sex with me?"

"Geez, Jeffy, I mean, well, I– yes. No. I mean, yes of course I do. What guy wouldn't? But I mean, the way you put it makes it sound so, I dunno, so cold, I guess. Let's just say I want to make love to you."

"Oh, wow. That was the perfect thing to say. So, then, will you make love to me?"

He swallowed hard. Didn't respond.

"Cam?"

He shrugged. "I'm older than you. I'm supposed to say, you're just a kid. You're only fifteen and you're a virgin. You don't know what you want."

"And you know that wouldn't be true because I'm very mature for my age, and I'm telling you, I very much want to be relieved of my virginity. So, what do you have to say now?"

"Uh," he said, trying to wrap his brain around what was taking place. He stopped trying to understand and went with it. "I guess I say I'll go get some condoms."

Jeffy giggled. "I'll take that as a yes." She jumped up, clapping her hands. "Oh, this is gonna be so wonderful. You go get condoms and I'll order pizza cuz I'm starved. Deal?"

He thought briefly, here is a girl offering to buy pizza and have sex with him. He just wasn't man enough to turn that down. "Deal." He sprang for the door. Stopped, came back and grabbed his keys. "Be right back."

Cameron beat the pizza guy back by twenty minutes. He'd half expected to get back and find Jeffy dressed in some sexy nightgown or something, but she was still dressed in her blue jean skirt and short-sleeved shirt. She had, however, removed her shoes and taken her hair down.

She sat on the bed against the headboard again. He tossed his keys and wallet on the dresser and his package on the bedside table and sat down on the side of the bed.

"Can I see them?" she asked.

He took the box out of the bag and handed it to her. "You're curious about everything, aren't you?"

"I have a very inquisitive mind."

He looked her over. She had amazing thighs, taught and muscular. Small breasts. The cutest mouth. Big eyes. And the way she was sitting on the bed he could see up her skirt, which made his throat dry and his eyes water. "Are, you uh, are you sure you still want to do this?"

"I think so. Do you?"

"If you want to."

"I think I do."

They chatted a little awkwardly until the pizza arrived. Cameron left to buy some soft drinks out of the vending machine. When he got back they turned on the TV and camped out on the bed, gobbling up greasy, cheesy pizza and guzzling sodas. When they finished eating Jeffy rose and cleaned up the mess, washed her hands and face and stood in front of the mirror brushing her long hair.

"Your hair is really pretty," Cameron said.

"Thanks. I get the color from my dad and the curls from my mom."

Setting her brush on the counter, she came back to the bed and sat next to him, cross-legged, her back against the headboard. Cameron's eyes were on the TV, watching some movie with a couple kissing. He looked over at her.

"You know, it will hurt the first time, right?"

She nodded. "I've heard that. I'm not afraid."

"So, are you ready?"

"I guess. It seems weird now, though. Not like before when you kissed me."

"Well, probably when I kiss you again, it won't seem weird anymore."

"Okay."

He stood, took off his shirt and sat down next to her. She started to pull her own shirt over her head, but stopped.

He'd been watching her, waiting for the exquisite moment and realized she stopped. He noticed she was trembling. He sighed. She was having second thoughts.

"I can tell you're not feeling it anymore, Jeffy."

She swallowed hard. "I'm sorry, Cameron. Are you mad?"

"I don't think mad is the right word. I guess disappointed is more like it."

"I guess I'm just a stupid little girl after all."

"Naw, I still think you're the coolest chick I know. I'll tell you what, we'll just lie here together for awhile. Maybe I'll kiss you again. And then, if you still want to go further we can. And if you don't, we won't. How's that?"

Jeffy nodded, smiled weakly. "Thanks, Cameron, that makes you pretty cool too. I see why Marissa likes you so much."

"Well, considering the alternative, it just makes me smart."

"What do you mean? What's the alternative?"

"I mean, the alternative is I could force you, but since I know who your family is, that would be a death sentence for me, so I'm just being smart."

Jeffy laughed. "Aww, that's sweet."

"What's sweet?"

"That you think you could force me."

He frowned for a moment, then accepted her declaration of superiority. He turned off the light, left the TV on and then they got under the covers. Jeffy lay on her back and Cameron on his side, facing her. They talked for a while about the next day's plans and then he bent his head and kissed her.

She moaned again, just like before. And kissed him back, just like before but he remained smart enough to take it no further.

~~~

Jeff softly knocked on Mickey's door in the very early dawn. He didn't wait for her to answer but just slipped inside.

"It's just me," he whispered, hoping not to startle her.

She rose up. "I was hoping you'd come to me last night."

He sat down on the side of the bed. "I thought about it, but decided to let you get some alone time to try to sort out some of your feelings."

She didn't say anything, only lifted the cover, inviting him in. He scooted in next to her. Mickey curled up against his chest as usual, sighing at the feel of his rough palm caressing her back.

He drew a deep breath and sighed. "Just want to let you know that so far, I'm still in love with you."

Mickey giggled. "Good. Just to let you know, me too."

"Good."

"If it changes, would you tell me?" Mickey asked.

"I hope I would. I mean, I believe in honesty in a relationship. Would you tell me?"

"I'm not sure. I think it would take me a while to realize it wasn't working anymore and then I'd probably try to do something to bring back the old feelings and then eventually, I'd figure it out and let go."

His finger ran gently over her shoulder and down her arm. "Well, maybe we should try to get to know each other better, I mean, other than carnal knowledge."

"Okay. So, ask me a question."

"Um, when's your birthday?" he said.

"February third. When's yours?"

"November eighth. What's your favorite color?"

"Purple, what's yours?"

"Blue."

Mickey snuggled closer. "Who's your favorite writer?"

"Mackenzie Daley."

She laughed. "Good answer."

"Do you want to have children?" Jeff asked.

"Sure. Maybe two or three. What about you?"

"Ditto."

"Jeff, I know I've been pretty weepy since I've known you. Do you think that is why you like me? I mean, maybe my wimpiness is bringing out your protective side."

He looked down at her. "Well, I guess giving you a night to be alone actually did give you time to think about things."

She sighed. "Then you think I have a point?"

"Nope. What I saw when I first met you was a woman with amazing strength. Remember, the woman I found in the woods had just ki— ." He stopped himself. "The woman I found had just escaped from an impossible situation."

She knew what he'd been about to say, but she let it go. "Maybe I am strong, even though it didn't feel like strength when everything was happening. All my life, it's only been me. I had to be strong. I learned at an early age that no one was gonna step in and make everything all better. I certainly didn't get any help from my mother. And my father left back when I was little. There's never been anyone, until you."

He squeezed her. "I'm glad I was there, baby. I want you to know that you can depend on me to 'step in' as you put it. No one is ever gonna hurt you again."

She looked up into his face, kissed his mouth softly, then snuggled back down. "Ask me another question."

"Okay. Ummm, what music do you like?" Jeff asked.

"Rock– and– roll," she said huskily.

"Oh, yeah. That's good. Okay, now we know all about each other, let's get back to the carnal knowledge."

Giggling, she pressed her face against his neck and breathed.

"You do that all the time. Like a kitten trying to get close."

"Does it bother you?" she asked.

"No, I like it. I think it's cute."

"I'm not sure what makes me do it. It really is as if I can't get close enough. And also because I like the way you smell."

He sniffed his underarm. "You're weird."

When she laughed, he grabbed her and held her still. "I love hearing you giggle and laugh. It's like, I want to be very funny so I can hear that sound all the time."

"Oh, Jeff, when you say things like that it tells me all I need to know about you. I do love you."

He kissed her. "Me too," he said when he pulled away. "How would you like to go for a walk?"

"It's still dark outside."

"I know, but the sun will be up soon and I love walking on the beach when the sun comes up. Besides, after that I have to join the Kinos for Tai Chi and training. When Grandmaster Kino extends a second invitation it wouldn't be polite to turn him down."

"Can I watch?"

"Sure, however, if you do, you'll probably be asked to participate."

"Okay, that's cool. Let's get going."

~~~

"Just follow along the best you can. When you get winded, slow down or stop for a few minutes and then join back in," Eric counseled.

"I jog almost every day so I'm in pretty good shape," Mickey said. She peered around her when she heard several snickers, but whoever had laughed had already schooled their features back to innocence. She looked back at Master Kino. "What?"

"They were being smart alecs, and they will pay for that," he said with a smile.

This time she heard a few soft groans.

"Let's begin."

She followed them through the warm up and stretching, keeping her eyes on Jeff, amazed at the extent of his knowledge and physical conditioning. And then things got tough. She pushed herself and yet ten minutes into the drills she thought she might pass out. At the fifteen minute mark she definitely felt like she might throw up. She stopped, breathing hard, her hands on her knees.

"Don't stand in one place," Jeff whispered. "Walk slowly in a small circle, breathe deeply."

Nodding, she did as instructed. And so it went throughout the lesson. Near the end, she was grateful when she was instructed to sit and watch as they went through their choreographed forms. It was an eye-opener for sure. These people were amazing. True artists. Perfect bodies, beautiful minds, angelic faces. It seemed they glowed with a golden aura. What an absolute treat to be able to share this experience with them. She was in heaven.

~~~

Cameron watched her walk away. This morning she had on some tight jeans with a little tank top that showed her belly. She'd braided her hair back. Even though he preferred it down like she'd had it last night, it was still appealing. He realized as he watched her that he didn't want her to leave. The moment she'd turned her back to him it was as if the sun had gone behind the clouds. He had to stop her if only for a few seconds. "Hey," Cameron called.

Jeffy turned with a smile on her face and the sun reappeared. "What?"

He crooked a finger at her.

She came back to the car, leaned toward his window.

"Be careful," he said softly.

"I will," she laughed.

"No, really. We haven't talked about it, but what you're getting ready to do, it could be dangerous."

"About the only thing I'm in danger of is being on restriction for the rest of my life."

Cameron frowned. "But what if—"

"Cam, I'll be careful. I promise." She leaned in and kissed him. "Thanks Cameron. For everything."

He sighed. He didn't want to say goodbye. "Can I give you a ride to the airport?"

She smiled. "I'd like that."

"Then I'll wait here."

"It could be a while."

"I'll wait."

"Thanks." She took off at a jog.

Cameron had dropped her off a block from the Daley's house. Once there she found the veranda on the side of the house easy enough. Her heart pounding like a bass drum, she eased up to the French doors and turned a knob. It gave a little click and opened. A rush of cool, air conditioned air blew wisps of hair back from her face. She moved through the room silently, thinking about her Ninjutsu training and how it finally was getting some practical use. She opened the library door and moved into the hall.

Voices traveled to her from the back of the house. She could hear Marissa asking her father questions about Mickey. Jeffy thought she was probably trying to keep his attention on her in case Jeffy made a mistake. Quickly, Jeffy moved two doors down and entered the office. It was the same room Mr. Daley had returned to after she'd met him yesterday.

Moving fast, she went to the file drawers. They were locked. She opened the drawer to his desk, found some keys and tried them. They worked. How simple was that? Still, after thumbing through the files for fifteen minutes she could find nothing of interest. No funny names. No bills or receipts. She gave up on the files and began searching the desk itself. She went through every drawer, even looked for secret compartments, but she could find nothing.

Gazing at the desk she noticed a PC and a laptop. The laptop was sitting front and center. Shrugging, she fired it up. It blinked on and she went to work. She was pretty good at computers, but she didn't have a lot of time left. Her fingers flew over the keyboard searching for some clue.

~~~

"But what if she never comes back? What will we do then?" Marissa asked, acting as if her heart was broken.

"Marissa," her father said sternly. "We've covered this subject enough for today. If Mackenzie doesn't come back then life goes on.

We will accept it and deal with it because that is what we Daley's do. Now stop all this whimpering, sit up straight and finish your breakfast."

"Yes sir," she mumbled, thinking of how much she hated him.

His cell phone went off. He looked down at it with disgust. It surprised Marissa when he actually answered it during their stupid sacred breakfast.

"Why are you calling me at this hour?" he said without saying hello.

"Because we may have some big problems."

"Speak."

"Martin and Yin were arrested yesterday at Ameritech."

"Yes, well, I told you to not underestimate those people."

"I got wind this morning they spilled their guts."

"Impossible. I've taken precautions to make sure they are loyal. If they want their wives or kids to—"

He stopped, realizing he was still at the table and Marissa was staring at him in horror. He stood. "Excuse me ladies, a bit of business that can't wait."

"No!" Marissa cried, jumping out of her chair and running after him. "Dad, wait. Where are you going?"

He stopped in the hall. "I'm going to my study to take care of this business. Now go back and finish breakfast."

"No, dad, I need to talk to you."

"It will have to wait."

"It can't wait."

"Marissa, you're being ridiculous and melodramatic. Are you sure you're well? Run along now." He started toward the door.

Marissa reached out and grabbed him by the arm. "No! Wait, Dad. This can't wait. It's, it's something really important. Really bad. You have to listen to me."

He smiled at her. "I'll be off the phone in a few minutes and whatever it is you have to tell me we can talk then." Wrenching his arm from her grip he turned the knob and strode into his office.

Marissa held her breath.

When her father didn't go berserk she peeked into the room. A quick glance around told her Jeffy must have heard them coming and hidden or had already left. She let out a sigh of relief until she looked up at her father. He stood stock still, his eyes teaming with anger. He was either staring at the computer on his desk or the slightly open drawer. As if in slow motion, his eyes shifted to her.

"What were you doing in my office?" he said between clenched teeth.

Marissa's mouth fell open. Her brain scrambled. "I, I—"

Her father grabbed her by the shoulders. "You what? What?"

The high pitch of his voice told her he was angrier than she'd ever seen him. Maybe she was getting a glimpse of what her sister had faced all those years. When she didn't answer him he shook her hard.

"What did you do?" he bellowed.

She couldn't get the words out. She couldn't think of what to tell him. "You're hurting me," she finally screamed at him.

"You little brat, you haven't seen anything yet." He hauled back his hand.

"Let her go!" Jeffy ordered.

Both Marissa and her father gasped loudly. Talmond spun around. "You!"

"Yeah, me," Jeffy said. She looked past him to Marissa. "Go, Marissa. Run."

Marissa shook her head. "No. I can't leave you," she cried.

"I don't know who you think you are, you little thief, but you have messed with the wrong person." He reached for her.

Jeffy snap kicked, knocking his arm away then side kicked right into his gut. The man doubled over then looked up, astonishment on his face.

"Yeah, how does it feel to have someone fight back," Jeffy said.

"You're dead little girl," he whispered fiercely, then louder. "Marissa, get out of here."

"No, I won't."

His face contorted with rage. "Yes you will!" he yelled. He spun, his backhand knocking the young girl out into the hall.

"What's happening," Marion cried as she and Ms. Dora came running.

Breathing hard, Talmond glared at her. "You and Dora put your daughter in the car and go somewhere. Now."

"Go somewhere?" Marion asked as she pulled Marissa to her feet. "Where? Why?"

"Don't you question me. Take her to the mall, take her shopping, just get her out of my house."

"I won't go," Marissa cried, wiping blood from her mouth. "What are you gonna do with Je– Chris?"

"Chris and I are gonna have a little talk and then I'm gonna send her home."

"You, you can't do that," Marissa sobbed. "Please, Daddy."

"Get her out of here," he ordered, glowering at his wife.

Dora put her hand on Marion's shoulder. "Come on, Marion, we'd better do as he says."

Marissa screamed as Marion and Dora each took one of her arms and dragged her away.

Talmond turned back to Jeffy. "Now then, suppose you tell me what you and my daughter were doing in my office snooping around in my computer."

Jeffy swallowed hard. "I don't have to tell you anything."

"You're not gonna get away with whatever you were doing."

"What're you gonna do, call the cops? I wish you would."

"I'm sure you wish that. I don't know what you think you know about me, and I don't have time to try to get the information out of you. I doubt that Chris is your real name, though it doesn't really matter. I have someone who has all the time necessary to find out what I want to know. I don't know what you think you were doing, but it's over for you."

Jeffy fought the fear that snaked up her spine. She knew he was capable of anything. He'd proven that. She also knew she needed to act quickly. Taking a stance, she raised her fists. He laughed, and then lunged at her.

She spun with blinding speed and kicked to his face connecting with a pleasant sounding thunk, punched to his throat, landing only a glancing blow then kicked to his groin. He sank to his knees.

It's now or never she thought and darted toward the door. She almost made it, but he reached out to grab her and caught her braid at the last second. Her head snapped back and she landed hard on the shiny hardwood floor, moaning. Before she had a chance to recover he'd pulled her up and had her in a headlock. He jerked her out of the room and down the hall to another room, slamming the door open.

She grabbed the door jamb and held on.

"Let go," he warned, tightening his arm and squeezing off her air supply.

When she didn't comply, he began to squeeze. Slowly, her arms went limp. He pulled her dazed body into the small area and tossed her literally across the room. She landed with a thud. Before she could get up and try to run out, he slammed the door shut and locked it from the outside, smiling when he heard her throw herself against the door, screaming at him to let her out. Straightening his shirt, smoothing back his hair he drew a calming breath and went back to his study.

When he found the phone he'd dropped in all the scuffle, he dialed Kurt.

"What happened?" Kurt asked.

"We have another problem I'm gonna need you to take care of."

~~~

"How could you, Mom?" Marissa cried in the back seat of the car. "What kind of a mother are you? How could you let him do this?"

Marion sat next to her, hands squeezed into fists. "Do what, Marissa? Your friend broke into your father's office and he's going to have a word with her, that's all. Then he's going to see her home."

"Oh, Mom, you are so blind. She didn't break into his office. I let her in."

"Why on earth would you do that?"

"To get information."

"Information on what?"

Marissa eyed her mother, realizing she really was in her own little world. She had no idea what kind of man she'd married, and Marissa just realized her mom would never believe all the things Marissa had discovered about her own father.

"You know what, Mom? I don't care that he hurt me. And I don't care that you don't care that he hurt me, but how could you let him hurt Mickey? How could you?"

Dora glanced at her passengers in the rearview mirror. Finally, the truth was gonna come out.

"What are you talking about?"

"You know he hurt her, Mom. You have to know. Your own little girl. You were all she had and you turned your back on her. I hate you. You're so weak. I hate you," she cried, turning away.

Back at the house in the tiny room, Jeffy looked around her. It had no windows and no furniture. There were boxes and boxes of what appeared to be ceramic tiles. She could see no way out and the fear factor kicked in completely. She needed her father, and she needed him *now*. Then she realized, Mr. Daley hadn't bothered to take her phone.

~~~

The Kino's breakfast table was a riot, Mickey thought. Lively, friendly, happy. It was a wonderful way to start each day. Remembering the breakfasts she'd endured all those years growing up, she shuddered.

Shelley was laughing with Mark and Joey over something that little Joey had said. Eric looked on quietly, love and kindness glowing on his face. He glanced at her and Mickey smiled at him and he smiled back and she thought all was right with the world. Beside her, Jeff chowed down with one hand and squeezed her thigh with the other. Closing her eyes, she gave thanks for her life.

Eric's cell went off.

"Who could be calling this early?" Shelley asked casually.

Eric pulled out the phone and glanced at the number. "It's Jeffy."

"Tell her to get her butt home," Joey said. "She's been gone long enough."

"Good morning, Jeffy," Eric said.

"Daddy?" Jeffy cried.

Eric's face changed. "Jeffy, what's wrong?" The entire table became silent.

"Daddy, I'm in big trouble," she sobbed.

Eric stood. "Where are you, baby?"

"I'm sorry, Daddy. I'm so sorry."

"Jeffy, tell me where you are. What's happened?"

"I'm in Seattle."

"Seattle?"

There was a collective gasp. Mickey rose, as did Shelley. Then Jeff, then Mark and Joey.

"Yes, Daddy. I thought I could help. I thought I could fix everything."

Eric swallowed, forcing himself to use his logical mind. "Sweetheart, I need you to calm down and tell me exactly where you are, okay? Deep breath. Talk to me."

"I'm at the Daley's house. I came to tell Marissa that Mickey was alive. I knew how much she was suffering, you know, like when Ricky was missing. I thought while I was here I could snoop in Mr. Daley's office and maybe find some stuff for Jason, but he caught me. I fought him, Daddy and I almost won, but he grabbed my hair and pulled me down. He locked me in a room. He told me I was dead. And he hurt Marissa. He made Mrs. Daley take her away. I'm not sure where she is."

"Okay. I'm on my way. You hear me? I'm on my way. When we hang up you hide your phone. Turn it off so he won't hear it if someone tries to call you. Don't put it in your pocket. Put it in your sock or your bra. Got it?"

She sniffed. "I got it."

"Jeffy, we'll be there."

"I believe you. I'm sorry, Dad. Tell Mom, I'm sorry."

"We'll talk about that later. Hang up and do what I said."

"Okay. Bye."

Eric held his hand up as everyone tried to talk at once. "Just listen," he said. He dialed Jason and started talking the moment he picked up. "Tell me you have a read on Jeffy's GPS phone tracker."

Eric waited impatiently for Jason's answer. Jason came back to the phone.

"I've got her. It's in Seattle."

"That's because she's in Seattle. Get in touch with the FBI up there, Jason. Daley has my daughter."

The family listened as Eric told Jason everything Jeffy had said. Mickey stumbled backward, plastered herself against the dining room wall. "It's all my fault," she said softly.

Jeff placed his hands on her shoulders. "No it's not. You're not responsible for anyone's actions but your own. Do you hear me?"

Mickey glanced over at Shelley's pale face, her eyes glued on her husband as he spoke. Pulling away, she ran up the stairs.

Chapter Nine

Eric hung up the phone and went straight to his wife. "She'll be okay. Trust God. The FBI will be there soon. Jason's getting his company jet ready."

"I'm coming with you."

"I'd expect nothing less. Go upstairs and grab what you need." He turned to the three other men in the room. "Jeff and Joey, Jason wants you on the jet. Mark I'm gonna have to ask you to stay here and take care of Mickey."

"However I can help the most," Mark answered. "Besides, I've got little Joey."

"Good. And please call Ricky and Bree, let them know what's happening.

Jeff ran up the stairs to see to Mickey. He found her sitting on the floor near the bed, her knees drawn up to her chin. He knelt beside her.

"Mickey, we'll get Jeffy back. Everything is gonna be okay."

"You keep saying that, but how do you know, Jeff? How? If he harms her, what then? And she said Marissa's hurt. How bad? I've got to get up there."

"Oh, no. You're staying right here where you're safe."

"Like hell I am."

"We're leaving on Jason's jet as soon as we can get to the air strip and you will stay here with Mark and little Joey."

"I don't know where you get off telling me what I can and can't do."

Jeff scowled. "Well, it was fine as long as you needed me to protect you, now wasn't it? Now that you're feeling a little more secure, all of sudden you think you know best?"

Mickey's mouth dropped open. She screamed at him calling him a list of pointed and insulting obscenities.

Jeff sighed, ran a hand through his hair. "Yeah, I guess I am. Bottom line, you're staying here where you'll be safe. I have no idea what's gonna happen and I need to be able to help find Jeffy without having to worry about you."

"I'm not asking you to worry about me and I *am* coming with you."

Jeff's face went blank. "No– you're not and this discussion is over."

Mickey stood, her body trembling. "Don't you dare tell me when a discussion is over. I'm going with you. I have to go."

"You are most definitely not going with me and unless you think you're brave enough to venture out alone you will stay here." He stopped, sighed at the wide-eyed expression on her face. "It's for your own good, Mickey."

"How in the world do you suddenly become an authority on what's best for me?" she shrieked. "I think you're reading way too much into our relationship."

His eyes narrowed as he realized what she was saying. "Maybe. So let's put our relationship aside for a minute. I'm not acting as your boyfriend, I'm doing my job, and in that area, I certainly know what's best. You've been through a severe trauma. You're not thinking clearly."

The tears came and she tried to choke them back. "Jeff, you don't understand. It's my fault."

"Even if it was your fault, that's not reason enough for you to come out of hiding. You stay here until we make a move on Daley."

Her chin trembled and Jeff blew out a breath. "Look, Mick, I'm sorry. I'm not trying to pull off some sort of male domination kind of thing. I'm supposed to be keeping you safe."

"Yet you're leaving."

"Yes, however, I'm leaving you with Mark."

"Is he a trained agent too?"

"No, but he's just as good as one because he's Grandmaster Kino's stepson. He's been trained by the people who trained me. Now, I don't have time to discuss this any further."

"Good. Then stop arguing with me. We need to get ready to go."

"Dammit, Mickey, I can't hash this out with you right now. You're just gonna have to trust me. Please. I need to know that you're here and safe. I'll call you the moment I know something."

"You're just like all the other men I've known. Pushy and bossy and unreasonable."

"You're comparing me to your stepfather?" Jeff asked incredulously.

"I didn't say that."

"You didn't have to, Mick."

She turned her back on him. "Maybe I've made a mistake."

The words were spoken softly, yet Jeff heard them loud and clear. Maybe his job just wasn't conducive to happy relationships. Or maybe it was him. Whatever it was, he didn't have the luxury of sticking around and talking it out. "I have to get ready. I don't want to delay them. They're worried enough as it is. When I get back I hope we can talk this through." He moved close, tried to hug her, but she stepped away.

Sighing, he stood. "Fine. If that's the way you want it."

He stormed to his room down the hall and she followed him thinking to continue their argument. She watched him gather a bag with a few clothes and personal items and mostly weapons. It seemed as if she'd seen him do that exact thing hundreds of times now. Strap on a holster. Check his gun. Un-sheath and re-sheath a knife. He was a professional and of course, he knew what was best– usually. However, *not* in this case. He started for the door, stopped and looked at her.

She looked away. When she looked back, he was gone.

~~~

Marissa didn't know what to do. They were parked in the mall parking lot. Marissa had refused to get out of the car. Her mother and Ms. Dora stood just in the front of the car, having a private conversation. Probably trying to figure out what they were gonna do with her. Then she did what she always did when she didn't know what to do. She called Cameron.

"Where are you?" she asked.

"I'm down the street waiting on Jeffy. I saw you leave with your mother. What's taking Jeffy so long and why aren't you with her?"

"My father caught her," Marissa sobbed. "He forced my mother to take me away from the house. He said he was gonna have a word with Jeffy and then take her home."

"Well, we both know that's not gonna happen, unless Jeffy makes him believe she lives nearby and he actually lets her go."

"I have a very bad feeling about this," Marissa said.

"A black Buick just pulled into your drive. Isn't that Kurt's wheels?"

"Yes. Oh my Gosh, Cameron, I don't know what will happen to her."

"Marissa, I won't let her out of my sight. I'll follow behind him. I won't let him hurt her. You need to try to contact her parents. And your friends at the FBI. Call them. Hurry, Marissa. Jeffy could be in big trouble. If he would kill his own daughter, he'd hurt Jeffy without blinking an eye."

"Do you think so? I don't think he's stupid enough to hurt someone from a famous family."

"Marissa, he doesn't know who she is, remember? He thinks she's some kid from the wrong side of the tracks. Just call the FBI and her parents. I'll try to keep you posted. I promise, I won't let her out of my sight."

Marissa didn't have the business card Agent Dodge had given her to call if she needed him, so she dialed information and asked for the number. Hands shaking she punched in the number. She explained to the woman who answered that she needed to reach Agent Dodge, that it was an emergency and she'd lost the card he'd given her. The woman asked her to wait while she patched her through. While she waited she silently begged him to answer, but it went to message. "Ugh!" she grunted, slamming her phone down.

~~~

Jeffy looked up when Mr. Daley opened the door of the room. Her face paled as she looked into the barrel of a gun.

"You're going for a little ride," he said.

He stepped aside and a tall man dressed in an expensively tailored suit walked into the room. The man wasted no time. He moved quickly, grabbed her wrist, twisted it behind her back and ushered her through the kitchen and into the garage.

"Where are you taking me?" she demanded, trying to keep her voice from shaking.

The man stopped mid-stride, turned her toward him and struck her across the face. "Shut up. I'll be asking the questions." Still holding her wrist, he opened the trunk of a dark sedan.

Jeffy's eyes grew wide as saucers.

The man leaned her against the side of the car and ran his hands over her body, taking extra time to check around her breasts. She gave thanks she'd put the phone in her sock and not her bra.

He moved close to her, whispered in her ear.

"You're not really a kid, are you? Who do you work for?"

Jeffy's body began to tremble. "I, I don't work for anyone."

"How old are you really?"

Jeffy began to cry. She'd give anything to have her father walk up right now. "I'm only fifteen– really, I'm fifteen, I sw —"

Suddenly, he moved away. "Shut up your whining. Just get in the trunk," he ordered gruffly, pushing her forward.

She readily complied, happy to put space between herself and him. She climbed in and lay on her side atop a thin, green comforter that was spread out across the space.

"On your back," he said.

She obeyed. He grabbed her hands and began to tie them together with some nylon rope. Once her hands were secure, he seized her legs and did the same. Jeffy was terrified he would find the phone. As long as she had it, her father could track her. His hands moved quickly, wrapping the rope several times around her legs and ankles. Suddenly he stopped.

"What have we here?"

Jeffy closed her eyes, her heart taking a dive.

He pushed her sock down, removed the phone. "I think I'll hold onto that," he said.

Jeffy watched as he pocketed her phone and she gave thanks that he hadn't tossed it aside or handed it to Mr. Daley.

The man spoke briefly to Mr. Daley. Jeffy couldn't hear what they said except the last part where he assured Mr. Daley no one would discover the girl in his trunk. He then produced a white cloth and placed if over Jeffy's nose. She bucked and fought, trying not to breathe in the sickening sweet smell. She knew exactly what it was. Trichloromethane and methyl trichloride. Commonly known as chloroform.

~~~

Talmond watched them drive away. His anger was palpable. The little thief had probably been looking for money. Yet, why would she use his computer? It didn't make any sense. He wandered into the dining room, eyeing the remainder of the breakfast dishes with disdain. He hated when things didn't go as planned and especially when things were out of order. Unable to stand the mess, he cleared the table of the dishes, polished the wood, replaced the centerpiece, then stood back and admired his work. He'd barely gotten back to his office before there was a knock at the front door. He opened it to Agent Dodge and Agent Stevens and an army of others.

"What is going on?" he blustered.

"Senator Daley, we have a warrant to search the premises."

"On what grounds? This is absurd. I'll have your badge for this. I'm a United States Senator. You can't just come bursting into my home."

"Yes sir, with a warrant I can."

Agent Dodge motioned and several agents stormed the house.

"You people are in big trouble. Let me see the warrant," he demanded.

The agent handed papers to him. Daley read them, his face turning a bright red.

"This is absurd. This is ridiculous. Fraud? Kidnapping?"

"There's more. That's all we could get this morning. We were in a hurry."

Men began walking out the door with files and computers. Some headed up the stairs.

"Let's step into a room and have a chat," Agent Dodge said.

"I believe I'll call my attorney first," Talmond answered, his voice not quite as forceful as before.

Two agents approached Agent Dodge. "We've searched the house, sir. She's not here."

Dodge pinned Daley with an icy stare. "You wanna tell me what you did with the girl?"

"What girl? I have no idea what you're talking about?"

"The young girl. The one who was a friend of your daughter. Where is she?"

"That little tramp? Is that what this is all about? Did she call you?" he asked, thinking of the phone Kurt had found on her. "I don't know what she told you, but she broke into my house. I should've pressed charges, but instead I sent her on her way. Told her to go home. That's what I get for being a nice guy. That little brat is who you should be questioning."

"We'd like to question her, if we could find her."

"I have no idea where she went. I kicked her out of my home and told her to make sure she doesn't come back. How do you even know about her? Did she call you? Or maybe it was my daughter who called you. Who was it?" he demanded. If it was Marissa he would take great satisfaction in beating his youngest daughter to a pulp. Apparently

Mackenzie had been a greater influence on her than he'd thought.

"The young lady in question called her parents, said you had her locked up in this house somewhere."

The agent watched as Daley's face visibly paled.

Talmond cursed himself inwardly for not being more careful. The little brat had gotten to him. Flustered him. She'd actually kicked him. He hadn't even thought of her having a cell phone on her. "This is all quite absurd," Talmond said

"You keep saying that. The funny thing is, I'm gonna have to agree."

"I sent that little brat on her way. I had my man take her home."

"Your story just changed."

Talmond sneered at the agent. "I have no idea what you're talking about."

"A few minutes ago you said you kicked her out of your house, but now it seems you had her escorted home? I doubt that."

"Don't you dare question my word. It could be fatal to your career."

"What's his name and number?"

"Whose name and number?"

"Your man, Senator. You said you had your man take her home. I'm gonna need his name and phone number."

Huffing out a breath, Daley gave him the information. Agent Dodge dialed immediately. The call went to message.

"He doesn't answer, Senator. Have you spoken to 'your man' recently?"

"As a matter of fact I have."

"And where did he take the girl?"

"She refused to tell him where she lived and so he took her to the school where he dropped her off. If you find her I believe I've just decided I will be filing a complaint against her."

"If we find her? You mean when, right? When, we find her. And let me fill you in on some information, Senator. You'd better hope we find her, because that little girl is the daughter of Eric Kino. And if anything happens to her it will be all we can do to keep him from killing you."

"Eric Kino?"

"Yes, you know, Ricky Kino's father. Does that answer your question?"

~~~

Mickey was pacing the Kino's living room, her bag packed with the few possessions she had. She turned to Mark who'd also packed a bag for himself and little Joey.

"Why? Why do you think we've suddenly been summoned to Seattle? Do you think it's because everything is over? Do you think it's because they've found Jeffy? Or maybe it's because something's happened to Marissa. Maybe she's—"

"Mickey, please, calm down. Ricky will be here any minute and we'll know the answers. Until then, why borrow trouble? You wanted to go and now we're going. We'll know why in just a minute," Mark said calmly.

Mickey stopped, nodded. "Of course, you're right. I'm sorry, Mark, I'm just so worried."

"That's understandable. I am too. Take a deep breath or two. We were about to have a prayer. Would you like to join us?"

She nodded and they bowed their heads and prayed for Jeffy's safety. Near the end of the prayer Mark also asked for Mickey's healing. "In Jesus' name, Amen," he ended.

Mickey looked up with tears in her eyes. Smiled at Mark. Mumbled a soft, "Thank you."

He nodded. "Picture the best possible outcome and focus on that, okay?"

She closed her eyes, drew in a deep breath. "Okay," she said softly. "Okay. Sorry I'm being so hard to deal with right now."

Mark smiled. "Did it seem like I was having any trouble dealing with you?"

She gave a slight chuckle. "No. None whatsoever."

Ricky and Bree came bursting into the house with their kids. Ricky was not the jovial, happy man she'd met a few days ago. Bree had obviously been crying. Ricky's eyes met Mickey's.

"I'm sorry," she whispered. "It's all my fault."

He came to her, took her hand. "How do you see that?"

"Jeffy and I talked. I told her she reminded me of my little sister. I told her how much I missed Marissa and how worried I was about her, thinking I was in captivity or dead. I said I wished I could somehow get word to her."

Ricky sighed. "It's not your fault. Jeffy is completely responsible for her own actions."

She shook her head. "That's the same thing Jeff said, but Ricky, she's just a child. I influenced her."

"Jeffy is *not* just a child," Ricky argued. He looked at Mark. "Are you ready?"

Mark nodded, grabbed his and Mickey's bags. "Joey," he yelled.

The little boy came immediately down the stairs. He was quiet as were Eric and Taylor.

"Get in the car, kiddos," Ricky ordered.

They quickly obeyed.

"So, why do I get to come now when a few hours ago I had to stay here?" Mickey asked.

"Things have changed," Ricky answered. "The Feds decided to stop handling the Senator with kid gloves while they try to put together a case against him. Thanks to Jeffy's stunt they've launched an outright investigation and they'll need your statements, so your well being is extremely important. They want you close at hand and Jason has promised them he'll deliver you safe and sound."

"I'm so relieved. I was going crazy. I need to be there."

"We all need to be there," Bree said. "I know Jeffy is gonna be just fine. I just know it, but staying home and waiting for word about her is beyond my capabilities. So, we're all going."

"Thank goodness. If only we'd known this a few hours ago, Jeff and I might still be together."

Ricky's eyebrows rose. "The two of you broke up?"

She shrugged. "I think so."

Ricky's eyes met Mark's. The younger man slowly shook his head. Ricky raised his eyebrows at Mickey, waiting for her explanation.

She huffed out an indignant breath. "I can't be with a man who thinks he can order me around."

"Let me guess," Bree said. "You wanted to go. He insisted you stay and he won."

"Yes."

Bree smiled. "And you're not speaking to him."

"Never again."

Ricky glared at his wife. When she glared back he shook his head at her. "I'm sure he was trying to do what he thought was best at the time, and probably also following Jason's orders," he said.

"I don't want to talk about it anymore," Mickey said, arching her brows defiantly, even though what Ricky said was absolutely correct. She changed the subject. "Anyway, there is a problem. I have no ID with me in order to fly."

"That's okay, we're chartering a jet. Jason has three company jets, but one is in New York, one is in Saudi Arabia, and one is on its way to Seattle with our family aboard," Ricky explained. "So it's a charter for us." He motioned toward the door. "No more conversation. Let's go."

Mickey nodded and rushed out the door.

~~~

Kimmie listened as her mother spoke on the phone to her closest friend, Shelley Kino. Something was terribly wrong and it had to do with Jeffy. Her mom was crying and trying to console Shelley over the phone. It sounded like they were saying that Jeffy was missing, but Kimmie knew exactly where Jeffy was. Well, not exactly, but she did know Jeffy was in Seattle. She'd promised not to tell, though now, she knew she'd have to break that promise.

Most days Kimmie's dad would be at the office, but it was Saturday morning and he was working from home. Nervously, Kimmie walked through to the west wing of their sprawling mansion and entered her father's office. He was speaking to someone on his headset as his hands flew over a keyboard. A red light flashed on a map, another phone was ringing. It sounded as if her father was on the phone with the FBI, Kimmie thought, because he'd used the words Special Agent.

"Dad," Kimmie said softly.

He spun, eyed her, held his finger up, meaning, 'just a minute,' and went back to his conversation. He was giving directions, saying something about a back mountain road, arguing and finally he punched a button to end the call. He turned to her and the worry on his face had Kimmie's stomach churning.

"Kim," her father said softly. "I need to tell you something. It's about Jeffy."

Kimmie nodded. "Me too, Daddy," she said. "I'm sorry, Dad, I know Jeffy's missing. I know where she is. She's in Seattle."

Jason's eyebrows arched. "Yes, I know."

"You do?"

"Yes I do," he said slowly. "The question is, how do you know?"

Kimmie chewed on her lip for just a second. "She told me."

Her father's face darkened considerably. "When did she tell you?"

"Yesterday."

"Did you know she went there without her parent's permission?"

Kimmie nodded her head.

"And you kept her secret?"

"I promised her I wouldn't tell."

Jason closed his eyes, shook his head.

Kimmie looked up hopefully. "Is she okay?"

"We don't know, Kimmie. She's in trouble. She's in the hands of some criminals and they've taken her off somewhere and we can't find her. Not yet anyway."

Kimmie's hands flew to her face, tears welled in her eyes. "Oh no, Daddy, you have to help her. You have to." She ran to him and buried her face against her father's chest.

He held her, stroked her long dark hair. "Okay now, Kim. I'm working on it, honey."

She sniffed, lifted her head as the tears continued to fall. "You always save everybody, Daddy. You always win. So you have to win this time. You have to. You have to save Jeffy. You can't let anything happen to her."

His daughter's words pierced his heart, and it took Jason a moment to clear his throat. "I'm doing my best."

"It's all my fault. I should've told. I should have."

"You were keeping a promise to a friend. You were being loyal. I understand that. It's not your fault, little Kim." The phone rang. "Now, I have to get back to work. You don't leave the house, you got it?"

"Why not?"

"Because I may need you, so stay close. And I need to know you're safe so I can concentrate."

She nodded. "I'll do anything to help."

"I know you will, Kimmie." He kissed her head, set her away.

~~~

When his cell phone rang Kurt reached into his pocket, but pulled Jeffy's cell phone out instead of his own. Cursing, he tossed it aside, reached back in and grabbed his own phone. He didn't recognize the number and so decided to not answer.

The second time it rang it was his boss. "Yes," he said, doing his best to hide the resentment he felt for the man.

"Listen carefully. I don't have much time. The Feds are here, they've taken all my files and my PC. They won't find anything on it, as you know. They want me to go downtown with them for questioning."

"The crap is about to hit the fan," Kurt moaned.

"No. You have to stay calm. Don't blow this. They have nothing. As it turns out, this Jeff Davis is still in good standing at Ameritech and Mackenzie is in their custody, accusing me of kidnapping her."

"Damn."

"There's no proof."

"There's proof that I knew where that cabin is. Davis saw me heading there. And are you forgetting that I met with this guy and made arrangements with him to deliver proceeds from the arms deal?"

"You driving toward that cabin is hardly a crime and only circumstantial. I will explain the meeting you had with Davis as my own ploy to get a crooked agent to bring back my daughter. Keep your mouth shut, Kurt. I don't need to remind you how bad things can get."

Kurt's jaw tensed. "No."

"The real problem is that little brat you have in your trunk. It seems she's not some two-bit kid off the street. Her real name is June Flower Kino as in Eric Kino's daughter, Ricky Kino's kid sister."

Kurt cursed.

"Somehow, someway, she knows something."

"What makes you think that?"

"It was something she said when she was in my office. Bottom line, she doesn't survive."

"We've already decided that, so why the call?"

"Because she's not some two-bit kid that nobody is gonna miss. She's the kid of a celebrity and they'll leave no stone unturned. So, make sure you leave no evidence. Clean the area well. I already have two eyewitnesses who'll say they saw you drop her off near the school. Make it look like some lowlife got her."

"Got it," Kurt said. He scowled as he hung up, his temper exploding. He threw his cell phone so hard it broke into pieces against the windshield. Kurt swore. How had he let a guy like Daley take over his life? It'd gone on too long and now there was no way out, not that Kurt could see. Kurt himself was no innocent puppet, not anymore. He'd done his share of bad deeds and gloried in the spoils more than once. He had no qualms offing this smart alec kid, and he would because he was told to do it, still, he could almost feel the walls closing in around him.

~~~

"Who was that?" Agent Stevens asked his partner as he slumped down in a chair in his small office, going over the stack of statements he'd already collected.

"That was Jason Lee, the guy who owns Ameritech Security. He's convinced that the Kino girl is being transported west, into the mountains. Says he has a new kind of GPS type tracker in her cell phone. Our tracker gave a weak signal for a few minutes and then stopped completely. He says he has a clear signal which has her headed west about two hours from here. Problem is, I told him we have two witnesses who saw the kid dropped off at the school. Nevertheless, he insists she's in a car and headed out west." He shook his head. "You know, Daley asked if the Kino girl was the one who called us. That makes me think he believed she was alive and well, so just maybe he actually did have his guy drop her off."

"But he's smart. And why can't we locate this Kurt Wells guy?"

"We know the guy intended to off his stepdaughter, so I believe he's lying."

"So we go after the kid?"

"Yeah. Her family just landed at the airport. We pick them up and head west."

~~~

Mickey realized she'd been chewing on her fingernails and forced herself to stop. The thought that she could be the cause of something terrible happening to Jeffy tore her up. And what about Marissa? Was she okay? What had Talmond done? She knew what he was capable of, but surely he wouldn't hurt Marissa, or an outsider like Jeffy. He wasn't that stupid, was he?

Mickey glanced over at Bree. Her daughter sat in her lap as Bree tried to keep her entertained by reading a book. Mark's son, Joey, was sitting next to his Uncle Ricky on the floor of the jet, their legs crossed, their eyes closed, their upturned hands on their knees, apparently in deep meditation. Ricky's son, Eric, was playing a video game with Mark.

Sighing, Mickey looked back out the window, her mind going over and over the crazy events that had taken place over the past few weeks of her life. It all seemed so surreal.

"Feeling a little displaced?"

Startled at the voice, Mickey turned to find Bree smiling at her. "That is exactly how I'm feeling."

Bree nodded. "With everything that's happened, it's no wonder."

Mickey eyed her. The book was gone. Little Taylor sat quietly eating a banana. "You sound so calm. Aren't you worried about Jeffy?"

"Sure, I'm worried, but somehow I have a feeling she's gonna be okay. I have to believe that anyway. Therefore, I will act as if that's fact."

Mickey nodded. "You and your entire family have some interesting philosophies on how to go through life."

Bree smiled. "I didn't always, but Ricky is a huge influence on me. He keeps me calm, and I suppose when he gets upset, I keep him calm. We believe God is very active in our lives. If we're going to integrate that into our lives we need to show our trust in Him."

"Integrate? So, you can't profess to believe in God and when something goes wrong fall all apart."

"Right. Instead of reacting to certain situations, I, we, try to act. We try to take control and be the author of every event, so to speak. So, in my mind I will write this little episode as ending with a happily ever after."

"But what if—"

"What if's are borrowing trouble and useless. Then again, I may have to do a rewrite."

Sighing, Mickey nodded.

Bree reached across the aisle, squeezed her hand. "Do you think you and Jeff will be able to talk things out?"

Frowning, Mickey shook her head. "Really, the little spat we had wasn't important enough to actually break up over. Not if we truly loved each other."

Bree waited, but when she didn't go on, she said the words for her. "You're saying maybe you didn't truly love each other?"

Mickey briefly closed her eyes. "I don't know. I mean, we've only known each other a very short time. I've said I love him and he's said he loves me. Yet we've both agreed that it's possible that we're just in over our heads with feelings that come from being through a traumatic situation together. You know, like, he's my hero, my knight in shining armor, and I'm the female who's brought out his protective tendencies. It could all be false."

"But what if it's not?"

"Exactly," Mickey whispered. "What if? I'm so confused. Having that little spat with him sort of woke me up. It made me realize I don't really know him at all, and he doesn't really know me. Maybe we should back off, you know? Take things a lot slower."

Bree nodded. "That sounds logical."

"Yeah, so why do I feel so miserable when I say it?"

"The chemistry is strong, huh?"

"To put it nicely," Mickey said with a sigh. "What do you think I should do?"

Bree glanced at her husband whose eyes had popped open at the question. She smiled at him. "A wise man once told me he couldn't tell me what I should do because then I'd have someone to blame when things went wrong. He said I had to make my decisions for myself and he gave me this advice; be honest with yourself. Only do what you truly feel is the right thing to do."

"And what if it turns out you made the wrong choice?"

"Then you fix it."

~~~

When Kurt stopped, Cameron stopped and slid quickly behind a tree. The old guy was doing pretty good considering he was carrying maybe a hundred and ten pounds over his shoulder. Cam was having no problem keeping up with him. For two hours he'd followed the guy. He found it was much harder to follow someone than he'd thought it would be, especially when you were trying to keep your distance.

They'd headed west out the state highway into the foothills. Just before they'd hit the town of Gold Bar, Kurt had swung north toward the pass, then turned left again at a road that was barely a road. From there they'd turned so many times Cam wasn't sure he could find his way out. He'd always had a terrible sense of direction. At one point Kurt had slowed almost to a stop and Cam had to pull over quickly. It looked as if the guy threw something out the window then kept going.

Once on foot, they moved through dense forest. So dense, at times it was hard to tell it was daytime. Now Kurt was doing this zig zag and circle stuff. Cameron was pretty sure he'd passed this particular fallen tree at least once, maybe twice before. With each zig and zag, Cameron was getting closer. He couldn't just charge in because the dude had a gun in his suit pocket. He knew because Cameron had seen him pull it out twice now.

He wondered how much farther into the forest they would go. He was pretty sure they'd been at it for over an hour. He peeked around the tree. Apparently finished resting, Kurt picked up his bundle which was wrapped in a green blanket, hauled her over his shoulder and started again. Cameron fell in step. It seemed they'd walked forever when Kurt stopped again, lowering Jeffy to the ground. He was panting, trying to catch his breath.

Cameron watched as this time, the man knelt beside her and

unwrapped her from the blanket. Cam's heart practically jumped out of his throat at the site of Jeffy, bound with rope, her eyes closed. She moaned and tossed her head.

"You waking up, little girl?" Kurt muttered. "Well, we can't have that, can we?"

He produced a white cloth and a bottle, poured something on the cloth and held it to her face. Jeffy kicked a few times before she fell limp. Cameron slipped a little closer as Kurt concentrated on untying the ropes that bound her wrists and ankles. Once Kurt finished with that, he removed her shoes and socks.

Cameron moved closer still, his heart racing, when Kurt looked up suddenly, his eyes scanning the forest. Cam forced his breathing to slow, forced his body to be completely still. Finally, Kurt turned his attention back to Jeffy. He grabbed the hem of her shirt and pulled it over her head, then removed her bra.

Good Lord, did he plan to rape her? Cameron swore he wouldn't let it happen. He inched closer, then ducked behind a tree that was large enough to hide his body and was only maybe twenty feet from them. Kurt unbuttoned Jeffy's jeans and pulled both them and her underwear off at the same time.

Cameron almost lost it. He decided to charge, but Kurt pulled the gun and spun around. Cameron remained where he was, safely hidden. Getting himself killed wouldn't help Jeffy. He had to use his brain. Peeking around the tree he saw Kurt scan the forest, then finally relaxing, he tossed the gun down onto the blanket. Cam watched as Kurt rolled Jeffy off the blanket to lie face down on the forest floor and then pulled her hands out straight. Next he moved behind her and spread her legs apart. Bile rose at the site of Kurt's hands on Jeffy's body.

And then Cameron finally understood. Kurt wasn't gonna rape her. He was positioning her, for death. Staging the scene. Realizing what the next step would be, Cameron charged.

Kurt looked up at the sound, reached for his gun, but Cameron was on him too fast. Cameron plowed into him with every bit of force he could put behind it, and being a defensive back, that was considerable. Kurt landed with a grunt on his back with Cameron on top of him. Before the man could even gain his wind, Cameron was pummeling him with his fists.

Kurt wasn't fighting back, mostly because he couldn't. It was taking all he had to try and keep the kid from breaking his nose.

There was no stopping Cameron. He swung until Kurt stopped moving. When Cam finally pushed himself away and stood, the man was completely unconscious. Breathing hard, his hands covered with blood, Cam pulled Kurt over to the nearest tree, grabbed the rope that had been used to bind Jeffy and secured him to the tree.

Next, he knelt beside Jeffy and gently turned her over onto her back.

"Jeffy," he said softly. "Can you hear me? Jeffy?"

He watched her, making sure she was breathing, then in relief, simply hugged her to him. He had no idea how long he stayed in that position, cradling Jeffy's body, rocking her back and forth, giving thanks that she was alive, but he knew he had to get moving. Daylight was burning and he didn't want to be this deep in the woods at night.

He was gonna have to carry her. He grabbed her shirt and tried to get it on her, but her body was so limp he gave up. Instead, he merely tucked her shirt and jeans and shoes around her and wrapped her up in the blanket. The gun he stuffed in his waistband. Then he went to Kurt and searched his pockets. All he found were car keys, which he took, a wallet, which he left and the stuff he'd seen him use on Jeffy. Pouring some into the cloth, he held it to Kurt's nose, figuring it would be best to keep him unconscious as long as possible.

Before he hoisted Jeffy up, he dug in his pocket for his cell phone to call Marissa and let her know Jeffy was okay, but it wasn't there. Frantically, he searched all his pockets, then realized when he'd spoken to Marissa earlier, he'd tossed the phone onto the passenger seat of his car. Great. Just freaking great. He looked down at the young girl whom he had quickly and easily come to care very much about and brushed a few leaves from her face.

"Don't worry, Jeffy. I'll get us out of here."

With that, he hoisted her over his shoulder and started walking.

~~~

The elation that came when they found the dark blue Buick quickly faded when they discovered Jeffy's phone in the front seat. From here on out they'd have to track them. The Feds had called for dogs, but Eric and Shelley had no intention of waiting around until the dogs arrived. It was getting late. Choppers were also called, yet they'd been told they wouldn't be much help due to the denseness of the forest.

Jeff and Joey took point, since they were armed. The rest spread out behind them. Agent Stevens stayed behind to wait for the dogs.

The group had been searching the woods for over an hour when Agent Dodge received communication from Stevens. First thing he told them was they'd found another car a few hundred yards further down the road. They'd know the owner soon. Then he let them know they had two bloodhounds and that, using the driver's seat in the Buick, they'd picked up a scent and were headed south.

Agent Dodge and the Kinos adjusted, turning south. They headed that direction for more than thirty minutes when they met up with the dogs, who were now headed north, in the direction the Kinos had just come from.

They adjusted their direction again. When they got to a point where the dogs seemed to lose the trail for a minute, Shelley began to panic. It was when they changed direction a third time she completely broke down.

Eric was quickly at her side.

"He's leading us on a wild goose chase," she cried. "I want my daughter."

"I know, Shelley. We're gonna find her. He walked a zig zag pattern trying to throw us off, but it took him time to walk the pattern. Eventually, we'll catch up to them. He's gonna expect us to get frustrated and give up trying to follow his pattern. He will eventually break away. He can't keep it up forever. You have to be strong. Don't give up."

She shook her head. "I won't give up, Eric. Just tell me, please, tell me you think she's alive."

"I do, Shelley. I think she's alive. Do you need to rest, or do we keep going?"

"No. No rest. We keep going," Shelley said firmly.

"That's my girl," Eric said, giving her a quick hug.

~~~

He was lost. Leaning against a tree, the sweat pouring from his body, he closed his eyes. Ugh, he was lost. He'd been walking for hours. When he first realized he should already be out of the woods he hadn't panicked. He'd taken a deep breath, looked up at the sky and tried to judge which way was east or west, but the trees were too thick. It was hard to see the sun and harder still to figure out which way it was headed since it seemed to be at a different angle each time he looked up.

He thought he'd been so smart when he came to the stream and began following it. It had to lead down, right? Down to a town or at least out of the mountains. Then he'd come to a point where on his side of the stream he'd have to climb down a steep cliff, so, he'd crossed the small river, no small task with Jeffy in tow, and continued on from there. Now he came to another place where there was a steep drop off, this time on both sides. Realizing he was gonna have to back track for miles to continue following the water, he began to question the wisdom of it at all. The only thing the sun was telling him now is that it was going down.

His attention was drawn by the soft moan at his feet. Kneeling down beside Jeffy, he brushed his hand over her cheek. "Jeffy? Wake up, baby."

Her only answer was to moan again, and move her head. Thank goodness, he thought. She's coming around. To help things along he reached inside the blanket, grabbed her tank top and rushed down to the creek. Taking a moment to wash the blood from his hands and to drink some water himself, he then plunged Jeffy's shirt into the cold water, wrung it out and went to her.

He wiped her face and neck as she began to stir. He hurried back to the stream, rinsed out the shirt and this time didn't quite ring it out all the way. Kneeling down next to Jeffy he twisted the material and let the cool water drip into her mouth. To his delight, she swallowed and licked her lips.

"There you go, Jeffy. Better, huh?" He stroked her face gently. She moaned.

"More water," she whispered.

He immediately complied, getting emotional at the sound of her voice.

He watched her tongue flick out to lick at the moisture, then her eyes fluttered open.

He smiled at her. "Hi."

She smiled back. "Cameron?"

"Yeah, it's me."

"What happened?"

"Long story short, I followed you. Kurt tried to off you, I beat him up pretty good and tied him to a tree. And now, well, now we're trying to find our way out of the forest, however, I seem to be hopelessly lost."

She gave a soft laugh. "My hero."

"Yeah, some hero. It's getting late. We're probably gonna wander around in the mountains until we either starve to death or get eaten by a bear."

She shivered. He sat and pulled her into his lap, pulling the blanket tighter around her, holding her close against his chest. She reveled in the beat of his heart and the warmth of his body. "It's a lot colder up here in Seattle then it is in L.A.," she said, her voice barely audible.

"Yeah, it may be summer, but it's always chilly up here in the mountains. Especially when the sun is blocked."

"The man, you said his name is Kurt?"

"Yeah. He works for Rissa's dad. He's a jerk."

"And he tried to kill me?"

"Well, I don't know for sure, but it looked to me like he was posing you. He had a gun and he was positioning you on the ground. For some reason it seemed to me like the next thing he was gonna do is pick that gun up and shoot you in the back of the head."

"Why did you think he was gonna do that?"

"Just instinct. I couldn't think of any other reason for him to be positioning your body like he was. I was afraid to wait any longer to see what he might do because I knew once he picked that gun back up I wouldn't be able to move fast enough to stop him. So I charged in and took him out."

"Thank you, Cam," she mumbled, her voice still weak.

"I guess we'd better get moving," he finally said.

Jeffy shook her head. "No. We stay put."

"But—"

"My father is looking for me. He'll find me."

"How do you know?"

"I know my dad."

"Okay, but how will he find you?"

"A tracking system in my cell phone. The guy, Kurt, he took my phone, but they'll at least be able to track us out here. I don't suppose you could find your way back to him?"

Cameron sighed. "I doubt it, but, listen, I checked his pockets. Your phone wasn't on him."

She frowned, then looked up. "Then it's in the car. How far are we from the car?"

"I don't know. Could be miles. Could be a few yards." He shook his head. "I'm sorry, Jeffy. I have a terrible sense of direction."

She snuggled against him. "It's okay. My father will find me. It's getting dark, so it may not be until morning, but he will find us. Don't worry."

"I'm too busy being happy you're alive right now to worry about anything."

She groaned. "I'm dizzy and nauseated." Her eyes fluttered closed.

"That freak put some stuff on a rag and held it over your face."

"Yeah, chloroform. It was used years ago as an anesthetic during surgery, and then they found it can cause kidney damage among other things and they stopped using it."

He grinned down at her. "Right."

"Doing it again, huh?" she asked without opening her eyes.

"It's okay."

"You wouldn't happen to have some matches on you?"

"Unfortunately, no."

"Well, then, I guess you're gonna have to keep me warm tonight in other ways," she sighed.

His gut clenched. "You just work on feeling better right now, okay?" he said.

She snuggled down into the blanket, then her eyes flew open. "Am I naked?"

"Yes."

"Wh– did he—?"

"No. He took your clothes off. Like I said, I think he was trying to make it look like someone had raped and murdered you. I never bothered to dress you because I just wanted to get out of here, and also because you were limp as a noodle. I brought your clothes, they're stuffed down there in the blanket somewhere."

Pulling the blanket away, she looked for her clothes. She found the jeans and one shoe. They stood together, shook the blanket out completely, but found nothing else."

Cameron sighed, as his eyes glided over her supple, perfect, body. "I, uh, didn't think to grab your underwear and socks, but I know I had both shoes. One must've fallen out. Anyway, you have your jeans, but, uh, I used your shirt to wipe your face and bring you water." He quickly pulled his own shirt over his head. "Here," he said helping to dress her.

The Madison High School t-shirt came to mid-thigh. She smiled up at him. "Thanks."

He held her jeans out to her.

"No, I think I'll just stay in this during the night so I can be comfortable." She put a hand to her head. "I'm still dizzy. I think I'd better lie down."

Cameron spread the blanket out on the ground and helped her to get comfortable, then sat down beside her. She looked up at him.

"Thanks, Cameron, for everything."

He touched her face, shook his head. "You could be dead right now. If I hadn't decided to stay and wait for you, if I hadn't been able to follow you, you'd be dead."

"I'm sure glad you decided to wait. I don't want to be dead and just the thought of the pain I would've caused my family, oh, man, that's a bad thought, so I won't dwell on it. I'll just stick with gratitude that you waited for me."

"You know, it's because, you know, after last night I was feeling close to you. I wasn't ready to say goodbye."

"I was feeling close to you too. Last night– it was amazing."

"Yeah, it was, and what I'm trying to say, Jeffy, is if we hadn't done what we did last night, I may have just dropped you off and waved goodbye and that would've been the last time I saw you alive."

"My father says playing 'what if' is a waste of time and only serves to create fear."

"Your father is a wise man. I've heard him speak before, at Washington State at a youth conference. That was two years ago. I never dreamed I'd be sitting beside his daughter one day, thinking about the makeout session we had."

Jeffy giggled, then shivered. "Cameron, will you hold me? I'm so cold. It must be another side effect of the chloroform."

He stretched out beside her and pulled the other half of the blanket over both of them.

She snuggled up into his arms. "Ahh, that's better already."

He kissed her forehead.

~~~

Once in Seattle, Mickey found that she would be left behind again. Apparently Ricky had been instructed to drop her off at her own home where two Ameritech agents were waiting to take over her protection. This time she didn't argue for two reasons. One– she knew she would be no help traipsing through the woods searching for Jeffy and two– she'd developed a little plan of her own.

Her home was located on the north side of the city in a trendy neighborhood known as the Avenues. She hadn't been prepared for the jolt that hit her as she approached the small craftsman-like dwelling. The last time she'd stood on the walk outside her front door she'd been on her way for an early morning jog. It'd only been a few weeks since that fateful morning, but it seemed like it'd been years.

She wandered around the house in a daze. The cops or feds had been here, she surmised, since the place had been dusted for fingerprints and the black dust was everywhere. Her computer was gone and she made a mental note to ask about it.

"Mickey?"

She looked up at Jack, the agent who'd come to the motel that first night with Jeff.

"You okay?"

She blinked, not sure if her emotions were in control enough to speak.

"I know it's a mess," Jack said, "but there are companies you can hire who will clean it all up for you. Or you can do it yourself. It will come up. I'd be happy to help you with it."

She looked up at the large man who looked so deadly and spoke so gently. "Jack, you must be one of the nicest men I've ever met." She looked at the other agent when he let out a snort. "But, no," she continued. "It's not the mess. It's just that, it almost doesn't feel like home anymore. I feel like I'm in a stranger's house."

He nodded. "I understand. Facing death gives us a different perspective on everything. Fresh eyes, I like to say. Sometimes it has a way of making us feel out of place. Between dimensions. Maybe when Jeff gets back you can—"

"Don't mention him to me, please."

Jack glanced at Nathaniel, his fellow agent. "But, I thought—"

"Me too. Apparently I was wrong. I find him to be a pigheaded jerk, who is only concerned with being the big man hero thing."

Jack used every ounce of will to control his smile. She couldn't have spoken more loving words. He covered by frowning deeply. "Maybe once you two get to talk about things, it will be better."

Mickey smiled at him. "You're a very nice man, Jack, but I don't think that's gonna happen and I'd appreciate it if you don't talk about it anymore."

Jack gave a nod of his head. "Whatever you say. Still, I just want you to know that if you want, I'd be happy to tell him off for you."

Agent Nathaniel Hawk choked, then coughed, covering his mouth with his fist.

Mickey turned her gaze on him.

"Uh, sorry . . . allergies."

She breathed a sigh. "I'm just gonna change clothes, grab my purse and I'll be right down. I want to go to my mother's house to see my sister."

Thirty minutes later, Mickey stood nervously on the steps of the Daley home. She was accompanied by Jack and Nathaniel. Her stepfather was being questioned by the FBI at the present time which left the coast clear for Mickey. The media had been mulling around trying to get a story and when they saw her they made a bee line, but were stopped abruptly in their tracks by Jack and Nathaniel.

It was Ms. Dora who opened the door. Her hands flew to her face. "Oh Mickey," she cried, clutching Mickey and pulling her into the house. The agents stepped in behind her, closing and locking the door.

"Oh, Dear Lord," the woman exclaimed. "Ms. Marion, come quick. Marissa!"

Dora threw her arms around Mickey, blubbering and crying and thanking God all at the same time. "We thought you would never come back. We thought you were dead for sure."

Mickey pulled her away, smiled. "Oh, you can't get rid of me that easily."

Marion came hurrying from the den. She stopped, her mouth agape. "Mickey?"

"Yes, Mom, it's me."

The woman moved slowly, much slower than Mickey was use to seeing her move. Her hands shook as she placed her arms around Mickey and hugged her tightly. She couldn't remember the last time her mother had actually hugged her. Maybe when she'd left for college. Mickey looked up at the sound of loud clumping coming down the steps. Her mother moved away and Mickey opened her arms. Marissa jumped onto her almost knocking her down. If Jack hadn't braced her, they both would've gone tumbling to the floor.

"Oh, Mick, I'm so happy to see you. I was so worried and then Jeffy came and told me you were alive. But now—"

"Wait," Marion said. "You knew she was alive?"

"As of yesterday. Jeffy told me."

"Who's Jeffy?"

"My friend who visited me. Oh, I told you her name was Chris, but really it was Jeffy Kino."

"How did this Jeffy know Mickey was alive?"

Mickey ignored her mother's sudden interrogation of her sister. "Rissa, have you had news of Jeffy at all?"

"Nothing yet. I'm so worried about her."

"Me too."

"Maybe the two of you need to have a seat and tell me what's going on," Marion said sternly.

Mickey's chin rose into the air, letting her mother know that there was no way she would ever be able to intimidate her again. Still, her mother was right. They needed to talk.

"Fine. Come sit down, Mom, and we'll tell you everything," Mickey said. "You too, Dora."

"I don't think I can sit right now. The Senator will be coming home soon and—"

"I, uh, doubt that," Jack said.

"This is Agent Jack Crandall and Agent Nathaniel Hawk," Mickey said quickly.

"Agents? You're with the FBI?"

"Oh, no, Mrs. Daley, much better than that. We're with Ameritech Security. We're here to make sure Ms. Daley stays safe since she'll be the principal witness against your husband," Jack said.

"What? How dare you come into my home and say that."

Mickey smiled at Jack. Maybe he wasn't quite as sweet as she'd originally thought. The remark was a well-placed barb. Apparently something in her mother's mannerisms had displeased Jack.

"Come sit down, I'll fill you in," Mickey said.

~~~

They'd hoped Jeffy would've been found before they'd arrived in Seattle but apparently, it was not to be. Bree and the kids were shipped off to a hotel where she took rooms for the family. Ricky and Mark hightailed it westward to the mountains with packs filled with supplies to help with the search. They carried things that Eric hadn't had with him, not expecting a wilderness search for his daughter. Things like flashlights, hunting knives, blankets, protein bars, water and night vision goggles.

Communicating with Joey, they were able to quickly catch up to the search party before dusk. Only a brief moment was taken for hugs and words of encouragement. Water and nourishment was dispersed to be consumed as they walked.

They walked steadily for another hour before the dogs began to whimper and speed up. Excitement and anxiety collided as they realized the scent the dogs had been tracking was getting stronger.

It was full dark when they came upon the man tied to a tree. He was awake and moaning. No sympathy was shown for his battered and bloody face. He was untied from the tree, given water, cuffed and pushed down to sit on a nearby log.

"Where's Jeffy?" Joey asked.

"I don't know who you're talking about," Kurt answered.

"Geez, the man is an idiot," Ricky said softly. He turned to watch his father, ready to grab him and hold him back if necessary. Ricky's eyes met Mark's and Joey's and realized they were thinking the same thing. Yet Eric appeared to be as calm as he always is. He also appeared to be in deep thought.

It was Shelley who moved forward. She knelt down beside him. "Listen to me carefully. Jeffy is my daughter. We know you brought her out here and yet, she's not here with you, and finding you in the condition you're in, I surmise someone was not happy with you. Whoever that was, tied you to a tree and took my daughter. Now, I'm asking you nicely, where is she?"

When the man didn't answer Shelley looked up toward her husband. Eric nodded at her, knelt down next to her. "Shelley, I'm thinking it wasn't anyone who took her. I'm thinking Jeffy did this to him. That's why he won't talk. He's embarrassed that he was bested by a young girl. She's probably trying to find her way out of the forest right now. It shouldn't take us too long to locate her."

"That little brat could never best me."

"It appears she has."

"It was the kid."

"The kid?"

"Marissa's friend. The Wallace kid."

Eric smiled. Ricky rolled his eyes. The man really was an idiot.

Eric looked up at Agent Stephens. "Before you take him in, I'd like a word with him alone."

"Uh, I don't think that would be a good idea."

"Just a few words, I promise. I won't harm him. I admit, I thought about ripping his heart out, but it was just for a split second. If I wanted him dead, he would be already. Just a few words, man to man."

Against his better judgment, Agent Stephens nodded. The group moved away, but each person kept a close eye on Eric.

Eric looked deep into the man's eyes. "I know you brought her out here to kill her."

When Kurt started to deny, Eric shook his head.

"I'm not asking you to confirm. I already know. And in order for someone to do what you planned to do, I assume you've killed before." He stopped, watched the man's face closely.

Kurt remained silent.

Eric nodded. "That's what I thought. So, I know you've killed for Daley. I'm told you've been with him more than twenty years." Eric shook his head, sighed dramatically. "Hell of life, huh, doing the dirty work for Senator Daley. I guess, when you have enough respect for a man you'd do anything for him."

Kurt made a short, choking noise.

Eric nodded again. "So, there is no love between the two of you. Then it must've been for the money. Daley must've made you a rich man, huh?"

Kurt rolled his eyes heavenward.

"No? Not for money? And not out of love or loyalty to the man you work for. There is only one answer, then."

Kurt remained silent. Eric watched him closely.

"I'm not a cop. I'm merely a man, a man of honor. This conversation is only between you and me."

No answer.

Eric shrugged. "That's okay. You don't have to answer. The answer is simple. I know why you've done what you've done. I don't think there is pure evil in you, so I don't think you committed murder, amongst other things, just because you wanted to see someone suffer. Oh, you're hardened alright. To life, to feelings. And you have a temper, that's obvious. Still, that's not why you've done what you've done. I know the answer. Just keep in mind, that there was always a choice. Always."

Eric stood, nodded at the Agents. "Let's find my daughter."

Agent Dodge nodded, as he finished punching buttons on his phone. He held it out to the group. "This is the kid that's with Jeffy. He's the one who drove Marissa in to see me one morning. He's a good kid. I don't know how he's involved or came to be out here, but if he has Jeffy, then I believe she's safe."

"As safe as one can be wandering around in the mountain wilderness in the middle of the night with no food, water, shelter or protection," Shelley added.

Dodge nodded, sighed. "Yeah, as safe as one can be."

While Joey walked around the area, Jeff spoke with the Kino family and Agent Dodge finished up with Wells.

Joey cursed softly, gaining everyone's swift attention.

Jeff, Eric, Ricky, Mark and Shelley all moved to where Joey was kneeling on the other side of the small clearing. Joey lifted some light-colored items from the ground, held them out. Eric took them from his hands. His eyes closed in pain, his hands balled into fists.

Shelley recognized the items immediately. A long wail came from her throat as she gathered her daughter's bra and panties from her husband. Eric wrapped his arms around her as she sank to the ground.

Joey took off. Ricky and Mark scrambled after him. Agent Dodge jumped in his path, but Joey easily pushed him out of his way.

Joey screamed at Wells. "I'm gonna kill you. You raped a fifteen-year-old girl?"

"No!" the man screamed, cowering, covering his head. "I didn't touch her that way. I swear!"

It was a struggle, but they finally pulled Joey off the already badly beaten man. Ricky had one of Joey's arms twisted behind his back, Mark had the other one. Each had one of Joey's legs scissored between their own. Still, it took Joey several more seconds before he stopped struggling.

Kurt finally looked up from the fetal position he'd assumed. "I didn't rape her."

"Then explain these," Shelley demanded, holding up the undergarments.

"I," he stopped. What was he gonna say? I didn't rape her, but I was about to shoot her in the back of the head? His eyes shuttered, his jaw clamped shut. "I didn't rape her. I don't care whether you believe me." He looked up at the FBI agents, letting them know he expected their protection.

Jeff ushered the family away and helped them to regroup. Agent Dodge and Officer Langston, whose dogs were Jeffy's lifeline, consulted. It was dark, but they had Jeffy's clothing and Langston was positive the dogs would be able to pick up a scent. They also had night vision goggles now and choppers still available though spotting anything through the dense forest was almost impossible, however, they would circle, looking for a possible camp fire. They decided, the agents would take Kurt Wells into custody while Officer Langston, the Kinos and Jeff would continue the search– at least a little longer. If they didn't come across the kids soon, they would have hundreds of searchers gathered by dawn.

Chapter Ten

Marion shook her head, wiped tears from her eyes. "I can't believe you knew Mickey was still alive and you didn't tell me."

Marissa's eyes flashed. "Why should I have told you? I finally realized that you never cared what happened to Mick. You were always on his side."

"What are you saying Marissa? There are no sides. How can you say something like that, especially right here in front of strangers?"

Marissa rolled her eyes. "You're worried about appearances?"

Marion eyed the two men in the room. "Would you be so kind as to excuse us?"

Jack shook his head. "Sorry, ma'am, we go where Ms. Daley goes. Just pretend like we're not here."

Her eyes glittered with indignant anger. She was the wife of a Senator. Most people treated her with great deference. Sighing, she turned back to her youngest daughter. "You and your father have always been close. Now you speak as if you believe all the lies being spread about him. I don't understand, I just don't understand." Her eyes moistened and she wiped at them with a tissue.

"I'll get you some tea," Dora offered. She scanned the others in the room, nodded toward Mickey and the two men in the room. Agent Crandall stood near a window, his arms folded across his chest. Agent Hawk leaned casually back in a Louis the fourteenth chair in the corner of the room. "Can I get anything for you gentlemen?"

"No thank you, ma'am. We're fine," Jack answered.

"Answer me, Marissa. What has come over you?"

"I woke up, Mom. I've been watching you and Dad this whole time Mickey's been gone. I knew Dad was faking it. I knew he and Mickey didn't get along and I knew he didn't love his stepdaughter like he kept saying in front of the cameras. I hate all that fake stuff. You both were so willing to just give up on her."

"I didn't give up," Marion argued. "I prayed every day that somehow she would come home."

Marissa shook her head. "I began to remember things. Times when Dad hurt Mickey."

"Marissa," Mickey said softly. "Don't. You don't have to bring this up and you don't have to defend me."

"If I don't, who will?" she countered, then turned an accusing stare at her mother. "I remembered a time when I walked in on Dad beating Mickey with a belt. He made me leave, and I think I like, pushed the horrible memory out of my mind. Then when Mickey was taken, I began to remember those things. I remembered there were a lot of times like that when I heard Dad and Mickey in her room. I remember hearing her cry. I was just a little kid, and there was nothing I could do, but where were you, Mom? Where were you when your husband was beating your daughter? Huh? Where were you? You let him do it. You turned a blind eye. You gave him your own child and let him do whatever he wanted. It makes me sick to think about what she went through."

Mickey started to intervene. She had no desire to get into all this. No desire to bring up the past. Yet now that her little sister had, she found herself being curious as to the answer. Her eyes met her mother's.

Marion scowled. "He's not the monster you're making him out to be. Mickey was very headstrong. A handful. She needed discipline. Your father took care of that."

Mickey's eyes welled, but she forced the tears back. Her mother's response was exactly why she'd never asked the question.

"Mom, you need to open your eyes," Marissa said. "He is a monster."

"How can you say that? He's been nothing but good to you?"

"Oh my Gosh, Mom! Are you kidding me? I think they say that serial killers are great with their own families too! Are you not listening? He ordered his men to kidnap your daughter and to kill her. It wasn't some silly prank, Mom. He wanted Mickey dead. And he's involved in some bad illegal stuff. He sent my friend off with Kurt and now she's missing. What do you think about that? Do you have an answer for that?"

Marion looked up when Dora entered the room with a tray. She let the woman put the tea cup in her hand, nodded politely. "I can't believe Talmond was behind Mickey's disappearance. How can you say that about him? Your father loves you, Marissa."

"That's hardly comforting. Funny thing is, I thought I loved him too. Until I realized what kind of person he is. Mom, it doesn't matter how good Dad was to me. It makes me sick to think about that now. How kind he was to me. He never raised a hand to me. How can I be grateful for that when I know what he did to Mickey? And even worse, Mother, I can't stand to even look at you, knowing you let him."

Mickey drew a deep breath. "It's enough, Rissa. I don't care about that. Bottom line, his dealings have caught up to him and I can only be grateful that his plan didn't go as expected. I escaped and I'm alive. Right now, I just wish I knew if Jeffy is okay."

"Me too," Marissa said.

Agent Crandall's phone sounded. The room remained quiet as everyone tried to eavesdrop on his conversation. When he ended the call, he eyed the women. "Senator Daley has been arrested. The judge has no intentions of convening especially for him and since this is Saturday, the Senator's attorneys won't be able to arrange his release until Monday."

Marion rose. "Oh, dear, Dora, what shall we do? He's gonna be in a very bad mood when he gets home."

Dora's eyes shifted to Mickey and Marissa, a look of apology and regret evident in their depths.

Marissa jumped to her feet. "You just don't get it, do you? Who cares what kind of mood he's in? Who the crap cares?" She ran up the stairs.

"Mickey," Jack said. "There's more. They found Kurt Wells up in the mountains. Jeffy Kino wasn't with him. They're still searching. They believe she's with a kid named Cameron Wallace."

"That's Marissa's friend. That's great. That means she's probably okay. She probably got away."

"That's what they seem to think."

She nodded.

"Will you be staying the night here?" Dora asked.

"No. I want to go home to my own place. I've always hated this house."

Dora nodded.

"I'm going with you," Marissa said as she came back down the steps carrying an overnight bag.

Mickey looked toward her mother who seemed completely unaware of Marissa's statement. She looked back at her little sister, nodded. "That's fine with me. Let's go."

~~~

It was the sound of choppers that woke them. Cameron sat up, trying to peer through the trees. They hadn't been right over head, still, he'd definitely heard them. Unfortunately, the sound faded away.

"It doesn't matter. My father will find us in the morning," Jeffy said.

"You sound very sure of that."

"I am." She stretched and rolled onto her back. "I can't believe how dark it is out here," Jeffy whispered. "If you peek right up there between those two big pines, you can see the sky. The stars, they're so beautiful."

"Makes you feel very much alone, doesn't it?" Cameron said.

"Oh, no, not with you next to me. It makes me feel peaceful, except for the occasional sound of some animal rustling through the brushes." She turned toward him. "I can just make out your eyes."

"I can see yours clearly. Jeffy, last night, did I tell you how pretty I think you are?"

"No, you didn't. I mean, you did say you thought my hair is pretty. Why? Do you think I'm pretty?"

"Heck yes."

Jeffy giggled, yawned, stretched. "How long do you think we slept?"

"I don't know. A few hours at least."

His hand cupped her face. "Earlier, lying here next to you, talking about our lives, sharing things with you that I've never shared with another living soul, not even Marissa, it was nice, you know?"

"And you don't hate me now that you know about the college thing?"

"Naw. How could I hate a beautiful girl with brains?"

"Cam, you mean a lot to me."

"You mean you don't just need me for your sex experiment," he joked.

"You're much more than that to me. When you were kissing me last night, I felt a real connection. I felt so much a part of you."

"Yeah, I felt that too. It's never been like that."

"Really? How many girls have you been with?"

"You're number three."

"Oh."

"You're not mad about that are you? I mean, you asked me if I was a virgin and I told you 'no'."

"No, I guess I'm not mad. A female has a tendency to become emotionally attached to her mate much easier than the male. I suppose I'm feeling a little territorial."

He chuckled.

"What?"

"The way you talk."

"Oh. I'll try to keep that in check."

"No. I don't want you to be anything but yourself with me."

She sighed. "Cam?"

"Hm?"

"I probably won't be able to see you for a very long time. I'll probably be on restriction for, oh, I'd say twenty or so years."

"Man."

"So, tonight, it's like—"

"Like goodbye."

"Yeah."

"I want you to kiss me again."

He turned to her. "I can do that."

She waited for him to kiss her. When he didn't she asked, "What's wrong."

"I was just thinking, what if it leads to something, you know, something more."

"Well then I guess I'll have my experiment, huh?"

"Yeah but I don't have any condoms with me."

"I don't care. I'll take my chances."

"Jeffy, that makes you sound so innocent. You'll care when you have to tell your parents that you're pregnant."

"I'm very close to the end of my cycle. It's highly improbable that I could become pregnant now. Given that there are twenty-eight days in the cycle and the egg remains alive for only a twenty-four hour period of time, I'd calculate my chances of conceiving at point five percent."

He sighed heavily.

Jeffy felt her body tremble, just like it did last night, and she suddenly realized something. Jesus was speaking to her. He was warning her, telling her it was not the right time. He'd tried to tell her last night, but she wasn't listening. It was Cameron who heard Him and obeyed. She just remembered that whenever she was about to do something, make a bad choice, do something wrong, her body would tremble, sometimes even her teeth would chatter. It was a divine warning.

She and her dad had talked about it. People are always asking God to lead them and guide them, and then they don't listen. If they continue to ignore God's warnings then He'll eventually stop talking to them. Her dad had realized what was going on when she had this feeling. He'd said God was giving her a tap on the shoulder, or even a little shake. She hadn't been listening to God last night, but she would listen now.

"Cam, I think you're right. I don't think we should have sex. But I do want you to kiss me goodbye."

When he remained silent, she reached for his hand, brought it to her mouth and kissed it. "Please, Cam. Give me one more wonderful memory to take with me."

"Oh man, Jeffy," he murmured. "How can I resist you?"

She smiled. "I hope you can't."

He leaned closer and lowered his head to kiss her. From the first touch of his lips to hers he was lost. He sunk into her, feeling his heart melt, bonding with her as if their souls became one. It had never been like this with the other girls. He had a feeling it would never be like this again.

Jeffy, completely immersed in the kisses Cam was placing over her face, gasped as suddenly Cameron was gone.

Cameron struggled for breath as he found himself in the air, his back braced against a tree and a muscular forearm across his throat.

"Give me one good reason why I shouldn't kill you right now," the man who held him growled.

Cameron gripped madly at the arm that was cutting off his air supply. "I, I—"

"Daddy, put him down. He saved my life," Jeffy cried from where she sat on the ground, her mother's arms suddenly wrapped tightly around her.

They were surrounded by men with flashlights who unmercifully had them trained on Cameron.

"You were having sex with my daughter," Eric said, loosening his hold just enough to let him breathe.

"I was– only kissing her– sir."

There was a murmuring from the spectators.

"You'd better pray she backs you up."

"The moment you put me down, sir."

Eric dropped him and Cameron made good his promise.

"Jeffy, please— "

"Dad, he was kissing me. I asked him to, now leave Cam alone. He risked his life to save me."

"You didn't have to pay him back like this."

"You insult my intelligence, Dad. Besides, this wasn't our first time making out."

Another murmur from the spectators.

A groan from Cameron.

Jeffy looked around to see all three of her brothers plus Jeff Davis and another man she didn't know who held the leashes of two ugly dogs.

"Wow, I can't believe I didn't hear all of you coming."

There was a snicker from one of her brothers.

"I'll just add that to the growing list of indiscretions," her father said, doing his best to sound stern.

Jeffy wasn't worried about him. She knew, in truth, her father was a big pushover. "Dad, this is Cameron Wallace. When Marissa told him I was being taken away he followed the car. If he hadn't I think I'd be dead right now. Did you find the man? His name is Kurt something."

"Yes, we found him. Why didn't you stay there?"

"Jeffy was unconscious, sir," Cameron put in. "I thought I could carry her out, but I got lost. When she finally came out of it and I confessed to her that we were lost, she told me to just wait right where we were and you would find us. So that's what we did."

"Obviously, you thought it would take us longer than it did."

"Uh, yes sir." He hung his head.

"Okay, that's enough," Shelley said. "My daughter is alive and well and I'm so grateful to Cameron that I could adopt him as my own and you men had better find your gratitude real fast."

Eric nodded. "You're right, as usual my darling wife. Let's get out of here. I'm sure these kids are tired and hungry." He reached down and pulled his daughter to him, tilted her face up to get a good look at her, ran his thumbs over her cheeks and then crushed her to his chest.

~~~

They'd been lying in bed in the dark, speaking in hushed tones of the very different lives they'd had under the same roof. Mickey realized she'd always thought of her baby sister as just that—a baby. Yet she was discovering that she was a lovely, mature, intelligent young lady with a good discerning head on her shoulders.

"What will happen?" Marissa asked.

"You mean with your dad?"

"Yes. Will he go to prison?"

Mickey sighed. "I don't know. I'm not sure if his being a United States Senator will be good for his case or bad. I mean, it could be really bad, you know, violating his oath of office, but it also means he has a lot of pull politically. I'm just not sure how it will play out."

"I won't live with him," Marissa said firmly.

Mickey remained silent, thinking of her mother. Talmond Daley had her completely submissive. It wouldn't surprise Mickey if her mother remained married to the man. And if her stepfather somehow managed to stay out of prison, would Marissa be forced to live with them? Surely the courts wouldn't force Marissa to live under the same roof with him.

"Don't you want me to stay with you?" Marissa asked.

"Of course I do. I was just wondering what the laws are. Don't you worry, though. I'll hire an attorney. I can try to work out me getting custody of you until you're eighteen. Is that what you want?"

"Yes."

"What about Mom?"

"What about her? She didn't care about you. Why should I care about her?"

"Don't be so harsh, sweetie. Talmond is extremely manipulative. He's always known just what buttons to push to handle Mom. In a way, she was just as abused as I was."

"She was weak. She allowed herself to be ruled by him. For what? Why didn't she leave him? I know why. She didn't want to leave the fancy house, the fancy cars, the clothes and the parties and all that wonderful publicity."

Mickey blew out a slow breath. "Forgive, Marissa. Hating her will only hurt you. Please, if not for your own sake, then for mine."

"I'll try, but only for you," she said, startling when her phone went off. Jumping from the bed, she dashed across the room to grab her phone. "Yes? Cam? Well? Is Jeffy okay?"

"Yeah. She's fine. Thank God you told me what was going on. I think he was gonna kill her, Marissa. I tackled him and tied him to a tree. I would've been back to you a long time ago, but I got lost. And

I left my phone in my car. Then Jeffy's parents found us and, anyway, everyone is okay. I'm in my car now and we're all headed back. I'll tell you all about it later. They've contacted my parents who have to meet us downtown and take me home and then I have to go back in some time tomorrow to meet with the FBI guys again. They said they're gonna talk to you too."

"Okay. I'm just so glad Jeffy is okay. It's weird. I only was with her a few hours and I already just love her."

"Yeah. Me too. I mean, I really like her."

"Whaddya mean? You mean, you like her? Like, *like* her?"

"Yeah. Like that."

Marissa grinned. "That is like, totally cool."

"I don't think her parents feel that way, but since they live so far away, I doubt it will matter. We'll probably never see each other again."

"Sure you will. And besides, there's always the internet."

"Yeah. The internet. Great," Cameron muttered. "Look, I gotta go. We'll talk more tomorrow."

"You can bet on that. Bye, Cam. And thanks. You're the best."

She hung up and whirled, a huge smile on her face.

"I heard," Mickey said, also smiling. "Thank goodness."

~~~

Jeffy lay sound asleep in the other bed in Eric's and Shelley's hotel room. Eric glanced over at her to make sure she was asleep.

"But did you hear what she called me?" Eric whispered. "She called me 'dad'. Not 'daddy', like she always has. She called me 'dad'."

"Sweetheart, you're little girl is growing up." Shelley cuddled closer to her husband, breathing in his essence, his power, his very male scent.

"Trying to lose your virginity doesn't necessarily make you grown up."

"Not to us it doesn't, but to her, it's like she was trying to cross a rite of passage. And from what she told me while you were in the shower, Cameron was honorable and gentle and took good care of her."

Eric shuddered. "Shelley, please don't say stuff like that when you're talking about our daughter."

Shelley laughed softly. "Well, it's true. He saved her life and he was gentle with her. That's two things we can be thankful to him for."

"If you think I'm gonna slap him on the back for trying to take my daughter's innocence you can forget it."

Shelley giggled. "First, he didn't try, Jeffy asked him to do it. It was Cam who decided she wasn't ready. Eric, it's gonna happen sometime."

"Not until she's married."

"It would be easier for us if she was older when she found this interest in her sexual being— "

Eric groaned.

Shelley giggled and went on. "But in Jeffy's special circumstance, attending college at the age of fifteen, it was bound to grab her interest earlier."

"I realize that, but she knows better."

"She's probably having a great inner battle."

"Her mind versus her body?"

"No, Eric, her intellectual mind craving knowledge versus her spiritual mind knowing the difference between right and wrong. And you, the big psychologist, would know that if you could step back a minute and be objective about your daughter growing up."

He rolled onto his back. Shelley followed, spoke in his ear.

"This could've been a lot worse. Don't forget a few weeks ago in that motel. Instead, this time she was with a boy close to her own age who genuinely likes her, respects her and was caring and gentle with her. Even if they'd gone through with it, I don't think you could ask for much more."

"What about sin? She was gonna willfully do something she knew she shouldn't do."

"That should tell you what a struggle it's been for her. And, remember, she didn't do it."

Eric sighed. "It's not just me, you know. Her brothers were ready to take the kid out somewhere and tear him apart."

"Her brothers take their lead from you."

"Don't sell them short. They're not puppets."

"No, of course not, but they do have a protective instinct that matches yours. Please help them to understand why they should be thanking Cameron, not beating him to a pulp. Besides, you have to hand it to him, he didn't cower and he tried to maintain a modicum of manly pride. I'm sure he was mortified, yet he held it together."

Eric laughed softly. "That's true. Poor kid." He sighed. "Bottom line, we wouldn't have Jeffy if not for him. He'll have my undying gratitude for that. I'll accept the other."

"That's my great, big, adorable man," Shelley murmured, glancing over at the other bed with her sleeping daughter. "Too bad we're not alone. All this talk about losing one's virginity is getting to me."

"I'm a Ninjutsu master," Eric said. "I can be very quiet. The question is, can you?"

Shelley smiled. "I accept the challenge."

She barely got the words out of her mouth before Eric's mouth covered it. In the other bed, Jeffy snuggled down into her pillow and smiled.

~~~

"Hi."

Mickey had been intently scrubbing the carpet but looked up at the softly spoken word. Now that Jeffy was back safe, she'd been expecting to hear from him, but hadn't expected the sudden punch in the gut. That's exactly what she got, however, when she gazed up at the man, making her plan of breaking things off a little more difficult.

He looked tired. There were still a few bruises on his face from the meeting he'd had with her only surviving kidnapper. She'd since discovered the van driver was none other than her stepfather's right hand man, Kurt Wells. She'd known the voice was familiar, yet she hadn't been able to place it. Not very astute of her. Then again, she had been under a great deal of stress.

"Hi," she answered, dumping the scrub brush into the bucket. She nodded toward the floor. "I got up most of that nasty fingerprint stuff the crime scene people left, but there were some places on the carpet that needed some extra attention. It's what I get for choosing such a light color."

Jeff's brow furrowed at the ridiculous chit chat.

Wiping her hands on her jeans, she started to rise. Jeff moved forward to help her up.

"I got it," she said shortly.

He pulled his hand back slowly, wincing at the first nick aimed at his heart.

"So, you're still angry." It wasn't a question, nor was it stated like one.

She shook her head. "No. I'm not angry." Her eyes darted toward the living room. "Where's Jack and Nate?"

"I dismissed them for now."

"Oh. You have the authority to do that?"

Another well-placed shot. He leaned back, bracing himself against the wall. "As a matter of fact, I do. I'm the senior agent. What's going on, Mick?"

She shrugged, wishing he wouldn't use that term of endearment. "I'm not sure. Maybe we'd better sit down and talk."

He watched her walk past him, careful not to brush against him. This isn't what he'd pictured in his mind yesterday or last night. He'd pictured showing up and them throwing their arms around each other and after a long, slow, satisfying kiss, they would begin apologizing for getting so angry over nothing and they would promise each other it would never happen again. He certainly hadn't pictured the woman he'd fallen in love with being aloof, or cold, or acting like a stranger.

Following her into her living room, he quickly took in his surroundings. He seated himself on the off-white, contemporary sofa. Rather than joining him, Mickey sat in a nearby chair, upholstered in light pink and purple flowers. Lilies, he guessed, as he looked around, thinking how completely different her home was from the one she'd grown up in – the one he'd just come from. This one was very casual and utterly feminine. Her parent's home was formal, stuffy, cold.

"Nice place," he said.

She smiled stiffly. "Thanks. Small, but cozy."

Their eyes met. He gazed into the depths of those dark brown eyes and thought he saw regret. "Look, I–"

"Jeff, I–"

They began both sentences at the same time and stopped at the same time.

Jeff started again. "I handled it badly back in Los Angeles. I was in a hurry. I should've taken the time to help you understand why it was important you remain safe and secure."

"I understand."

Her words were short and cool and he wasn't sure at all that she understood. He grimaced.

"I was under orders, Mick, but I can't place the whole blame on Jason because I wanted you safe, too. I'm very close to the Kinos and I've known Jeffy since she was a kid and I needed to do everything I could to get her back safely. I couldn't do that while I was worried about you."

She nodded. "I understand that, Jeff. Really, I do."

"I've been over those few minutes in my mind a hundred times since then, thinking of better things to say, thinking I should've taken the time to make sure you understood."

"You didn't do anything wrong, Jeff. I was angry and frustrated and we were both worried about Jeffy."

"If that's so, then, what's this all about?"

She stood abruptly, wringing her hands. "Would you like something to drink?" She didn't wait for an answer, but hurried toward the kitchen.

Jeff rose and followed her, his heart stumbling, his arms aching to touch her, and his fear building. She was pulling a bottle of water from the fridge, offered it to him. When he declined, she uncapped the bottle and gulped from it. His gaze swept the room, the agent in him quickly registering the details– white appliances, white cabinets with apples painted on the fronts, white curtains with red ribbons woven through and pictures of more apples. Cute, quaint, utterly unpretentious. Enough of this.

He approached her, took the bottle from her hands and backed her up against the counter, his palms resting on either side, effectively trapping her.

"I'm still feeling it," he said softly. "I take it things have changed for you."

She looked down, stared at her own feet. The heat emanating from his body being so close seemed to engulf her. Drew her. She looked back up at his face. Her eyes lowered to his lips. She licked her own.

"Tell me you don't feel that," he said, as if reading her mind.

She swallowed, looked up and ignored his statement. "Being angry with you, Jeff, gave me the chance to step back for a second, to use my logical brain for a second. It gave me time to think. It made me realize that maybe rushing into our relationship like I did, was silly and crazy and irrational and made me think that maybe we should pause, take a breath. You know, like, take some time."

"Some time?" He could certainly understand her needing some time.

"Yes, and you know, maybe see other people and see how that goes."

He stepped back, forcing himself to draw breath into his lungs. Those last words were fatal to any relationship. And they hurt. Man they hurt. The whole thing had only lasted a few days. It had been like heaven. And he wasn't ready for it to be over. "Mickey, I'm not the overbearing, dominating lowlife I appear to be. I was in agent mode that day, speaking to you as your protector. I'm asking you to give our relationship another chance. I don't beg well, but I will, if that's what you want."

"No, of course I don't want that, Jeff, and I have a feeling you would never beg for anything anyway. You strike me as the kind of man who takes what's offered, but you would never beg." She shrugged. "I offered and you took."

He scowled. "That's not how it was and you know it. Geez, Mick, break it off with me, tell me to go to hell, but don't you dare make less of what we had, even if it was for only a few days."

She nodded. "Okay."

He waited. When she didn't say anything else his temper began to kick in. "Okay? That's it? Okay?"

He moved fast. Her eyes grew wide as he grabbed her and lowered his head. At the first touch of his lips, she thought to push him away, but instead grabbed his shirt in her fists and held on. He kissed her hard. His arms pulled her hard against his body. She moaned, melted.

"Oh! Oh, well, excuse me," Marissa said with a giggle.

Mickey broke the kiss and shoved Jeff away.

Frustrated, Jeff turned toward the young girl, thrust a hand through his hair, forced a smile. "You must be Marissa."

"I am. Who are you?"

He glanced at Mickey before he answered. "I'm Jeff Davis."

"Agent Davis," Mickey put in.

"Oh, yeah, you're the one."

"The one?"

"The one who found my sister and took care of her until she was able to come home." She grinned. "Looks like you take your job very seriously."

"Hush, Marissa," Mickey hissed.

The younger girl looked him up and down. "He's a hottie, Mick."

Mickey rolled her eyes.

"She didn't tell me she had something going with you," Marissa complained. "We spent half the night talking and she never even mentioned you."

Again Jeff's eyes slanted toward Mickey. More pain.

"Well, don't let me interrupt," Marissa said. "You just go back to whatever it is you were doing."

"Cute, Marissa. Actually, Jeff was just leaving."

Jeff drew in a breath, pushed the hurt aside. "Actually, I'm not leaving. At least, not alone. What I am doing is getting ready to escort the two of you down to the FBI field office. They need official statements from both of you."

"Cool. Cam, said they were gonna want to talk to me today. I'll go get ready. Nice to meet ya." Marissa turned and dashed up the steps, taking them two at a time.

Mickey pushed some hair back from her face. "I guess I need to get cleaned up."

He grabbed her wrist. "Wait. I just need to hear that what you felt for me, if even for those few days, was real. You loved me. You weren't lying. You weren't just saying the words out of some sick sense of gratitude."

"That's what I'm trying to tell you, Jeff. I don't know. I'm not sure."

"Hell," he mumbled, his voice thick with emotion. Running a hand over his face, he turned away, got himself under control. When he turned back, she had tears in her eyes. He forced himself to ignore them. "That kiss just now, are you telling me you didn't feel anything?"

"Of course I did. I'm not saying there isn't an attraction. I'm a woman. You're a gorgeous, hottie, as Marissa was so quick to point out. What woman wouldn't want to be kissed by you?"

For several moments he could only stare at her incredulously. Her words made him feel used and hurt more than he thought he could be. "Well, damn me," he finally muttered, as he stormed out of the kitchen. "I'll be waiting in the car." The sound of the front door slamming reverberated through the house.

~~~

While Mickey and Marissa were being interviewed, Ricky Kino, his brothers Mark and Joey Adams, Ameritech agents Jeff Davis, Jack Crandall and Nate Hawk, and several FBI agents and staff stood in a circle in the east lobby of the FBI field office. It seemed whenever Ricky Kino was around, people came out of the woodwork to get an opportunity to meet him and chat with him. The added bonus that two of them, Ricky and Joey, were Kino Challenge competitors made the crowd a little larger than usual. Add in the fact that Jeff was the famous agent from the big bust of the child trafficking ring five years earlier, and the rescuer of MacKenzie Daley, there was a lot of buzz and excitement with a lot of separate conversations going on.

The group stood chatting and joking with each other. Jeff was obviously in a mood and Ricky had taken notice. He made his way over to his friend.

"Jeff."

Jeff blew out a breath. "Rick," he responded shortly.

"Lookin' a little antsy there, my man."

Jeff only nodded.

"Wanna talk about it?"

"Nope, don't really wanna talk right now, Rick."

Jeff's words were spoken sharply and garnered the attention of the group at large. It seemed everyone quieted to hear the exchange.

"I get the idea you're presently a bit unhappy."

"Oh, ya get the idea do ya?"

"Come on, tell me how you feel. It always helps to get something off your chest."

Jeff glanced around at the audience and decided he just didn't care. "What I'm feelin' right now is I'd like to plant my fist in someone's face."

A murmur from the crowd.

Ricky smiled. "Someone in particular or will anyone do?"

Jeff only rolled his eyes and shoved his hands down into his pockets.

"I mean," Ricky continued, "there's a Kino studio a few blocks from here. If you wanna go a few rounds with me, I'm game."

If there had been anyone who wasn't listening before, they were definitely all ears now.

Jeff, stilled, looked Ricky over, finally shook his head. "I don't think so."

"Aw, come on, Jeff, I promise to go easy on ya."

A large murmur from the crowd. A snicker or two from Mark and Joey.

Jeff's eyes narrowed. Ricky was an experienced pro in the ring. The only fighting Jeff ever participated in was usually life and death. Not that Jeff didn't realize that Ricky was lethal in his own right. But the way Jeff was feeling right now, he'd probably accidentally snap Rick's neck or something. He smiled at Ricky. "I appreciate that, but out of deference to Bree, I respectively decline."

"What does my wife have to do with it?"

"I don't want Bree to have to plan your funeral."

A lot more snickers and several "Oh-ho's."

Ricky laughed too. "I'll take my chances, if it would help you out."

"Really don't want to fight you, Rick."

Ricky put his arm around his friend's shoulders. "Well then, at least let me buy you a drink."

Jeff nodded. "Now you're talking. But I'm on watch."

"I can take Marissa and MacKenzie back home to change and escort them to the restaurant where their having dinner with Grandmaster Kino," Nate volunteered.

"Good man, Nate," Ricky said. "Let's do this."

~~~

Ricky Kino motioned at the waitress and she came hurrying over, all smiles.

"Yes sweetheart," she said in a sultry voice. "What can I get you?"

"My good friend here would like another drink. Wild Turkey, on the rocks." Ricky looked around at the others at the table. "Anyone else? It's on me," he said.

"Give me a Jack and coke," Mark said.

"Long Island Iced tea," Joey added.

"Bud Light," Jack said.

"And what about you, Mr. Kino," the waitress purred.

"I'll stick with my Perrier for now, thanks."

All five men watched her walk away.

"What about you, Mr. Kino," Joey mocked. "How do you deal with that crap, Rick?"

He shrugged. "Been dealing for a long time now. It's not like you don't get the same thing. Ever since you started fighting in the Kino Challenge, you're havin' to beat 'em off with a stick."

"That's not what I see," Mark said. "He's not fightin' it. He's turned into a regular playboy."

"Bull," Joey answered. "I just don't know how to get rid of them without hurting their feelings."

"Mostly, I just ignore them," Ricky offered.

"With my sister for a wife, that would be the healthy thing to do," Mark laughed.

Ricky grinned. "Absolutely."

"I can't believe she didn't insist you go to the dinner with her." Jack said.

"Bree thought it might get interesting so she elected to go that route. I, on the other hand, needed a little bit of down time. She's cool with that."

"Who all is at the dinner?" Jack asked.

"Well, there's Dad and Shelley, Bree and the kids, little Joey, Jeffy and her new boyfriend Cameron Wallace and his parents. Then there's Marion Daley and Mickey and Marissa and their housekeeper Dora Suarez."

Jeff looked up at the mention of Mickey's name.

Ricky rested a hand on his shoulder. "I know it's tough man. I think she'll come around."

"Women all suck," Joey muttered.

"Here, here," they all said in deference to Jeff's feelings, regardless of how they actually thought about the subject of women.

Jeff smiled briefly. "Thanks guys."

"You need to bash women, we're just the ones to do it for you," Jack said, slapping Jeff's back.

The waitress returned with their drinks. Jeff lifted his glass and took a large swallow.

"I only wanted her to stay safe, you know? Just needed her to stay safe."

"Bree and I had it out once a long time ago about me trying to protect her. I gave her a little lesson in how easy it would be for a man to take her down. That was right before she drugged you, Jeff my man and snuck off to do her thing with the enemy. Obviously my demonstration went right by her. I almost lost her that day." He shook his head. "Like you said, I was only trying to protect her."

Jeff tipped his glass up and finished it. Motioned for another. The waitress delivered it in only a few seconds.

The bar they'd chosen was dark and dank and filled to capacity. Music blared and voices rose from the half dozen or so pool tables on the far side of the room.

Jeff glanced over.

"Wanna go shoot a few rounds?" Ricky asked him, thinking to distract him from his misery.

"I'm game."

The party moved their operation to surround the only empty table. Sticks chosen, balls racked, Jeff broke with a vengeance.

They played several games, Jeff getting more and more inebriated with each one. The guys kept him happy, though, laughing and cajoling. They were minding their own business, so they were pretty surprised when a few guys began to argue with them, accusing them of using more room than they required.

Ricky shook his head. "Sorry, man. Didn't realize we were hogging the space. We'll move over."

"So, then, you're not as tough as they make you out to be in the flicks, huh?"

"Uh oh," Mark murmured.

Ricky shrugged. "Naw, that's just movie magic. However, I'm every bit as tough as I look in the Kino Challenges."

Usually no one had the nerve to pick a fight with Ricky, especially since the Kino Challenge had shown just how lethal Ricky could be.

"Rick?" Mark said. "Let it go, okay?"

Ricky grinned at his brother. "I'm good, Mark. I got no problem, right guys?" he asked, directing his question to the three big guys shooting pool at the next table.

"You might not have a problem, but I got one with you. You think just cuz you're some big movie star you get special treatment? You come in here like some big shot, spending the big bucks, flirting with the waitresses."

"Flirting? No man, you got that wrong. I'm a happily married man. Really. I don't want any trouble."

The three men all smiled, stood toe to toe.

Jack muttered a curse.

"Well, you found trouble pretty boy."

Ricky sighed. "Look, perhaps you guys should rethink this. I don't want anyone to get hurt. And you guys are outnumbered. And we're all trained fighters here."

"Trained like that Kung Fu crap?"

"Trained like Special Forces kill your ass crap," Jeff said loudly, slurring his speech badly.

"Shut up, Jeff," Joey ordered.

Suddenly they had the interest of the other four pool tables. A few more men came to stand with the original three instigators.

"Was that a threat?" one of them asked. "Cuz it sounded like a threat."

"No," Mark said quickly. "No, that was not a threat. Listen guys, we have no problem here. We're just gonna play our game and move on."

A few more arrived, and few more and a few more. Suddenly, instead of three men standing toe to toe, there were about twenty.

Mark moved to play his turn. One of the guys knocked his stick just as he hit the ball.

Ricky shook his head, held his hand up. "Okay, really now, that was uncalled for. I guess I'd better warn you, I trained him and one of the things I taught him was to avoid a fight at all costs, which is why he didn't just take your head and shove it up your butt. Now, I have to say, the past twenty-four hours for me have been hell, and I'm right on the edge of just not caring anymore." He paused a moment. "And by the way," Ricky added with a smile, "*that–* was a threat."

"And here we go," Joey muttered.

"Oh, yeah," Jeff said, clapping his hands together.

"If we don't count Jeff," Ricky began, "we'll each need to take five."

"You can freaking count me, bro," Jeff snarled. "I'm not too far gone."

"Okay, then four apiece. Anybody can't handle that?" Ricky asked. The speech was made to hopefully make the other men think twice. It didn't work.

The bar erupted.

Chapter Eleven

"It's enough I had to pull my own brother away from his law practice to fly up here and bail your butts out of jail, but the harm done to the reputation of my company is ineluctable and for that there is gonna be hell to pay," Jason said, his voice quiet and controlled. Always a bad sign.

"To have three of my agents, top agents, in a bar brawl, the day after you were involved in the arrest of a US Senator gives us little credibility."

"It was my fault, sir," Jeff said.

Jason looked him over. "Why was it your fault, Agent Davis?"

"I was uh, feeling sorry for myself. I wanted to go out and get drunk. Went out specifically for that purpose."

"And you picked a fight?"

"Well, no sir, but I certainly didn't help avoid it. Actually, to be honest, I wanted a fight. Needed one."

Jason paced the room quietly. Stopped, zeroed in on Jeff's battered face. "This about the girl?"

Jeff's head lowered.

"Next time you need a fight you come see me. I'll be happy to beat the crap out of you." He whipped his head around to face Ricky. "What are you grinning at? The same goes for you, Ricky boy, and you know I can do some damage."

"Sorry," Ricky said, still smiling, not bothering to argue the point. Jason was nine years his senior and like an uncle to Rick. They'd both been trained by Ricky's father. Whichever way it went, it would be a battle.

Jason eyed the group. "I don't buy this all being Jeff's fault. You could've walked away and not one of you did because you were all itching to show off your gonads. Someone gets hurt bad, it changes everything. Suddenly, your life and the lives of those you love are on the line. Ricky you should know that. If you'll recall a few years ago you faced felony charges for letting yourself get carried away. Mark, you have a kid who looks up to you. Ricky, you have two. Jeff, what would your parents say? Get your acts straight."

He paced away, abruptly turned to Eric. "Anything you'd like to add Grandmaster Kino?"

Eric's calm gaze took in the bunch. He drew a breath. His words were spoken slowly and calmly. "This shouldn't have happened for several reasons, but mostly out of respect for Jason. You owe him an apology for that. He gives his all for you and for the world renowned company he runs. The admiration and respect the world has for Ameritech Security has been built on Jason's back and on the blood of other agents. That respect is what allows him to pay you extraordinary salaries. Yeah, I'd say you owe him big time."

Eric gestured toward Justin Lee, Jason's brother and the family attorney. "And you owe Justin just as much, though I'm sure his fee will be stiff enough to teach you a lesson of sorts. Now, as far as the fight itself, I'm gonna assume, based on your injuries, that you were careful not to hurt anyone?"

Jason's eyes met Eric's. "I hadn't thought of that."

Eric nodded. "You were upset. It's understandable. I can't imagine that Ricky would let anyone punch him in the eye, or even let anyone get close enough to punch him in the eye if he wasn't trying to be very careful not to hurt the guy. I don't know Jack as well, but I think I can say the same for Mark about his strained shoulder, or Joey and his split lip. Jeff's face is pretty battered and I'm thinking, under normal circumstances, sober circumstances, he would've killed the man who did that, and there were no deaths reported, so I assume he too was trying not to hurt anyone." He eyed the five men. "I suggest next time you try just as hard to walk out of the bar."

"But—"

"Period." Eric said, effectively ending the conversation.

"Okay, then," Jason said, blowing out a breath. "Ricky, Mark, Eric, I guess I'll see you back in L.A. Jack, Nate is waiting at Mackenzie Daley's home to be relieved. Joey, I'd like you to arrange transportation for those needing to get home and then I need you back at headquarters ASAP since I'll be detained here. Jeff, you and I have a meeting with the Feds. Let's move."

Eric joined Justin and Jason as the meeting broke up.

"Eric," Jason began, "I meant to ask how your little dinner went last night with Jeffy's new, uh,— "

"Yeah, just what do you call him? Her boyfriend?" Eric asked, shaking his head.

Justin smiled at his friend. "Some guys would call him lucky."

Jason snorted in laughter as Eric's eyes narrowed. "Lucky to be alive is, I'm sure, what Justin meant," Jason added.

"That he is," Eric stated.

"Seriously, Eric, what's your take on him?"

He shrugged. "I have to admit, he seems like a good kid. Smart, strong, athletic, with a good head on his shoulders. Mature, kind, and as Shelley has pointed out to me more than once— gentle."

The brothers both pressed their lips together to keep from laughing.

"It's a shame though, his parents don't seem to appreciate the good young man he is. Oh, they pretended to be proud that their son saved the day, but it was all show. They never even looked at him. Literally, I watched. There was no eye contact between the Wallaces and Cameron. From what I can gather on a first meeting, his father is some big real estate guru, rolling in dough and the dough is what's important. His mother is quite the socialite. As long as Cameron stays out of their way, they have no problem with him. They'll even ride his glory bus with him for a while.

"I asked Mr. Wallace what Cameron intended to study in college and the man had no idea. It's sad really, that his parents aren't interested, because he *is* a good kid. And I owe that kid everything right now and so I'll step in and see if I can mentor him a bit. He plays high school football, so I've asked Mark to speak with him also. I won't let him fall through the cracks."

"So are you gonna let him see Jeffy?"

Eric heaved a giant sigh. "Good question." He shook his head. "Never thought I'd feel so protective, but if Jeffy wants to see him, I'll pretty much have to allow it. Poor girl, she's walking this fine line between being a kid and an adult. It's hard for her."

"Eric, you have to know, now that she's decided she wants a taste of what sex has to offer, well, you know– what I mean to say is, every time they get together they're gonna want to, uh, go a little further."

Eric nodded. "You're right. That's exactly what they'll want. What did you want after the first time you dabbled in sex?"

"I wanted to do it again. And again. And again."

"All right already."

"Genius or not, she's only fifteen. You can restrict her," Jason said.

"Spoken like the father of a teenage daughter," Eric laughed. "But you know circumstances are different for Jeffy. I'll have to speak with my wife about this, of course, figure out the best course of action. I have a feeling we're gonna have a long talk with Jeffy about God's will for her, responsibility coming with privileges and," he paused, "and protection."

Justin laughed. "Hard to get that word out of your mouth?"

"Yeah, wait until you have a daughter."

"I do have one! Don't you know I live vicariously through you."

"Eric, maybe you can talk to her about how she speaks with Kimmie from here on out," Jason said. "Because I don't want my daughter following in Jeffy's footsteps, no offense."

"None taken. Yes, that will be one more issue we'll have to cover with her."

"Next subject, quickly, because I have to get to that meeting, your take on Marion Daley?" Jason asked.

"Mickey's mother is a zombie, a robot, and she doesn't really believe her husband tried to have Mickey killed. In order to prove her faith she's willing to alienate both her daughters. Another shame, as far as parenting goes. The housekeeper, she's been with them almost from the beginning. Her eyes are wide open, but she's not talking. Daley has threatened her in some way. I'm almost sure of it. This man has been able to get away with too much for too long and usually that's because the people that work for him are either extremely loyal, or afraid to step forward. I'm leaning toward the latter."

Jason nodded thoughtfully.

"Marissa is all about being her big sister's champion and she's a great kid," Eric continued. "Mickey, on the other hand, is a mess."

"A mess?"

"Her hands shake. She's nervous. Her eyes tear up. I see her force control over it, but I'm telling you, the poor girl is suffering. She feels totally alone. You know what? I just decided I'm gonna see if she wants to talk a little before I leave Seattle. Maybe I can recommend her to a professional in the area."

"She dumped Jeff."

"Defense mechanism."

"You mean, dump him before he can dump her?"

"Sure. Everyone she's depended on in her life, her father, her mother, her stepfather, they have all betrayed her in the worst way. They've either thrown her to the wolves or they are the wolf. She's not gonna let that happen again."

"I am a rock and a rock feels no pain?"

"Exactly."

Jason nodded his head. "You're pretty good, Master Kino."

Eric smiled. "That's Grandmaster, and don't you forget it."

Both Jason and Justin smiled and bowed. "Yes, sensei."

"I'll speak with you later," Jason said. "I have to get to that meeting." He shook Eric's hand, turned to Justin. "Thank you, brother, for taking time to fly up here and get those bozos out of jail."

"Like Eric said, my fee will make it worthwhile. Glad to help."

Jason shook both men's hands and took his leave. He headed out of the police station. Jeff leaned against the wall just outside the building, waiting for his boss. Jason joined him, noticed Jeff's unhappy demeanor and placed a hand on Jeff's shoulder in consolation. Jeff winced.

"That sore, huh?"

"Pretty bad."

"Let's get down to the Federal building and I'll fill you in on my conversation with Eric. Maybe it'll cheer you up."

Jeff glanced over at him. "Why, you got a miracle cure? Some Chinese herbal tea maybe?"

"Something better than that."

Shrugging, Jeff limped beside Jason as they left the building.

~~~

Marissa wrapped her arms tightly around Jeffy. "Ugh, I'm gonna miss you so much. I know I just met you, but it feels as if I've known you forever."

Jeffy hugged her back. "I know, it does for me too. I promise we'll keep in touch, and after my three months of prison time locked in my room with no amenities, I'll come and visit, and maybe you guys can come and visit me!"

"I'd like that," Cameron said from where he stood near a tree in the hotel courtyard.

Marissa turned and smiled at him. "Oh, Cam, don't be so sad. You'll see her again."

"Yeah, I know. The thing is, I can't stand to be away from her for even a few hours. What the heck did you do to me, Jeffy?"

She crossed the small courtyard, took his hands. "I know, Cam. I feel the exact same way. I don't want to leave you."

"You love birds are so cute," Marissa sighed.

Cameron smiled at his friend.

"I'm going to wander over to the other side for a minute so you two can say goodbye," Marissa said.

"Thanks, Rissa. You're a good friend," Cameron said.

He took Jeffy's hand, kissed it. "I'm gonna miss you, June Flower Kino."

"Me too, Cam. This is so hard. Please, just hold me a minute."

He pulled her close and held her tight against his chest.

"Did I ever say 'thanks' for saving my life?"

"Not straight out to me, but I'd say you keeping your Dad from killing me was thanks enough. I've been giving thanks myself, that Marissa called me, that I was there."

"God did that."

"God?"

"There are no coincidences. You were meant to be there."

Cameron considered her words, nodded his head. "Cool. All I know is, I can't imagine the world without you in it."

"My mom said the exact same words." She sighed. "Cam?"

"Yes?"

"I know, with us living in different states and being so young, I mean, I know you're gonna have more girlfriends, but somehow, I'm hoping that what we've shared has been special to you, because it was really special to me. I don't intend to overwhelm you, I mean, I know that with me being female, psychologically, I see things differently than you. I'm more prone to an emotional attachment once I've given myself to a mate, not that we went to fruition with it, still I offered myself completely, but don't let that scare you away because I promise that me being aware of that will keep me on a more level field. What I'm trying to say is, I'm hoping that what we shared has been special for you, because I don't know—"

"Jeffy." He took her face in his hands. "It has been special. It's been the most important thing that's ever happened to me in my life." He lowered his head and kissed her.

Jeffy melted against him.

Eric had just arrived back at the hotel and stepped into the elevator when he glanced out the courtyard doors and saw his daughter wrapped around the young man who'd saved her life. He caught the closing door and stepped back out, headed for the courtyard. Then, he stopped himself, drew several deep breaths. Running a hand through his thick, black hair, which he was sure now had several more streaks of gray then it did yesterday, he tried hard to get control.

He watched for a few more seconds. The kiss ended. The young man raised her chin and used his thumbs to wipe tears from his daughter's cheeks. Praying for guidance, Eric turned and headed back to the elevator.

~~~

"He's out as of about an hour ago," Agent Dodge said. "There's probably going to be a Congressional hearing called. It's not going to be pretty for him."

"I don't want him to have any access to Mickey," Jeff said.

"That goes without saying. We'll move her to a safe house."

Jeff shook his head. "She'll go crazy with that."

"Either way," Jason began, addressing Agent Dodge, "you have to pay agents to be with her. Ameritech will be happy to contract out to take care of that."

Special Agent Dodge nodded. "I'm sure I can get that approved, given your reputation." He shrugged. "Barring last night's activities," he added.

"Point made," Jason said, never flinching as he took his medicine.

"What about the arms deal?" Jeff asked.

"Nothing. We have nothing. Nothing on his computers. No bank accounts. Not a trace of information anywhere."

"There's gotta be something somewhere. The deal is real. They were scared that Mickey would talk and their little deal wouldn't happen. The irony is, she doesn't know anything about an arms deal. No more than we know anyway. The dead guy, Butch, was the first to mention it to her. My little meeting with them confirmed it for me. We're talking eighty million dollars. That's got to be a hell of a lot of weaponry or even a jet or artillery. I've ID'd Kurt Wells as the one running things for Daley. He's definitely the one who beat the crap out of me in Reno. You can't get anything out of him?"

"He's not ready to roll over yet."

"Daley has something on every one who works for him. He believes it keeps them loyal," Jason said. "Look to their families, make them safe, someone will talk."

"How do you know this?" Agent Stevens asked.

"I consulted with an expert this morning. That's his opinion. I think he has something."

"We'll check it out," Dodge said.

"So what has Daley been charged with?" Jeff asked.

"Accessory to kidnapping."

"That's it? Who's kidnapping?"

"June Flower Kino."

"What about Mickey?"

"Hearsay. The only thing we have linking Daley to the kidnapping of his stepdaughter is what she says was told to her by one of the dead guys."

"You believe her, right?"

"Sure, but there's no one to corroborate her story. The guy is dead."

"Maybe he told someone else. His family. Girlfriend. Someone."

"We're looking into all that."

"Daley's man, Wells, drove the van that kidnapped her," Jeff said.

"Mackenzie never saw him and couldn't immediately identify his voice."

"He was definitely driving the van when I ran into him on the road."

"It'll help to build a case, but by itself is only circumstantial. You didn't see him committing a crime."

"He sure as heck made a deal with me to keep Mickey silent until after the arms deal."

"Thanks to you and Mr. Lee that will add a great deal of weight to our case against Wells and since he's on the Senator's payroll it will go against him too. We're building slowly. We will eventually nail Daley."

"Mickey can tell you how badly she was treated as a child. Her loving stepfather beat her constantly. It even came very close to sexual abuse."

Agent Dodge nodded. "Yes and her sister has corroborated much of the abuse. That will destroy his political career, but probably won't put him behind bars."

Jeff blew out a breath, his frustration mounting. "So, if Jeffy hadn't come up here and gotten herself mixed up with that idiot, you'd have nothing on the Senator."

"Pretty much. We'd be waiting for this arms deal to happen."

"Jeffy's got him good though."

"He locked her in a room. Arranged for his man to take her away in the car. Jeffy says he threatened her, but—"

"Threatened her? What did he say?" Jeff asked.

"Two words. 'You're dead.' Still, she didn't actually hear any orders to terminate between Daley and Wells, even though you and I both know Kurt Wells didn't drag her into the mountains for a picnic. He intended to kill her. Daley claims Wells came up with that plan on his own. We're using that to try to get Wells to turn, yet so far his loyalty to the guy is complete. And Wells insists he wasn't gonna kill the girl. He was just having some fun."

"Hell."

"Yeah. It comes down to the word of two kids, June Flower Kino and Cameron Wallace. One who'd lied to her parents and snuck up to Seattle. The other is fairly credible."

Jason shook his head. Even though he hadn't mentioned it, Jason was sure Eric realized his daughter's credibility was in question. The damage was done and only time would erase that. But it is painful for a member of the Kino clan to be labeled as not credible.

"Okay," Jason said. "So, why did Daley panic when he thought Jeffy had been in his office? What does he think she discovered?"

"Of course he denies being upset about anything except the fact that some kid broke into his personal space, yet obviously, he thought she was some sort of threat. He thought she'd discovered something that he didn't want discovered. And, don't forget, he thought she was some kid off the street Marissa had befriended," Agent Stevens added.

"So when he gave the execution order, he thought she'd never be missed," Jason said.

"Surprise, surprise," Jeff muttered. "Wait, back up. He says he wasn't upset? He was so angry Marissa Daley has a fat lip from the good Senator knocking her out of the room."

Dodge nodded. "We have her statement and took pictures yesterday."

Jason sighed. "So really, as of right now, we have very little to go on. He'll get a slap on the wrist, lose his election and move on, unless we can be there when the arms deal takes place and are able to pin him to it. According to what was disclosed to Agent Davis, we don't have long before that goes down."

"That would be the long and short of it," Dodge answered. "Unless we can get Wells to turn on him, which is my strongest hope. We do have the two guys we arrested from your office, Jason. They're willing to spill their guts. Problem is, they know very little. Still, they'll add a little more credibility to our case. It may take a while, but we will build a case against Senator Daley. Jason, if you can spare Jeff, I'd like him to work with us on this since he's been involved up to his elbows."

Jason nodded. "He's all yours."

The meeting adjourned and Jeff grimaced as he stood, stretching his sore muscles. He shook hands with the others in the room and stepped out the door. Jack was there. Jeff approached him, brow furrowed. "I thought you were with Mickey."

"Feds wanted to have another go at her." He nodded down the hall. Mickey sat on a padded bench in the corridor. Her face lifted toward him, her eyes opened wide. She rose and quickly approached, reaching up to gently touch his face.

"Jeff? Look at your face!"

He shrugged away her concern. "No big deal."

"No big deal? It looks horrible. You must be in pain."

"Yeah."

She sighed when she realized he wasn't speaking of the physical. "Jack told me about the fight and you guys getting arrested. I heard you were pretty banged up, but I didn't realize, I mean, it looks worse than I pictured it."

If it hadn't been for what Jason told him earlier, her gentle, caring tone would've pissed him off. Now, it made him realize that she truly did care about him. She wasn't putting on an act. She was terrified of being abandoned again by someone she depends on.

He smiled at her. "It looks worse than it is. I'm okay."

She looked down as if she just realized she'd shown too much of her hand. He touched her chin. "How are you holding up?"

Her eyes met his. "I'm okay. They wanted to talk to me again. I hope that means something good, like they're gonna be able to throw the book at him."

Jeff shook his head. "Look, Mick, I don't want you to get your hopes up just to have them crushed. I just came from a meeting. They don't have a lot on him. Not concrete evidence."

"Are you kidding me? He kidnapped me?"

"Three guys kidnapped you. He wasn't one of them."

"But Butch said—"

"Unfortunately, Butch isn't here to testify."

"But, he tried to kill Jeffy."

"Jeffy broke into his home and he had her escorted off the property."

"He told Kurt to kill her."

"An assumption on our part. Jeffy never heard what Daley told Kurt. Daley says he only had Kurt escort her home."

"In the trunk of a car."

"One of the few valid points and incriminating, yet not on its own."

"But he didn't escort her home, did he? He took her out to kill her."

"Kurt says he was just trying to scare her and that it was his own idea. Luckily, Cameron saw him do three things. Take her out of the trunk, remove her clothes and drug her, so charges against him should stick. Daley loses his right hand man, but that's about all."

Her chin quivered, she covered her mouth with her hands, her eyes wide with fear. "My God, he's gonna win, isn't he? He's gonna win."

Jeff caught her around the waist as she sunk against him. "Okay now, he won't win. We just have to build a better case. The feds are committed to doing just that."

"What about Kurt and those guys meeting with you in that warehouse? Will anything come of that?"

"When Jeffy disappeared the feds threw caution to the wind and raided Daley's house, confiscating everything, certain they'd find what they needed. Instead, they found nothing. It was a mistake. They blew my cover as an agent gone bad, they blew your cover as my hostage. We'll have to start over."

"But Talmond still believes I know something about an arms deal, right?"

"I'm guessing, yes."

"And he thinks I know something just because he found me in his office and he also seemed to think that same thing about Jeffy just because she was in his office. Why, if there was nothing incriminating?"

"Good question. We must be missing something. There must be something and we'll find it eventually. In the mean time, we keep you safe, because he believes you know something."

"So you're saying you think he might come after me?"

Her voice shook, her hands trembled. Jeff worried she might go into one of her panic attacks. He reached out, took her hands, pressed them between his own. "Please don't worry, Mick. An Ameritech agent will be with you at all times. We're considering moving you to a safe house. At least until this is all over."

She shook her head. "Can't you just have someone stay with me at my house? I mean, I can't go away now, I have Marissa."

"What do you mean? You intend to have her stay with you?"

"Yes. I called an attorney this morning. She's started working on it. She feels like we can get immediate temporary custody under the circumstances."

Jeff drew a deep breath, blew it out. "Okay, I'll talk to Jason. I don't want to mess up your getting custody of your sister."

"Thank you," Mickey said softly.

"So, where is Marissa right now?"

"Cam picked her up and took her to say goodbye to Jeffy at the hotel."

Agent Dodge approached. "Ms. Daley? Will you come in now?"

Jeff smiled down at her. "Try to relax and tell them everything you can think of, even if it doesn't seem important to you."

Mickey nodded. "I will."

"Jack will be right here when you come out."

"Where will you be?"

"I have some detective work to do."

Mickey frowned. "Be careful."

He smiled at the sincerity in her voice. "I will."

~~~

"Senator?" a female reporter asked. "Would you like to comment on your situation? What do you have to say about the allegation that you were behind the kidnapping of your daughter?"

Talmond turned from his limo and smiled sweetly at her. "Actually, I will make a statement." He paused, straightening his tie and smoothing his hair as the other networks positioned themselves.

"It's unfortunate that my daughter's mental illness has to come to light in this way. It appears she's been free of the kidnappers for over a week now and has been in hiding. She has delusions that I was behind the kidnapping. I can only vehemently deny the allegations. Mackenzie and her mother and I have tried to handle her mental illness privately. We've done the best we could. She's always had a vivid and morbid imagination, hence her writing of her crime novels. I'm not a bit surprised by its authenticity because these things are very real in her mind."

"Well, sir, she certainly didn't imagine the two dead guys in the cabin where she was held."

Talmond shook his head sadly. "Whoever they were, I'm sure they had no idea when they kidnapped her that she would be capable of the violence she demonstrated. Mackenzie is my daughter, and no matter what she does or what she says, her mother and I love her and we will stand behind her and get her the help she needs. The fact that she wants to blame me is not surprising. Somehow, in her mind, she believes I wasn't there for her when she needed me most. And I suppose I wasn't." He stopped to wipe at an invisible tear. "I'm sorry, that's all I have for now."

~~~

"Our daughter is down in the hotel courtyard cuddled up to Cameron Wallace," Eric said the moment he walked into the hotel suite.

"She's saying goodbye."

"Fine, but that's it. From now on, I don't want her out of our sight until all this is over."

"It's not over?"

"Not until Senator Daley and Kurt Wells are permanently behind bars. Until then, they have power to move and manipulate people. Someone might be stupid enough to try to shut Jeffy up. Or be unbalanced enough to hurt her out of vengeance. You and I of all people know that the human mind is completely capable of revenge."

Shelley nodded as she pulled out her cell phone and called her youngest daughter.

"Yes, Mom?" Jeffy answered.

"Where are you now?"

"In the courtyard with Cam and Rissa."

"Have Cameron walk you up to our room please."

"Now?"

"I'm afraid so. Play time is over."

"Yes ma'am. We're on our way," Jeffy said, resigned to her fate.

At the same time Eric called Joey.

"Yes sir," Joey said.

"How long until our flight?"

"A little over an hour."

"Can we delay it?"

"Yes sir, it's your call, of course."

"I want a chance to speak with Mickey once more before we leave and I have one more errand I need to run."

"An errand? Anything I can do?"

"No, something I need to take care of myself."

"May I ask what?"

"No you may not. So any problem delaying our flight?"

"No problem, I'll contact the pilot."

Eric hung up and turned as Jeffy came through the doors with her new friends.

"Cameron," Eric said, extending his hand.

"Sir," Cam nodded nervously as he shook hands with the stern-faced man.

"Marissa, nice to see you again."

"Thanks, Mr. Kino."

"Cameron, our flight will be delayed a little while and I'm gonna drive over to speak with Mickey. Why don't you stay here to keep Jeffy company and I'll take Marissa home. Would that be okay with you, Marissa?"

"Sure," Marissa said, stepping forward and hugging Jeffy once more. "I'll keep in touch. You're A-number one on my list, Jeffy." She turned and said goodbye to Shelley and left with Eric after he kissed his wife.

Marissa watched the man who was Ricky Kino's father, as he drove, deciding the movie star looked almost exactly like his dad. "Mr. Kino?"

He smiled over at her. "Yes?"

"What do you think is gonna happen to my father?"

Eric sighed. "It's hard to tell, sweetheart. Do you think he's done anything wrong?"

"I know he has. Mickey wouldn't lie."

"What if the man who told her that your dad was involved was lying to Mickey."

"What reason would he have to do that?"

Eric's brows rose. "That's very astute of you. I can see why Jeffy likes you so much."

Marissa smiled at the compliment then went back to her questioning. "He told her the truth because he knew she was gonna die. And Mickey believed him because she knows my father hates her. He always has. He's made her life hell."

"Really? Did you tell this to the FBI when they spoke with you?"

"Yes. I told them everything I could think of."

"Would you mind telling me what you told them?"

"Sure, if you think it would help."

She started from the very first memory she had of Mickey, of her father and mother, even of their housekeeper. Eric asked probing questions and she answered them the best she could. When they arrived at Mickey's home, they stayed in the car until their conversation concluded.

"And then, I knew my father was pissed, oh, sorry, I mean, angry, because he was staring at the desk, his eyes were all bugged out and his face was red."

"He was staring at the desk? Anything in particular?"

"At the computer, I think."

"Jeffy had gotten into his PC?"

"No, I don't think so. It wasn't on."

"I thought he was angry because she'd accessed his files on his computer."

"He was, but it wasn't his PC. It was his laptop."

"Oh, I must've misunderstood," he said.

"Yeah, he gets real mad if anyone touches his laptop. He's weird that way. He's always throwing them away and getting new ones."

"That's interesting."

"Ya think? I used to think he was just, you know, OCD, but now, I just hate him. Everything about him. I even hate that he was so nice to me. I think I would rather him have beat me too. It's like he was nice to me in a sort of, 'in your face' to Mick, like he used me to be cruel to her. I'm surprised Mickey doesn't hate me."

"I don't think anyone could hate you, Marissa. Least of all, your sister, whom I'm sure was grateful that you didn't have to face what she did. Come on, let's go in."

~~~

"Where's my daughter?" Talmond demanded the moment he walked in the door of his home.

"She's gone to—"

"Gone where?"

"She's staying with Mickey."

He grabbed his wife by the front of her expensive silk blouse and pulled her close. "Are you out of your mind letting her go over there? You get on the phone or you take Dora and you get over there and bring my daughter home."

"Dora's gone home for the evening, but, Marissa won't come home, Talmond."

"What do you mean, she won't come? She has no choice."

"Actually, she does. Mickey got a temporary court order to allow Marissa to stay with her."

The news floored him. He didn't move for several seconds as his fingers dug into Marion's arms. "That whore," he finally said, his eyes boring into his wife's blank stare. "That kid of yours has been a thorn in my side from the day I met you." He shook his head as he thought back. "It was such a perfect setup. The instant family. Cute kid.

Beautiful wife. Perfect for my political aspirations. I could train the wife, but apparently, not the kid." He shook her. "And we would've only had that one troublemaker if you hadn't gotten pregnant."

Marion blinked up at her husband, her brow furrowed as his words made their way through her brain. "Talmond, you know you love Marissa."

"As it turns out, she's just like all the other females I've ever known. And you can believe me when I say she's gonna regret crossing me and taking sides with that slut daughter of yours. Mackenzie always was an uncontrollable little brat."

"She wasn't a brat, Talmond. She was a lot like her father, though. Headstrong. Independent."

Talmond moved very close to his wife. "Don't you dare defend her to me. Do you know what she's saying about me to the world? Do you?"

"Y-yes."

"She's trying to destroy me. Well, we'll just see who wins, won't we?"

~~~

Jack moved aside and opened the door.

"Hi," Mickey said as Marissa and Eric came through the door. "I was wondering if you were ever coming in."

"We were talking," Marissa explained. "Mr. Kino brought me home because he wanted to talk to you before he left." She started up the stairs, stopped, turned. "Um, excuse me, I was gonna call some friends. You don't mind do you?"

Mickey smiled after her sister. "Of course not. Go on." She turned to Eric. "Well, can I get you something to eat or drink? Jack and I just got home a few minutes ago and were just having some sandwiches."

Eric shook Jack's hand. "No, I'm fine. You two go ahead and eat though." He glanced into the kitchen which was just to the right of the entrance foyer. It was a long, narrow space, a galley kitchen that opened up into a small dining room on the other side.

Jack moved into the kitchen and began piling sandwiches onto a plate. "I'll make myself scarce," he said. He threw a mound of chips on top of one of his sandwiches, grabbed a bottle of water, and headed toward the living room which was at the back of the house.

Eric smiled when Jack flipped on the TV. Now he could speak to Mickey in the dining room without being overheard.

Eric gestured toward the remaining sandwiches. "You need to eat."

Mickey nodded, placed a sandwich on a small plate. Grabbed a soda.

"Let's sit in here," Eric suggested as he moved through the kitchen into the dining room.

Mickey followed him, took a seat at the table and waited for him to speak.

Eric smiled. "Eat. You need take care of yourself. You're under a lot of strain, and your physical body is using up the vitamins faster than usual. Especially the B's. Stress will do that."

Mickey grinned as she took a small bite of her sandwich. "Is there anything you don't know about?"

Eric picked up Mickey's soda, went back into the kitchen, rummaged through her refrigerator, poured her a glass of apple juice and brought it to her. "Sorry, didn't mean to come across as an arrogant know it all."

"Oh, no, I didn't mean that. I'm just really impressed by all your knowledge."

He shrugged. "I'm older. I've had a lot of time to learn things. I've studied nutrition, alternative healing and medicines, everything I could about the human body in order to help my students be the best they can be."

"And you became a psychologist for the same reason?"

"Yes. Being able to understand how our mind functions is helpful. My students must become one with themselves, bringing their physical selves together with their higher selves and with God. I strive to learn all I can in order to help them and myself to obtain the ultimate."

"Shelley is a lucky woman."

"I'm a lucky man, where she's concerned." He motioned at her plate. "Eat."

She smiled and obeyed. "You love her very much."

"Words cannot express."

"I can't imagine having someone love me like that."

"Yes you can," he said, neatly swinging the conversation in the direction he wanted.

"Excuse me?"

"Again, I apologize if I sound arrogant, but I think you know what I meant by that. Mickey, I wanted to speak to you about the trauma you're going through."

"I'm okay."

"I know you think you are, yet there are telltale signs that tell me you're suffering. Your hands shake, your voice quivers, your eyes tear up periodically, there are dark smudges under your eyes, your body is shrinking. I'm concerned for you."

She looked down at her plate. "I want to be angry with you right now."

"But?"

"But somehow, I can't find the energy to do it."

"I believe that makes my point for me."

The tears he'd spoken of welled and spilled over. "So, what am I supposed to do? It's not like I can keep from feeling the way I do."

"How do you feel, sweetie?"

She shrugged. "I don't know. I guess I feel alone." She stopped, waited for him to say something. When he didn't, she went on. "I feel dirty and disgusted with myself. I feel ashamed and maybe angry and very much alone."

Eric smiled, reached across the table and opened his palm. "Give me your hand."

Slowly, she placed her hand in his. He had the kindest smile. She watched as Eric closed his eyes, drew a deep breath and blew it out slowly. Mickey could swear that she felt a warm, tingling sensation move up her arm, across her shoulder and into her heart.

"The angry part is natural and healthy," Eric finally said. "And it will fade. Tell me about the dirty and ashamed."

She sniffed. "I killed a man."

"It was self-preservation."

"I know. I keep telling myself that, but I keep hearing that choking sound he made as he struggled to breathe." She winced at her own words and the tears spilled again. "I keep remembering how he struggled to try to get away from me, but I held him tight while I– oh, God forgive me." She clutched at her abdomen with her free hand.

Eric refused to let go of her other hand. He squeezed it gently. "It was self-preservation, Mickey. If you hadn't held onto him, he would've gotten away and then he would've killed you. Do not think for one moment that he would've had mercy on you. He intended to take your life and from what you described, he intended to use you first. You did the right thing. It was survival instinct and there is nothing wrong with what you did. You were strong and I'm proud of you. You did something not many have the strength to do."

"I don't even know how I had enough strength to hold him still."

"I do."

She looked up. "What? Are you saying God gave me strength?"

"He most assuredly did. In the Bible it says, 'For the Lord your God is the one who goes with you to fight for you against your enemies to give you victory.'"

She shook her head. "But isn't it also God who said, 'vengeance is mine'?"

"You weren't reaching for vengeance. You were fighting the enemy. God uses his warriors to help fight the enemy."

"I am hardly a warrior."

"You are in my book."

She shook her head as tears coursed down her cheeks. "What about Butch? I ended up not having to kill him, but I had intended to try. Even after he was so kind to me. After he saved me from Richard's rape attempt."

"Butch was kind to you because he felt guilty that he was about to take your life, but make no mistake, Mickey, he would've gone through with it."

"I'm not so sure. I mean, he kept saying the same thing you just did, but I think I'd convinced him to work with me to make it look like I'd gotten away."

"And then the other guy killed him. So if, as you say, Butch had decided to come to the light and do the right thing, the forces of darkness took him out. So, what happens to Butch is now between him and God. And our Father is loving and forgiving, so I'm not worried about Butch."

"Then you truly believe there is a God and a life after we leave here?"

"I don't believe. I know."

She nodded, contemplating what Butch was doing at this very minute. "You know, he told me that morning that we could work something out. I think he *had* decided to help me. I think it was because of his brother."

Eric sat up straighter. "His brother? Who's his brother?"

"He never mentioned a name, but he loves him. I could tell that."

"Did you tell the FBI this?"

"Actually, no. I hadn't thought about it until just now. I think I'm already suppressing memories."

"I'll speak with Jason, fill him in. They still don't know Butch's real identity. No family members have stepped forward to claim his body."

"What about Richard?"

"They found his family. They're from Iowa. They hadn't seen him in eight years. They had a small memorial service several days ago."

"Do they– do they know I killed their son?" she asked as the tears came again.

"They know what happened. I don't think they hold you responsible. Jason said they were horrified by what their son had done."

Mickey nodded her head. Eric squeezed her hand. "Now, let's tackle 'alone.' You said you felt alone. You're not alone. Yes, there have been people in your life who've abandoned you. There are also some in your life who've stood by you."

"Who?" she whispered. "My father left me. I thought we were so close. I thought he loved me. And my mother, she let Talmond– she gave– she just turned me over to that horrible man."

"Your mother has her own demons. Marissa stood by you. And my entire family will, from this point on, always be here for you. And then, most of all, there's Jeff."

She shook her head. "I pushed him away."

"I know. Why did you, Mickey?"

"You're the doctor, you tell me."

"I know the reason, I want you to tell me." He squeezed her hand. "Please."

Shrugging, she shook her head. "Actually, I'm not really sure. It just seemed the logical thing to do."

"Because he wouldn't let you come with him?"

"No, I don't think that's it."

"You were angry with him."

"Yes. Well, more like frustrated. I wanted to come with him to Seattle, though, that's hardly a reason for breaking up."

"He was thoughtless toward your feelings."

"No, he felt terrible about making me have to stay. He tried to comfort me about it but I wouldn't let him."

"He should've known how you would feel if he left you there in Los Angeles. He should've realized you would feel abandoned."

"No, really, it wasn't like that. He was following orders. At the time, I was supposed to be kept hidden and protected. He couldn't have known that would change just a few hours later. And he did feel bad about leaving me. He was very upset to have to leave and he was worried about me. He's a caring, wonderful man. Really."

Eric said nothing, only smiled kindly.

Mickey rolled her eyes. "Okay, I get it. Only, you see, once I stepped back for a moment to think about our whirlwind relationship, I realized breaking it off was the rational thing to do."

"Why?"

She sat quietly trying to come up with a good answer. Finally, she looked up at him, shaking her head. "We rushed into declaring our love to each other under traumatic conditions. Maybe our feelings weren't real. Maybe they were just based on the moment. You know, a hero worship kinda thing?"

Eric nodded. "You would've rather met him at a bar instead of rescuing you?"

"No, I mean, I don't know. Maybe. I'm glad he was there, but, oh, I don't know."

"Mickey, do your feelings for him seem real to you?"

"Yes."

"And his seem real also?"

"Yes, but what if they're not? What if he realizes he doesn't really like me? What if he comes to his senses?"

"Jeff is in perfect control of his senses and his mind. Why should he change it?" Eric prodded.

"Why should he be different from anyone else?"

He smiled at her. "You do realize what you're saying, don't you? You pushed Jeff away because you're afraid he'll betray you like everyone else."

She sniffed, dabbed at her eyes with her napkin. "I am afraid. I can't help it."

"What you and Jeff have may not last. You can't know what the future will bring, sweetie, but you can't close down your heart because you're afraid he'll betray you like your parents did. If you're afraid to love, if you're afraid to live, then it's as if you're already dead. Are you gonna let your stepfather win? From the way you fought to free yourself I would think you wouldn't give up so easily, simply because you're afraid. Admit it, with Jeff, you drew first blood so that he couldn't."

She lowered her eyes. "I hurt him. I didn't mean to."

"He's a big boy and he can take it."

Her eyes met his. "I miss him."

Eric nodded. "It's good when you begin to be honest with yourself."

Mickey smiled. "It felt good, to say those words."

"It felt good because your honesty put you in harmony with God.

You see, God will tell you, through your body and heart, when you're on the right track in any situation. You just have to quiet your mind enough to listen and be honest enough with yourself to hear."

Her eyes glistening, she smiled at him. "I'll try to remember that. Thank you, Eric, for taking the time to speak with me."

He shrugged. "The pleasure was mine. I felt strongly that I see you before I leave Seattle."

"And you always listen to yourself?"

He laughed softly. "It's not myself, it's my Father, and no, I don't always listen, and I find those are the times I suffer." He drew a deep breath, stood. "I have a plane to catch. I'd better get going. Would you object to me praying with you before I leave?"

"No, I don't mind." She stood.

He took both her hands in his. "Father, we come before You, first, to thank You for Mickey here, for her life. Thank You for saving her. We understand that means You have a plan for her life, Father. We ask now that You heal her heart, mind and soul. We ask that You surround the current circumstances with Your wisdom and light so that everything will work out according to Your will, Your plan. Give Mickey strength to go through whatever is coming her way, and help us both to rise up and do whatever You need us to do. In Jesus' name we pray, Amen."

He opened his eyes and smiled at Mickey.

"Thank you,"she whispered. "I feel better already."

There was no need for him to say anything else. It was time to be quiet and let God touch her heart. He opened his arms and Mickey stepped into his warm embrace. She looked up at him with wonder.

"What?" he asked.

"Your children are so lucky to have you as a father."

He patted her back, stepped away. "An exquisite compliment."

"Do you stay on top of all of Jason's investigations?"

He laughed. "No. I actually have a life. It's just that once you came to our home, and we saw how it was with you and Jeff, you became special to us. Then Jeffy threw us all in. From here on out, what happens in this case is personal." He reached out, placed his fingers under her jaw and lifted. "You keep your head up. You can call me anytime you want to talk. Even if it's three in the morning. Got it?"

She nodded. "Thanks."

"Mickey, you're gonna need some counseling. Will you let me recommend someone for you? Just someone to help you sort out your feelings? Can you trust me enough to see who I recommend?"

She sighed. "I trust you completely."

~~~

Eric Kino walked brazenly up to the large, cherry door and rang the bell. Marion Daley opened the door. Eyes wide, her mouth opened and closed a few times before she finally spoke.

"Mister Kino, uh, what, I mean—"

Eric smiled kindly at her. "It's okay, Mrs. Daley. I understand what you're thinking. Why am I here? What do I want? And mostly, you're afraid because you don't know how your husband will react to my visit."

Her face hardened. "I'm not afraid of my husband's reaction."

Eric nodded. "Good. Then let him know that I'm here to see him."

She started to shut the door. He put his foot in it. "I suggest you invite me in if you don't want to let the neighbors in on your personal life any more than they already are."

She looked into his eyes. They weren't the kind, compassionate eyes she'd seen the night before when they'd had dinner together. These eyes were hard, steely, and determined.

She opened the door and made a sweeping gesture. He stepped inside.

"He's upstairs in the bath so it may take a few minutes." She motioned toward a chair just inside a formal front room. "You can sit there if you'd like."

"Don't worry about me. I'll occupy my time."

She nodded and walked slowly up the steps.

Eric moved stealthily down the hall, opened the door on the left and gazed into the library. Two walls of dark, cherry wood shelves were filled with expensive, gold-trimmed books, valuable vases, statuettes, and crystal figurines. His eyes moved to the far wall, to the French doors covered in gold drapes. He envisioned his small daughter coming bravely through them, doing her best to use her Ninjutsu skills just as she'd described to him.

He closed the door, moved to the study, Daley's personal office space to which no one was allowed to enter. He quickly took in its layout. Again, he projected the images of Jeffy fighting with Daley. Of her trying to run past him from the desk to the door. Of Daley grabbing her braid and pulling her back. He moved on.

He came to a hallway. To the right, under the stairway led toward the kitchen. To the left there were three more doors. He moved down the hall, opened the first door. It was an empty room, obviously under construction. Boxes of imported tiles sat next to tools and buckets. Strips of cedar wood lined the walls. No window. This is where Jeffy was when she made the call to him. He could almost feel her in the room now. Her fear must've been sizable, her adrenaline pumping. Sighing, he shook his head as he walked the room.

Talmond Daley appeared at the door. "What the hell?" Daley said, looking accusingly at the intruder.

Eric gazed calmly at the man. "Daley," he said softly. As with most of Eric's students, a soft, calm voice was not a good sign.

"What are you doing roaming around my home?"

"The question is, what were you thinking, when you locked my daughter in this room? What were you planning?"

Brows raised, his eyes met Daley's. Talmond's eyes immediately retreated.

"We will go to your office and have a few words," Eric ordered.

Daley looked up quickly, thinking to bluster his way out of this, but saw that this man would not be easily shaken.

Eric nodded politely. "You may lead the way."

Talmond opened his mouth to give a sharp reply. No man was gonna barge into his home and order him around. He was a United States Senator, by God. "How dare you–"

"How dare I? I'm gonna need for you to think about your words before you speak, Senator. We can do this standing up or seated in your office like the civilized people I know you believe yourself to be."

Talmond's brow furrowed at the slight. Blowing out a breath he drew his shoulders back and led the way to his office. He moved around toward his chair behind the large desk and stood waiting for Eric Kino's next move.

Eric motioned toward Daley's desk chair. "By all means, have a seat," he uttered softly as if giving him permission.

Eyes glittering with anger, Talmond lowered himself into the chair. Eric took one of the chairs opposite the desk.

"I have nothing to say to you," Talmond said fiercely. "I don't understand why you would even think to come to my home."

"The reason I'm here, Senator, has to do with honor. I realize this is something you are hardly familiar with, still, please try to follow along."

Talmond drew a deep breath. "It was your daughter who broke into my house. I had her escorted—"

"Save it." Eric stated firmly bringing Daley's tirade to an immediate halt. "As I was saying, honor dictates that I pay a visit to confront the man, and I use that term lightly, who intended to terminate my daughter's life."

"I did no—"

"Interrupt me again and I will make sure that this is a completely one-sided conversation."

"You threaten me, Kino?"

"The moment I walked into your home." Eric smiled ferally as he watched the blood drain from the Senator's face. No amount of blustering could hide fear, and it was emanating from Talmond Daley's entire body.

"So, as I was saying, you thought to end June Flower's life as if she were nothing more than a pesky fly. That tells me much about you, Daley. That tells me you've killed before and that also tells me you will try to kill again. Up to now you've had free reign, no one has dared to stop you. That time has come to an end. I know about the investigation into your affairs. I know you've been charged with a crime against my daughter."

"There's no proof that I did anything to your daughter."

Eric's brow raised in warning. "You can lie to everyone else, but not to me. I've never been gullible. So, again, as I was saying, I'm very much aware of who you are, what you are, what you're capable of, and probably your next move. No matter what happens with the law, no matter what fancy lawyers you hire or even what the verdict is, your slight against my family will not go unpunished. So, if you somehow, wiggle out of the mess you're in, don't think for a minute that you've avoided your fate. Your life span has shortened considerably. As a matter of fact, given what I know about you, I predict you don't make it to the new year.

"Are you threatening to kill me?"

"I won't have to. One of those you've crossed in the past will do it for me. So, you'd probably better think real hard if you want to go to jail and live, or, die very soon. Either way, there is no out for you, Senator. I will make sure of that."

Eric stood.

"You barge into my home, you threaten me, I should call the police."

Eric snorted. "Your antics are almost laughable. Almost." He gave a slight bow. "I'll see myself out."

Talmond rose, brandishing the gun he'd slipped out of the center drawer of his desk. He grinned at Eric. "Maybe you're not as smart as you think you are. The great Eric Kino barged into Talmond Daley's home today in a fit of anger vowing to avenge his daughter. Senator Daley, having no other choice, drew his weapon and fired as Kino tried to attack him."

Eric smiled, shook his head. "You realize you're giving me a reason to take your life right now? Do you know *anything* about me?"

Talmond leered. "I know I'm the one with the gun."

Eric sighed, shook his head.

It happened so fast, Talmond stumbled backward in confusion. Pain shot through his wrist and fingers. He looked down at his now empty hand and up at the man standing across from his desk. Eric Kino pointed the gun at the Senator's chest. He fingered the trigger. Talmond held his breath.

Sighing, Eric pointed the weapon at the floor, quickly unloaded it, pocketed the gun and ammo. "I think I'll hold onto this," Eric said, smiling. "Rule number one, always know your enemy. Keep looking over your shoulder, Daley. I'll be there." He spun and walked out the door.

Marion Daley stood in the hall, wringing her hands. Eric stopped, looked her over. "You don't have to go down with the ship," he said softly.

She looked into his eyes. Blinked. He nodded, opened the front door, stepped out and closed it softly behind him.

He paused only a second when he realized Ricky, Mark and Joey were there, on the porch, apparently waiting either for him to emerge, or for them to have to rush in. They followed him out to his car. He looked at them over the top of the car. "She's my daughter," he said in explanation.

Ricky shrugged. "Understood. She's our sister."

Eric nodded. "Understood. You guys never disappoint me."

Chapter Twelve

"You sure you don't want to join the game?" Jack asked Mickey.

She smiled at the large man who was at the present moment sitting cross-legged on the carpet in the middle of the living room, teaching her baby sister how to play poker. "No thanks, Jack. I don't feel like playing anything. I'm just feeling antsy. I wish I'd remembered to ask for my computer back, then maybe I could write, take my mind off things."

"You wanna talk about anything?" Jack asked. "I'm a good listener."

She tucked her legs up under her. "I imagine you are, but no. You two just go on playing. Do you mind if I turn on the television?"

"Of course we don't mind, Mick, it's your house," Marissa said. "You want me to make some popcorn?"

"Maybe later, sweetie. Thanks."

Mickey took up the remote and switched on the TV. The seven o'clock news was just coming on. The top story was the arrest of Senator Talmond Daley and the fact he'd been charged with accessory to kidnapping. The room quieted as its three occupants listened to the report.

They didn't hear anything new until the very end of the report. It showed the Senator being questioned by reporters as he was getting into his limo. Mickey wasn't surprised that he'd granted the impromptu press conference. He'd always loved publicity, good or bad. It was what he said that caught her off guard.

Marissa gasped in surprise at her father's words as he painted a picture of her sister as being unstable and violent. Her head snapped around to look at Mickey, who stood, her mouth gaping open, her eyes wide. Marissa and Jack both rose. Jack's arm went around Mickey's waist to support her. He eased her back to sit down, worried she might collapse. Marissa knelt in front of her, and took Mickey's hand.

"Don't worry 'bout what he said. It doesn't matter."

When Mickey didn't respond, Jack tried. "It'll all come out in the end, Mickey. The truth will come out. Try not to take it so hard."

"Mick?" Marissa said, the worry evident in her voice.

Mickey's eyes flicked down to Marissa and then slowly moved over to look at Jack. "I'd like to go upstairs to bed, now," she said, her voice barely audible.

"Let me help you up the steps," Jack said. "Marissa, you come and help her get undressed, okay?"

"No. I don't want any help. I just want to be alone. Please. You two just stay here, play your game. I need to be alone." She rose and went slowly up the steps.

"I hate him," Marissa said vehemently before she ran up the steps to the room she'd commandeered as her own.

Jack pulled out his cell.

"Yeah," Jeff said when he answered.

"Where are you?" Jack asked quickly.

"I met Agent Stevens at Dora Suarez's home. We interviewed some of her family. I'm on my way back now. Why, what's wrong?"

"Daley took a stab at Mickey using the media." He went on to describe exactly what Daley said in the interview.

"Damn him," Jeff mumbled. "How's she holding up?"

"Not good. I think you should get over here."

"I'm on my way. I'm about twenty minutes away."

"Hold on, I think I hear a car in the drive."

Jeff waited while Jack checked it out. He heard Jack curse. Heard footsteps running. Heard Jack call Mickey's name twice. "What is going on?" Jeff said.

Jack was breathing hard when he spoke into the phone. "She's gone. She snuck out the door, got in the car and drove away."

"Okay," Jeff said calmly. "Okay. Don't go after her. Stay there with Marissa. I know where she's headed. I'll take care of it."

"Man, Jeff. I'm sorry."

"It happens. I know that all too well."

"Yeah. Keep me informed. I'll call Jason."

"Thanks." Jeff ended the call and floored it.

~~~

Marion Daley hurried to the door, wondering who would be pounding on the door this time of evening. She hoped it wasn't one of the reporters who'd been hanging out all day. The police had come and ushered them away twice now. She'd thought they'd all gone home. Whoever it was, she intended to let them know just how rude they were. She jerked open the door.

"Mickey! What are you doing here?"

Mickey pushed her way into the house. "I've come to see that monster you're married to."

Marion gasped and stepped in front of her daughter. "You– you can't see him. It's been a hard day for him, Mackenzie. Besides, your father is at the dinner table and you know how he is about mealtime."

"First, he's not my father and second, get out of my way, Mom," Mickey said through gritted teeth.

"I'm sorry, Mickey, but I have no choice. I can't let you in to see your father right now."

"You're right about one thing," Mickey said as she grabbed her mother's arm and slung her away. "You have no choice."

Mickey stormed into the dining room.

Talmond looked up at her calmly, touched his napkin to his sneering lips and replaced it in his lap. The finest china graced the table, apparently in celebration of his being home from jail. Mickey eyed rare roast beef, new potatoes, blackened asparagus and chocolate layer cake. She glared at the slim, distinguished man sitting at the head of the table.

She called him a string of names and ended with, "I despise you."

"Mickey, you know how I hate to be disturbed at mealtime."

"I don't freakin' care how you hate to be disturbed."

"Don't you speak to me like that in my house, young lady," he warned, his eyes narrowing.

"Or what, Tal-mond? What will you do?" She moved closer to him.

"And don't you dare call me by my given name. You, young lady, are pushing your luck."

"It didn't work, did it?" Mickey shouted, moving closer. "I'm supposed to be dead. It didn't work and now you have no choice but to try to sway the media."

"I have no idea what you're going on about."

"Mickey," Marion said from behind. "Get yourself under control. You know better than this. How dare you come in here using that kind of language and making crazy accusations."

Mickey whirled. "Screw you, mother dearest." She turned back quickly.

"You're not gonna get away with it, you cowardly pile of crap."

"Now, now, Mickey, we'll get you the help you need," Talmond said, a sly smile on his lips.

Mickey screamed and lunged. She was on him in seconds, her hands around his throat. His chair tipped over backwards and she lay sprawled on top of him doing her best to choke the life out of him. He struggled to breathe while he tried to get his hands around her wrists. Finally he was able to wrestle her hands away from his throat. He pushed her over onto her back, reversing positions and pinned her hands down beside her head.

"You'll pay for that little girl. Like always."

"What are you gonna do, daddy, take me upstairs and beat me again? You'd like that wouldn't you?"

He grinned. "Oh, yes. I would." He hauled back and struck her across the face. "I dearly would," he said, swinging again, backhanding her this time.

Mickey gave all she had, struggling against him, bucking and finally toppled him enough to get out from under him. She rose quickly, but he swung at her again, catching her in the eye this time. She stumbled back against the sideboard. Wine glasses crashed. She picked one up and threw it at him, hitting him in the chest. She grabbed another and let it fly, but he ducked in the nick of time.

He rounded on her. She didn't back away. She charged him again, this time pummeling him with her fists. He reared back and punched her in the mouth sending her to the floor. Disoriented and moaning, she rolled over and tried to stand. Talmond stood there, waiting, his eyes gleaming. "Come on, brat. You think you can take me on? Come on."

Mickey rose, holding onto the table. Her hand closed around the knife lying next to the platter of beef. She lunged at Talmond. He jumped back just in time. She lunged again and again. He dodged the knife several times before he grabbed her wrist and hit her hand against the table until she let go of the knife.

"This time you're going to jail, girl. A mental ward. You won't see light of day for years."

She screamed and picked up his plate and cracked it over his head. He stumbled back. She picked up a smaller bread plate and threw it at him. Then another. Then a glass. A fork.

"Stop it, Mickey!" Marion cried. "Stop!"

Mickey fully intended to kill the man. So it surprised her when, as she went to throw the bowl of potatoes, an arm snagged her around the waist and lifted her off the floor.

Mickey struggled against whoever it was.

"It's me, Mick. It's me. Stop it now. No more," Jeff said.

She glanced back at him briefly, then let go and threw the potatoes. She struggled again to get at her stepfather, her arms and legs reaching out toward her intended victim. "Let me go, Jeff. I'm gonna kill him. Let me go."

Jeff held her tight. Talmond advanced. Jeff pointed a finger at the man. "Stay right there, Daley. Or I'll kill you myself."

"Don't think you can come into my house and threaten me. I'm calling the police."

Jeff nodded. "Go ahead."

"I'll have her arrested and it will only go to prove what I said today. The girl is mentally ill."

"That's not what I saw here. I saw her coming to confront you about what you said about her to the media today and you lost your temper and beat her up."

"That's a lie," Talmond said.

Jeff shrugged. "Look at her face."

"They won't believe you."

"You think? I'm much more credible than you right now."

"My wife will attest to the truth."

"Your wife? The one doing so many prescription drugs she doesn't know up from down?"

Mickey gasped and looked over to her mother. The woman's eyes lowered.

Jeff tightened his hold on Mickey and began backing out toward the front door. "We're leaving, now."

Mickey surged forward, but Jeff jerked her against him. Since she couldn't throw punches, she threw words instead. "I hate you," she hollered. "I hate you both. I hope you burn in hell. But first I hope you die a horrible, painful death!"

"Hush now," Jeff said as he got her out the front door. He moved quickly. Tossed her into the passenger side of his truck. He closed the door, but before he could make it to his side she opened the door and ran full speed back toward the house. Jeff grabbed her again and put her back into the truck. "Stay– dammit," he growled at her. He quickly hopped behind the wheel and took off.

Jeff leaned over and rummaged through the glove box. When he found some tissues, he held them out to her. "Here, Mick. You're bleeding."

Shakily, she took the tissues, but said nothing. They drove in silence the rest of the way home.

By the time they'd gotten back to her house she was practically comatose. Jeff opened her door for her, but when she merely sat, staring straight ahead, instead of getting out, Jeff lifted her into his arms and carried her in. Jack opened the door for them. Marissa hovered nearby.

Jeff sat on the couch with Mickey in his lap. "I need ice and some antiseptic, and a wet cloth," he said.

Jack went to find the essentials. Marissa knelt down in front of her sister and took her hand.

"Mickey," she mumbled as tears ran freely down her cheeks. "I'm so sorry. I'm so sorry." Her head dropped into Mickey's lap. Marissa sobbed. Mickey's hand came up to rest on her sister's head, stroking her hair gently.

Jack came back and Jeff began cleaning the blood from Mickey's face. She winced a couple of times and he mumbled apologies as he worked on her. Finally, he applied some antiseptic to her cut lip and two ice packs, one to her lip and the other to her eye that was already showing signs of a real shiner.

Mickey rested her head against Jeff's chest and breathed deeply, inhaling his scent. He stroked her head as he told Jack and Marissa the part he'd seen. Wanting to know the rest, he asked Mickey some questions to get her started talking. Her story came out in bits and pieces.

When she finished the telling, Jeff and Jack sat quietly, thinking how it could've ended much worse. The room was completely silent except for the mini pendulum clock sitting on the desk, so it caught everyone's attention when Marissa began to giggle.

Mickey sniffed, looked up at her. "What's so funny?"

"I just wish," Marissa began, her giggles turning into outright laughter. "I– I just wish, I could've been there to see," she laughed harder. "To, see you on top of Dad, trying to choke—" She had to stop to hold her stomach as she laughed. Mickey began to giggle too. "To see you choke him. What did– what did his face– his face look like?" She fell over onto her back, laughing.

"His face was bright red and his eyes," Mickey said, also beginning to laugh. "His eyes were all bugged out."

Marissa shrieked with laughter. "And when you said," she held her hand up to ask everyone to wait on her, "and when you said, 'screw you, mother dearest,' was it just the best?"

Mickey wiped tears from her eyes. "It was fabulous," she laughed.

Jeff's eyes met Jack's. They shook their heads.

~~~

I'm dreaming, Mickey said to herself. This is the same dream. He's not real. He's not real, she chanted to herself as she watched Richard, blood dripping from his neck, crawl on top of her. He took his hand away from his throat to reveal a large, gaping black hole. He reached toward her, touched her, leaving bloody streaks on her pale skin.

It's a dream, it's a dream. Wake up. Please, wake up. She looked away, but when she looked back it wasn't Richard any longer, it was Butch. His face was sad, and there was a large red stain on his shirt. "I'm sorry," he said. "I have to do this. I have to for my brother. I'm sorry, little girl."

Please wake up. Wake up, wake up, wake up. Gasping, Mickey sat straight up in bed.

Jeff was at her side. "I'm here, Mick. I'm here. It's okay. Just a bad dream."

Mickey gazed up at him. "Jeff? What are you doing here?"

"I stayed to watch over you. You were so out of it last night, I couldn't leave you. I love you, Mickey. I know you're probably upset that I stayed here, but it just seemed—"

She put a finger on his lips. "I'm not upset. I'm glad you're here."

"You are?" Jeff asked, a smile crossing his lips.

"Yes, I am."

"But I thought—"

"I know, Jeff. Please don't ask me to explain it. I'm so confused and tired. I don't want to think."

"Okay. No thinking. Maybe you'd like to tell me about the dream."

She shuddered. "It was horrible. The thing is, I knew I was dreaming but I couldn't make myself wake up."

"Trapped, huh? Tell me about it."

He held her tighter as she told him the bloody details. She didn't leave anything out. When she finished Jeff sat silently thinking for a time as he stroked her arm and shoulder.

"So, I guess there's no need to analyze it," Mickey said. It's pretty straightforward."

"I don't know about that. The only thing I know is it's probably gonna take some time before the nightmares stop and I think you really need to think about seeing a shrink."

"Mr. Kino came by yesterday to talk to me and asked if I would allow him to recommend someone for me. I said yes."

"Good. Eric will find you the right person. He's a good man."

"He's more than that. He's like, I don't know, powerful? He has an aura about him. I can't explain it."

"I know what you mean and powerful is a good description. Some of us guys have talked about being around him feels like we're standing just outside of a nuclear power plant. He's very spiritual. Really into Jesus. He, and Jason too, are responsible for the conversion of many of the Ameritech agents. They believe that as long as we stay on the right path, God will be with us."

"You too? Did he convert you?"

"God converted me, the night Keegan came for me."

She nodded in understanding. "I didn't realize you were a Christian."

He frowned. "Well, that means I'm not very good at it. It's kind of a hard road to walk, having to do things, hard things, violent things, and still remain Christ-like."

"But like you just said, or like you said Eric said, if you are doing those things for the right reasons, then God will be with you."

He nodded. "Yeah, but kill a man first and then come and tell me how easy it is to keep things straight. Things can get confusing."

At her muffled sound he looked down at her and realized his mistake.

"Sorry, Micky. That was an automatic statement that I say inside my own head a lot, so it just came out. I wasn't thinking. Of course I know that you know how it feels."

"It's okay. Mr. Kino really helped me work through things in my mind. But you have piqued my curiosity. Have you had to kill many men?" she asked softly.

He grimaced. "Even one is difficult, as you well know."

She nodded. "So, you've only had to kill one man?"

"I wish." He scrubbed his hands over his face. "I'd rather not talk about this."

"I'm sorry. I sort of went off on a tangent. I believe we were talking about how powerful Eric Kino is."

"Yeah, he's been like a second father to me. I have a great deal of love and respect for him and Shelley both."

"Where did you tell me your parents live? It was Utah, right?"

"Yes, Utah. I have an older sister in Texas. She has two kids. Boys.

Great kids. I'll get to see them on the 4th of July."

"And you're close to your parents?"

"Very."

"Must be nice." She raised her head and looked over at the other side of the bed. It didn't look slept in. "Where were you sleeping?"

"In the chair over there by the window."

She looked down, licked her lips. "I'm sorry, Jeff, I know I hurt you."

"Yeah. Well, I love you, Mick, so you not wanting to be with me hurts. Still, I can handle it."

She turned in his arms so she could see his face. "The thing is, I'm so mixed up. Eric says I broke it off with you because I'm afraid you're gonna abandon me. I can see that. I *am* afraid. It's just that, well, I don't know what to do." Her voice choked with emotion.

"Oh, baby," Jeff soothed. "It's okay. We can take it slow. You don't have to make any decisions right now. I'll be here for you, Mick. I'm not going anywhere. When you're ready, I'll be here. I won't abandon you."

"When you're not around, I think of you constantly. When you're near me, I feel calm and safe."

"All you have to do is call me and I'll be at your side."

"Thank you Jeff." Sighing, she leaned closer. "Listen, I don't want you to read anything into this, but, will you lie down with me? Will you hold me?"

He smiled at her. "I'd be happy to, and you can read anything you want into that."

She gave a soft laugh. Jeff kept his slacks on but removed his shirt and belt. They snuggled down under the covers. He waited with great anticipation for her to turn into him and snuggle her face up against his throat as was her habit. When she did, the expected jolt of lust forced a soft moan from him, but he kept it under control, feeling only gratitude that she wanted him beside her. He closed his eyes and fell into a warm, peaceful slumber.

~~~

"What time will you be here? ...Yes sir... I'll be ready," Jeff said into his cell phone, his back leaning against the headboard of Mickey's bed.

The door swung open and Marissa stepped into the room. "Oh!"

Jeff held a finger up to her while he finished his conversation. "Yes sir. Thanks. See ya soon." He closed the phone. "Hi, Marissa."

She grinned. "Hi."

He rolled his eyes. "Mickey's in the shower. She had a bad dream last night. I only kept her company."

"You don't have to explain anything to me. I think it's great that you two are, uh, together."

"We're not actually. I mean, we were, but she wants to slow things down. So, now we're not."

"Whatever." She came forward and sat on the bed. "So, you saw the cabin right? The one where they held Mickey."

"Yeah, I saw it."

"Was it bad?"

"It was bad. Bloody. Your sister's been through a lot. She'll need you as much as you need her."

"Do you think that Butch guy was telling the truth?"

"I can't imagine why he would make it up."

"Yeah, that's how I see it too. I believe it. I've been remembering stuff about my father. Things I think I must've like, what's that word?"

"Suppressed?"

"Yeah, that's it."

"Things like what?" Jeff asked.

"Him doing things to Mickey. You know, hitting her, using a belt on her, pushing her, tripping her, smacking her around."

Jeff muttered an obscenity.

"I was only five when she left home. If I can remember all that, just think of what my mother or Ms. Dora probably saw."

"Yeah. Just think. We're gonna be hearing some of that real soon."

"What do you mean?"

"Can't talk about it right now. Just wait and see. Your father doesn't have much time left. He's going down."

Marissa smiled. "Thanks, Jeff. I mean, for caring about Mickey. I'm glad she has you."

"Are you two talking about me?" Mickey asked as she emerged from the bathroom.

"Of course," Marissa answered. "Man, your eye is really black."

"Yeah. Looks great, don't ya think?"

Jeff only shook his head. He couldn't wait to bring down the man who'd tortured a young girl her entire life. He headed into the bathroom to shower and dress. Fifteen minutes later the three of them and Jack sat at the table in the small dining area.

"Nate's coming to relieve you," Jeff informed Jack. "Jason and I have another meeting with the feds."

"Making any headway?"

"Actually yes. I'll tell you about it later."

Jeff rose at the knock on the door. "I'll get it. It's probably Nate." He opened the door to a fiftyish looking woman dressed in a navy blue business suit. "Hello," Jeff said cautiously.

Her eyebrows rose haughtily. "I'm here to see Mackenzie and Marissa Daley," she said.

Jeff raised his brows right back. "And you are?"

"I don't believe that's any of your business."

"Actually, it is. I'm here at the request of the FBI to offer protection to Mackenzie Daley as a witness for their case against Talmond Daley. I have no idea who you are and until I'm satisfied you mean her no harm, you don't come in."

"I'm with CPS," she said, looking down her nose. "That's Child Protective Services."

"I know who CPS is. Have any ID?" Jeff had no doubts she was who she said she was and the two cops he'd spotted standing beside their car out by the curb was a very bad sign of things about to become unpleasant.

The woman blew out an indignant breath as she pulled her credentials from her purse. Jeff took them and examined them thoroughly for no other reason than he didn't like her attitude. Finally, he opened the door and ushered the woman inside.

Mickey and Marissa had heard the conversation and stood nearby. Mickey assumed the woman was there to make sure Marissa was safely ensconced in her new residence. She was sadly mistaken.

"Please come in," Mickey said pleasantly.

They moved into the living room and sat down. Jeff and Jack held back. Jeff nodded toward the front window. Jack peeked out and saw the cops. "Aw hell," he mumbled.

"Ms. Daley," the woman began without preamble. "I'm afraid I'm here to remove Marissa Daley from the premises."

Mickey's face paled.

Marissa bounded to her feet. "No way. I'm not going anywhere."

"Did Talmond arrange this?" Mickey asked, her voice shaking.

The woman looked up toward Marissa. "I'm afraid you have no choice in the matter."

"Answer me," Mickey said, louder this time. "Did my stepfather arrange this little show?"

The woman pierced her with a venomous stare. "The Senator has nothing to do with this."

"I have a temporary order of custody issued from the judge yesterday."

"Yes ma'am, I know that. The judge himself called CPS this morning and rescinded that order. He said it was in light of what he learned last night. He didn't want to be responsible for anything happening to Marissa."

"In light of what he learned last night? What did he learn?" Mickey shrieked.

Marissa whirled. "It was that stupid interview Dad did with the reporters, wasn't it? That was all a lie. You have to know that. He was lying."

"I can't believe the judge is gonna remove my sister from my care because of some rumor he heard on television. What kind of quack is he?"

"That kind of talk will get you nowhere," the woman said snidely. She turned toward Marissa. "You will get your things now."

"When hell freezes over," Marissa yelled. "I'm not going back to that house."

The woman gasped. "Such language."

"You ain't heard nothing yet. See what happens if you try to take me."

"Where are you taking her?" Mickey asked, trying to stay calm.

"I'm afraid that information is confidential. I can however, tell you she's not going back to her mother and father's home either. She will be placed in foster care until the matter is brought before the judge in a hearing scheduled in three weeks."

"Three weeks! You're crazy." Marissa turned to Mickey. "Tell her, Mick," Marissa pleaded, her voice shaking. "Tell her I'm staying with you."

Mickey's heart broke at the desperation in her sister's voice. She turned back to the woman as her eyes welled with tears. "Please, is there no way around this?"

"I'm afraid not. My hands are tied. Ms. Daley, may I ask, what happened to your eye?"

Mickey looked toward Jeff where he stood in the dining room. Jeff shook his head. She looked back at the woman. "I ran into a door."

Lips pressed tightly together, the woman rose from the sofa, nodded at Marissa. "Get your things, young lady. We need to go."

"I already told you, I'm not going anywhere with you."

"I have two police officers waiting outside to enforce the judge's orders if necessary."

Mickey looked to Jeff again, who'd moved into the room to stand near the wall. He nodded his head. She stood and placed her hands on Marissa's shoulders. "Rissa, I love you with all my heart. I promise I'll get you back. Please, sweetie, be brave."

"It will be much better for you if I don't have to use the police escort."

"Don't you threaten my sister," Mickey said fiercely. "I'll handle this. You shut your mouth."

Jeff smiled.

"Thatta girl," Jack said.

Mickey looked back at her sister. Tears poured over Marissa's cheeks, causing Mickey to start crying too. "Rissa, if there was any way I could keep this from happening, I swear I would."

Marissa, affected by her sister's tears, wiped her own away. "I know that, Mick. It's just that, all this time I thought I'd never see you again. Now, here you are and they're taking me away from you." Her brow furrowed and she looked at her sister with resolve. "You know what? I just realized something. Jeffy went through so much, and so did you. And Cameron too. I guess it's my turn."

"Oh, Rissa, you're so grown up," Mickey cried. She held open her arms and Marissa threw herself against her sister.

The old bat wisely remained quiet as she waited for them to finish embracing.

They pulled away from each other, wiping their tears. Marissa glanced at the woman. "I'll be down in a minute." She turned and went up the stairs.

Mickey scowled fiercely at the woman. "You'd better hope nothing happens to her and no one mistreats her while she's in your custody or I'll bring suit against CPS and against you personally."

"There's no need to get personal, Ms. Daley."

"On the contrary, this is very personal. Just remember my words."

"I can assure you your sister will be well taken care of."

"You'd better pray she is," Mickey said. "And you know what? You can tell the judge—"

"Uh, Mickey, didn't you want to go upstairs and make sure Marissa has everything she needs?"

Mickey's eyes met Jeff's. He smiled and nodded at her.

"Excuse me," Mickey said as she made her way upstairs.

A few minutes later the sisters reappeared, the tears flowing once more. Marissa hugged her sister again then moved to Jack and hugged him.

"Keep that chin up," Jack said. "You never know what this little adventure will bring."

Marissa smiled at him. "I will," she promised. She hugged Jeff next. "Take care of Mickey," she said, her voice breaking.

"You know I will. I'll tell you a secret," he said softly.

Marissa leaned forward and Jeff whispered in her ear. She smiled up at him, threw her arms around his neck and kissed his cheek. She strode to the door, opened it and walked bravely out. The woman hurried to catch up.

Only a few minutes after Marissa was gone, Nate arrived and Jack took his leave. Jeff filled Nate in on what had transpired with CPS and then called Jason and told him. Jason made a call to his brother to make sure they had things under control where Mickey's sister was concerned.

Jeff pulled Mickey into the kitchen with him. "I have to go now. Are you gonna be okay?"

She nodded. "I think so. I hate that Marissa has to go through this, but I feel better knowing that Mr. Lee's brother is looking into things. Just wondering where she is, what she's doing, it makes me crazy."

"I get that for sure. I mean, when Jeffy was missing, the things running through my mind that she could be experiencing, where she was, what she was doing or even worse, what was being done to her."

Mickey nodded. "I bet the Kinos were about to have a heart attack."

"You know, they were concerned, but their modus operandi in times of stress is trusting God."

"They are pretty amazing people. I guess I should follow their lead. Heck, Marissa hasn't been kidnapped by some evil sicko."

"Exactly. She's a strong girl, Mickey, just like you. She'll be okay. It's not forever."

"I know. I just worry." She smiled up at him. "Anyway, I'm glad you were here. Thanks for that. Thanks for everything."

"You're welcome."

"So, tell me, what did you whisper to Rissa?"

"Hmm, it was a secret. If I tell you then it's not a secret anymore." Brushing his hand over her cheek, he smiled. "I have to go. I'll call to check on you. You can call me if you need anything, okay?"

She smiled. Nodded. Leaning forward, she rested her head against his chest. His arms came around her, holding her tight. She looked back up at him and he couldn't resist. Using his fingers to tilt her head up, he gently touched his lips to hers. He lingered right there, for a few seconds and then the moment ended and Jeff pulled away. "Sorry," he said, not really meaning it. He turned and left the house.

~~~

Jeffy stood in front of the mirror, gazing at her body, the memories of Cam's kisses running through her mind. They'd arrived home late the evening before. She'd endured the ministrations of her mother and the lecturing and admonishments of her father and then fallen into bed thinking she would sleep like the dead. Yet the dreams and visions came more than ever before. The dreams were mostly of Cam. Ashamedly, at times it would begin with Cam and end with someone else, someone familiar, yet she couldn't quite place him. The visions were not so pleasant. She'd wake from a dream only to have pictures of events flash through her mind like some horror movie trailer.

Now, as she stood in her room in the light of day, showered and dressed, she gazed at herself and realized something about her had changed. She felt more grown up. She had not crossed that rite of passage, as she'd overheard her mother speak about the other night. Yet there was something else. She felt much more connected, like her mind and body were finally beginning to understand the vastness of what a living, breathing, conscious human being was capable of. It was a beautiful thing. Though she'd almost ignored God's warning the first time, the second time she'd recognized His voice and listened. Maybe that is why she was feeling different. She was more connected than ever.

Smiling, she remembered the feel of Cam's mouth as he'd kissed her. How amazing is this body that can feel so much both physically and emotionally, she thought. No matter what, she would never regret offering herself to Cam, and being close to him.

Hearing the front door open, and people being greeted, she counted to ten with a smile. By the time she reached the last number, Kimmie came bursting through the bedroom door.

"Jeffy! Oh, Jeffy," Kimmie said, throwing her arms around her and hugging her tight.

Jeffy smiled warmly at her friend. "Hi, Kim."

"Hi Kim? Is that all you have to say?"

Jeffy shook her head. "No. I have a lot to tell you, even though I've been instructed that there are some details I'm not allowed to speak to you about."

"And you intend to follow those instructions?"

Jeffy grinned. "Actually, I'm gonna try, but don't worry, you'll get the gist of everything."

Kimmie's nose turned up, her lips pursed and then she smiled. "I'm just so glad you're okay I'll have to forgive anything else."

"Thanks, Kimmie." Jeffy held out her arms and they hugged.

The world went gray and cold. Suddenly, she felt as if the floor had fallen away from beneath their feet. Kimmie's hands grabbed her shirt, pulling her as if she were trying to pull them down. Their hair flew out around their shoulders as if in a great whirlwind. She couldn't breathe. Kimmie looked into her eyes with a look of abject terror on her face. It seemed she was sinking, sinking. She tried to pull Kimmie's hands away from her, but her friend held fast as if her very life depended on it. She heard Kimmie scream. And then, slowly, her senses came back to her. She lay on the floor, the soft white carpet feeling warm and dry and secure beneath her.

Kimmie was kneeling next to her, shaking her. "Jeffy, what's wrong? What's happening?"

The door burst open. Jeffy blinked, looking up at her father as he rushed into the room, and then, she was in his protective embrace, her head pressed against his chest. She could hear her mother's soft voice, feel her hands on her hair.

"Kimmie. Where's Kimmie?" Jeffy asked, panic in her voice.

"I'm right here, Jeffy," Kimmie said. "What happened? Are you okay?"

"Of course I am. I'm fine."

"What happened, Jeffy?" her father asked.

"I don't know. It seemed like, it seemed—" The tears came. She buried her face against her father's chest and wept.

"What did it seem?" Shelley asked softly.

Jeffy sniffed, shook her head. "I don't know. It's all a blur now. I don't want to talk about it, I mean, not now."

Eric gazed deep into his daughter's eyes, nodded in understanding. "We'll talk later," he assured her.

Jeffy smiled. Her father understood. He always understood. She'd had a vision, a very unpleasant vision, and it concerned her friend, and she was frightened that it just might come true.

~~~

"This totally sucks," Cameron said.

"Yeah, it does. I mean, the lady here, she seems nice enough, but it's not home. It's so weird, ya know, it's like, in a few days time my whole life has fallen apart."

"It fell apart the minute your father decided to off your sister."

"You're right. I don't wanna talk about it anymore. How's Jeffy?"

"She's good. She told me to tell you to call her. So, listen, what are the ground rules? I mean, will these people let you date?"

"I don't know. I'll have to check it out. Why? You askin? I mean, I'm all the way over in Olympia."

"Only an hour away. That's not bad. So, yeah, I'm askin'. We'll go get a pizza or something. Go to a movie. Do something."

"I'll find out and let you know."

"Hang tough, Rissa. And don't forget to call Jeffy."

"I will and I won't."

~~~

"You didn't have to cook dinner for us," Nate said.

Mickey looked up at him through bleary eyes. "I'm going crazy. I had to do something." She held her glass of Baileys up, shook the ice. "Sure you won't have one?"

"I don't drink, Mickey. And I'm not sure you should be drinking either."

She giggled. "Why not? What difference will it make? Everything's gone to hell anyway. My baby sister has been taken away to God knows where. My mother is a drugged out zombie. The whole world thinks I'm mentally deranged. I'll probably never sell another book. And the man responsible for it all is sitting over there in his fancy mansion probably eating some fancy meal in his fancy dining room being waited on hand and foot by my mother and her faithful housekeeper."

The knock on the door saved Nate from the conversation. He went to answer it. "Jeff, I'm freakin' glad you're back."

"What's up?"

Nate nodded toward the kitchen. "Mickey's decided to tie one on."

Jeff heaved a sigh. "Well, this should be entertaining."

"Oh, there you are," Mickey said loudly as she set a salad on the little dining table. "I decided to cook. Hope you like it."

"I'm sure it's great," he said. "It smells fantastic." His eyes swept the frilly, flowery dress she wore that flowed around her as she moved. She'd carelessly twisted her hair up in a clip. Strands fell loose around her face and at the back of her neck. Swaying slightly, she returned to the kitchen.

"This looks great. I love lasagna. It's one of my favorites," Nate said. "Can I help set the table?"

Mickey returned with a basket of garlic bread which she placed on the table. "Sure. And Jeff would you mind opening the wine for me?"

"Not at all."

"I'll just have some water," Nate said as he got his glass.

Jeff washed his hands, found the wine and joined Nate and Mickey at the table.

Mickey eased down in her chair, turned her attention on Nate. "So, Nathaniel Hawk, why don't you drink?"

He smiled. "My body is a temple."

Mickey hiccupped loudly. "Oops, sorry. Well, that's very ingenious of you, Nate."

He smiled, glanced at Jeff. "Thanks."

"I understand you actually live here in Seattle." she said.

"Yes, just north in Redmond."

"And you're Native American, aren't you?" she questioned.

"Blackfoot."

"Well, I think that's lovely, just lovely. And terribly interesting. Are you married?" Mickey asked as she scooped some lasagna from the pan and placed it on her plate.

"Married six years and have three kids." He took a bite. "Oh man," Nate said, his mouth full. "Now *this* is good."

"I'm glad you like it," Mickey cooed with a smile. She glanced over at Jeff, lifted her wine glass. "So did you accomplish anything wonderful today, Agent Jefferson Davis? Catch any bad guys?"

He smiled at her. "We made some progress." He nodded at his plate. "This is good stuff. You should eat."

She downed her wine and set the glass by her plate. "I think I will."

"So, tell me what you have so far," Nate said to Jeff.

He crunched down on the buttery garlic bread. Gave a soft moan before he spoke. "Last night we drove out to speak with Dora Suarez and her family. She has two sons and a daughter, all grown. Ms. Suarez was holding back and so I took her aside and let her know exactly what we think."

"We?"

"Eric, Jason, me, and now the feds."

"And that is?" Nate asked.

"Daley threatened her family in some way."

Mickey drained her glass and poured more.

Nate nodded. "Did she admit to it?"

"Yes. We have to make arrangements for her family before she'll come in and talk to us, but that should be taken care of by tomorrow. I can tell you this, she's terrified of him. Apparently she knows things that would put him away for a long time."

"Anything else?" Nate asked.

"Oh yes. Eric found out from Marissa that Daley had a laptop computer. It was the laptop Jeffy got into. Not the PC."

"But there was no laptop confiscated."

"Right. And the feds arrived only a few minutes after Kurt Wells left with Jeffy. Daley didn't have time to get rid of it, so, they're thinking he gave it to Wells to get rid of."

"Is he talking yet?"

"Not yet. In the morning, we're going back out to the mountains with Cameron."

"For?"

"We spoke with him again today and he thinks he remembers Wells slowing down, maybe tossing something out the window of the car when he drove Jeffy into the mountains."

"So you find the missing laptop, retrieve the hard drive. I bet we find something there."

"Hopefully dates, times, locations of an arms deal. We're also looking for this Butch guy's identity. Mickey told Eric that Butch had a brother. If we can figure out who Butch really is and who his brother is, it might help." Jeff turned to Mickey. "Butch didn't say anything else about his family?"

Mickey smiled sleepily, shook her head. "Butch said he didn't have a family. Said his mother was some crack whore who died when he was young. He never knew his father."

Jeff nodded. "That's the information we already have. I was just hoping there was something more."

Mickey shook her head. "I told them 'bout the old girlfriend back when he wuz eighteen," she said, her words beginning to slur. "Her father had him thrown in jail for statutory rape."

"The feds are trying to narrow that down. A lot of ex-cons did time for that. We're talking fifty states and we can only guess at the approximate year."

"He had a northern accent. You know, like Brooklyn," Mickey

said, pouring another glass.

Frowning, Jeff reached for the bottle, poured himself some wine and placed the bottle away from Mickey. "You need to eat something, Mick."

Mickey picked up her glass, swirled the contents. "Poor guy. He never had a chance. Dick blew him away just like that," she said, snapping her fingers as her eyes filled with tears. "He was holding my hand when it happened. Did I tell you that? I couldn't see past him, he was blocking my view, standing in front of me, like he was trying to protect me. His hand jerked, you know? Squeezed my hand tighter before it went loose. Poor guy."

"By your own admission that 'poor guy' intended to end your life," Jeff reminded her.

She shrugged, choosing to ignore his statement completely. "I wizh I had my computer back. I need to do sumpin. I could at leeez pull up my new book and work on it, ya know? Can you get it back for me, Jeff?"

"I'll check into it tomorrow."

Mickey finished off her glass of wine and held it out for Jeff to refill.

"I think you've had enough," he said.

She wiggled the glass in her fingers. "I'll be the judge of that."

"Actually, why don't we let me be the judge tonight."

"They took my sister from me today," she said, vehemently. "Juz came and took her like they had a right."

"I know, sweetie. We'll get her back."

"Juz took her," Mickey said again. "I hate him, whaddya think about that? Huh? I despise him. He liked to hit me, ya know? I think he got off on it. He, he– oh, whatever. I hate him."

Jeff nodded at Nate. "If you want to go home to your family, we're good here for the night."

Nate cleared his plate. "Let me help with the dishes."

"I got 'em," Jeff said. "Go, kiss your wife."

"You don't have to ask me twice," Nate said. He leaned over and kissed Mickey's cheek. "Go easy there, champ. You're gonna feel it tomorrow."

"Bye Nate," she said sweetly.

Jeff frowned at Mickey. "Eat."

"Stop being so bossy. I don't want to eat. I want to get sloppy drunk. You get that, Jeff?" she said angrily.

He sighed. "Yeah, I get it. However, I want you to drink less and eat more."

"You can't tell me what to do."

"Fine. You're absolutely right. I'm just concerned for your well-being. You wanna make yourself sick, you go right ahead." He rose and began clearing the table.

Mickey grabbed the wine bottle, poured the rest in her glass and drank it down, then rose and joined Jeff in the kitchen. "Where do you get off sounding so self-righteous? From what I understand, the other night you did the exact same thing."

"And I paid for it."

She shrugged. "And I'm sure I will too. Maybe that's what I'm looking for– some sort of self-flagellation. She found her original glass of Baileys, added ice and filled the glass to the rim then stood with her back to the counter, eyeing Jeff as he rinsed dishes and put them in the dishwasher.

Jeff thought about her words as he worked. He'd gotten drunk the other night because he was feeling sorry for himself. She was doing it tonight to punish herself. Judging from what she'd said earlier, she felt guilty for Butch's death. Plus it sounded like she was having a hard time getting the memory of how it went down out of her head. Maybe he could help her work through it. He certainly had enough experience with therapy that he could practice a little amateur session with her. He put the leftovers away, wiped the counter and turned to her.

"How you doin'?" he said.

She shrugged. "Thangz for doin' the dishes."

"No problem." He smiled kindly at her. "Why don't we go sit on the sofa and talk some things out."

She turned up her glass, drank down the contents and slammed it down on the counter. Smiling, she crooked a finger at Jeff.

Eyebrows raised, he moved forward. "What?"

She grabbed his shirt and pulled him close. "Kiss me."

He started to refuse, however, the temptation was too great and a kiss was not asking that much. Why not? His head dipped and he gently took her mouth, but pulled away when her hand drifted down. A kiss was one thing, but she was in no shape to do anything else.

"What?" she asked innocently. "I can tell you want me. Come here."

He shook his head. "No, Mick. Not like this."

She moved forward, rubbed her hand over his chest. He gently but firmly pushed her hands away.

"Come on, sweetheart, let's go sit down. We'll talk."

She pushed away and leaned back against the counter. "I don't want to talk, Jeff. I want you, right now."

"Geez, Mick."

She jumped up onto the counter. "Tell me you don't want me. I dare you."

"Oh, I want."

"Then let's do this."

He shook his head. "I can't do that when you're drunk, Mickey."

She slammed her hands down on the counter beside her. "Why? Is this some kind of attempt at chivalry?"

"Not really. It just wouldn't be right. If you were sober and told me you wanted me, believe me, I'd be really considering it right now. And that is saying a lot because we just had that talk about me being a Christian, and I'd like to think I'm stronger than that. But not like this, when you can claim you weren't in your right mind."

"I'm telling you, Jeff, make love to me."

"Mickey, I—" He closed his eyes.

"Please, Jeff," she begged.

He moved close to her. "I'm glad you need me. I need you too, but I won't make love to you when you're not in your right mind." He reached up and lifted her off the counter, pulled her against him.

"At least kiss me," she demanded.

He didn't argue with her. He tilted her face up and kissed her.

"Please, Jeff, I need you. Please," she said softly as her tears flowed.

He kissed her softly.

She looked up at him. She wanted him to make her forget. No more pain. No more memories. No more terror. Please, no more terror.

Her head fell onto his shoulder. Jeff lifted her into his arms and carried her upstairs to her bed.

Chapter Thirteen

Agent Stevens tossed a report on the desk in front of his partner. "Kurt Wells has a brother."

Agent Dodge quickly read through the document in front of him. "Donald Harris?"

Stevens nodded. "Governor Donald Harris. The honorable Governor of South Dakota. His older brother, Kurt Anton Harris, left home at the age of seventeen. He hasn't heard from him in over twenty years. Kurt took on his mother's maiden name of Wells. Apparently, the Harris household was strict and unyielding, the father pushing both boys to achieve ultimate success. Kurt never wanted to follow the rules and bailed as soon as he could. He was arrested in New York at the age of eighteen for grand theft auto. Paroled at twenty two. After that, he disappeared."

"I'm guessing that's when Daley picked him up. He needed a malleable soul to do his dirty work for him," Agent Dodge surmised.

"And he's been with Daley all these years."

"He spent his life trying to protect his brother." Dodge shook his head. "Starts with a little rebellion against an iron hand and ends with messin' up your whole life. So, anyway, do you think the Governor is dirty?"

"Already spoke with him. From what we can tell, he's a straight shooter. Hasn't had contact with his brother since the day he graduated from college."

Dodge leaned on his hands, as he thought. "The Senator found a soft spot in Wells. Ex-con, proud of his little brother and what he's made of himself. Brother Donny will remain on top as long as Wells keeps in line, does what he's expected to do for Daley."

"I think you got it. So, guess who did time with Wells?"

"Fill me in."

"A young buck in for statutory rape. Eighteen years old. Name is Alan Bradshaw. Mother dead from a drug overdose. Father unknown."

"Butch?"

"Yes. And again, a famous little brother. Matthew Wilson."

"Matthew Wilson, running back for Dallas?"

"One in the same. You've probably heard his story. Put in foster care as a young kid, fell in with a decent family. Big kid, gets to high school, excels, valedictorian, captain of the football team. Picks up a scholarship to the University of Texas, breaks all kinds of records, fourth round draft pick. Now making millions for Dallas."

"And again, he's clean."

"As a whistle."

"So Butch did what he was told in order to protect his little brother."

"Just like Dora Suarez has been doing for twenty years, in order to protect her family."

"She's ready to talk now that they've been placed in protective custody," Dodge said. "She's being brought in as we speak. She insists Jeff Davis be present. She trusts him."

Stevens nodded. "I got no problem with that. Jeff is a good man."

"You know he's involved with Mackenzie Daley?"

"I would be too if she'd have me," Stevens said with a lusty sigh.

Dodge chuckled. "You know, this entire case is strange. It involves so many prominent figures. Talmond Daley, the Senator, Mackenzie Daley, the writer, Matthew Wilson, the pro-baller, Governor Harris."

"And don't forget the Kinos. The entire family is famous."

"No, couldn't forget them, and even Jeff Davis is famous."

"To think, he's that agent who went missing back several years ago in Savannah. If I recall the story correctly, he was abducted and tortured."

"More importantly, they were able to rescue those kids."

"That was also when the bureau tried to fry one of our own for doing our freakin' job."

Agent Dodge nodded. "Keegan Tanner. Good man. He saved Jeff Davis, he saved those kids, he returned hundreds of kidnapped kids to their parents." Dodge shook his head.

"Did you know Tanner?" Stevens asked.

"We worked a case together once when we were both in Virginia. He was a newbie, just out of Quantico. Tough. Sharp. Reminded me of me."

"Yeah, right," Stevens laughed. "I hear he works for Ameritech now."

"He does and Jeff Davis is one of his closest friends, which is one of the reasons I have no problem with Davis being in on anything. So did the two of you pick up the Wallace kid this morning?"

"We did."

Dodge eyed his friend. "And? Did you find anything?"

"I've been waiting for you to ask. Heck yeah we did. A laptop, a few miles south of where Wells pulled off the road and took the Kino girl into the woods. It's at the lab as we speak. We're about to nail this sonofagun."

"One of my favorite pastimes. Let's go interview the housekeeper."

~~~

Jeff handed Dora Suarez a tissue and waited while she blotted her eyes. Dora looked down at the tissue, folded it once, twice, drew a deep breath. "It was my day off, but I came in to make sure the house was just right. There was this big political dinner being given the next day." She shook her head. "My own children were only babies then."

"Do you remember their exact ages?" Agent Dodge pressed. "It will help to document every single fact."

"I remember," Dora said bravely. "I remember everything. I wrote it all down. It's in the journal."

Dodge nodded. Before they'd even begun she'd walked in and handed him a journal. For an agent it was like manna from heaven. She'd already given them enough information for an indictment. "And the day you came in on your day off was *after* the first time he raped you?"

"Well after. I came in because I was afraid of displeasing Senator Daley, which wasn't a hard thing to do. We constantly walked on egg shells around him. I was afraid he would follow through with his threats to deport me and take my children away from me, and so I came in to make sure everything was ready."

She gave a humorless laugh. "Ironically, coming in was my big mistake."

"Why is that?" Jeff asked.

"I came in the kitchen entrance like always. I found some laundry in the dryer and decided to fold it. I went to Mackenzie's room to put it away and walked in on the Senator having his way with a young girl."

"How young?"

"I don't know for sure, but young. Maybe about thirteen or fourteen. The girl appeared to be asleep or drugged. I remember just standing there, not even sure that I was actually seeing what I was seeing. Then, I regained my senses and ran out." She stopped, looked out the window as if she was seeing what had taken place. "But the Senator, he was always quick on his feet. He caught up to me before I could get out of the house. He slapped me around, shook me, threatened me. I told him things had gone far enough. There was no way I could ignore what I'd seen. He warned me to think again, but I refused. How could I let him get away with what he'd done to that young girl?"

"Do you know her name?"

Dora shook her head. "Sorry. I never did find out who she was. Poor child. I always wondered about her."

"It's okay," Agent Stephens said with a sigh, trying to help her stay on track. "What happened next? Did you try to blow the whistle on Daley?"

She shook her head again, her eyes staring straight ahead. She spoke slowly. "I went home to wait for my husband to get back from his job at the transportation department so I could tell him about Senator Daley. I was gonna tell him everything. About the times the Senator raped me, about the girl in Mackenzie's room and all the other things." She stopped, shook her head. "My husband never made it home. He lost his brakes, went off the road, hit a roadside boulder and flew through the windshield."

Jeff cursed.

"At the wake, in the guise of offering condolences, Senator Daley came up to me, took my hand, told me he was sorry he'd had to demonstrate his power and he let me know he would always be there for me and more importantly, for my kids. Always. I understood his meaning. From that day forward my life became a nightmare. The Senator had an appetite for young girls. I think it had to do with Mickey."

"How so?" Agent Dodge asked.

"It was like he became aroused beyond his ability to contain it whenever he'd had to discipline Mackenzie. When Mickey turned eighteen and finally left the house, the Senator seemed to settle down."

Jeff reached out and took her hand. "Did Daley ever rape Mackenzie or Marissa?"

She shook her head. "I don't think so. If he did, I wasn't aware of it. He *did* have other girls, though. Girls off the street. Sometimes willing. Sometimes drugged. Kurt joined him too. Disgusting. Disgusting, filthy, pigs."

"How many times would you say he raped you?" Agent Dodge asked.

She closed her eyes, blew out a breath. "I lost count. For awhile it was weekly. Then it dwindled. The worst times would be when he'd have one of his sessions with Mickey. Such a sweet little girl, but she could never please him, and she pushed him. Even at seven years old she knew how to push his buttons. It was eerie, the way he'd calmly lock his fingers around her wrist and pull her upstairs to punish her. He'd come out of her room with a wild-eyed look on his face and I knew it would either be me or some young girl he'd have Kurt find. I started offering myself to him hoping he would take the bait and not go after some poor young thing. It usually worked."

Agent Dodge sighed heavily, Agent Stephens paced, Jeff cursed softly. The evil in this world seemed to infiltrate every part of life. Every corner. Even where there is innocence. This woman had sacrificed herself in order to keep young girls from the Senator's clutches. She was more than a victim. She was a hero.

"And where was Mrs. Daley when all this was happening?" Jeff asked.

"Poor bird," Dora said, shaking her head. "He kept her so doped up on meds, she never knew what was going on around her."

"She had to know her daughter was being abused at the hands of her husband," Jeff said.

"Maybe, but he had her where she couldn't think. She couldn't make a rational decision. Still can't. And I'm sure she didn't realize all the things that monster did to her daughter."

Jeff swallowed, sat up straight. "Things like what? Are you talking about the beatings?"

"The beatings, yes, but so much more. The terror. The dread. The humiliation. The worst one was when Mickey was thirteen. I'll never forget it."

"What happened?" Jeff asked, dreading the answer.

"She was headed out to a birthday party for one of her friends. He told her no way could she go in a shirt so low-cut. She smarted off, as she had a tendency to do." Dora shrugged. "It was the only way she could assert herself. The only way she could rebel against his iron hand. Anyway, when she smarted off, he took her by the hand and led her up the stairs. I think she instinctively knew this time wasn't gonna be a normal beating. She'd tried to get away, you know, tried to jerk her hand free, but he just smacked her several times before he ever got her to her room."

Dora's tears started anew. Jeff's expression remained stony.

"There was a lot of screaming and yelling and hitting and then there was silence. I was worried. I waited in the upstairs hall for him to come out. When he didn't, I thought maybe he'd hurt her, or, even killed her. I was terrified, but finally, I opened the door. Mr. Daley, he was just standing there in the middle of the room, staring into the corner. I looked over and little Mickey, was standing there in the corner, standing tall, completely naked."

Cursing softly, Jeff stood and paced the room, coming to stand by a small window. He stared out while she continued.

"Her nose was bleeding and her hair was all tangled. Her entire body shook, but she stood there unmoving, her eyes glaring at Mr. Daley. She was so young, so young, but so old at the same time. The Senator glanced at me and seemed to snap out of the trance he was in. He looked back to Mickey and said, 'you like to show off your body so much, you will stand there, young lady, until showing off gets old.'" Dora sighed. "She never could keep her mouth shut."

"What did she say?" Stevens asked kindly.

Dora swallowed. "She started screaming at him. Things like, 'F' you daddy.' She said, 'The only reason I'm standing here without my clothes is because you wanted to see me naked. The only reason you didn't want me to wear that shirt is you're jealous. I know what you really wanna do, you sick old man.' Stuff like that. He charged at her, then stopped when he was only inches from her. She stood her ground. Always did. Even when he towered over her like that she held her chin up."

Jeff closed his eyes as he imagined the proud girl standing there, naked, defying death.

"He just stood there looking her up and down. I thought he was gonna jerk her to the floor and rape her. Instead he hauled off and slapped her so hard she hit the wall. Then he turned to me, forced me down on Mickey's bed and raped me."

Jeff made the decision right then and there that if they weren't able to put the Senator away, he would kill the man. No idle threat. Daley was a dead man.

Dora wiped her eyes and continued. "That poor baby stood in that corner for three days. Three days!"

"Where was her mother during that time?" Agent Stephens asked.

"Marion was nine months pregnant with Marissa. She had no idea what was going on and I couldn't tell her because I was afraid she might confront him and he might hurt her and the baby."

"What happened after three days?" Jeff asked.

"I went in the room to take her water and found her collapsed on the floor. I went to tell Mr. Daley. He picked her up from the floor and carried her to her bed. I watched every move he made. I was so worried he would, you know, lose control. She was unconscious and it scared me the way his hands lingered. That's when I moved close and took his hand in mine and drew him away. Thank God, I was able to distract him. Marion went into labor the next day with Marissa. After that, it seemed like he tried to keep his distance from Mackenzie."

"The beatings stopped?" Dodge asked.

"Maybe not stopped completely. They did slow down. Instead of a weekly thing, it became every few months. The moment that child turned eighteen she left home. She very seldom came back unless there were a lot of people around. She acted like she'd completely forgotten what he'd done to her."

"Did she ever confide in you?" Dodge asked.

"Never. She knew I knew what he'd done to her, and I knew she knew what he'd done to me, but we never spoke about it." Dora shook her head as the tears coursed down her cheeks. "I don't know, it was like, if we didn't talk, then it didn't really happen."

Jeff approached, knelt down by her side. "You will testify against him?"

She bit her lip.

"I give you my word I'll keep your kids safe. My word."

She nodded slowly. "I trust you."

He stood. Nodded. "Thank you."

"Ms. Suarez, did Daley ever abuse Marissa in any way?" Dodge asked.

"I was so scared that he would. When Mickey left home Rissa was only five. I thought maybe he would transfer his attention to her, ya know, but he seemed to be real loving towards her. He never yelled at her. She sat on his lap a lot and I was suspicious of that. I watched his hands, though. I watched him whenever he was with Marissa and he didn't seem to have any interest in her."

"Ms. Suarez, I'm sorry for the loss of your husband. We will nail this guy, but you'll have to be strong a little while longer."

"I'll do it. Mickey was strong. It's my turn." She turned to Jeff as he moved toward the door. "Agent Davis?" Dora called softly. "Do you think she'll forgive me?"

He smiled kindly at her. "There's nothing to forgive. He played you. You're as much a victim as everyone else. To me, you're a hero. You did what you could to protect the innocent. Then again, I can't speak for Mickey. I suggest you speak to her yourself. Maybe it's time to get things out in the open."

She nodded. "I think you're right."

~~~

Talmond screamed curses as he slammed down the phone.

Marion appeared in the doorway of his study. "Talmond? Can I get you something?"

He glared up at her. "Where's Dora?"

"She didn't come in today. She said she had a family emergency."

"I don't pay her to take time off."

"She's never asked for a day off in all these years, Talmond. Is there something I can get for you?"

"You can get the hell out of my room."

Wringing her hands she went to pull the door closed.

"I'm gonna punish your daughter," Talmond said quietly.

Marion stopped, gave a soft gasp. "Marissa?"

"Both actually. Marissa has proven to be just as much trouble as Mickey. Punishing her, however, will have to wait a few days since I'll have to track her down."

"What do you mean, track her down?"

"Judge Whitcomb had Marissa removed from Mackenzie's care. They've put my child, a Senator's daughter, into foster care. Can you believe that?"

Marion's hand flew to her mouth. "I, I didn't know. I guess it's because of what you said to the reporters the other night," Marion said with a sigh.

"Come here," Talmond ordered.

Marion moved forward, suddenly realizing the mistake she'd made. Fear mounting, she moved forward until she was in front of his desk. He rose slowly. Pointed a finger at her.

"Do you think to tell me what I should or shouldn't say to the media?"

"No, of course not."

The blow came quickly, knocking her against the bookshelf on her right. She crumpled onto the floor. "I'm sorry, Talmond. I wasn't thinking."

"No, you weren't, but that's just par for the course, isn't it? Do women ever think clearly?"

Marion wisely didn't answer the question.

He came around in front of the desk, knelt down beside her, offered his hand, which she took, and helped her up. "There now." He motioned her into a wingback chair. She sat cautiously on the edge.

Talmond began to pace the room.

"I'm surrounded by idiots. Things are not going well for me, Marion."

"I'm sorry, Talmond. Let me do something to help."

He stopped, looked her over. What little comfort her body could offer him he'd take advantage of soon enough. Right now, he just needed to work out a plan of action.

He shook his head. "Kurt's in jail, denied bond. Two of my men Kurt sent to do a job are also in jail. My daughter is in some stranger's home being kept from me. My campaign manager just quit. Polls have me about as likely to win an election as Charlie Manson. My career is over. I may even face a jail sentence on this ridiculous kidnapping thing. My aides and most of my staff have turned in their notices. The only ones still beside me are my attorneys and that's only because I'm paying them big bucks. It's all over, everything I've worked toward all these years, and you know who's responsible for all of it?"

Marion shook her head.

"That brat daughter of yours."

Grimacing, she looked up at her husband, eyes pleading. "Talmond, surely you don't believe Mickey could do all this to you? The poor girl was kidnapped, held hostage for over a week. She's not in her right mind. Unless," she hesitated, looked up. "Talmond, please, tell me, did you arrange to have her kidnapped? Did you order men to kill my daughter?"

He stopped pacing in front of her chair, grabbed her by the shoulders and pulled her up. He smiled, spoke surprisingly soft. "Think, Marion. After all the time and effort I spent in molding that headstrong little girl into a successful young woman, would I have her murdered? Of course I didn't. She's lost her marbles. I can't even imagine what's going through her head." He hugged her against him, stroking her back, then pulled her away, his eyes gleaming. "And Marion, don't ever question me again." His backhand knocked her to the floor again.

He immediately felt contrite. Sweet Marion had stood by him through everything, always believing in him, always backing him. He knelt down beside her, pulled her head into his lap, stroked her hair. "There now. Everything's gonna be alright. You know why, Marion?"

She shook her head.

"Because I'm gonna make it right. I'm gonna fix everything. And that daughter of yours is gonna get just what she deserves. Then, in a few days, nothing else will matter. Would you like to go on a long vacation, Marion? Someplace warm?"

She sighed. "That would be wonderful. Somewhere in the south Pacific?"

"Maybe. Somewhere far away. We'll spare no expense."

"What about the girls?"

"Don't worry about them, they'll be taken care of. This is just for you and me. Would you like that?" he asked, gently stroking his hand through her hair where she lay on his lap.

"Yes, Talmond. It would be so lovely to get away, lie on the beach, get a tan. It's always so cold and wet here."

He rubbed his hand over her face, still surprisingly smooth for her age. He realized she looked a lot like Mickey. Or, Mickey looked like her. But Marion didn't do it for him. MacKenzie, he sighed, he'd always wanted her. His young daughter Marissa he'd never had any interest in. That Kino kid was hot, but who was he kidding? It'd always been Mackenzie.

~~~

"How's she doing?" Jeff asked as he came in the door and set Mickey's computer on the dining room table.

"I think she's okay," Jack said. "She had a pretty good hangover this morning, but I fixed her up. Then I took her into her appointment with the shrink."

"How'd that go?"

"Hard to tell. Her face was all swollen from crying and stuff, but her mood seemed lifted. Then Marissa called and they talked for a few hours. That was another crying jag, but I'm thinking it helped her too. Tell me you accomplished great things today."

Jeff grinned. "I accomplished great things today. We're gonna nail him. They're trying to reach some famous family of Kurt Wells and Butch a.k.a. Alan Bradshaw. They think Kurt will turn states evidence and then that's all she wrote."

"Famous?"

"Yeah. Wells' little brother is a Governor and Alan Bradshaw is the older brother of Matthew Wilson." Jeff nodded before Jack could ask. "Yes, of the Dallas Cowboys."

"Amazing. Are they crooked?"

"Don't appear to be. Daley used the gov and Wilson to keep Wells and Butch loyal."

"And how'd it go with the housekeeper?"

"Dora rolled over today, but the feds want all their ducks in a row this time before they take Daley in and charge him. Cameron went out with Stevens and I early this morning and we found the computer he saw Wells dump. We're still waiting to hear about what they found on the hard drive."

"Well, heck, you weren't exaggerating, Jeff. Did you solve world peace while you were at it?"

"Not yet, but I'm getting ready to start on that one person at a time. Is she upstairs?"

"No, actually, she's on the patio, sunbathing and good grief, you should see her in that tiny, black bikini."

Jeff's brows rose.

Jack shrugged. "Sorry, man, but I'm human, ya know?"

"As long as you're also outta here, I'll forgive you for lusting after my woman."

"Man, I just ordered pizza."

Jeff pulled out two twenties. "Be a friend, go back to the hotel and order again."

Jack grabbed the bills. "I'm outta here. Hope you like pepperoni."

Jeff grinned, closed and locked the door behind Jack and turned to find Mickey. He watched her through the sliding glass doors as she lay in the late afternoon sun. He figured she was the most beautiful woman he'd ever seen. She had her dark tresses up in a pony tail and wore sunglasses. Sweat beaded on her upper lip. Her skin glowed in the sun. The strings to her top were loose and fell forward, exposing a tiny triangle of lighter skin. His mouth went dry.

When he slid open the door, Mickey raised her sunglasses to the top of her head and smiled up at him. "Hi, Jeff."

He knelt down beside her. "Hi yourself. You doing better today?"

She looked down self-consciously. "I'm sorry about last night. I don't usually drink."

He smiled. "Yeah, I could tell you're not real good at it."

She gave a soft laugh.

"I love that sound. You laughing."

"I've not had a lot to laugh about lately."

"Hopefully that will change soon."

She nodded, sighed. "Let's talk about other things tonight. Just things that are up and positive and have nothing to do with Talmond."

"That would be my pleasure," he said, forcing the images of what he'd learned today out of his head. It was hard though. The guy had beaten her with fists and belts, clothes hangers and extension cords. He'd beaten her bare skin, he'd touched her. He'd humiliated her. And he would pay for what he'd done to his Mickey. His. That's exactly how he thought of her. His. His girl. His woman. His wife. He cupped her face, ran his thumb over her mouth. "May I ask you a question?"

"As long as it's not about the forbidden subject."

"I want to ask you to give our relationship another chance. I want to ask you to trust me enough to believe I won't hurt you. I know it's difficult, under your circumstances, to believe in me. But I'm not leaving you, Mick. I'm here. Right here. And I'm not going anywhere."

She smiled at him. "I would've thought after I begged you to have sex with me last night that you would've figured out that I wanted us to resume our relationship."

He breathed a sigh of relief. "That's really good to hear."

"That doesn't mean I'm ready to have sex with you now."

"When we're ready for that, we won't be having sex, we'll be making love. And I'm not ready for that either. The time is not right. I want only what's good and right for you."

She sighed. "I love it when you talk all forceful and manly."

He smiled. "Do you?" She didn't love it last week, but he was smart enough not to bring that up right now. Instead he lowered his head and kissed her softly.

Mickey whimpered, arching her back, straining to press herself upward. Touching a finger to her nose, he smiled. "I love you, Mickey. I have a feeling I will always love you. They will never go away, these feelings I have. I want to make you happy. I want to come home to you every night."

"Jeff."

"No, don't say anything. You don't have to reciprocate. Not yet. Just accept it. Accept that you are loved, by others, yes, but especially by me."

He kissed her softly and pulled away. "Jack ordered pizza. It should be here soon."

"Then I think I'll go take a quick shower," she said, tying the strings of her top so she could stand without it falling off.

"I'll be waiting."

~~~

They sat on the sofa snuggling when Mickey jumped up at the knock on the door. "Steady now," he said with a chuckle.

She started toward the door and he grabbed her hand. "Um, I'll get it. I'm not trying to order you around, but you are still under protective custody."

She caught herself and stifled her automatic response.

He grinned. "You hungry?"

"Starved."

He came back with the pizza box and put it on the coffee table. "Let's have a picnic on the floor in the living room."

"Sounds fun," she said as she jumped up to grab plates and napkins.

Jeff headed into the kitchen as well, started to grab some wine then quickly changed his mind and grabbed a couple of sodas.

Minutes later they sat cross-legged on a comforter, the pizza box between them.

"It seems like it was months ago we ate pizza together that first night in a motel room in Red Bluff," Mickey said. "It's weird to think it's only been a few weeks."

"A lot's happened since then, and a lot more is gonna happen, but we're not supposed to talk about anything bad tonight, remember?"

She licked some sauce from her lips. "That's right, so instead let's talk about you."

"What do you want to know?"

"Umm, how long have you worked for Ameritech?"

"Ten years now. I was twenty when Jason hired me."

"Wow. That's a long time. I mean, most people have been through several jobs by the time they turn thirty."

"Yeah. I've always known what I wanted to do."

She smiled seductively. "So, you're a man who knows what he wants."

"I am. Maybe that's why I knew the moment I saw you that I wanted you."

She thought back to that moment and pushed it from her mind. No bad thoughts. "You say you're going to visit your family next month?"

"We always get together for the fourth. Why don't you and Marissa join me?"

Mickey's lips pursed as she thought. "That's an idea. Can I think about it?"

"Of course. It would be great fun and my parents would love to meet you."

"Do they know about me, and that you're the one who found me?"

"Yes. When Daley plastered my face all over the television they contacted Jason. He filled them in. I spoke with them a couple of days ago. They asked me if you are as pretty as you are on TV."

She giggled. "Yeah, right. What did you say?"

"I told them you were absolutely gorgeous, but it was much more fulfilling to see you up close and personal."

"Oh good grief, Jeff, you didn't say that did you?"

"Sure. It's true."

She shook her head. Sipped her soda, while Jeff finished off the last piece of pizza. She watched him. He was so strong. Physically and mentally. So self-assured. So kind. How could she not love him? Leaning over, he took her soda from her and set it down, pushed the box out of the way and sat with his back against the sofa. Crossing his ankles, he patted the spot next to him and Mickey scooted over.

Jeff draped his arm around her shoulders and they sat in companionable silence for a long time before Jeff finally spoke.

"Jack tells me you had a counseling session today. How do you think it went?"

She looked down. "Sharon Denton, that's her name. She's like, sixty and she's very good."

"Sort of grand-motherly?"

"Not at all. At first glance you might think she's a lawyer or some high corporate exec. She's sharp. Professional."

"And you felt comfortable?"

"Yeah, it was weird. It's like, she had such an air of professionalism and confidence that I felt I could trust her. We really hit it off. I think she's gonna be good for me."

"Eric recommended her?"

"Yes. I guess he knew what he was doing. Remind me to call him and thank him."

Jeff pulled out his phone, dialed the number, handed it to her. "No time like the present."

Smiling, Mickey took the phone. Jeff watched her face as she profusely thanked Grandmaster Kino, answered some questions and then spoke to both Shelley and Jeffy. When she handed the phone back to Jeff, she had tears in her eyes.

"What's wrong?" Jeff asked.

"They're just so nice. They act as if they'd just heard from their long lost daughter or something. They act as if they love me."

"They do."

"They don't even know me."

"They know your heart. Mickey, you are so easy to love."

"Eric said he was proud of me. For being strong. All three of them ended their conversation by telling me that they missed me and that I could call on them for anything at anytime. Have you ever heard of people like that?"

Jeff smiled kindly. "I grew up with people like that. However, the Kino's, they're special. With them on your side, you'll never be alone."

Mickey yawned and slid down to lay her head on Jeff's thigh. Jeff stroked her arm and back, until she rolled over to look up at him. "Do you still think you love me, Jeff?"

He rubbed his knuckles over her cheek. "With all my heart."

"It still feels like I love you too."

His eyes closed briefly in thanks, before he smiled down at her. "That is so good to know."

~~~

Eric Kino gave a soft moan as he lay in the dark, kissing his wife. He wasn't sure how it was possible, but he was more in love with her now than when he'd fallen hard and fast sixteen years ago. Life with her had been glorious and at times scary. Frustrating, and rewarding, yet never dull. Never. She'd taught him so much, though he was supposed to be her teacher. Tonight, the lesson being taught was that a forty-nine year-old woman could have complete power over him with just the touch of her fingers.

Shelley ran her hand over his chest, feeling the familiar ridges of muscle, and the heat and warmth that seemed to seep from him always. She sighed in pleasure just before the door burst open.

Eric was out of bed immediately. Shelley sat up, swung her legs over the edge of the bed.

"Jeffy?" Shelley said.

Jeffy sniffed loudly. "Something's wrong. Please, help me, Daddy."

Eric was at her side. "What is it, baby girl?"

Jeffy shook her head.

Shelley placed her palm against Jeffy's forehead. "Are you sick?"

"No, not sick," Jeffy said, her speech beginning to slur. Her body jerked and both hands flew up to cover her ears. "Oh, no, Daddy! Make it stop. Please!"

Eric caught her as she went down. He laid her on the bed while Shelley got a cool cloth.

"It's another vision, isn't it?" Shelley asked as she came back in the room. She placed the cloth on Jeffy's head, ran her hand over her face. Jeffy opened her eyes, sighed in relief.

Eric eyed his wife. He would never lie to her and he hoped the news wouldn't upset her too much, yet it seemed Jeffy was in for some bad times. He'd had visions and dreams himself over the years. As a matter of fact, he'd had a recurring dream starring Shelley long before he met her. That is how he came to be involved with her.

Now it seemed their daughter too would have dreams and visions, but hers were beginning to prove much more powerful, much more real, and much harder for Jeffy to separate from her waking reality.

"Well?" Shelley demanded.

"Well, yes, it seems to be a vision."

Shelley stroked her daughter's face. "Jeffy? Sweetheart, can you tell us what you saw?"

Jeffy blinked up at her parents. "I'm not sure. Everything was dark except for flashes of light here and there. I saw shadows of people running through the dark. I heard loud bangs, maybe like gunshots. And that last one, the last one was so loud it hurt my ears. I felt pain shoot through me and then I felt so sad." She shuddered. "I don't ever want to feel that again, that sadness. It was horrible." Tears ran down her face. "Daddy?"

"Yes, baby."

"It seems the visions are escalating, doesn't it?"

He sighed. "It appears so."

"Do you know why?"

"I have a theory."

"Will you tell me?"

Eric glanced at his wife, unsure if he should go into it.

"Daddy, you always say that talking about things, communicating, is a powerful tool. You say that communication is a tool not only for learning but for healing too."

Eric smiled. "Then I suppose, since you're so good at throwing my words back at me that I should tell you my theory, huh?"

"I want to learn. I want to understand what's happening."

Eric nodded. "I know you do, sweetie. So, here it is, I believe things have escalated because you are becoming more conscious, more awakened to who you are."

"Who I am? You mean, like when we talked about people being more than just biological beings?"

"Yes, like that. I'm speaking of our connection to something much greater than ourselves. Our connection to God. Who we are here and now is just a small part of who we really are."

Jeffy nodded. "I can feel that. Especially when I can see things, or know things psychically, I mean, it makes me feel like there is so much more to this world than what we can experience with our five senses."

"Exactly. And you know that I believe your being psychic, your having an abnormally high IQ, your physical capabilities and your having visions and dreams, is all because you have something extremely important to do. Maybe even something special you were sent to the world to accomplish. I feel this only intuitively, but I believe it to be true. Well, it's more than intuitively, God's been whispering this to me a long time, maybe even since the moment you were born. And now, I think things are escalating because you are coming into your own. You are growing and changing and part of that, maybe a lot of that, is because you recently toyed with the idea of crossing the line from being an innocent young girl to being an awakened young woman."

Jeffy sat quietly a moment, mulling over her father's words. Finally she looked up. "You're saying it's because I thought about having sex?"

Shelley smiled as Eric grimaced. "Yes," Eric said. "Because of that. Because of how it awakened you to another entire dimension to your human existence."

Jeffy sat up, nodded with a smile. "Oh yeah, it certainly did that."

Eric closed his eyes. Shelley chuckled and took his hand in comfort.

Jeffy grinned. "Sorry, Dad, I know it's hard for you to have your little girl grow up, but I have to say, I am surprised at you. I mean, you of all people talk about how we all must grow and progress."

"Yes, well, I'm merely human and I suppose I wasn't quite prepared for the time with you as my baby girl to come to an end."

"Merely human? Eric my love, you have never been merely human," Shelley quipped.

He smiled, touched her cheek. "Thanks for the vote of confidence, sweetheart, still, you need to take me down off that pedestal."

Jeffy smiled.

"What?" Eric asked.

"Nothing. I just love you guys, that's all. I hope one day I have what you have."

"That would make me happy to know that my daughter is as happy as I am," Shelley said softly.

"So, what do you think about my explanation as to why your visions have escalated?" Eric asked.

"It's cool. I can deal with that."

Eric sighed. "I just hope your mother and I can."

"I understand that it's hard for you, Daddy, to accept my growing up."

"Yes, well, thank you very much for your understanding," he said dryly.

"And I'm sorry if I scared you and mom just now when I came bursting into your room. It just seemed so terrible. And real. It seemed so real. So, do you think my vision will come true?"

"I hope not, yet experience shows you are usually pretty accurate."

Jeffy shuddered. "I wish I could do something to keep it from happening. I wonder if there is anything I could do."

"I suggest some prayer, some fasting, some meditation, and ask God what you can do to help. The answers will come to you if you can quiet your mind and let the information flow. God *will* talk to you."

She smiled at her father. Hugged him and kissed his cheek. "Thank you, Daddy. I will do just that." She turned and took her mother's hand. "Mom, will you come to my room with me for a little while?"

"Sure I will, sweetie." Shelley turned and kissed her husband's cheek. "Gotta go. Girl talk."

Sighing, he kissed her softly, his disappointment obvious.

She leaned close, whispered in his ear. "At least she called you 'daddy' again."

He laughed.

"If you're good, I'll come back later and call you anything you'd like."

He smiled. "I'll look forward to it."

Eric watched them go. He felt uneasy. He rose and headed downstairs to check that the house was secure. Just in case.

~~~

Jeff lay next to Mickey in her bed, watching her as she slept. She'd had another nightmare and she'd been so frightened, he couldn't bring himself to go back to his place on the sofa. He was contemplating their life together as husband and wife when he sat straight up in bed, listening intently. Someone was in the house. In seconds he was out of bed, one gun tucked in the waist of his jeans, and the other in his hand. He touched his pockets making sure his cell phone, wallet and keys were still there in case they needed to make a quick getaway.

"Jeff?" Mickey said sleepily.

"Shh." He whispered in her ear. "Don't make a sound."

Chapter Fourteen

"What's happening?" Mickey whispered.

"Listen to me carefully. Get your phone, go in the bathroom and lock the door. Call Jason. Tell him we've got company."

"But– oh no, no, no." Her nails dug into Jeff's forearm in panic as she realized what was happening. "Someone's in the house? They've come for me, haven't they?"

"Mick, come on now, don't freeze up on me. You have to trust me. Please just do as I say. Lock the door and don't come out until I come to get you." He handed her the phone off the night table. "Here. Go. And Mick, I love you."

She scrambled up off the bed. "Please be careful, Jeff."

But he'd already left the room.

Moving silently on bare feet, Jeff eased down the steps. He saw a ray of light, obviously from a flashlight, skim down the wall near the front entrance. Another one hit the front door simultaneously so he knew there was more than one intruder. As Jeff neared the halfway mark of the staircase a third man stepped into view looking up the steps as if he'd been waiting for him. The surprise in his eyes told Jeff the man had been assigned to watch the stairs and had failed in his duty.

The intruder raised his weapon, but Jeff fired first, hitting him square in the chest. Jeff dove left, over the railing then scrambled toward the living room as several shots peppered the stair and wall where he'd been standing. He rose immediately and took out the black shadow that'd been coming from the dining area, but not before he felt the sting in his shoulder. That's two down he mentally calculated. Another gunman squeezed off several shots. The sliding glass patio doors behind him shattered as Jeff barely dodged the bullets and threw himself behind the sofa.

The house became deadly silent. Jeff couldn't be sure there was only the one left. Crawling on his belly he made his way into the dining area. Satisfied there was nowhere for an intruder to hide in there, he rose and stealthily made his way into the kitchen which was only a narrow corridor-like room with doorways that led from the front entrance area near the stairway to the dining room on the other side.

"Jeff?"

He looked up in horror as Mickey stepped from the stair landing and moved toward him where he stood in the kitchen. "Dear Jesus," he began.

He heard the steps before he saw the man charge her. Mickey gasped as the guy grabbed her from behind, his forearm locked around her neck. It was the gun pressed to her temple that had Jeff's heart stuttering.

"Drop the gun. I'll kill her. You know I will," the man said.

Jeff pressed his lips together, shook his head. "Why haven't you? Isn't that what you came here to do?"

"Drop the gun," the man yelled.

"I drop the gun you'll kill us both."

"No, I just wanna get out, that's all. Drop it. I'm not playing around." He jerked his arm making Mickey gasp for air.

"Okay, okay. I'll drop," Jeff said.

"Now."

But Jeff's eyes narrowed as the gunman did something strange. He raised his arm and glanced at his watch.

"Now, I said!"

"Okay, okay, I'm dropping it right—" He squeezed the trigger.

Mickey screamed. The gunman fell back against the wall, a small black hole gaping between his eyes. Jeff moved forward, grabbed Mickey. "Come on. Hurry."

"What's—"

"No time," he yelled as he pushed her ahead of him through the broken shards of the sliding glass doors.

The room exploded. Mickey knew a strange sensation as she and Jeff both went airborne and landed in the backyard. Afterward, like the dawn after a storm, there was silence.

Mickey didn't know how long she'd been lying there. She realized there'd been a bomb. She realized her house was on fire. She knew help was close because the siren's were loud enough to be nearby. She realized Jeff's heavy body lay on top of her, protecting her as always.

Slowly, she finally realized, he wasn't moving.

She pushed up, against his chest, but he didn't respond. "Jeff?" she cried. "Jeff?"

Terror gave her the strength to crawl out from under him and turn him over. "Jeff!" she screamed. "Jeff!"

She bent over him. He wasn't breathing. Blood oozed from his nose. She started mouth to mouth. She blew life into him until she was so dizzy she couldn't tell up from down.

Hands tugged at her, pulling her away. "No, let me go. Jeff!"

"Let the paramedics work on him," a familiar voice said. "Come on, you can't help him that way."

Mickey slowly looked up into Jack's face. "Jack? Is he, is Jeff—"

"I don't know."

She flung herself against his chest. "No, no, no," she sobbed.

Jack held her tight while he watched the paramedics work on Jeff. Jack himself was mesmerized by the limpness of Jeff's arms as they moved him around. That wasn't Jeff. The lifeless guy lying there couldn't be Jeff. He heard them call out the numbers for his blood pressure. Forty something over twenty something was not good. Then things got worse.

Mickey looked up when she heard the medic team call, 'clear.' She watched them put paddles to Jeff's chest and shock him, which meant they were trying to either regulate his heartbeat or restart his heart. She collapsed to the ground in a daze. Not real. Not real, she thought. Can't be real. This is another dream, right? Jeff is strong. Jeff is practically immortal. He can't die. Not Jeff. Not her Jeff. She closed her eyes and willed him back to life. You said you'd never leave me, she thought. You said you weren't going anywhere. Don't leave me, Jeff. Please don't leave me.

Jack knelt down beside her. "Mickey?"

She looked up at him, not really seeing him.

"Mickey, he's alive," Jack said.

She became alert. "He is?"

"Yeah. His heart's beating. He's breathing. Now, we have to see to you."

"To me?"

A paramedic put a blanket around her shoulders. "Let me check you out," a woman said softly. Mickey nodded, keeping her eyes on Jeff until they placed him on a stretcher and took him around front of what was left of her house. Jason appeared, stopped the gurney, spoke briefly to the paramedic before they went on. He didn't seem to be his usual reserved self. He walked toward her, worry etched on his face.

"Is he okay?" she asked.

"He's alive. He has a concussion. His heart tried to stop, but they were able to remedy that. He was grazed twice by bullets, but those are just flesh wounds. Looks like he's gonna be okay."

Tears coursed down Mickey's cheeks. "Thank you. Thank you. Thank you," she whispered.

~~~

Mickey sat in a chair in a waiting room, her knees drawn up, her arms wrapped tightly around them. She watched Jason walk back from the vending area, two cups of coffee in his hands. He offered her one. She lowered her legs and accepted the styrofoam cup with a nod.

"How much longer do you think it will be before we can see him?"

"It's already been well over an hour. I don't think it'll be too much longer."

She nodded. Agent Dodge and Stevens had left not fifteen minutes ago. She told them all she knew. They said they'd be back to speak with Jeff. She looked out the window, noting the pink tinges of dawn creeping over the horizon.

"He did this," she said vehemently.

"He's going down," Jason said.

"Everyone keeps saying that, but he's alive and well isn't he? He's asleep in his comfortable custom bed with the silk sheets. Soon, he'll rise with a smile on his face and be anxious to hear the top news story of the day. He'll sit down to his stupid ritual breakfast and force my mother to sit with him for exactly one hour." She smiled. "Oh, but he'll be furious to know he missed again. That I survived." She gave a soft chuckle. "I'd love to see the look on his face when he hears I'm alive."

"Thank God for that," Jason mumbled. He briefly closed his eyes, pointed upward.

Mickey watched him. She'd seen Jeff do something like that, and the Kinos, and Mark and Joey Adams, and even Agents Jack and Nate. "What you just did, Jason, tell me about that."

He glanced at her, "Um, what did I do?"

"You pointed upward."

"Did I? I guess I do it so much it's become second nature to me. I was thanking God that you made it through alive, and Jeff too." He shrugged. "It seems I'm almost in a constant state of prayer. I'm either thanking God, or asking Him for some assistance all the time."

Mickey frowned trying hard to understand. "And He answers you?"

Jason smiled at her. "He does."

"How? I mean, do you hear a voice in your head?"

"Actually, sometimes I do. It took me a while to realize I was hearing His voice. I used to think these random thoughts I had were just my mind chatter, you know, just my own thoughts. But I began to recognize His voice. It would usually be accompanied by a strong feeling of peace or of clarity, or of motivation. And then, as if He knew I, in my humanness, would need confirmation, He would give me that confirmation."

"I don't mean to be dumb, but, how would you receive a confirmation?"

Jason nodded. "That's not dumb. It's a good question. The confirmation could be something like a synchronicity, or what some people call a coincidence. But there are really no such things as coincidences. For example, back when I was trying to decide if I should invest everything I had to start Ameritech, I had five different people, who had no idea what I was thinking about doing, in the course of a simple conversation, tell me they wish they could hire their own FBI to help them with whatever problem they were having. After the fifth one, it finally got through to me it was the right course of action. And then, as I sat out under the stars, and was thanking God for the confirmations, a shooting star shot straight down in front of my eyes. And because I had my mind in heavenly places, I knew in my heart that was God acknowledging me." He stopped, wiped the tear from his eye.

Mickey watched him, her eyes wide. "Wow. That was amazing. It's like, I can feel what you're talking about in my own heart."

Jason smiled. "Remember that feeling. That is God talking to *you*."

"So, I'm assuming you're a Christian?"

"I am. And Jesus is my constant companion."

"And is everyone in your company a Christian?"

"No. But I can't even tell you how many people who work for me have become Christians. It's in the hundreds."

"Really? Do you have some kind of missionary initiative?"

"Nope. We teach– by example."

"What do you mean?"

"Well, for example, this whole conversation just happened because you saw me offer a quick prayer of thanks. I set the example, it led to you asking questions. God touched your heart as I spoke. That's how it works."

Mickey nodded in understanding. They sat in companionable silence for some time.

Jason looked at her. "You know, you're closer to God than you think."

"How's that?"

"Back at your house, you asked me about Jeff's condition. When I told you he was gonna be okay, you said, 'thank you, thank you, thank you.'"

"I was thanking you."

"Were you? I had nothing to do with Jeff's condition. I'd just arrived. You were grateful Jeff was alive, and the only one to thank for that at that moment, was God. So just naturally, automatically, you offered a prayer of thanks."

She sat thinking about that for several minutes.

It was Mickey who broke the silence on what she thought was a completely different subject. "You should've seen him. Jeff, I mean. That guy had a gun pointed at my head and Jeff, he was so calm. He never even hesitated. He fired his gun and got me outta there so fast. Two seconds slower and we'd probably both be dead."

Jason smiled kindly. Eyebrows raised he pointed upward.

"Oh, I think I'm beginning to understand," she said.

It was Jason who changed the subject. "You love Jeff very much, don't you?"

"I know we haven't known each other very long, but yes, I believe I do."

"I know Jeff well, and I've seen him go through several relationships. You're it for him." He smiled. "But you didn't hear it from me."

"Thank you," Mickey replied, smiling sweetly.

Sighing, Jason looked out the window. He had business he needed to take care of. Once he saw Jeff for himself, he'd have to get Nate over here to stay with Mickey. He'd already contacted Jeff's parents and they would be arriving sometime today. "Your stepfather will probably be taken into custody today," Jason informed her. "We've built a decent case against him."

"Really?" Mickey asked, disdain in her voice. "And how fast will they let him out on bail?"

"That's purely at the judge's discretion."

"He'll keep getting out. He won't go to jail. I doubt he'll go to trial."

"He will go to trial and he will be found guilty. Kidnapping, accessory to kidnapping, rape, child endangerment, child cruelty, attempted murder, murder, and I'm just getting started."

"Rape? Murder?" Mickey asked softly.

"Dora is gonna testify."

Mickey's face paled. She set her cup down. "Are you sure?"

"Yes. We're putting her and her family into protective custody. Daley murdered her husband. She realizes she let him get away with everything for too long. It's time to step up."

Mickey looked down at her feet as memories surfaced. She didn't raise her head when Jason's hand covered hers and squeezed.

~~~

"Good morning, dear," Talmond chirped at his wife as he entered the dining room. "Something smells wonderful. Is Dora back?"

Marion wrung her hands. "No, she's still out. Says she'll be out for a while."

Talmond shrugged. "Doesn't matter. We'll be leaving for our extended vacation tomorrow. So, what have you cooked up in there?"

Marion smiled at him. This was the man she remembered. The one she'd fallen in love with. "I've made a spinach quiche and buttery croissants."

"Sounds lovely. I'll have my coffee first, if you don't mind."

"Not at all. I'll just be a second."

She exited the dining room, humming softly to herself. Talmond opened the doors of the hutch that sat atop the large buffet and turned on the television, anxious to hear the news. When Marion returned with his coffee his expression brought her up short. Nervously, she set the cup by his right hand.

"Talmond? Is something wrong?"

He spoke to her without looking at her, his tone dangerously soft. "There was an explosion at Mackenzie's home last night."

Marion's hands flew to her face. "Oh no! Are you sure?"

"Yes. Mickey escaped unharmed. Her little boyfriend is in the hospital."

"I have to see her," Marion said, untying the apron at her waist.

"You will do no such thing."

"Talmond, she's my daughter. I have to see her. Did they say how it happened? Did they say what caused the explosion?"

Talmond looked up at her with derision. "I never realized you were such an idiot."

Marion gasped.

Talmond shook his head. "Oh, Marion, what did I ever see in you, huh?"

She didn't answer. Only stood with a bewildered look on her aging face as she struggled to understand the direction the conversation had taken. It sounded like he no longer wanted her. No, wait, there was something much more important to attend to, wasn't there? Yes, it was Mickey. Her house was destroyed in an explosion. Then again, it was just a house. Something material. And here was her husband of twenty-one years speaking to her as if he were about to leave her. That was much more important than a house, right?

"You've been much more trouble than you were ever worth. Nothing has worked out the way it should– the way I'd planned. Not one thing."

"I– I don't understand."

"I know you don't. Part of that is my fault, I guess. I definitely encouraged your little prescription drug habit."

"I don't have a drug habit, Talmond. I'm sick. I need my medications. You know that."

"Yes, dear. I know. At least, I know that's what you believe, but look at yourself, Marion. All those pills, they've aged you. You look like an old, used hooker. Too much makeup, skinny and haggard. Breasts like dried up prunes. Now that I'm really looking at you, I can't believe I've actually stayed with you and even allowed you in my bed."

Tears welled up in her eyes. "Talmond, it's not like you to say such mean things to me."

He gave a short laugh. "Isn't it? You don't know me at all, Marion. Not at all." He found himself wanting to hurt her. He wanted to break her down completely. He wanted to make her suffer. Nothing had worked out. He'd endured her idiocy all these years just to have everything fall apart right here at the end. An exchange will be made tonight that will bring him more money than God. He'd originally planned to buy his way right into the presidency. Now all those plans were gone. Thanks to Mackenzie.

Still, he thought, he'll have the money by morning. There is no reason why he can't go on with his secondary plans which are to disappear and live like a king in another country. It just won't be as much fun knowing Mackenzie survived. Then again, with the money he'll have, he can hire a real professional. As a matter of fact, he could drag it out for years. Terrorize her. Make her suffer. Make her life as miserable as she'd made his. A shame he couldn't do to her what he'd never let himself do all these years. There was nothing left of his political aspirations thanks to her. If only he could get in one more shot at her before he left tomorrow. And then he realized– he could.

She was probably at the hospital watching over her boyfriend. With him out of commission and all the excitement over the explosion, she would probably be alone. He needed to get to her. However, him arriving at the hospital would not go unnoticed. No, he needed her to come to him. She wouldn't do that, of course. She would never come at his request, but he was sure she would come for Marion, or, his face brightened, for Marissa. Yes, that was the way to go. He'd need Marion, though, to pull it off.

"Talmond?"

His eyes shifted back to his wife. Had he actually planned on bringing her with him when he left for his new life? What had he been thinking? She was nothing more than a nuisance. He watched as she stood waiting like some homeless dog, for him to speak to her, to offer her a bone. Her hands shook. She looked toward the kitchen. He knew what she was thinking. She needed a pill. She truly disgusted him. How he'd like to be rid of her. Maybe tonight, when she goes to bed, he'll make her a nightcap. One she won't wake up from. The idea gave him a jolt of excitement and pleasure. How good would it feel to rid himself of the pesky fly he'd endured all these years? Yes, what a wonderful idea! Why hadn't he thought of it sooner? For now though, he needed her for a few more errands.

He smiled up at her. "I apologize Marion. I don't know what came over me. I was so distraught I guess I took it out on you. Forgive me?"

She smiled at him. "Oh, well, of course, Talmond. We all have our little moods, don't we?"

"Yes, yes we do."

"Why with all this with Mickey, first her being kidnapped, and then her saying what she said about you, you getting arrested and then Marissa being taken away— "

"I don't need a recap."

"Oh, of course you don't, dear. Sorry."

"Marion, can we just sit and eat breakfast? You know how much I look forward to our morning breakfasts together. Just you and me."

She re-tied her apron. Sighed happily. "Let me warm your coffee and I'll get your breakfast."

"Thank you, dear. And then maybe we'll talk about you giving Mackenzie a call."

"That would be great. I really want to go see her."

"Actually, I want her to come here. The judge says I'm not allowed to get close to her, but I'm so worried about her, Marion and I'm hoping I can get you to talk her into coming here."

"But—"

"I want you to call her and tell her to come here."

"Talmond, she won't come here. She's very angry at you."

"I know, nonetheless, don't you think it's time to put a stop to all this foolishness? I think it can all be solved if we just all sit down together and really communicate. Like they always say, communication is the key."

"That would be wonderful, but I'm trying to tell you it won't make any difference if I call her. She won't come."

"Sure she will," he said softly. "She will when she learns I have Marissa here."

Marion's brow wrinkled. "But Marissa's not here."

He closed his eyes, forced himself to stay calm. She is a freaking idiot, he told himself. Be patient. "Marion, I want you to try hard to follow what I'm asking you to do."

Her eyes welled with tears. "I'm trying, Talmond, but I don't understand."

"You will call Mickey and tell her I have Marissa here and she is to come if she ever loved her sister."

"You mean you want me to pretend that you're gonna punish Marissa?"

He looked at her incredulously. "Yeah, that's it, Marion. Tell her you don't know what I'm gonna do to Marissa, that I'm so angry and you're worried about her. And Marion, tell her to come alone. Tell her I'll know if she's not alone."

"Oh, dear, if I tell her that, she'll be even angrier and when she gets here she'll never be willing to sit down and talk things out."

Talmond nodded. "It's just a way to get her here. Once she gets here I'll explain to her why I had you say those things. I'm sure she'll understand once I tell her how much I want this big misunderstanding to be over."

Marion smiled. "I should never have questioned you."

"That's correct, Marion."

"I'll get your breakfast."

"You do that."

~~~

Mickey stood near Jeff's bed, his hand squeezing hers. He glanced up at her as Jason gave him a rundown of what had transpired. She smiled, he smiled back. He had a few cuts on the side of his face and a bandage around his upper left arm. Otherwise he was whole and healthy and swearing he was gonna take the IV out himself if someone didn't do it soon.

He'd been told to calm down, they would be releasing him shortly. He'd already stripped off the hospital gown and pulled his jeans back on. His chest was bare. They'd begged him to stay to let them monitor him for a few more hours. Mickey had only been able to have a few quick personal words with him before the world converged on him. The police department, the FBI, the media.

"And so, I have to take care of business," Jason finished up. "Nate will be here soon. He'll take care of whatever you need. Oh, and here—" he said, setting Jeff's gun down.

"I had two on me," Jeff said.

"Yep. Feds confiscated the one you used so they could put together the crime scene. We literally had to pry it out of your cold, dead, hand."

Jeff chuckled at Mickey's indrawn breath.

"Sorry, Mickey," Jason said. "I couldn't resist, he's used that line so many times." He held the gun out to Jeff. "Put this away so no one freaks before you get out of here."

"Got it," Jeff said, reaching out for the weapon. He quickly checked it, locked it, placed it in the metal bedside drawer.

Jason leaned forward, took Jeff's hand, started to speak then stopped as his emotions got the better of him.

Jeff nodded at him. Jason nodded back, then moved quickly toward the door.

Mickey watched him go until Jeff jerked her hand and pulled her down to him. "You okay, baby?'

She nodded. "You're alive. I'm more than okay."

"You know, if you hadn't disobeyed me, you'd probably be dead."

She grinned. "You should never have brought that up."

"You're probably right about that." He sighed. "You'll never listen to me again. So, tell me, what made you come downstairs."

She thought a minute. "I heard the shots. Then everything got so quiet. All I could think was you'd been shot and were lying there dying while I was hiding like a coward in the bathroom. I had to find you."

"You are such a warrior."

She shrugged. "I just love you."

"You love me, huh?"

She smiled. "I do."

"All I can say is, I'm very glad you came looking for me." He tugged at the IV. "And now, all I want to do is get out of here."

"We'll get out soon enough. Besides, Nate will be here soon. At least we should wait for him."

"Okay, and then we'll go. I want to go back to the house, look things over."

"There's not much left to look at."

He rubbed his hand up and down her arm. "I'm sorry, Mick."

"Not your fault. Insurance will pay and I'll rebuild. And then, I'll probably sell. Bad vibes, ya know?"

He nodded. "I understand."

They both looked up as Nate walked through the door loaded down with bags.

"Hey, bud," Nate said, grinning. He tossed everything on the nearest chair and came to take Jeff's hand. "Glad you're still with us."

"Thanks, man. Glad to be here."

"But not glad to be *here*," Nate said with a laugh. "Don't worry, you're leaving soon. I brought you a shirt, some shoes and socks, and money."

"Did my truck make it through?"

"Yeah, everything out front was okay, so your truck, Mickey's car and Marissa's room made it through." He turned to Mickey. "Your room though looks to be a total loss as does most of the downstairs living area."

She sighed. "I didn't think much survived."

When the room phone rang Jeff picked it up. He raised his eyebrows in a gesture of surprise, then with his hand over the mouthpiece he handed the phone to Mickey. "It's for you. It's your mom."

"You're kidding," Mickey said. She shook her head. "I don't want to talk to her."

"Come on, Mick, be brave. She said she saw the news and couldn't believe what happened. She needed to hear your voice for herself."

Mickey blew out a breath and took the phone, but turned her back so she could have a little privacy.

"So," Nate said. "Tell me what the hell happened."

"You haven't heard?"

"Sure I have, but I want the dirt from you."

While Nate and Jeff talked, Mickey spoke softly into the phone. "Tell your husband not to hurt her. Tell him I'll be there. I just have to figure out a way to get there, but tell him I'm coming. And you'd better believe it won't be pleasant."

She hung up the phone and put it back on the bedside table, smiling and easing into the conversation. A few minutes later Jack walked through the door and the conversation started all over again. Thirty minutes later, the door opened again and a nurse took Jeff's vitals and left. Fifteen minutes after that Jeff's parents walked in the door.

"Mom! Dad!" Jeff said. "I didn't think you'd be here so soon."

"We got lucky and managed to grab an earlier flight," Mr. Davis said as Jeff's mom leaned over the bed and threw her arms around him.

Mickey backed away to give them room, but she didn't get very far before Jeff's mom approached her.

"You're Mackenzie aren't you? Jeff's right, you're even prettier in person. It's so nice to meet you."

Mickey brushed at the soot and streaks of dirt and blood on her clothing, the mismatched clothing she'd pulled on quickly when she went in search of Jeff. "Thank you, I'm afraid I'm a mess right now."

"Mom, Dad," Jeff said. "Obviously, this is Mackenzie Daley. We call her Mickey."

Mr. Davis extended his hand, smiled warmly. "Nice to meet you, Mickey."

Mickey nodded. "I'm sorry you have to come see your son in the hospital all because of me."

"Don't be ridiculous," Jeff said.

"It's my fault. You've been through so much just trying to protect me."

"If not you then someone else," Mr. Davis stated matter-of-factly. "I'm sure he's glad it's you."

Mrs. Davis smiled. "We've almost gotten use to Jeff's career choice." She turned, placed her hand on Jeff's shoulder. "Almost. If we had anyone to blame for him being injured, it would have to be his Grandpa Jared who bought him his first video game. From that moment on it's been guns and rifles and cops and robbers."

Jeff jumped in then defending his grandfather. Mickey tried to pay attention, but her mind was circling so fast, it seemed the conversation was merely background noise. There was laughter and jokes and then the story of what happened last night along with the nurse coming in to remove Jeff's IV with the good news that they were preparing his release paperwork. Mickey knew she had to make her move. She made her way around the room covertly collecting what she needed, then uttered some inane excuse about finding a more private restroom in which to freshen up.

A few minutes later she was climbing into a cab headed for the Daley mansion. She sat nervously, trying to make her mind think about the actions she was about to take. When Mickey had been a child, no one had ever defended her. Today, she would defend her sister. She patted the gun in her purse, hoping her mother wouldn't try to intervene.

The cab pulled up in front of the house and Mickey shoved the two twenties she'd stolen from Jeff into his hand and got out. Looking up at the house she'd grown up in, suffered in, the house she hated, she drew a calming breath and walked up the wide circular steps. When she tried the door, it opened. She slipped inside.

Marion came hurrying to meet her.

"Mickey, oh Mick, I'm so glad you're okay."

"Where's Marissa?" Mickey asked, ignoring her mother's ridiculous statements. Mickey never understood how her mother could say things that sounded like she actually cared, yet ignored her husband's actions. She figured it was an act. A role. One her mother had been playing since she married Talmond Daley.

"Marissa's, um, I mean, your father told me to tell you to go to his study."

Mickey turned on her. "Let me tell you this one more time, Mother. He's not my father. Stop calling him that." She looked toward the study. "Leave this to me. You go see to Marissa."

Marion only wrung her hands and nodded, knowing full well Marissa was nowhere around.

Mickey went to the study and slipped inside. Talmond sat at his desk, calmly waiting for her.

"I see you cared enough about your sister to come," he said quietly. "Come in, have a seat."

She stepped closer to the desk. "I won't be sitting down. Where's Marissa?"

Talmond laughed, rose and circled around behind Mickey. "Marissa's not here, Mackenzie. You don't really think I would hurt her, do you? After all, she is my flesh and blood."

"Then why—"

He shook his head. "You always were so rash. Rushing off and doing things before you thought them through. I knew you would come running over here. And why did I want you here? Is that what you were about to ask? Well, of course, to finish what three freaking professionals couldn't do last night."

This time Mickey laughed. "I don't think it's gonna turn out the way you think, Talmond."

"I suppose we're about to find that out." He pulled a small handgun from his suit pocket and pointed it at her.

Mickey took a few seconds to let her heart settle. He may have pulled his weapon first, but she had a big surprise for him. He'd never think that she'd actually come armed and ready to fight back. Him holding a gun on her is actually a good thing, she reasoned. It will give her a defense when they put her on trial for murder, because she did intend to kill him today. No matter what, he was going down. Last night he'd almost killed the man she loved. He'll never hurt anyone again.

She'd been more than willing to accept that she'd had an abusive childhood and to move past it. She done just that, hadn't she? She hadn't been sitting around feeling sorry for herself. She'd put it all behind her. Moved on. Pushed the ugly scenes from her heart and mind. It was his paranoia that led him to come after her again. Well, she's not a weak, frightened little girl anymore. His soft laughter brought her thoughts to an end.

"What's the matter, Mackenzie? I've never seen you at a loss for words. Usually you can't hold that smart tongue of yours. You've always been so defiant."

She ignored his barbs. She wanted to know his plan so she could figure out the best time to pull Jeff's gun from her purse and blow him the freak away. "So, what now? You just gonna shoot me right here? I can't imagine you taking the chance of getting blood on any of your precious things."

His eyes traveled over her, lingering. "Oh, no. I'm gonna have some fun first."

"Fun?"

He licked his lips. "You and I, Mackenzie. We're going up to your room just like the good old days, only this time, I'm gonna do exactly what I want to do, no holding back."

Mickey's stomach took a dive at the thought of what he wanted to do. He'd never get the chance, still, he was admitting what he always wanted to do. Her mind raced to figure out how she should handle it.

Maybe she should pretend to submit. She'd done that briefly with Richard while she worked to get her weapon in position. It had relaxed him enough to give her the chance to put that piece of glass against his neck. Bile rose in her throat at the thought of what she'd done. Realizing the trauma of that event may affect her today, she wondered if when the time comes will she be able to point her gun at Talmond and pull the trigger?

Talmond swirled his gun in a circular motion. "Turn around."

When she did as instructed he moved close, pushed the gun against her back. His free hand moved around her waist, pulled her in tight against his body. He leaned close, put his lips against her ear. "You and me, Mackenzie. I'm guessing you've thought about it before. Have you ever wondered what it would be like?"

Mickey closed her eyes as the fury built. Nope, she was not gonna have any problem at all blowing him away.

He let go and took a step back. "We're gonna walk slowly, go up the front stairs to your room. Got it?"

She nodded, holding her purse close against her abdomen, as she worked her hand inside. No way was she gonna let him take her up to that room again. No way.

They walked down the front hall toward the front door. It was as they turned at the bottom of the stairs to head up that she made her move. Jumping up onto the first step she spun as she let the purse fall to the floor, leaving only the gun in her hand.

The look of surprise on her stepfather's face was so worth the wait. She reveled in the feeling of triumph for several moments. Then his look of surprise changed quickly to rage.

"Drop the gun, daddy dearest," Mickey said.

He grinned and shook his head. "You drop yours."

"There is no way that's gonna happen, now drop the gun," she yelled.

He just stood there, that snide, ugly smile on his face. "No. You drop yours."

"Drop the freaking gun!" she screamed. "I will shoot you. I swear it."

"What's going on? What's happening?" Marion cried as she came running from the kitchen.

In a flash Talmond grabbed his wife in a headlock and planted his gun against her temple.

The house was quiet except for the women's heavy breathing.

"What are you gonna do now, little girl? Put the gun down or I blow your mother's brains out."

Mickey's hand trembled. "She's your wife. She's never done anything to you, but she's done everything for you. She's stood behind you all these years and you're gonna just kill her?"

He shrugged. "I'll do what I have to do."

"I don't think you will," she said.

He chuckled. "There's so much you don't know about me, Mackenzie."

"You'll never get away with it."

He shook his head. "Stupid girl. I'm not trying to get away with anything. I don't care anymore, Mackenzie. I've lost everything. And it's all your fault. And now, you're gonna pay. I received a call a little while ago from my attorney. He's gonna pick me up in a few hours and I'm supposed to go with him to turn myself over to authorities."

Marion gasped, tried to pull away, but he kept the gun firmly against her head.

"It's over for me, Mackenzie. Your mother and I, we were gonna take a vacation, go away, but you messed that up for me. You and Dora. My attorney tells me Dora has come forward and told all about our little relationship."

Mickey swallowed hard as she looked into her mother's bewildered eyes. He had nothing to lose. He'd kill her mother, and yet, she knew if she put the gun down there was no doubt he'd take her upstairs and rape her just like he said he would. What if she could stall? Certainly Jeff has realized she's gone by now. He won't sit around waiting to see if she'll come back. He'll know where she is. He'll come looking for her. Her mind shifted to Jeff realizing what she'd done. He'll be furious, though she couldn't blame him.

"You can save your mother's life, Mackenzie. All you have to do is put the gun down and I'll let her go."

Mickey gazed at the pitiful woman. "Did you know about Dora, Mom?"

The confused look on her mother's face told her what she wanted to know.

"He raped her. And not just once. So many times, Mom. For years."

Marion began to cry.

"You think you know it all, little girl. You don't know half." He jerked Marion, tightening his hold on her throat. "Shut up," he yelled at his wife. "Stop your incessant crying." His finger flinched on the trigger.

"Why don't you tell her Talmond? Tell her all the things you've done."

"What do you want me to tell her Mackenzie? That I raped Dora, or that I killed off Dora's husband all those years ago?"

"You're a monster," Mickey whispered.

"I'm powerful, Mackenzie. Your mother knows I'm powerful."

"Tell her the rest, then," Mickey demanded, hoping to waste more time and gain more evidence against him for her imagined trial.

"What? That I arranged to have you kidnapped and murdered? Or that I hired men to end your life last night? Or that I told Kurt to off that Kino kid? Or that I'm about to make eighty million dollars on an arms deal that's been ongoing for years? Or is it something more personal you're after? Like how much I enjoyed beating your young, soft body and bringing you pain, or how I looked forward to getting my hands on you."

Mickey's eyes met her mother's. There was terror there, and regret and sorrow. Mickey suddenly realized the woman had been no match for the powerful, manipulative man and that Dora knew that and that was why she hovered over her mom like a mother hen. Dora had done all she could to protect her.

"Put your gun on the floor and slide it toward me," Talmond said. "This is the last time I'm gonna ask you. I count to five, your mother dies."

"One."

Mickey's hand trembled. She had no choice.

"Two."

"I hate you with every fiber of my being."

"Three."

"Okay." Stepping down from the step she carefully placed the gun on the floor and pushed it toward him.

He stopped it with his foot, then kicked it. The gun slid to the far side of the formal living room. Talmond lowered the gun from Marion's head, jerked his arm and threw her away from him. She sprawled onto the hard wood floor, then still crying, rose to her knees and crawled away like a wounded animal.

"She'll go curl up in a corner and cry herself to sleep like the pathetic, weak dog she is." Talmond nodded toward the steps. "Let's go."

Nate came back into the room after Jeff sent him to find out what was taking Mickey so long. She'd said she wanted some privacy and would find a restroom near the waiting area. With his parents there, he understood she would want to clean up the best she could. After all, she was a mess. Her clothes had been covered in soot and dirt and blood. Her hair was a tangled mess. Her face was dirty and tear streaked. He couldn't blame her. After a lengthy conversation with his parents, Jeff realized she'd been gone quite a while. He'd sent Nate to find her.

"Well?" Jeff asked.

Nate shook his head. "I can't find her. Checked every restroom I could find. Spoke to the nurses. One remembers her heading out. Said she got on the elevator so I went down to the cafeteria, but she wasn't there either. I thought maybe she went to buy some clean clothes, so I went to the gift shops. She's not here, Jeff."

Controlling the mindless terror that wanted to take him over, he moved quickly, nodded at the stuff Nate had arrived with. "Toss me my clothes."

"What's going on?" his mom asked. "Do you think something's happened to Mackenzie?"

"I shouldn't have let her out of my site. Daley is still out there. He could've sent someone to take her."

Sitting down he pulled on his shoes and socks. "I gotta go find her. Nate, call Jason for me."

He finished dressing, opened the drawer of the bedside table. "Oh no, wait, Nate."

"Hold on," Nate said into the phone. "What is it?"

"My gun is gone. She must have taken it."

"That means she left here on her own."

"And if she took my freaking gun—"

"She went hunting for the Senator," Nate said, as he filled Jason in.

"Jeff, can we do anything to help?" his father asked.

He shook his head. "No. I know where she is. Nate and I, we're headed to Daley's. You guys go check into a hotel. I'll be in touch."

"Be careful, Jeff," his father admonished.

Mickey shook her head. "There's no way I'm gonna go up there with you and let you touch me. You're a sick pathetic pervert. It makes me wonder what happened to you that made you so depraved. What was it, huh? You're mommy refuse to breast feed you? Your daddy like little boys? Why are you such a sicko? Are you sure you're gonna be able to do it once you get me upstairs?"

His free hand struck out. Mickey's head turned violently with the blow and she stumbled back against the railing. He leveled the gun at her. "I guess you're about to find out. You were always so stubborn. You always made me have to prove that I would do exactly what I said I would do. Now move up the steps. You don't really have a choice in the matter. You'll do as I say or you'll die."

She shrugged. "You're gonna kill me anyway. I won't submit to you. Ever."

Talmond stood there calmly. "You think you're smart. You've been a pain from the moment I met you. Do you remember, Mackenzie?"

"I remember it clearly. I knew from the very first day when you came to take my mother out to dinner that you were a jerk. Nothing's changed."

His eyes flared before he got control. "You don't know the half of it. If not for you it would've been so easy."

"Yeah, well, life sucks."

"I had it planned out so well. Everything I needed to make it. I could've been president."

Mickey gave a short burst of laughter. "Hah! In your dreams."

He moved forward, swung again, catching her in the mouth and knocking her to the floor. Moaning, Mickey rose to her knees, wiped the blood from her lip.

"Feel better?" she asked.

He placed the gun against her forehead. "Take your shirt off."

"What happened to going upstairs?"

"We can finish our business right here." Still pressing the gun against her head he grabbed the edge of her shirt and jerked. The material ripped.

Mickey found herself wincing as she imagined the gun accidentally going off as he tried to tear her clothing away. She needed to stay alive and keep him talking. "Okay, okay. Hold on," she said. "I'll do it."

He stopped, stepped back and watched in fascination as she pulled the torn material away from her body. He felt the familiar pull of lust. The one he'd felt whenever he'd looked at her. Especially when she was in a state of submissiveness as she was now, on her knees, hurt and bleeding. She'd tortured him since she'd been a little seven-year-old brat. Her tiny body, trembling whenever he came near. Back then he'd lived in almost a constant state of arousal, so he'd used Dora and others to appease him. Why he'd never just gone ahead and forced her, he didn't know. Maybe he liked the state of need he was always in around her. Maybe he'd been afraid if he gave in and had her, she would lose her appeal.

She was trembling now, like she used to, her eyes filled with tears that she would try to hold back no matter what. It pleased him so much. He motioned at her with the gun. "The rest, now."

He smiled when he saw her hands tremble as she moved to obey him.

She was moving in slow motion, trying to stall as long as possible. Her eyes met his. "You're such a degenerate."

"You can blame me all you want, but really, Mackenzie, it's all your fault. You've done this to me. All I ever wanted was to take the money your stupid father flaunted in my face, take his family and build my career. And it—"

She paused her task. "Wh– what are you talking about? You knew my father?"

He laughed. "Oh, yes, Mackenzie. Your father and I were partners. Only his aspirations were much lower than mine."

Circling behind her, he knelt down over her and pressed the gun to her throat. He wanted her to suffer, wanted her to cry and whimper like she used to do. He placed his hand on her back. "That's right, little girl. Your father had no gumption." Mickey winced, not because he hurt her, but because she lost control and a tear made its way down her cheek and she knew it would please him.

She sniffed. "My father would never have been your partner. He would've hated you."

"He did hate me. At the end." He moved the gun up to her head and placed his lips on her cheek. "He hated me when I told him I would relieve him of the forty thousand dollars he won on the horses. When I told him I would use the money to further my political aspirations." His hand gripped her arm. "When I told him that after I killed him I would take his family and use them to gain respectability."

She stiffened more from what he said then from his hand squeezing her arm in an iron grip. "You killed my father?" she sobbed.

"Oh, come on now, that was a long time ago."

She reached down and grabbed his hand, tried to pull it away from her. He pressed the gun harder against her head. "Calm down, Mackenzie. It will all be over soon. Now do as I say and take your clothes off."

The tears welled over. "You killed my father."

"Water under the bridge. Don't make me mad. Take off your clothes, Mackenzie. Now. I'm gonna finish this." He moved his hand up to grab her cheeks. "But, you know what? I've just decided that first I want you to use this smart mouth of yours for something other than backtalk."

She turned her head and tried to bite his hand.

He pressed the gun harder against her. "Did you forget who has the gun?"

"Shoot me. I don't care anymore, but I know you won't. You won't because you don't want a corpse. You want me alive and kicking and fighting you."

He chuckled. "I guess you do know me. So, I guess I'll just have to make you a little more cooperative."

His fist tangled in her hair as he stood, dragging her to her feet. He placed the gun down on the hall table, pulled back his fist and punched her.

Mickey punched back. She kicked, scratched, fought with every ounce of strength. Though he had the definite advantage, she had the satisfaction of hearing him grunt a few times when she connected. His fist drove into her face, her chest, her stomach. Into her kidney when she tried to turn away. Into her ear when she tried to block him from her face. In the end, he straddled her barely conscious figure, breathing hard, exhausted from the fight.

Stroking her cheek he leaned down. "You messed up everything in my life, Mackenzie," he whispered softly. "A little girl. A stubborn, spoiled little girl. Well, little girl, you're gonna pay now, just like your old man. That's what happens when someone crosses me. Dora knew that. So did Kurt and Butch and all the others."

"Let's do this," he said as he tugged on her jeans.

The blast from the gun shocked them both.

Even though dazed from the beating she'd just taken, Mickey realized she'd been given a reprieve. Talmond grabbed at his shoulder as he was knocked back. He rolled over and came up. Mickey moved her head slightly to see her mother standing just behind her, holding Jeff's gun in her outstretched hands.

"You're gonna pay for that with your life," Talmond said as he advanced.

"No," Mickey moaned, trying to grab at him, but her body wouldn't obey. As it turned out it was unnecessary for her to move at all. The next shot hit her stepfather square in the chest.

~~~

Nate and Jeff pulled into the gate and up the circular drive to the front of the Daley mansion. They sprang from the car. The feds were right behind them. When he heard the gunshot a myriad of pictures ran through Jeff's mind. It felt as if he were moving through quicksand as he headed for the front door. Nate circled around to the side entrance.

Jeff held Nate's spare gun in one hand and twisted the doorknob as the second shot was fired. He barged in. Of all the things he'd pictured, this scene never crossed his mind.

Daley lay on his back, a hole in his chest, blood pooling around him. Mickey, dressed only in jeans lay opposite him, battered and semi-conscious, her feet almost touching Daley's. Marion Daley stood as still as a statue, the gun she held firmly in her hands pointed straight at Jeff.

"Mrs. Daley," Jeff said calmly as he tucked his gun away. "It's okay. I'm here to help you and Mickey."

Her eyes shifted down to the prone man and back to Jeff.

He smiled kindly at her as he edged his way forward. "Give me the gun now. He can't hurt you anymore."

Jeff kept his eyes on hers as Nate came up behind her and gently removed the gun from her hand. The woman collapsed in Nate's arms. Only a moment later the feds came through the door.

Jeff knelt down next to Mickey's prone body. Bruised and bloody and covered in perspiration, she looked much like the first time he saw her. Only this time she appeared to be unconscious. He put fingers to her throat, searching for and gratefully finding a pulse.

Gently, he lifted her onto his lap. His heart leapt when Mickey moved her battered face up, burrowed in against his neck and breathed deeply.

Agent Dodge removed his suit jacket and placed it around Mickey's shoulders.

"Thanks," Jeff said.

"Ambulance is on the way," the agent answered, squeezing Jeff's shoulder. "Ms. Daley, can you speak?"

She kept her eyes close. "Yes."

"Is there anything you want to tell us before the EMTs get here?"

"He killed my father," Mickey mumbled. "He told me he killed my father back when I was a kid. He did it to take some money my father won, and to take my mother for his wife."

Sighing, Agent Dodge shook his head in disgust. Talmond Daley, a United States Senator, was one of the worst criminals he'd ever encountered throughout his long career as a Federal Agent.

Mickey looked up. "He was gonna rape me and then shoot me. My mother, she had no choice."

"She won't be charged," he assured her.

Chapter Fifteen

Jeff stood in the doorway of the crowded room. Mickey lay on the small emergency room bed while nurses worked on her. She moaned a few times in her half-conscious state. Every time she did, Jeff's gut wrenched. Her face was battered and bloody. There were scratches on her arms and neck.

He needed to hold her. Needed it bad.

"Excuse me," a deep voice said behind him.

Jeff moved aside. The man moved into the room, turned, looked Jeff over.

"You need to wait outside," he said.

Jeff finally gave the man his attention, read the name tag, Dr. Haralson. Looked up into his eyes. "I'm waiting right here."

"Do I need to call security?"

Jeff began to chuckle.

"Is something funny?" the doctor asked.

"He's okay," another said behind Jeff.

Jeff turned to see another doctor and beside him, Jason Lee. Jason moved up beside Jeff, put his hand on his shoulder, while both doctors moved past to attend to Mickey.

"How's she doing?" Jason asked.

Jeff shrugged. "He beat her up pretty bad. There's a lot of facial swelling and bruising. I heard them say there might be some internal bleeding. She's in pain, I know that." He stopped, shook his head. "Do you realize how hard he'd have to hit her in order to cause internal bleeding?"

Jason sighed. "The important thing to focus on is she's gonna be okay."

Jeff turned, looked at his boss. "She'll live. Will she be okay? I don't know."

"She will with God' help— and yours, Jeff. Now would be a really good time to put your faith to work. Some prayers, some of that positive thinking, you gotta walk the walk."

Jeff nodded.

Mickey moaned and both men turned their attention toward her. Dr. Haralson was pushing on her abdomen. He looked up, consulted with the elder doctor, nodded his head, before he continued his exam. A few minutes later, the elder doctor joined Jason and Jeff.

The man extended his hand to Jeff. "I'm Dr. Meir. I'm Chief-of-Staff here."

Jeff shook his hand. "How is she?"

"She's obviously taken quite a beating, but I think it looks worse than it is. No major damage. We believe she has at least one broken rib. We're sending her for a full body scan and MRI to make sure there's nothing more than that. She's gonna have some major bruising and swelling, again, nothing critical. We'll keep her a few days, monitor her. Poor kid has been through enough and we want to make sure she's okay before we release her."

Jeff nodded. "Thank you."

The doctor spoke briefly to Jason before he took his leave. Jeff watched as they covered Mickey and pushed her bed toward the door. He stepped aside. As she passed him, she opened her eyes, reached out.

Jeff moved close, took her hand. "You're gonna be okay, Mick."

She closed her eyes. He kissed her hand and gently placed it on her stomach. Stepping back, he watched as they wheeled her down the hall.

Jason's cell phone began to vibrate. He pulled the phone from his pocket and glanced at the readout before he answered. "Special Agent Dodge, what can I do for you?"

"Trying to reach Agent Davis. Kurt Wells finally talked. The arms deal is going down late tonight. Exchange of cash to take place in Nevada. Thought Jeff would like to be in on it."

Jason eyed Jeff before he answered. "I'm pretty sure Jeff would love to be in on the bust, but I'm afraid he's out of commission right now. You know he just barely left the hospital earlier today, and now he's here with MacKenzie. I'm thinking he won't be much good to you in his present state of mind."

"Yeah, that's what I thought, but I just wanted to give him the option. He deserved first dibs on the bust. I guess he's earned some well-deserved R&R. Give him and Ms. Daley our best."

"Will do."

"Excuse me, Agent Davis?"

Both Jeff and Jason turned to one of the nurses who'd worked on Mickey.

"Yes," Jeff answered.

"When Ms. Daley gets done with the MRI they're gonna take her straight to her room. You're welcome to wait for her there. It's room 220."

Jeff nodded. "Thank you."

He turned back to Jason. "What bust am I not gonna get in on?"

"The cash exchange for the arms deal that's not gonna happen."

Jeff sighed. "I'm too tired to argue with you about it."

"That right there should tell you I made the right decision."

~~~

Marissa sat on the sofa with her arms folded across her chest. Next to her sat a four-year-old, pig-tailed little girl, who was mimicking Marissa's every move. On the floor in front of them the girl's older brother had control of the remote and was at present scrolling through every channel of the four or five hundred that was available on their current cable plan. She really didn't care what they watched, she just wished he'd stop at one channel and leave it there.

They weren't bad kids, as kids go. They were just– kids. It was as eight-year-old Jimmy scrolled through the channels that Marissa got a quick glimpse of her father's face.

"Wait," she said quickly.

"What?" Jimmy asked.

"Go back."

"To what? It was only news."

Marissa glared. "I said go back."

Jimmy frowned. "No, I don't wanna watch the news."

Marissa jumped up and grabbed the remote from him. "I said go back you little brat."

Jimmy jumped up and went crying to his mother. Marissa pointed the remote and scrolled back. What she saw took her breath away. "Oh my gosh," she whispered as tears spilled over her cheeks.

Jimmy's mom came in the room. "Marissa, what is going on? Jimmy tells me—" She stopped at the expression on Marissa's face. Her eyes went to the TV. They stood there watching until the end of the report.

Marissa turned her face up to the woman, her tears still running freely. "Please, I need to see my sister. Please."

The woman stood, indecisively ringing her hands.

"She's all I have left," Marissa whispered.

"Jimmy, Angie, go get your shoes on. We have to go bye-bye."

~~~

Both her eyes were blackened and swollen shut. Her bottom lip was busted. Her top lip swollen. Her right cheek was blue and yellow. Angry, red scratches marred her neck and her forearms. Jeff sat examining her as she slept. The anger for what Daley had done to her was eating him alive. He wanted to make the man suffer. In a way, Daley had hurt Mickey again and gotten away with it. No closure for Mickey.

Jeff realized his thinking was skewed. The man had paid with his life. It was Jeff's need for revenge that was wreaking havoc with his equilibrium. Grandmaster Kino was always speaking about revenge being a poison to the mind and heart. Jeff was beginning to understand.

Mickey stirred and reached out in startled reflex. Jeff took her hand. "Hey, I'm here. Mickey? Can you hear me?"

Her eyelids moved but she was unable to open them. "Jeff?" she said softly.

"Yes, baby, I'm here."

"Talmond, he's dead?"

"Yes."

"My mother shot him?"

"Yes."

"Where is she?"

"She's at her house."

"Alone?"

"They called Dora. She's with her now."

"They?"

"The FBI."

"Oh."

"How are you feeling?"

"Sleepy."

"They have you on some pain meds."

She remained silent for several minutes. "She told me he had Marissa."

"Who— your mother?"

"She said Talmond had Marissa and that he would hurt her if I didn't come right away."

"I see."

"Are you angry?"

"Yep."

"At me?"

"Yeah, at you. At Daley. At your mother. At the world."

"Can you forgive me?"

He squeezed her hand. "Not yet, but that doesn't mean I don't love you. Because I do. If I didn't, I wouldn't be angry."

She sighed. "I think I understand."

"I doubt it. You scared the crap out of me."

"I'm sorry. I thought I could handle it."

"Did you really think you could go over there and shoot the man?"

"I don't know. I guess I thought I could use the gun to make him let Marissa go."

"Haven't you ever heard it said that you should never point a gun at anyone unless you intend to kill them?"

"Yes, I've heard that."

"And?"

"I intended to kill him. I guess I wasn't thinking very clearly."

"That's an understatement."

"You really are angry aren't you?"

"Anger, fear, very closely related."

She reached up to touch his face. "I wish I could see you."

"When the swelling goes down you'll be able to see."

"Jeff?"

"Hmm?"

"I don't like you when you're mad."

He chuckled. "Good. Then don't make me mad ever again."

"Okay. Jeff?"

"Yes."

"I love you."

"I love you too, Mick."

The soft knock on the door ended their conversation. Jeff's parents poked their heads in.

"Mom, Dad, come in," Jeff said.

"How's she doing?"

"I'm okay," Mickey answered for him. "I just can't open my eyes."

"Oh, you poor dear," Mrs. Davis crooned. She came closer, ushered Jeff out of the way, stroked Mickey's hair. "Just look at what that man did to you. Don't you worry about a thing. You'll heal quickly, and I'll be here for you. I want you to know, you can depend on me. I mean, I know Jeff is in love with you, and that's wonderful, but a girl, she needs women friends. Someone she can go to for camaraderie and understanding. I just want you to know I'm here for you."

"Thank you, Mrs. Davis."

Jeff stood back near his father, so proud that his mother was showering the woman he wanted with so much love.

"Please, call me Jen. Everyone does. I brought you some things."

"You did?"

The woman smiled broadly. "I went shopping. I mean, your house is gone, right? You're gonna need some things to wear until you're able to get out and shop for yourself. I brought you a few outfits, some underwear, some shoes, some toiletries. You know, things you'll need."

"Thank you so much. I don't know what to say."

"Oh, pooh, you don't have to thank me. Just concentrate on getting better."

"I will. I promise."

Jen bent down and kissed Mickey's forehead. "Things will get better. I promise."

Mickey sniffed as the tears began to flow.

"Oh dear. Have I upset you?"

"No, it's just that, a stranger is showing me more kindness and caring than I ever remember my own mother showing me."

"Stranger? Don't ever think of me as a stranger."

Another knock had them all turning toward the door. Marissa burst in, practically threw herself onto the bed.

"Mickey, oh, Mickey."

~~~

Talmond Daley was laid to rest with a minimum of flourish, even though he did have more people, press and dignitaries there than the average funeral. Most were there to show support for his widow and daughters even though the trio did not attend. After all, Marion Daley was the one who'd ended his life and was advised to stay home, Mickey was his intended victim and Marissa stayed away out of the righteous indignation of the young. Talmond had no other living relatives.

Though Mickey and Marissa had both refused to attend the funeral, they received a great outpouring of love and support from former friends and colleagues of her stepfather as well as the public. Some expressed guilt for somehow not seeing through his charade. Others wanted to share similar stories with her.

Mickey and Marissa planned to spend the day of the funeral with their mother. Mickey had supposed that the woman might need to unburden herself or might need comfort or might need to know that she wasn't alone. However, that's not how it turned out.

They arrived at the house at nine in the morning. Marion Daley was just sitting down to breakfast. When she answered the door she insisted on setting places for Mickey and Marissa and then serving them much like she used to serve Talmond. Mickey watched suspiciously as her mother performed these tasks. Once each place was perfect, Marion sat down. What she did next turned Mickey's stomach. She made note of the time. Marissa also knew exactly what was happening and glanced at Mickey, her brow furrowed.

"Mom," Mickey said softly. "You know, you don't have to do breakfast like this anymore. You don't have to sit in this room for an hour, you don't have to set formal places, you don't even have to eat breakfast at all if you don't want to."

Her mother glared at her. "I'll thank you to stop disrespecting your father on the very day he is being placed in the cold earth."

Marissa gasped, momentarily stunned by her mother's words. Mickey wanted to retort as she usually did by stating firmly that Talmond was not her father. Somehow, she held herself back.

It was Marissa who found her voice. "Mom, you do understand what he did? You do realize that he actually killed people? You do realize he killed your first husband, and he was gonna kill your daughter. You must realize it because you were the one to pull the trigger."

Marion turned quickly toward her younger daughter. "And I'll not have you taking after your sister. I did what I had to do," she stopped, looked over at Mickey, "but if not for Mackenzie's behavior, none of this would have happened. Just like your father said, she was always taunting him, pushing him. She knew just what she was doing." Though she spoke to her younger daughter, she kept her eyes on Mickey, eyebrows cocked.

Mickey's eyes filled as she stared at the woman who was suppose to love her and protect her. She'd done neither for most of Mickey's life. It seemed her mother finally coming to her rescue was a fluke. Nothing had changed. Could it be that she was still ready and willing to pretend Talmond could do no wrong? Probably her mother was simply confused. She'd been under so much stress. Mickey decided to give her the benefit of the doubt. "Mom," Mickey said softly. "I think maybe you need some help. I think you're having trouble handling all the horrible things that have happened."

"I don't need your kind of help."

"Please, Mom, let me call someone for you. Let me help you."

"Oh, I think you've done enough, don't you?"

The tears spilled over Mickey's cheek. Her hands shook. "You can't truly think that I had anything to do with what happened. He arranged to have me kidnapped. He arranged to have me murdered. He intended to rape me. Even when I was a child, Mom, I was a little girl and he hurt me. And Mom, he killed my father. *Your* husband. And *you* kept telling me my father left, that he didn't care about me. Talmond hurt you too, Mom. Why can't you admit it?"

Her mother rose. "If you hadn't come over here that day none of this would've happened. If you hadn't been here, I wouldn't have had to do what I did. I guess that makes you feel great, huh? You got me to turn on Talmond."

"You were the one who called me, remember?" Mickey shrieked.

Marissa reached for her sister's hand. "It's okay, Mick. She's not in her right mind. I think we need to go."

Marion frowned down at her. "You're leaving with her?"

"I don't want to stay here, Mom. Not here where, you know, where everything happened. Come with us. We're gonna stay in a hotel for a few days until we figure out where we're gonna go. Please, Mom, come with us and we'll all start over again."

Marion sat, placed her napkin in her lap, lifted her fork. "I have no desire to leave my home. This is my home. Mine! And no one is gonna make me leave. No one, do you hear?" she yelled.

Mickey stood. "Let's go, Marissa. I don't think there's anything we can do here." She looked at her mother. "I'll have Marissa's things packed and sent to us when we figure out where we're gonna be."

Marion swiped her hand in the air as if they were pesky flies. "Do whatever you want, Mackenzie. You always have."

Epilogue

Two days after the funeral, Marion Daley tried to end her own life. Her lifelong friend and protector, Dora Suarez, had come to check on her and found her unconscious next to an empty bottle of tranquilizers. By her side lay a note addressed to her husband begging forgiveness for taking his life.

She was resuscitated and transferred to a state mental hospital. A week later, Mackenzie Daley was awarded custody of Marissa and advised to attend regular counseling sessions with her.

Mickey obtained power of attorney over her mother's estate. She contacted Dora and offered to pay restitution to her and her family. Dora refused, knowing Mickey had already paid many times over. Mickey, though, wouldn't take no for an answer and in the end Dora accepted trust funds set up for her grandchildren. Dora herself was offered a publishing contract to tell of her years with Talmond Daley. Financially, she would be okay. Mentally, was another story.

Mickey's publisher is anxiously awaiting her next book. Planning stages of the reconstruction on Mickey's home in the suburb of Seattle had already begun. In the meantime Mickey and Marissa were preparing to fly down to Los Angeles with Jeff. They would stay in his apartment until they left to visit his parents for the Fourth of July.

The goodbye between Cameron and his lifelong friend, Marissa, was a tearful one. He was appeased however, when he learned they were all invited to the Kino's home after the fourth for the remainder of July.

~~~

"Do I look okay?" Mickey asked nervously, smoothing her hair.

"You look amazing, Mick," Jeff answered. "Why do you think *People Magazine* just listed you as one of the most beautiful people in the world?"

"It wasn't the most beautiful, silly man, it was most intriguing."

"Shoulda been most beautiful."

Mickey ignored him, turned toward the hall mirror in Jeff's small Los Angeles apartment.

"But the bruises—"

"The makeup covered what's left of them. Really, hon, you can't tell, and who cares if you can? It's just an interview. Everyone knows what happened."

Mickey blew out a breath, calmed herself and smiled back at the man she loved. "Everyone doesn't know everything. I just hope I don't screw up and say something I didn't want to say."

"You'll do fine. Trust yourself, Mick."

She nodded. "How do you stay so calm? Like, when you're about to do something really hard or scary, like the night of the explosion. You just calmly shot that guy like it was nothing."

He shook his head. "It's never like it was nothing." His lips pressed together tightly. This was a subject he didn't like to discuss. He blew out a breath, finally shrugged. "I'm trained to stay calm under duress. I've been doing this a long time, so I stay calm and do what has to be done."

Not liking the turn of the conversation, he smiled. "Or, have you ever heard the one about picturing the audience naked?"

"Yeah," she answered, waiting for the punch line.

"Well, I just picture you naked."

Frowning, she placed her hands on her hips.

"What?" he asked innocently. "It works for me."

"You are incorrigible."

"I was just playing around."

She shook her head, sighed.

"Okay, now, Mick, you're starting to worry me. What's wrong? You're not just worried about this interview. What is it?"

"Nothing really."

"More second thoughts about our relationship?"

"No, I don't think that's it. I mean, yes, I do have second thoughts, all the time."

"Great. That's really great to hear."

"Sorry. Just being honest."

Jeff sighed. "I get the feeling that second thoughts about us is not what's bothering you right now."

She nodded, eyed him. "I'm not sure what the problem is. I feel a little lost. A little displaced, you know? And if I'm feeling that way, how must Rissa be feeling. New town, soon to be a new school, new friends, no real home and even suddenly no parents."

He moved close behind her, looking at her gorgeous reflection in the mirror. His hands rubbed up and down her arms. "Rissa seems to be happy, but sometimes people cover well, but I know that Eric has spoken with her whenever she goes to see Jeffy. Look Mick, I understand completely. You go from your happy little life in your own little house to being squished in my tiny apartment with almost nothing salvaged from your former life. And I imagine it's got to be hard being squished in here with me."

She smiled. "It's you being displaced, Jeff. Sleeping on the couch, giving up your bedroom for Rissa and I. So, what would the Kinos say about how we're feeling?"

"Well, first, let's make sure we get the answer to that question by giving Eric a call soon. He said you can call anytime, right?"

She nodded.

"But for now, I can tell you what I think they would say."

"Okay."

"They would tell us to be grateful, you know, to count our blessings. We sure have a lot to be grateful for. Like you got away from your kidnappers, and then I found you, and Cameron decided to follow Jeffy, and remember, we got out of your house in the nick of time, and thank God, Marissa wasn't there."

Mickey looked up, her mouth open. "Oh, I hadn't thought about that one. I guess that judge changing his mind and CPS coming to get Marissa was a blessing."

"Exactly. Now you're talking."

"And now, here we are safe and sound. And really, Rissa doesn't seem to be having a problem sleeping with me in your bed. I mean, at least when she's here and not spending the night with Jeffy."

"Are *you* having a problem sleeping in my bed?"

"No, Jeff, that's not it. It's just that it's all happening so fast. I can't seem to get oriented before the next thing happens."

"What's the next thing?"

"Who knows?" she said sarcastically. She turned, circled his neck with her arms. "I love sleeping in your bed. I love you, Jeff. I just need to take things slow."

"No problem. I'd prefer that much more than you doing something crazy without thinking it through."

"Me doing something crazy? Like what?"

"You know, like stealing my gun and heading out to kill a man?"

She looked down. "Oh, that." Pouting, she rubbed her hands over his chest. "You still haven't forgiven me for that, have you?"

"For heading over to shoot the Senator while I'm laid up in the hospital? For stealing my gun? And worst of all for putting your life on the line without a thought as to how Marissa and I could live without you? No, I haven't forgiven you."

"I should've trusted you. I know that. I wasn't thinking clearly. Please, Jeff, what will it take?"

He sighed, shook his head, pulled her close. His hands cupped her face as he looked deep into her eyes. "I'd say it will take at least fifty years of marriage."

She smacked his chest. "Really, Jeff, I'm not kidding."

Leaning forward, he nibbled on her cheek. "Neither am I. Marry me, Mick."

Surprised, she quickly looked up into his eyes. He certainly seemed serious enough. "You're serious?"

"I'm very, very serious. I love you, Mickey. With all my heart. I think you feel the same way."

"What if, you know, what if when things calm down, we stop feeling this way?"

His jaw clenched, he nodded. "Okay. Since you seem terrified that what we feel is all gonna fade, we can have a long engagement. Let's say, a year. If we still feel this way next June, we'll plan the wedding. Is that taking things slow enough for you?"

Looking up at his beautiful, strong, almost angelic face, she tried to think of life without him and couldn't bear it.

"Just say yes," he whispered.

She smiled. "Okay, yes, but we wait a year."

"Yes? You mean it?"

She laughed. "I said it, didn't I?"

He picked her up and twirled her around. "Oh, Mick," he sighed when he put her down. "Oh, baby, I love you so much." His head lowered and he kissed her, slowly, gently, thoroughly. It was the clearing of Marissa's throat that interrupted them.

"Uh, it's time, you guys. Let's do this stupid thing."

Mickey grinned at her sister. "Jeff just asked me to marry him."

Marissa clapped her hands together. "Finally. I knew he was going to, I just didn't know when."

"You did?"

"Yeah, he told me the day the old hag came to put me in foster care. He was trying to take my mind off my troubles."

"Well, aren't you just so smart," Jeff laughed.

Marissa shrugged. "Child psychology. Easy stuff."

~~~

Friday afternoon Shelley knocked softly and slipped into her daughter's room which overlooked the front lawn. Jeffy sat in the window seat, knees drawn up, gazing out. Shelley herself had sat in this very window many years ago, when she'd first come to California for the MART. Shelley peered over her daughter's shoulder, took in the lush green of the lawn, the splash of pink and yellow flowers that bordered the walkway that circled the fountain. She and Jeffy had played in that fountain many times. Her eyes traveled the length of the drive down to the security gate. "Getting anxious?" Shelley asked.

Jeffy nodded, rubbed her hands up and down her arms. "It seems to be taking forever."

"Traffic is probably a nightmare between the airport and here this time of day. They'll be here soon enough, or should I say, he'll be here."

Jeffy sighed. "I miss him, Mom. So much."

Recognizing her need to talk, Shelley sat behind her daughter and wrapped her arms around her. "How much, baby girl?"

"I feel so empty when he's not here. I try to concentrate on other things, but I can't. I know it's silly. I understand the emotional pull that happens with a first love. I understand the rush of hormones and the pheromones and everything else involved, yet logic doesn't seem to help me stop feeling this way."

"And it won't. Only time. Believe it or not, I still miss your dad whenever he's away."

"But you're so strong. So independent."

Shelley gave a soft laugh. "You think so?"

"Yes. Everyone does."

"Oh, everyone, huh?"

"No really, Mom. Bree, Aunt Angel, Uncle Jason, Uncle Justin, Jeff."

"That's hardly everyone."

"People come up to me all the time when I'm at school, ask about Bree and Ricky and Joey and you. They always say stuff like what a great example you are for being a strong role model for women."

Shelley shrugged. "I won the MART, and that's something I'll always be proud of, but I didn't do it alone. Your father trained me not just physically, but emotionally too. He helped me to see my worth. He taught me to love myself, to have confidence, to trust my instincts. There was a time when I didn't think I could function without your dad by my side, but I've learned that, though I would miss him desperately, I can stand alone."

"Yeah, that's the way I feel."

"That you can stand alone?"

"No. Desperate. How do you learn to stand alone?"

Shelley took a moment to think about her answer. She didn't want it to be something trite, like, it will come with time or maturity. She truly wanted to help her daughter find her way through the maze. She didn't want her to think that women couldn't stand on their own, but she also didn't want her to think that strong, protective men were a bad thing. She sighed. "I think, my sweet June Flower, that women must learn to not give themselves away."

"What do you mean?"

"Women are taught to give, give, give. It's the loving, motherly, even saintly thing to do. And that is true. We give and we love freely and unselfishly, at least we should. Most of us want to be the best mother, the best wife. That doesn't take a weak woman. That takes a strong woman. We want to be a force for good in the world, but it doesn't help anyone when we give ourselves away."

"I still don't understand, Mom. How does one give themselves away?"

"I'll give you an example. Suppose Cameron asks you, what movie you'd like to see. To please him, you tell him to choose, offering no opinion when he says he'd like to see something that you have absolutely no interest in. Pretend you marry him. Not that I think you should, but I know you've imagined it. So, you're married, he suggests you live in a two-story brick home in Montana while you've always wanted to live in a stucco ranch in Arizona. He suggests a blue sports car while you've always wanted to drive a yellow jeep. He thinks you should have five children. He thinks you should be vegetarian, he thinks you should vote the way he votes, he thinks—"

"Okay, Mom, I get it, but how many women really would concede to all that?"

"You'd be surprised how many, Jeffy. Sometimes they don't even realize they're doing it because it's just little things, and little by little, women end up giving themselves away. You must always be aware that the most important thing in any relationship is to be honest and true to yourself first. That's how you be strong. Don't give yourself away in hopes to make a relationship last. How happy a situation could that be? How long could that last? Do you understand what I'm trying to say?"

Jeffy nodded thoughtfully. "I think I do. No matter what, continue to be the person I am or the person I want to be. And if I do that, I'll have relationships with people who can appreciate who I am and who wouldn't want to ask me to change to suit them."

"Right, but now I'm gonna backtrack a bit. That doesn't mean you can't compromise. When he wants one thing and you want another, you can discuss it, giving respect to each other's ideas, and somehow either arrive at a meeting of the minds or agree to disagree."

"You make it sound so simple."

"Honesty is simple."

Jeffy nodded. "I suppose it is."

"Two people can love each other but not be good for each other. But that is mainly because what they think is love, is just chemistry. But that flares and dies out. Unless you have a few other things."

"Which are?"

"Well, first and foremost, if you both love God above all else, and want to please Him, then you will be able to trust each other, because you know the other person is striving to be the best they can be, and is repentant, and prayerful."

"And?"

"And the other things are you must have respect and admiration for each other."

Jeffy's brow furrowed. "Hmm, go on."

"I respect your dad, and I admire him. He respects and admires me. Above any other human. So, even if we disagree with each other, we have the respect for each other to listen and understand. If I didn't admire your dad, it may not be that way."

"How could anyone not admire Dad?"

"Right? But let's say he got lazy, stopped training, got out of shape, started drinking, or doing drugs. Even stopped loving God. I wouldn't stop loving him right away. But I would stop admiring him and I would lose respect for him. And eventually, the love would die and I would start looking at other people to fill the void. So, tell me June Flower, what would be the answer to keep that from happening?"

Her mom had used her given name a second time, which to Jeffy meant this was a very important question. She thought for a few minutes, finally looking up at her mother's lovely face. "As individuals, we each need to do and become the best we can be. It doesn't matter what we work at, as long as we DO work at it. You admire Dad, because he works very hard at being a great teacher, a great martial artist, a great father, a great friend. And I think mostly, a servant of God. He progresses. He doesn't get stagnant. You both keep growing and progressing."

Shelley smiled. "You got it, baby girl. We keep growing and progressing so we continue to admire and respect each other." She leaned over and kissed her cheek. "So, anything else you want to discuss about your relationship with Cameron?"

Jeffy chewed on her lip. "Even if I learn to be without him emotionally, I still feel desperate physically. I mean, it's embarrassing to say it to my mother, but it's like, my entire body aches and hurts and the only thing that can make it feel better is being close to him."

"Wow. You do have it bad."

Jeffy turned her head and leaned it against her mother's breast. "Yeah, I do."

Shelley stroked Jeffy's silky curls. "Don't ever be embarrassed to say anything to me, sweetheart. Bree and I, we share everything. I'm thinking you're old enough to be admitted to that club."

Jeffy hugged her mom then turned at the sound of an approaching car. She lunged at the window, knocking Shelley in the chin. "Oh, sorry, Mom. They're here!"

Rubbing her chin, Shelley moved out of the way before Jeffy bowled her over. Jeffy dashed from the room. Eric joined his wife as she came out of Jeffy's bedroom.

"Our daughter's in love," Eric said sadly.

"Yeah, she is, and I think all we can do is ride it out."

Eric nodded. "Wise as always, my love."

"Let's go greet our guests."

"Wait." He grabbed her, leaned her against the wall, and pressed his lips to hers.

Shelley sighed as he deepened the kiss. Her body felt just what her daughter had described. "Oh, Eric," she whispered. "I do love you so."

"Graaanddaaad," little Joey complained as he came out of his room into the hall on his way to greet the company.

Eric straightened quickly, looked up with a smile. "Sorry, JoJo. I didn't realize anyone was upstairs. I'll try to restrain myself."

Jeffy ran out the door, down the wide steps, across the circular drive and stood in the middle of the green grass as the car approached. The car stopped, the doors opened, and two teenage girls screeched at the top of their lungs as they threw their arms around each other and jumped up and down.

Shelley stood in the doorway and smiled at the comforting sight of her daughter acting like any other teenage girl.

"That does my heart good," Eric murmured.

Shelley nodded. "So very– normal. I love it. You'd think they hadn't seen each other in months. Marissa just spent the night the day before they left to visit Jeff's parents."

Mark and Joey moved past their parents and went down the steps to help unload luggage. Mark ruffled his son's hair. "You help too, little man."

"I'm not little," the younger Joey insisted.

"You're not a little boy. You *are* a little man."

While the guys unloaded the trunk, Eric and Shelley watched as Cameron emerged from the car and stood silently waiting for Marissa and Jeffy to calm down and break apart. It took only a few seconds once Jeffy knew he was standing there waiting on her.

Marissa broke away and stood back smiling. It was like something out of a movie. Cameron moved first then Jeffy ran to him. They wrapped their arms around each other and Jeffy buried her face against his chest and that's how they stayed for what seemed to Shelley like an eternity. Finally, Jeffy tilted her face up and there in front of everyone, Cam bent and kissed her, albeit briefly.

"I've missed you so much," Cam whispered softly in her ear.

"Me too," Jeffy said.

Cam pulled away, realizing her family was watching every move. Gently, he caressed her cheek with the back of his knuckle.

"Such a good looking young man," Shelley whispered to Eric.

He only grunted.

Jeff and Mickey emerged, grabbed some luggage and made their way up the steps. Shelley warmly and lovingly hugged them both and welcomed them to their home.

Eric took a suit case from Jeff's hand so that he could shake hands with him. "Welcome as always," Eric said, then turned to Mickey. He looked deep into her eyes, searching for and touching on her pain. When her eyes filled with tears he bent and kissed her cheek. "I'm glad you're here Mickey. May I speak to you later?"

She smiled, drew a breath. "I'd like that."

Eric gave a slight bow. "Please, make yourselves at home." He ushered them inside.

~~~

It was only noon on Saturday, so Mickey was surprised by the amount of people already arriving, dozens of them being agents who worked with Jeff. The Kinos had insisted on throwing Jeff and Mickey an engagement party. Preferring the informal to the formal, everyone was out back preparing a giant barbecue. However, informal did not preclude catering. Eric said if he didn't have it catered Shelley would wear herself out trying to see to all the details and he wanted her to have fun too.

Mickey and Jeff sat cuddled in a swing under a palm watching the kids play in the pool. Cam and six-year-old little Joey just finished tossing Marissa into the pool and were now chasing Jeffy who screamed as she darted away. Good luck on that, Jeff thought. Jeffy's quickness could be likened to Ricky and the only way they would catch her is if Jeffy wanted to be caught. Though, considering it was Cam doing the catching, Jeffy just might concede.

Ricky stood in the three feet giving his three-year-old daughter, Taylor, diving tips because she'd been crying in frustration that she wasn't an expert yet like her six-year-old brother, Eric, who was doing half gainers off the board. Watching Ricky, with the sun glistening on his very ripped body, Mickey couldn't help but admire him. A few feet away, Ricky's wife, Bree, devastating in her bikini, slathered on lotion and stretched out on a lounge chair.

Mickey's brow furrowed as she puzzled over what it would take to make a happy marriage when both parties were as famous as Ricky and Bree.

"What are you frowning at?" Jeff asked.

Mickey turned to him with a smile. "Just wondering about Ricky's and Bree's marriage. You know, the old Hollywood curse. Will they stay together? Are they happy?"

"I think they're happy. I think they'll always be happy. I mean, look at their relationship. It's not based on fear, you know?"

"No, I don't know. Are you making a comment about me being afraid of my own shadow?"

"No, Mick, not that kind of fear, sweetheart. You've been through hell and have good reason to feel afraid, though I'm hoping you'll eventually work through that, because the past should not define you.

I'm talking about fear of losing each other. It's like, they have confidence in themselves and they have confidence in each other. And trust. They trust each other. They allow each other to be just who they want to be. No restrictions."

"And what if Ricky decides he wants someone else?"

"Well, that would hurt Bree, I'm sure. Since they're married, and they are extremely honorable people, they would never cheat on their spouse. But say, they weren't married. Pretend they were just boyfriend and girlfriend. If Bree were to live in fear of Ricky finding someone else and be all clingy and possessive, then it could bring about the exact thing she fears. Should she live always in fear that she may lose him?"

"No, of course not."

"He wouldn't feel the need to go searching for anyone else because he feels happy and free right where he is. It's like, try to hold onto someone too tight and they will for sure want to be let go."

Mickey nodded. "But give them freedom and space, have trust in them, and the time together will be happy and no one will want to go anywhere."

"Exactly."

She leaned her head against his chest, sighed. "I hope our relationship will be like that."

"We'll make sure of it. How about I promise to always let you be you, to respect your opinions, even if I disagree, and to work things out as equal partners."

She smiled. "And that we will communicate. Talk to each other about our hopes and fears. Communication is the real key."

"That sounds like Grandmaster Kino talking."

"He's taught me a lot in a short amount of time."

They looked up as more people arrived.

They saw Nate and his family making their entrance. Nate's kids headed straight for the pool, while Shelley was busy welcoming their parents. Down on the beach, Jack sat, his legs crossed, his hands palms up on his knees. Boss man, Jason Lee, and his wife, Angel, had also appeared sometime during Jeff and Mickey's conversation. They mingled with Eric and Shelley while their daughter, thirteen-year-old, Kimmie, sat neatly on the side of the pool, her feet dangling in the water.

Mickey worried that the girl might feel a little left out with Marissa being here and occupying Jeffy's attention, but she discovered her worries were for naught. Cameron headed straight to Kimmie, introduced himself, shook her hand, and jerked her into the pool. She let out a brief scream before she went under.

Jeffy dove in, grabbed Kimmie, hugged her tight and asked her if she was okay. Kimmie laughed at Jeffy. "Of course I'm okay, silly."

"What's the problem?" Cam asked. "Did I do something wrong?"

Jeffy's brow creased. "I dunno," Jeffy answered. "It's just that, well, Kimmie, I just don't want her to be hurt."

"Don't be silly, Jeffy," Kimmie answered. "He didn't hurt me. Besides, how many times have *you* pushed me in the pool?"

Jeffy nodded, backed away, climbed out of the pool and went to sit alone. Wisely, Cameron went to join her.

"What do you think that was all about?" Mickey asked.

Jeff shook his head. "Don't know, but I have a feeling it's the beginning of a new episode in the crazy life of the Kino family."

Jeff raised his hand in greeting to Justin Lee, Jason's attorney brother, who he just noticed sitting at the bar with his wife, and chatting with the bartender.

A moment later Mark and Joey entered, each with a girl on their arms. Mark handed a lemonade to a beautiful Latino girl while Joey escorted his girl down toward the ocean to walk along the beach. How hard was it, Mickey wondered, to be a member of a famous family like the Kinos and find a companion who was genuinely interested in you?

Sighing with pleasure, Mickey gazed around at her surroundings. The place was like a tropical paradise. The deck they were on was huge and extended down the hill toward the beach in several tiered levels. Surrounded with palms and huge pots of flowers and greenery, it was as lush as a jungle. Below the deck was a flat beach area with a volleyball pit surrounded by beach chairs and umbrellas for spectators. Everywhere you looked there were large coolers of beverages not to mention the fully stocked and manned Tiki bar. Closer to the house were tables filled with delectable dishes. Barbeque, salads, fruits, desserts. So yummy.

Jeff laced his fingers with Mickey, lifted her hand to his mouth. "You okay?"

She smiled at him. "I'm good. Really good I think."

"How'd it go with Master Kino this morning?"

She knew he was referring to her talk with Eric shortly after breakfast. "There's something about that man. It seems just being in his presence makes me feel calmer, or, I don't know, grounded I guess. He's so close to God, he talks about Jesus as if they were close friends, he's so full of love and peace. I think I love him."

"Should I be jealous?"

Moving closer to him, she ran the palm of her hand over his chest then reached up to cup his cheek. "I think I'd like that, but, I can't lead you on. I mean, I love him like a—" She stopped, unable to say the words.

"Like a father?"

Her eyes filled. "Yes. Like that."

"Ah, sweetheart, knowing Master Kino like I do, he'd be more than willing to step into the role."

"I think he already has."

"I think so too." He took her hand from his face and kissed it, then lowered his head to kiss her.

Mickey closed her eyes, let the feelings take her. The power and heat that emanated from this man, the strength– she felt protected, loved, safe. So very safe. He took care of her, yet, he allowed her to stand up and be strong. Her strength didn't threaten him at all. He encouraged it. He wanted only her happiness. And she wanted his. She wanted him. The chemistry was incredible. Even now, with people all around she wanted to lose herself in him.

He ended the kiss, his eyes burning into hers and she knew he felt the same way.

"Jeff," she began.

He smiled sweetly at her. "Yes, baby?"

She smiled back at him. "You're still feeling it?"

"Yeah, I am. You?"

She laughed, nodded. "Yeah. I am."

At that moment Marissa came from behind and threw her soaking wet arms around her sister and hugged her hard.

"Oh, Rissa, you're getting me all wet!"

Marissa giggled. "I know. Just wanted to let you know how happy I am. How light I feel now that Dad's, I mean now that we're out from under, oh, heck. I can't seem to say what I mean. Does it just make me a horrible person to be glad he's gone?"

Mickey patted her sister's arm which was still wrapped around her, resting on her upper chest. "You could never be a horrible person, Rissa. I understand what you mean, sweetie. I feel happy too. Like a weight's been lifted off my shoulders."

"Yeah, like that." She kissed her older sister's cheek. "You guys come play volley ball with us."

Mickey grinned. "Okay, but Jeff and I get to be on the same team."

"Fine, come on."

"Where's Jeffy and Cameron?"

Marissa's lips pressed tightly together. "Um, they, uh, went inside to, uh, change clothes."

Jeff sat up straight, glanced up toward the balconies. "Maybe I'd better—"

"Don't you dare, Jeff," Mickey said.

Marissa giggled. "The whole family knows those two are gonna need some alone time. They're okay with it."

"How do you know that?"

"Cam told me he's been approached by every single one of them. They keep telling him how young Jeffy is, how they believe in not having sex unless you're married, reminding him that they are all some kind of level of black belt, and a few of them have asked him if he has protection with him."

Jeff chuckled.

Marissa went on. "Jeffy says they've accepted that she's in a little different situation than most fifteen year olds and will allow certain things for now, or until they see things differently. She said her parents admit they're in uncharted waters and could be making a mistake. I just love how open and honest everyone is in this family. When I grow up and get married I want my family to be just like this one."

"A great aspiration," Jeff said with a nod. "Come on, let's play."

They played Olympic indoor rules, six man teams, the best of three. Two full teams waited to take over for the next losing team. Marissa's team had consisted of Justin Lee and his wife Lori, Jack and Nate and Kimmie. They'd already been eliminated. On court now were Jeff, Mickey, Ricky, Bree, and two Ameritech agents playing against Eric, Shelley, Mark, Joey, Steven, a good friend of Rick's, and Angel, Jason's wife. Cam and Jeffy had yet to rejoin the party.

Kimmie and Marissa, having grown bored with the competition walked with the kids around the bend to some rocks where the children began climbing, pretending they were doing something their grandfather used to do in Hawaii, which was climb waterfalls. Since little Joey and Eric were in the lead, it appeared they'd played this game many times, with tiny Taylor trying to keep up.

Meanwhile, inside the house, upstairs in the pretty lavender room that overlooked the front yard, Cam had just pushed Jeffy onto her back as his lips moved over hers. She sighed with pleasure. Her mind scattered. Her heart lurched. She let go completely. And then she gasped loudly.

"What is it?" Cam asked casually. "Did I hurt you?"

Jeffy wrestled her way back to a sitting position, her eyes wide, her mouth open.

"Jeffy? What is it?"

"Something is wrong. Something is terribly wrong. I have to go."

She ran for the door.

Back on court, the score into the second game of the current match was seven– five. Eric served the ball right at Mickey. Heart pounding, she cupped her hands and knocked the ball straight up, then moved out of the way. She breathed a sigh of relief that she hadn't messed up. Ricky moved in, set the ball and Jeff jumped high and powered it over the net, cruelly, Mickey thought, right at Shelley. Yet Shelley dove and popped the ball up, Joey set and Mark retaliated by slamming the ball right back at Mickey. Mickey didn't fare as well as Shelley had, landing flat on her face and missing the ball completely.

Mickey pouted when Jeff offered his hand and pulled her to her feet, brushed sand from her face. "Okay?"

She nodded. "Sorry."

"Oh, that's okay, baby." He turned back at Mark with a grin, pointed. "You're gonna pay."

"Bring it on," Mark taunted.

"Six– seven," Eric called before he tossed the ball up to serve. Strangely, though, he caught the ball and stood still, his eyes looking off into the distance.

Mickey noticed then that Ricky had turned in the same direction, started off the court. Then Shelley, Mark and Joey. They all started walking off the court.

"What's happening?" Mickey asked. The answer came a few seconds later.

Jeffy came running from the house. "Dad! Daddy! Something's wrong. Where are the kids?"

Eric didn't have a chance to answer before the next cry.

"Dad!" little Joey screamed as he came running from around the bend. "Dad– Uncle Rick!"

Eric, Ricky and the others ran toward the boy. Joey pointed behind him. "It's Eric. He fell. He's hurt."

Ricky didn't wait for whatever else Joey had to say. He took off. The rest of the family was close behind. Ricky came around the bend to see his son's small body crumpled on the sand at the bottom of a cliff of rocks. His daughter Taylor was in Marissa's arms, crying. Kimmie Lee, on her knees, knelt over Eric, talking to him. She looked up as Ricky approached, pointed upward.

"He was way too high. I told him to come down. He slipped. He hit the rocks a few times on his way down."

Ricky knelt next to his son, struggling to remain calm. Little Eric moaned and opened his eyes. "I fell Dad."

Greatly relieved to hear him speak, Ricky allowed himself to breathe. "I see that." He brushed his hand over his son's face, noting the blood oozing from a cut on the side of his head. "Can you move at all?"

Little Eric squeezed his eyes shut, shook his head. "It hurts so bad. I don't wanna move."

"Okay, son. You're gonna be okay. Tell me where it hurts the most," he asked, noticing the ugly bulge on his forearm. Ricky looked up as his father and wife arrived on the scene. Bree knelt down by her son.

"My arm, it hurts so bad."

"Is that the only place? What about your back?" he asked, glancing at Bree when she gasped, noting the tears running down her face.

"Nuh uh. Just my arm."

"Eric, can you wiggle your toes for me?"

He did as requested. "Good. Listen, son. I think you've broken your arm. I'm not gonna lift you until the ambulance gets here just in case anything else is injured, okay?"

"I'm gonna ride in uh ambulance?"

Noting the gleam in his son's eyes, he smiled. "Yeah, you are. I guess that's okay with you?"

"Sure. I guess so."

Ricky looked up at his Dad. "I assume you've already called?"

"You assume correctly."

"What were you doing?" Bree asked, trying to keep the hitch out of her voice.

"Sorry Mom. I know we're not supposed to go up so high. I don't know why I did."

"I do," Ricky said, eyeing the many children standing around. "And we'll talk about it when you're feeling better."

The paramedics arrived quickly and left quickly with their precious cargo. Mickey didn't know what to think about continuing with the party while Ricky and Bree left to follow the ambulance to the hospital, however, Eric and Shelley insisted that they shouldn't let such a little thing ruin everyone's good time. They were just extremely happy and grateful little Eric wasn't hurt with anything worse than a broken arm.

As the party resumed Mickey cornered Master Kino. "May I ask you a question, Eric?"

"Of course."

"It seemed as if you and Ricky and the others knew something was wrong with little Eric even before Joey came to tell you."

Eric nodded. "I knew something was wrong. I didn't know it was Eric."

"So, how did you know something was wrong? Some sort of parent connection type thing?"

"Yes, some sort," he answered with a smile. "One of the things I teach my students is to become one with themselves, with the earth, with their fellow man and mostly with God."

"I hear that expression all the time," Mickey said. "To be 'one' with God, but the idea is pretty vague, don't you think?"

"It can be. I try to teach a way to actually accomplish it."

"And how is that, I mean, nutshell version if you wouldn't mind sharing your thoughts."

Eric laughed. "Sharing my thoughts is what I do. I'm a teacher. I teach them to surround themselves with love, forgiveness, compassion, and positive thoughts."

"Still sounds vague to me. How does one surround themselves with those things?"

"By being those things. I simply teach them to give only love, forgiveness, compassion, and positive thoughts out to those they come in contact with and then no matter what others are offering to you, see only the love, forgiveness, etcetera." He waited to see if she understood.

Mickey nodded.

"There is more to this than just that, but there's not much room in a nutshell.'

"What would you add?"

"The first thing I would add is prayer and faith in God. And then I would add that there are some things we do not tolerate, and that–is evil. We confront evil with strength, but that is a lesson for another time."

"Okay, I think I get it, but, what you're asking sounds like sainthood. I mean, who can accomplish that?"

"We can only work toward the goal of perfection and not be frustrated because we're not there yet. Sometimes, but not always, I and my students, accomplish this oneness. And when we do it seems we can sense things as they happen. Shelley would tell you it's like sensing a 'disturbance in the force.' Today, it seemed something came over me. I knew something was wrong. As did the others. Sometimes I get these feelings before the bad thing happens and sometimes I've been able to stop it. Sometimes I'm not as in tune as I should be. I've had to learn to forgive myself for this. Today, I was only partially in tune. Probably because I was thinking about the score of the volleyball game. Hardly an important venture."

Mickey gave a soft sigh. "You have a way of putting things in perspective. You and your family are like, not even real."

He laughed. "We're real, and completely imperfect which you'll find as you get to truly know us. Yet, even with all our imperfections, we'd like for you to think of us as your family now too."

She smiled and gave a nod. "I'd like that."

The party-goers continued in their revelry. Babies and children were taken inside for afternoon naps and while food was inhaled and drinks were guzzled Jeffy tried to explain to Cameron why she'd known what she did. Before anyone knew it, Ricky, Bree and Eric were back with everyone gathering around to sign Eric's cast.

Over the course of the day, Mickey, had been introduced to, hugged and kissed by dozens of people many whose names she was sure she'd never remember. She was asked about the kidnapping and offered condolences by well-meaning, compassionate people. Nevertheless, it began to wear on her, which was her reason for taking up yet another frozen daiquiri. When she stumbled slightly as she passed the pool, Jeff took her by the arm and escorted her inside.

She smiled up at him. He returned the smile and gracefully removed the glass from her hand. "Let me take that for you."

"Hey, give that back."

"I'm thinking you've had enough."

"I'll be the judge of that."

He smiled. "That's what you said the last time you decided you were gonna get wasted. Sweetheart, are you upset?"

She shrugged.

"Talk to me," he said, ushering her down the hall and into Eric's study, where he knew they would be alone. He sat on the leather couch and pulled her down.

She snuggled up to him. "I don't know what to say when people say they're sorry about what happened. It's like I want to tell them to not be sorry. I'm glad my mother blew away my stepfather. I know Marissa asked me the same question earlier, but what kind of horrible person does that make me?"

"It makes you a human person."

"You don't feel that way, do you? You're not happy she blew him away."

"Yeah, well, that's only because I wanted to watch his face as he was prosecuted and put behind bars for the rest of his life, but really, I secretly thought about killing him myself. So you see, I'm human too." He leaned back, rubbed his hand over her arm.

Mickey snuggled up against his throat, kissed his neck. "I want you, right here, right now."

He chuckled. "You're definitely drunk, Mick."

"And you won't do it when I'm drunk, right?"

"Correct."

"But I need—"

He kissed her. Slowly, softly.

"What you need is to know that you are the most amazing woman I've ever met. You're beautiful, and strong, and important."

"Important?"

"Yes, important. You are a survivor. An overcomer. A role model. You are a person of great worth, in Marissa's eyes, in my eyes and in the eyes of God and I love you and I won't abandon you and we are gonna live happily ever after."

Mickey smiled at Jeff. With Jeff she felt safe, warm and loved. So very loved. She hadn't realized until her most recent session with Eric that she'd felt unloved almost her entire life. That she'd felt fear and resentment on a daily basis and that realizing someone really can and does love her is a goal she must reach. Her mother and step-father had made her feel expendable, like she had no worth. But Jeff valued her and helped her to see that she did have worth.

Her eyes met his. He looked deep into her soul. He loved her. He did. And she loved him back. How could she not? He looked at her with such devotion, such passion.

As if reading her mind, he leaned down and kissed her again. "I love you, Mackenzie Daley."

"I love you, Jefferson Davis."

"Oh, there you are," Shelley said.

Jeff grinned. "We, uh, Mickey was feeling a little weepy," he said.

Shelley smiled sweetly. "Well, it looks like she's feeling much better now. I guess playing doctor suits you."

Jeff only rolled his eyes.

She touched his arm. "Will you come out front? We have a surprise for you," Shelley said with a grin before she turned and headed toward the door.

Mickey headed toward the large window. "What do you suppose is the surprise? Do you think someone bought us a new car?"

"Wouldn't that be great?" Jeff answered.

He looked over at her where she stood by the window. "What are you smiling at?"

Mickey motioned out the window. "Some more guests have arrived and there are five of the cutest little blondes I've ever seen."

"What?" Jeff said, hurrying over to the window. He laughed out loud. "Oh, man. It's Keegan!"

He left Mickey and sprinted out the front door.

Keegan Tanner turned from shaking hands with Eric as Jeff tore down the steps. The two men threw themselves into the other's embrace, completely unashamed of the emotion two big, burly guys were showing. They slapped backs and backed off then Keegan slapped Jeff's cheek affectionately. "You've been in the news, buddy."

"Yeah. Trying to keep up with you."

"You can have my fame. I don't want it."

Elizabeth Tanner came around the car, smiling her sweet smile as always. "Lizzy," Jeff said. He hugged her close, and patted the head of the dark haired little boy she held. "Hello there, Gabriel. You've gotten so big. How old are you now?"

The child scrambled down from his mother's arms. "I'm four," he said, grinning a mischievous grin.

"Hi, Uncle Jeff," Heather said as she approached. She was the eldest at ten.

"Well, you've turned into quite a little lady, haven't you?"

She giggled. "Yes sir."

He smiled warmly at her, shook his head. "It's amazing how much you've changed just since the last time I saw you."

Jeff turned and looked over the two sets of twins as they stood amazingly quiet, waiting for his attention. "Okay, let me try." He pointed at one with her hair in a pony tail and a frown on her face. "This must be Rose," he said.

The nine-year-old grinned. "Yep. Good job, Uncle Jeff."

He touched Violet's head. "So that makes you Violet. And you," he said pointing at the smallest one, must be Lily, and you're Daisy."

Eight-year-old Daisy smiled. "You did it. Daddy says you're getting married."

"Yes I am." He turned, looking for Mickey who stood at the top of the front steps. She came down slowly.

Jeff put his arm around her. "This is Mackenzie, but everyone calls her Mickey."

"Hello," Mickey said softly. She shook hands with each child. "I swear you must be just the most adorable children I've ever seen."

"Too bad they're not as sweet as they look," Keegan said.

"Daaddyyy," Heather whined playfully.

Keegan stroked her long, blond hair. "Sorry, I let the secret out."

Mickey offered her hand to Keegan Tanner. "I heard about you in the news several years ago. I'm so glad I get the chance to say thank you in person. By saving Jeff's life, you saved mine too."

Keegan nodded. "I'm just glad I was able to get to him. Jeff is a good guy."

"You would've done the same for anyone," Jeff put in.

Lizzy moved forward, linked her arm in Keegan's. "That he would." She smiled up at her husband.

Keegan lovingly brushed the back of his hand over his wife's cheek before he turned back to Mickey. "This is Lizzy, my angel whom you can see is very good for my ego."

Lizzy moved forward, hugged Mickey. "It's so nice to meet you. I hope we can be great friends. And I hope you'll come visit us down in Pine Forest. The girls seem to live for the day Jeff comes to visit."

Mickey smiled. "I'd like that. You have a beautiful family."

"Thank you," Lizzy said softly. She touched her husband's arm. "I'm so grateful for them every single day."

"Well now," Shelley said. "Was it a good surprise?"

Jeff ran over, picked her up in a big bear hug. "The best. Thank you so much."

"You're welcome. We're just so glad they came. Eric doesn't know what he'd do if his angel girls didn't come see him at least once a year."

"Exactly," Eric said as he knelt down. "So, where's *my* hugs?"

Five giggling blondes and one small, dark-haired boy ran at him.

The boy stopped right in front of Grandmaster Kino and bowed slowly.

"Hello, Gabe," Eric greeted.

"Hello, Grandmaster Kino," little Gabriel said reverently. It was a ritual they always shared.

Then all six children bowled him over. Mickey watched in delight as it turned into a giant kung fu brawl, with little voices yelling keyais fiercely as they punched and kicked at the Grandmaster.

Mickey stood mesmerized by the adorable scene. There was so much love in this family, in this home. She glanced over at Shelley and Lizzy and Keegan. They stood patiently, smiling, obviously enjoying it as much as her. Jeff took her hand, smiled down at her. "That will be us one day."

Mickey looked up into his eyes. "I want that."

He bent and kissed her softly. "You'll have it."

"Okay," Shelley commanded. "Enough. Come in. There's lots of food and drinks out back and the kids can swim if you like. We had some excitement here today. Get the kids to tell you about it. Well, what are you waiting for? Come in, come in," Shelley waved emphatically.

The kids ran ahead, followed by Keegan and Lizzy. Jeff smiled at Mickey, offered his arm. "May I escort you to that life you want?"

Mickey grinned, hooked her arm in his. "Please."

~❀~

About the Author

McCartney Green is dedicated to serving God. Striving to learn His will for her own life, she loves helping others to connect with God for she knows it is that connection that brings true joy. Her goal is to empower, heal, enlighten and awaken everyone to discover that God is real. Really real. And He speaks and heals and gives life. McCartney is the mother of seven children and fifteen grandchildren. She lives in the suburbs of Atlanta. Her amazing, loving, husband recently passed away from Covid and she very much looks forward to seeing him again. Until then, God is with us.

You may write her at mccartneygreen@gmail.com.

Readers talk about The Dandelions Series
(Real comments by real readers. Permission for names was not obtained before this printing.)

"*Angels* is my new favorite book! I had the weekend off and all I did was read. I couldn't put it down. I only have a few pages left but I don't want it to end. Plus when I finish I will have to wait until your next book comes out. I just wanted to tell you how much I LOVED reading this book!"

"Just when I thought your books couldn't get any better I was proven wrong with *Weeds Grow*! What an exciting, great book. I am having trouble getting my work done because I can't put it down. You are an amazing writer and I have to say WOW!"

"I absolutely love *DND#1*. I can't wait to start reading the other books in the series. I was amazed at how addicted I became to the book. I can't stop thinking about the characters and their stories. I can definitely relate to Shelley's self confidence issues. Her strength is so great and makes me feel like I can be as strong as her in whatever situation life has to throw my way. Thank you for writing such an inspirational and motivating book."

"I have read the first three books and I love them all. They are addicting! The problem is, I don't get enough sleep when I read them because I can't put them down! I am now having withdrawals because I don't have the 4th book. McCartney- you are great."

"I have read everything you have put out and have been patiently waiting for more. I love them all as they are all unique and different. Can't wait for more.(a thankful fan)"

"Just wanted you to know I loved all your books. Now, I am doing something I only do with my all time favorites. I am going back and reading them again. Thanks for sharing your gift. P.S. You are the real deal!"

"Hey McCartney~ Thanks so much for sending me your book. (#1) I absolutely loved it! As a fellow writer and "professional romance novel reader" I can honestly say you are truly gifted with writing talent. I've added you to the list of my favorite writers and I'm looking forward to reading another one of your books soon. Hugs!"

Coming up next- DND #7...
Warriors-In Jesus' Name

Mark and Joey Adams, sons of Shelley Kino and stepsons of Grandmaster Eric Kino, have grown up and are taking the world by storm. Mark, a fledgling attorney and part-time martial arts instructor for the Kino schools, and Joey, Ameritech Security's top agent, usually end up doing everything together, so it's no surprise when they become interested in sisters. It's also no surprise that their relationships throw them into a world of intrigue and violence. Their training under the Kino umbrella comes in handy as they come face to face with the dark secrets that threaten to destroy those they love.

"I wondered how McCartney was gonna fit both brothers into one book adequately. I should never have doubted her. She hits, once again, on some sensitive subjects and also teaches us that not everything is black and white all the while entertaining me with action-packed suspense. Loved it! Wow!"
~Kristel Carey~

"Oh, yes, I knew Mark and Joey were gonna grow up to be like their role models, hunky, deadly, sensitive men who aren't afraid to make things right. So enjoyable! And I love Bella and Breez, totally likeable characters. Oh, and the kids... I can see more books!"
~Eryn Clements~

"Amazing! I couldn't put it down. It's impressive the way McCartney pulled me in. The moment I started reading she took me into another world, one that isn't perfect. Yet we learn that love and family can overcome even the worst obstacles. I love the characters and McCartney takes you to the edge of reason as they try to decide whether to cross those fine lines of morality. I absolutely enjoyed every minute of this story!"
~Sandra Lindsey~

"As usual, I really enjoyed the book! Every book in *The Dandelions Series* is the best one. Now, I am truly looking forward to reading about June Flower, our little psychic! I find her to be my favorite character."
~Becki Kelly~

*And now
a sneak preview of...
DND #7*

WARRIORS
IN JESUS' NAME

Joey Adams streaked through the parking lot in his silver Ferrari, headed toward the back of the sleek, blue glass building. It wouldn't do for him to be late again, but darn it, he wasn't used to punching the clock. He was one of Ameritech Security's top agents. Highly trained. Highly skilled. Highly deadly. And this week, highly bored. He'd been forced by his own aspirations to work a month of eight to fives in the accounting department of the company that he would one day run.

He sighed heavily. An entire month. Thank goodness there was just one more week to go. Man, what he wouldn't give for a little action, a stakeout, a missing person, heck, even a bar fight. Yet, he knew he had to know the inside workings of the company and so he forced himself to exercise the patience he'd been taught by his stepfather, Eric Kino, a man for which Joey had great respect. Besides, Joey wanted to make sure Jason Lee, the owner of Ameritech, never felt he'd made a mistake in choosing Joey as his successor. Yes, they were like family and yes, Joey was a logical choice, but he knew Jason wouldn't turn his company, his pride and joy, over to just anyone, family or no. Besides, even though Joey had called the man who was now his boss, Uncle Jason for the first ten years he'd known him, they weren't really blood related. All that aside, it's Friday, Joey thought, certainly he could offer some assistance to some ongoing cases over the weekend.

He screeched to a halt as he swung toward his reserved space, stopping just inches from the shiny bumper of a dark blue Mercedes. He watched impatiently as the driver of the vehicle stepped out, closed the door and pointed her remote at it. His eyebrows rose as he waited for her to look his direction so he could point out the reserved parking sign that hung on the wall in front of her car like a beacon. Yet completely ignoring him, she pointed her little turned up nose toward the building entrance, dropped the keys in her purse, adjusted her sunglasses, turned her back and walked away.

As annoyed as he was, Joey couldn't help but appreciate the view from his angle. She wore a black skirt, black heels and a white silky blouse. And she wore it well. Shiny, black curls bounced around her shoulders as she walked toward the building's entrance, moving in rhythm to the bounce in her step. She seemed to be a woman on a mission.

Pulling his eyes from the scenery, Joey searched for another parking space, as he focused his mind on business. He found an empty spot several rows back and headed in. Once he made it to the third floor where much of the company's internal workings took place, he forced a pleasant smile on his face and prepared himself mentally for the task at hand.

"Good Morning, Mr. Adams!"

Joey turned to smile at the pretty, blonde who manned the front desk of accounting.

"Hi, Didi," he said as he tapped her desk with the palm of his hand. "And please, stop with the mister stuff. Call me Joey. You make me feel old."

She giggled and Joey tried not to roll his eyes. "Okay, Joey it is. So, Joey, I caught your movie last night."

"Really? Which one?" he asked, feigning interest.

"The one where Ricky Kino is accused of treason. Some friends and I rented some vids and vegged out at my sister's apartment. You were awesome."

Joey sighed. "Yeah, well, thanks. Listen, I'd better—"

"So, some of us are getting together for drinks tonight on the strip. Wanna join us?"

Not wanting to cause hurt feelings, he tried to ease his way into the turn down. His eyes sparkled at her. "Are you sure you're old enough to drink?"

"I'm twenty-two," she said indignantly. "You're not that much older, are you? Why don't you join us?"

"I'm twenty-nine, and I can't join you because it would be against company policy."

"You mean, since you're the boss and all? Heck, that wouldn't bother me."

"I'm flattered, Didi, but it would bother Mr. Lee. So, sorry, no can do. You have a great time though." He walked through toward the manager's office, smiling as he thought of how some of the agents thought the girl's name fit her. Double D. He reprimanded himself as he turned his mind back to business.

"He's absolutely dreamy," Darla purred, joining Didi as they watched Joey walk away.

"He told me to call him by his first name." She heaved a sigh. "He's just too cute. Why in the world did he stop making movies and come to work here?"

Darla shrugged. "I read he really hated the Hollywood scene."

"Yeah, well, lucky for us," Didi giggled. "Too bad he wouldn't come out with us tonight, though. I bet he's a lot of fun with a few under his belt."

✪

Her heart beat faster and she could barely catch her breath. Bella knew it wasn't because of the workout she was receiving in her martial arts class, but because of the instructor who'd decided to stop right in front of her to correct her movement. She had no right to be attracted to him. Yet, whenever he came near, her body and heart thought along other lines. She was a married woman with a son, but her husband had never made her feel like this man did; important, a person of worth, safe, protected.

How silly of her to be attracted to a man whom she barely knew and who probably wouldn't even recognize her on the street. She and Logan had been taking taekwondo classes at the Kino studio for almost two years now. Master Mark, as they called him to show respect, was Grandmaster Kino's stepson. He was a fifth degree black belt who taught only on Saturday mornings. Even though he always acknowledged her, they'd never really had a conversation. Admittedly, he'd tried a few times during their open houses and demonstrations, but she'd always shied away.

She was sure his kind treatment of her was simply professional courtesy. In her mind, she knew that, but in her heart, her imagination took over. What would it be like to have such a strong, gentle man interested in her? He'd smile at her, speak softly to her. He'd probably open doors for her, carry groceries in from the car for her.

He was large. Several inches taller than her husband. Her husband, she thought, was a complete opposite of this man. Gordon had blond hair, and blue eyes. Her instructor had brown hair and large brown eyes and a kind smile that would put anyone at ease. He had broad shoulders and narrow hips. She'd seen him change from his t-shirt into his uniform top and knew he was ripped with muscle. Another student told her he'd been some big time football player in college and would've gone pro except for a knee injury that had taken too long to rehabilitate.

"Ms. Bella?" he said softly. "Am I confusing you?"

She blinked, looked up into his eyes. "I'm sorry, what did you say?"

His brow wrinkled. "I said to keep the fist closed, like this," he replied, grasping her hand and folding it into a fist. He held her hand up in the air, over her head. "Tighten your elbow and shoulder. Good. Now, as I strike, you thrust sideways to block, using my momentum against me. Good. See the difference?"

He struck slowly toward her face, coaching her through the block. Then went low, forcing her to throw a low block.

"Good. Now, high again."

He came in faster this time and she thrust out her forearm against his fist.

Before she could stop herself she gave a small cry of pain and jumped back, holding her forearm.

"You okay?" Mark asked. Grasping her wrist, he raised her arm. The sleeve of the dobak she wore fell back revealing several bruises along her forearm. Mark's brow furrowed as Bella jerked her arm away.

His solemn eyes met hers and she smiled timidly. "Uh, Logan and me, we've been practicing a little too much."

He smiled at her, putting her immediately at ease. "I'd say. I think the two of you need to back off a little."

She nodded. "Yes sir, Master Mark."

He bowed slightly and moved on to work with the next student while one of the class black belts led them through their motions. Bella blew out a breath as she watched Master Mark walk down the row, relieved, for more than one reason, to have him move away. Her eye caught her son's. Logan stood two rows up from her, a look of unease on his young, eleven-year-old face. She gave him a stiff smile and went on with the class.

Thirty minutes later, dripping with perspiration, Bella headed to the locker room to change into her street clothes. Logan sat on the floor pulling on his shoes and watched her go, fighting the feeling of dread that always crept into his heart when it came time to go home.

"Hey."

Logan turned his head to acknowledge JoJo, who was Master Mark's son. They call him JoJo because his real name is Joseph, which of course, is Joey which is also his uncle's name. To keep the confusion down he'd been dubbed Little Joe which he hated so that morphed into JoJo. He was twelve and already a black belt. Logan liked him because he wasn't cocky. He seemed pretty ordinary despite the fact that his family was famous. Logan didn't speak but nodded his head.

"That was some pretty good sparring you did today," JoJo said.

"Thanks."

"You excited about testing for your red belt next Saturday?"

"Yeah, I guess."

JoJo eased down beside him. "So, we're having a belt party at my grandparent's house after the test. We're all gonna play on the beach and sleep over and stuff. There's about twenty kids coming, but the girls can't spend the night. Anyway, I hope you can come."

Logan's jaw clenched. His father didn't like him being away from home.

"Come where?" his mom asked as she walked up.

"Hi Mrs. Landow. We're having a belt party next Saturday. Can Logan come?"

Bella glanced down at her son, catching a brief glimpse of the hopeful look in his eyes before he was able to hide it. "Of course he can come. Sounds like fun."

"It's a spend the night party," Logan added.

Bella frowned, wrung her hands. "Oh. Well, I'm not sure about the spending the night part, but he can come for the evening. What time?"

Before JoJo could answer his father joined them and answered for him. "We'll get started right after the testing so we'll go straight there from here." He turned toward Bella. "You're invited too."

"Me?" Bella said nervously.

"Sure. You're part of the class, even though you're not testing. We promise we won't make you spend the night."

Bella laughed nervously. "Okay, well, I'm not sure how long I can stay. I'd better check with Gordon to see what he has planned first."

"I understand. Why don't you ask Gordon to come along?"

"Sure. I'll do that," Bella said smoothly, knowing her husband would never agree to come and not wanting him to anyway.

"Just a sec," Mark said. He hurried to his desk, grabbed a couple business cards. "Here. One for each of you. In case you need to ask any questions about the test or the party. Probably better to try my cell first. Don't want you to get lost in the shuffle if you call the office."

Bella fingered the glossy card, read the top line: *Mark Adams, Attorney at Law*. "Okay. Thanks. Well, we'd better get home. I have some fancy dinner I'm supposed to attend tonight and it will take me hours to get presentable."

Mark's eyes quickly moved over her, taking in the blue eyes fringed by dark lashes, the flawless complexion, the soft, black hair. "I doubt that," he said softly before he gave himself a mental shake. "Well, have a great time. And call me if you need to, about anything." He eyed Logan. "Even if you just need to talk."

"Thanks," Bella said as her cell phone went off. "Excuse me."

Mark watched her glance at the number before she answered, her teeth biting down on her full lower lip. His gut involuntary reacted to the sight.

"Hello?....Oh, no!...I, I'm not sure...no, of course I understand...please, don't think another thing about it. I'll figure something out.....okay, and tell Bill to get well soon." Sighing, she snapped the phone shut.

"A problem?" Mark asked, knowing it was none of his business but not being able to help himself. She'd been his student for two years and she'd made very little progress. She didn't seem to have it in her. She was the most gentle soul he'd ever met and over the years he'd found himself thinking about her at odd times. There was just something about her that intrigued him, more than the obvious delicate beauty. He had to constantly remind himself that she was married.

Bella put a hand to her forehead almost in a panic. "Logan was gonna stay at a friend's house tonight while Gordon and I attend this important dinner." She glanced at her son. "Barrett's dad has the flu. I don't know what I'm gonna do. Your father will not be happy about this."

Mark could've sworn Logan's face turned three shades paler.

"It's okay, Mom. I'm old enough to stay home by myself."

"Oh, honey, I know you are, but you know how your father is so . . . protective."

When Logan didn't answer, Mark smiled at Bella. "Why don't you let Logan come out with us. JoJo and my nephew, Eric, and I are going for a man's night out. You know, pizza and a movie and maybe some video games if there's time."

Bella wrung her hands. "Oh, I don't know."

"Please, Mrs. Landow," JoJo pleaded.

"Logan?" Bella asked.

"That'd be great, Mom."

"I promise to have him home by midnight and if you and Gordon are still out we'll stick around until you get home."

"I don't want you to go to any trouble," Bella said.

"It won't be any trouble at all. We'll have a blast."

Logan looked hopefully at his mom.

"Well, I guess it will be alright."

"Great. We'll come pick him up around six. Will that be early enough?"

"Uh, yes, that would be perfect."

"Okay, then it's settled. We'll be seeing you tonight," Mark said pointedly to Logan. He stepped back, nodded at his son. "We'd better get a move on JoJo." He gave both Logan and Bella a slight bow.

They returned the gesture and started out as Mark watched. On a whim, Mark called Logan back. The boy turned and trotted back toward his instructor.

"Yes sir?"

Mark smiled at him. "Just wanted to remind you to back off your mom."

Perplexed, Logan's brow creased. Did Master Mark know about the beatings his mother had endured? Did he think that Logan himself had caused the damage? His heart began to pound in his chest. He glanced over his shoulder at his mom, then fearfully back toward Master Mark, who strangely, was smiling.

"Your training," Mark said. "Your mom said the two of you have been training hard, sparring against each other. Sometimes young guys your age don't realize your own strength. Her arms are getting a little bruised. She probably wouldn't tell you that, but I thought you'd want to know."

"Oh, uh, thank you, sir," Logan mumbled.

Mark ruffled his hair. "No problem. See you later."

"Yes sir."

"See ya," JoJo added.

Logan turned and hurried off.

JoJo looked up at his father's concerned face. They were close, his father and him. Joe had been born nine months after his father's eighteenth birthday. His mother had died a few weeks later. He'd been raised by his dad with the help of his grandparents. Now it seemed they were more like best friends sometimes, rather than father and son. "You don't really think Logan is the one who put bruises on his mom's arm, do you?"

Mark sighed. "No, son, I don't. I was just feeling him out. The question is, what the heck am I gonna do about it?"

JoJo smiled. "You'll think of something. You always do."

"Thanks for the vote of confidence."

A Prayer and Some Pi

I pray that all who read this book and especially those who identify with the domestic violence story line will be blessed with healing. I pray that circumstances will change for the better, for Christ Jesus can work it all for your good. May you be blessed with true love and real joy and may you help others to do the same. In Jesus' name, Amen.

3.141592653589793238462643383279502884197169399375105820974944592307816406286208998628034825342117067982148086513282306647093844609550582231753594081284811174502841027019385211055596446229489549303819644288109756659334461284756482337867831652712019091456485669234603486104543266482133
My, my, how I love pi!

Look for these books by
McCartney Green

#1 A Healing-In Jesus' Name

#2 Suffer the Children-In Jesus' Name

#3 Finding Home-In Jesus' Name

#4 Weeds Grow-In Jesus' Name

#5 Angels-In Jesus' Name

#6 The Worth of Souls-In Jesus' Name

#7 Warriors-In Jesus' Name

#8 June Flower-In Jesus' Name

Coming Soon . . . . .

#9 Circle of Life-In Jesus' Name

and a little while later ... #10!

ALSO AVAILABLE . . .

(DND Prequel)
Messages From God-The Memoirs of Grandmaster Eric Kino
[What happened to young Eric Kino at the age of ten that set him on the path of becoming one of God's warriors?]

Kino Martial Arts Student Handbook
[Grandmaster Kino's Daily Regimen- A Guide to Living on Purpose]

Made in the USA
Columbia, SC
19 June 2023